"Potentially, a government is the most dangerous threat to man's rights: it holds a legal monopoly on the use of physical force against legally disarmed victims."

—Ayn Rand

"But surely for everything you have to love you have to pay some price."

—Agatha Christie

CHRONOS UNBOUND

THEODOR RICHARDSON

authorHOUSE®

AuthorHouse™
1663 Liberty Drive
Bloomington, IN 47403
www.authorhouse.com
Phone: 1-800-839-8640

Published by AuthorHouse 10/4/2012

ISBN: 978-1-4772-6875-9 (sc)
ISBN: 978-1-4772-6873-5 (hc)
ISBN: 978-1-4772-6874-2 (e)

Library of Congress Control Number: 2012916765

DEDICATION

To my beautiful, insightful, demanding, whip-cracking editor and benefactor, Katherine. Thank you for putting my dreams in print.

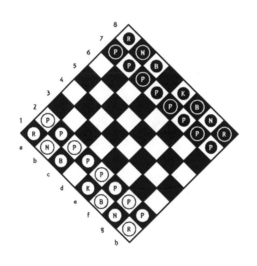

PROLOGUE

As he walked, the young writer examined the note in his hand. It had been meticulously printed and appeared more generated than scrawled. He was wary of engaging in the kind of meeting this unknown contact had arranged. Though he had gathered some perspective and even inspiration from such reclusive types before, the idea did not sit well with him in this instance. Something internal, however, compelled him to the task despite his stomach's position on the matter.

By the time he forced his body back into the obedience of his mind, the writer had arrived at the destination. The uneasy feeling inside of him intensified with the realization that this particular office building had been abandoned for some length of time. He rechecked the address, and was both assured and disheartened by the confirmation it offered. As he eased into the front entrance, he saw that the reception area was a perfect imitation of a haunted house lobby. He crossed the floor, unconsciously holding his breath; the ghostly echo of his footsteps on the marble was the only noise he could hear. His finger found its way through the resting dust to the elevator control. The loud creak that followed the renewal of activity within the gears sent the writer back from the closed shaft. Unsteady feet carried him forth into the elevator car, and he was glad when the device delivered him safely to the third floor.

He found his way to the office door marked with the name Jeannette Fitzgerald. The lockless door opened before him at a touch. The dusty, smudged windows inside barred all but a scant few rays of light and the weight of disuse hung almost palpably in the air. A cobwebbed reception desk, a chess set atop it, and the chair in which he was to be seated represented the whole of the room's furnishings. Scanning his surroundings in the dim overhead lighting, the writer casually noted that the chess board, though set up for play, lacked both of the queens. He seated himself cautiously in the cramped chair, pulling a miniature tape recorder from his jacket and fumbling with the small pile of cassettes that spilled onto his lap. He had refused to adopt more modern devices for interviewing. He felt it ruined the purity of the pursuit.

After several minutes, he reread the note for what seemed to be the hundredth time. The short letter still said for him to come alone and revealed very little else, except that this writer's entire future depended upon this meeting. The man began to wonder if this letter was a hoax.

As if in answer to the unspoken question, an all-encompassing shadow crept into the room, hungrily swallowing every sparse bit of light in its path. The vast, forgotten room suddenly became very small. The shadow heralded the monstrosity that cast it.

A technological creature in deep-hued blue metal regalia strode into the room. It gave a penetrating stare from what appeared to be its eyes and continued. A dim red, roving light offset on the creature's enclosed face seemed to satisfy itself with the scene, and the being's long dark cape swirled in the path of its gate. The budding writer's lightly tanned skin went very pale and he found himself frozen in the greatest terror of his life. The blond hair that barely rested on the writer's forehead along with his white shirt gave him the appearance of a ghost. He had just enough time to wonder if he was about to become one when the creature spoke.

CHAPTER 1

THE TECHNOLOGICAL CREATURE moved naturally and fluidly without any of the halting, jerking movement of machines. Whoever or whatever was behind the helmet wore an astounding suit of armor, the likes of which neither the reporter nor any contemporary engineer had dared fathom. Somewhere in the sudden maelstrom of the reporter's thoughts, he realized the obligation of the meeting. The writer reached slowly for his tape recorder. Distracted, he did not notice the disappearance of the segmented helmet. The face behind the armor, although definitely human, was no more comforting. The stranger's face was hard set and unnaturally pale, accented only by his flowing, thick brown hair. The stranger's face held no trace of expression except that of a grim brooding. The plates on his shoulders, which held his long, deep blue cape, were set at a decisive downward angle. The lack of reflection in the dark metal covering the whole of his armor added an incongruous sense of privacy, or possibly humility, which accompanied the obvious power. The chest plate, forcing itself inches above the interlaced body sections, accented the muscles of his upper torso just as the gauntlets accented his arms. The only object that stood out in contrast to the strong and alien nature of the figure was the hand-carved wooden cross hung about his neck, reaching to his heart.

"Relax," the stranger said in an almost mechanical tone, "it is only armor. I am a relic of the future, and I ask that you listen to the entirety of what I must say before you inevitably cast your judgment upon me and my story."

"How?" Realizing his interjection only too late, the writer snapped back into silence, praying he would not be killed.

"That is a reasonable question, and quite simplistic, actually. You see, all forms of energy are relatively interchangeable. My technology converts the very energy of life into temporal energy. It is quite an exhilarating and exhausting experience as I have found. This trip alone, however, has taken years off of my expected life span. Others fear this technology for good reason, so its exploitation remains limited to my person alone. As to how time travel is even possible: the universe is not as solid and stable as you may wish to believe." His tone was stilted and strange, nothing like the casual slang the reporter usually heard. "We exist in the instantaneous intersection between two times, as time is seen as the fourth dimension. To avoid overwhelming you with the physics, suffice it to say that it becomes a matter of forcing the right intersection." The writer thought that the stranger's voice seemed strong and serene, embodying a gale force brimming with unrealized thunder. "Now as to the reason for such travel, I have come a very long way to bring you this story. It is the story of my life, and it begins twenty years from now. I suspect you should find it more to your liking than the news you are used to regurgitating. In my telling, you will realize it is also the story of this planet and the life that is to come for every person aboard it."

The blood flow was slowly returning to the writer's face. The reporter saw a lifetime of struggle in the stranger's darkened eyes, but the man's face was untouched by physical tragedy, thanks most likely to the armor he wore. The stranger's face was as unrevealing as the helmet that preceded it, giving no quarter or hint of solace.

"My father is a very important man in the future history and I seek to change that. He controls over half of the world in my time. At first, I was pleased with the prospect of inheriting such a powerful position. Then, I suppose in a manner of speaking it can be said that my father's spirit possessed me. I suddenly sought to conquer the conqueror. I have my own reasons for that, as you will know in time. I was not in the position, being his son, to lead a revolution as you may imagine, so instead I appealed to both his vanity and his loathing of me. I chose to battle him in something much more personal but no less decisive.

"I challenged him to a game of chess; it was the only game he ever taught me," the stranger said, sucking air in through his closed teeth. "The rule of the empire and the fate of the world rested on this game. We each had our 'pieces,' most of them living people, and a complicated series of moves ensued. Eventually though, checkmate came. I have now come back to assert my victory. This is a dark tale and I weave it for you now as the worst kind of sinner: one who does not regret.

"I had planned my challenge, and the time had come to begin recruiting." The man picked up one of the white knights from the chess board delicately in his armored fingers. He turned the horse head to face him, staring into its empty plastic eyes.

CHAPTER 2

"I AM OPERATING on the opinion that forewarned is forearmed; therefore, I shall tell you as much as I can of the events that are yet to transpire. I remember when my campaign really began. It was a rather overcast day, not at all unpleasant. The sky had an ominous purple cast to it, not unlike today, waiting to see if the storm could be mustered out of the ambience. At the time, I was, or is that will be, having lunch in a rusted out neutral bar and grill in the outskirts of the capital city, New Charleston. As I sat alone at the bar, a ruckus erupted from outside the prefab structure. This was common enough in the neutral areas, especially if the military personnel that patrolled them got bored, and they usually got bored very often. This time, it sounded as though someone was being unceremoniously thrown into an alley, which also tended to happen quite frequently.

"The man that walked through the sliding steel and glass doors with his long black hair badly mussed looked as though he had experienced just that. He looked to be a teenager, and he was wearing a most peculiar garment. It was composed of a singular black strand of material nearly two inches wide covering him from neck to foot. The crisscross pattern of the fabric was reminiscent of the wrappings of an ancient Egyptian mummy, and I surmised that the band was not a simple single layer. A belt and boots of the same chemical composition completed his outfit, but somehow the most striking feature of the slight young man was the scar that ran the length of his face just beside his left eye. Whatever had caused this had dug deep into him yet had left him functional.

"Intrigued and otherwise constantly seeking recruits, I offered him a meal, being that it looked as though his last had come a week ago. As he crossed the room and prepared to sit down, the youth caught a faint glimpse of his reflection in one of the shards of glass scattered throughout the establishment, remnants of rather messy entanglements with my father's less than chivalrous soldiers. He looked to be surprised by his own appearance. He approached a mirror that hung on the wall with the same trepidation as a pup that sees its reflection for the first time. His face blended into the shadows as he gazed at his visage. Emotion overcame him in an instant.

"When he noticed the scar, a scream escaped his lips before he could even open his mouth. The resounding noise raged with years of pain. The scream also added a new depth to the mystery of the man. As the youth stood reeling from the sight of his own visage, a spark sizzled from his wrist. I was certain it was neither an artificial limb nor an illusion. The scope of the situation soon became clear to me.

"Someone had altered the youth through genetic engineering. His memory would most likely have been wiped, and a weapon had certainly been implanted in his wrist. I had an old friend who was famous for hiding surprises like that in his subjects. He was quite the prankster in work and play and he always tended to enjoy it more when it had real consequence. This had to be his work. We are two of a very close trio of friends in your present day, and I knew his style and signature quite well.

"After a time, I managed to calm the youth to the point where he picked over a plate of tough and greasy chicken, the best the capitol had to offer. As expected, the other patrons paid no more attention to the boy than was required lest they be drawn into the situation and risk their own precarious freedom. In the course of my quiet conversation with him, I decided it was high time to enact my plans and asked him to accompany me in my plot, provided he could prove himself. He reluctantly agreed, but he was obviously doing so in his own interests. My new companion desired knowledge of his origin, and there was no better resource available to him than my own vast networks, databases, and connections. I knew from the beginning that the side he would join after the game would clearly be his own if he managed to survive.

"After I settled the bill, we took the forest route to my estate, partly because I was reluctant to offer any explanation of the boy's presence to my father's soldiers. Since my father put me under such scrutiny, he had his guards and allies spy on me, benign yet nevertheless troublesome.

Even though most of the roads in that area had been destroyed, they were not above patrol.

"The boy knew nothing of his past. Midway through the journey, the boy decided on a temporary name, Jake, until he could find who he truly was. We walked in silence most of the way. I should also tell you that I owned the vast stretch of forest that held our trail within it. I had the forest stocked with as many animals as the woods could accommodate, and I was free to persecute any who violated that area. It was quite the coincidence that one of the last free roaming, though genetically-enhanced, grizzly bears on the entire American continent found us on our way without even needing the signal from my armor to coax it.

"Jake and I froze in place at the majestic creature's approach, but the fifteen foot bear was not content with that. The bear sniffed the boy and, sensing something aggravating, reared up to pounce. I had enough weapons with me to easily fend off the creature, but it was not my fight and I wanted to test Jake's abilities and a snarling wild animal easily five times his size seemed fitting enough.

"The bear's claws were rapidly descending towards Jake's face as he spun backwards and rolled behind the creature. Jake delivered a very strong kick to the crux of the bear's back as it rose. My guess is that such a kick would have crippled a person. The bear roared in agony, spun with startling speed, and struck hard. The claws should have sunk deep within the boy's abdomen, they should have gutted him, yet they stopped. The nails struck against the folds of the malleable fabric and stopped, merely forcing Jake backwards. The boy gripped the bear's paw with both hands and, to my own amazement, slowly forced it away. Jake flipped over the beast with the moves of a gymnast and landed on the creature's neck with a loud crack. The bear rose to its hind legs and growled wildly. Twisting, the ravenous monster ripped Jake from his back and pinned him to the ground, dripping foaming saliva on his face. Frustrated and enraged, Jake released a blue-white bolt of electricity from his wrist straight into the animal's paw. The smell of burnt fur singed my nostrils as the bear backed cautiously away towards my forest. It sulked away in search of less deadly prey.

"The violence of those two primal spirits ignited my soul. Almost drunkenly I wanted the looming confrontation more than ever. I vowed to myself that my father would never be shown such mercy.

"We reached my home without another spoken word. I told Jake that there were bandages and extra clothes in the closet and that he was welcome to them. However, something told me he would not accept, and he did not. While he took a well-deserved rest, I pondered how I could ask my oldest friends to join my treasonous little quest."

CHAPTER 3

"MY OLD FRIEND Max's laboratory was as cluttered as it was hidden. I knew its location only because of my ranking in my father's military. The neighborhood barely qualified as New Charleston territory and I was not supposed to know that Max was housed there. Our mutual curiosity about the way everything worked served as the closest bond between the two of us, and it strengthened our friendship into brotherhood as we each found our individual niche. In each other's eyes, we were equals, but I held much greater power on the political and economic scale. Even though Max worked for the government, I was the son of the country's supreme ruler.

"Max was brilliant. He would have been famous for his genetic and viral engineering in any other setting. However, my father turned him into a virtual slave before he could even be acknowledged for his accomplishments. Regardless, Max was a mismatched sort. You see, he tested his research on himself, the very action that gained my father's respect. The practice cost him dearly, though. While he had greatly increased his muscle strength, his massive right arm was covered in rough, bestial fur. His entire left side had been replaced with living robotics, semi-organics to be exact. I was somewhat involved in that particular transformation. Patches of reptilian scales and spines ridged his right shoulder and tinged the surrounding flesh with a sickly, greenish hue. His face was the last truly human part of his appearance except for his stained white shirt and vintage denim jeans.

"When I saw him, it was obvious he had not shaved in days. He looked tired, overworked, and overwhelmed. My father was pushing him too hard with the unreasonable demands for success. I had become accustomed to having these laid upon me as well. The last time Max was subjected to such stress, the situation cost him half of his body. Ironically, that was exactly how my father controlled him from that time forward. My father had a chip implanted in Max's chest plate that, when shut down, would disconnect him from the left half of his body. While Max rightfully feared this contingency, he somehow remained a few degrees beyond my father's control.

"When I asked him to join me, he naturally agreed, faster and easier than I had expected. I was not expecting it to be a hard sell, but he was quite eager. Max decided that it would serve best to destroy his laboratory as opposed to allowing its contents to fall freely into my father's hands. Taking only a small bundle of vials wrapped up in a satchel with a set of clean yet tattered clothes, we prepared to depart. We would have to face the issue of the control chip at some point. I asked him if there was anything that could be done about the chip, but he was convinced finding a solution was a worthless endeavor at that point.

"I was not so certain. I had never replaced it before then because it would have triggered Max's execution. I knew that if we tried to remove the chip, my father would deactivate it. Therefore, our only viable option was to give my father the impression that Max was dead. I suggested burning the laboratory and hastily programmed a disturbingly realistic hologram of Max screaming and burning. I found the programming quite unsettling, but it was necessitated by the situation and it was a simple enough exercise.

"Max exited through the hidden back door of the building as I started the blazing fire with the most combustible substances within my reach, such things being uncomfortably plentiful in the lab. I tossed the hologram pod on the floor and left quickly before the chemicals reacted in the air. I regretted leaving his test subjects behind, but the blazes were mercy compared to the fate that awaited them in Max's hands through engineering and imagination.

"I ran down the blank gray corridor and yelled for the guards, telling them Max was trapped inside the lab. From my gauntlet, I quietly keyed the projector to begin and took strange comfort in the faint sound of the projector's speakers starting, though it erupted in the synthesized sounds of Max's pained screams. The scenario played itself out well enough to protect him for some time, but the duration of that protection remained to be seen.

"We met once more back at my mansion. I was about to formally introduce Max to Jake when I saw in my old friend's eyes that he indeed remembered the boy. Since Jake did not share the expression, I assumed his brain was wiped like a chalkboard, leaving only basic knowledge and functions. I had previously discerned that Max had experimented on Jake, but there was something deeper there. I did not inquire about it though, trusting my friend to reveal the information if and when he desired.

"The problem of the chip presented itself much sooner than I had anticipated. It began when Max felt a sort of numbness in the fingers of his left hand at dinner. Though his sensations were limited by the metallic implants throughout that side of him, numbness in semi-organics was the equivalence of the normal response of pain receptors. The sensation meant that the electric impulses from his brain were not reaching the circuitry I helped design. The only answer blaring in my brain was the chip, and I realized the mistake in my judgment. If my father suspected that Max was alive, he would shut the chip down immediately, but even if he believed Max was dead, he would not waste power on the remote device or take any chances that it was a trick.

"Max continued to lose feeling. It began in his toes and spread to his wrist and ankle. As Max lost feeling, I lost time. If the electric flow to the robotics stopped, they would 'die' as quickly as any human tissue without blood. Then even if he survived, they would then have to be rebuilt, and that was not a luxury we could afford by any means. There was nothing to ensure that the living tissues incorporated with the devices could handle a shutdown.

"Without hesitation, I threw the armor off of my wrists and grabbed an electric generator in one hand and a screwdriver in the other. Lacking time for notification, I pried the metal plate off of the control panel in Max's chest, much to his surprise and pain. While my oldest friend winced with the electric feedback into his brain, his technological guts began spilling from the opening I had made. As soon as the chip was exposed beside his encased living heart, I slammed the screwdriver tip through the control chip. He roared in agony, and it took considerable physical effort on my part to restrain him from thrashing.

"Every bit of the power grid's wireless energy, which was monitored and allowed into Max's system by the chip, ceased, and he was then less than thirty seconds away from losing his left half permanently. I jammed the positive and negative electrodes into their respective sockets at the output end of the chip. It wasn't the same modulation of power his circuits were used to receiving, but it had to suffice. As I slowly turned the dial to an acceptable energy level, Max's circuits thankfully hummed with renewed life. While I began fashioning a new chip that would pirate energy from the grid, I gazed upon my now somewhat comfortably resting friend."

The stranger grew silent before the journalist. The armor clad man's mind flashed back to the day he found his best friend again and, for what seemed like the first time in his life, a miniscule smile crossed his face. It was barely perceptible, but even that was an uncomfortable concession to emotion for him.

CHAPTER 4

THE MAN WHO would grow to break the restraints of time remembered walking through the halls of his father's newest research base accompanied by a host of his father's guards. It was only a few short years before his breach of the fourth dimension. He walked along the hallways oblivious to his surroundings. In theory, he was supposed to inspect the facility; in reality, his mind was elsewhere as usual. He survived by living mostly in his own head and contented himself with that level of existence. Abruptly, a voice broke through his self-induced daze; it was present for a moment and gone again. The recognition had not yet set in, but the stranger grabbed the nearest guard by the collar, disregarding rank. He asked the hapless guard whose laboratory was beyond the doorway.

"Maximus Fitzgerald, sir," the hapless guard squealed.

"Max," the stranger said. The recognition struck him, and he stood staring at the door with his mouth agape. He had long given up hope of ever finding his childhood friend again. The last shred of his disbelief melted away as the armor plating on the dark steel door slid open before him. He dropped the guard to his knees and started forward.

Max Fitzgerald's back was to the stranger. His light brown hair was as ragged and unkempt as it had been in school. The only clothing Max wore in the unnatural heat of the biological subject lab was a pair of jeans which had seen better and cleaner days. His charcoal colored, plastic molded boots lay where they had been hastily thrown. His back was exposed as he sat the wrong way in the rotating chair. The years faded as the stranger stepped closer to his lost confidant. Max sat brooding over a rotating hologram of a DNA strand and a cup of coffee. The break was obviously well-deserved.

Max turned at the resounding sound of the clanging metal footsteps. His eyes caught on the armor covered feet and worked their way up the figure. Max was greeted with only a slightly less astounding sight that the one witnessed by the journalist, but his acceptance was faster and easier. "Oh my-"

"God? Sorry to disappoint you," the stranger answered with quiet sarcasm.

"If it isn't young Mr. Stone," Max said, leaping to his feet, "come to crack the whip."

"If it isn't old Mr. Fitzgerald," Stone said, clapping Max on the arm, "slacking again." Then, his friend's appearance really settled into Stone's mind. The patch of scales and spines on Max's right shoulder were offset only by the short, bristly fur covering his arms. "Wait, how did this happen?"

"What?" Max took a moment to register that it had been so long since they had seen each other and the wearing of age was not the most influential change in his him. "Oh, you mean this!" He held up his right arm with its various affectations. "I guess I've gotten used to it. I infected myself with several positive gene-altering viruses," Max said, looking down at his arms with satisfaction.

"I've never heard of a positive virus, but that still doesn't explain how you got here," Stone questioned. "How did I not know about this?"

"It explains more than you might think. This is why your father sought me out. There's not much glory in it, but it pays well, right?" Max's bitter laugh did not go unnoticed. Stone's father did not employ people, he threatened them into service: work loyally and get rewarded, or everyone you care about dies. With the utterly corrupt corporate world left standing to appease the upper ranks of the dictator's military and regional supervisors, Stone's father impressed the most promising talent available into his own private service before the ravenous vultures of the business world could hire them. Since there was no economy to speak of within the government, payment simply meant a meal the next day and medical care if the person was worth enough; in military service, even that was never guaranteed, but it was a better hope than most people had.

"I had no idea you were here or even that you got conscripted. Why didn't you get in touch with me?"

"Your father forbid it, and it's not like it's very inconspicuous to call the second most powerful man in the Americas," Max apologized.

"You pick now to start obeying the rules," Stone laughed bitterly.

"There are worse places than this, I suppose, and worse things that can happen. Now that you found me, let's see if you're still a genius!" Max magnified the image of the DNA strand and brought it into three dimensions. "I want to increase this man's metabolism and cellular division rate with a virus. I need the strand size fixed to fill the protein coat of the delivery system," Max continued.

"Child's play," Stone shot as he dropped his gauntlets, ceremoniously cracked his knuckles, and punched a series of keys. The image changed and the viral blueprint appeared on the neighboring monitor. "I always have overestimated you, Max. No wonder I always got better grades."

"Very funny, but let's not forget eighth grade phys. ed. when I got an 'A' and you didn't. I will admit, though, that it has taken me an hour just to get as far as I did."

"You worked nearly an hour without a break?" The armored figure gestured down at the mug casting its residual moisture ring on the desk. "How do you do it? It must be torture."

"Oh, your wit is as sharp as ever, twice as dull as mine. You forget that other people's torture is my pleasure."

The distinctive clack of the tape recorder brought Stone out of the memory induced reverie. The last trace of the barely visible smile faded from his lips. He resumed his tale as coldly as it had begun.

"This gave me both of my knights already. I was unsure whether or not my father was aware of my challenge at that point; he would find out quickly in any event. I had to complete my army soon. The rooks I had planned could easily be created with Max's assistance, but I still needed bishops.

"When Max was sufficiently recovered, I sought out one such bishop; more accurately, I sought out a monk. His name is Marcus and he was my mentor for a time. The elaborate temples of legend had long since crumbled to dust, so he trained me out of his own modest home. He was eccentric, but he was an exceptional fighter.

"Marcus is the end result of a careful line of breeding. A few decades shy of a century ago, his predecessors claimed to have come into possession of a box of prophecy. It warned of the Apocalypse, and, with my father in power, the monks may have been correct. Once they found this box, they converted themselves from their peaceful and religious ways into modern crusaders. They were rekindled Templar Knights with the belief that they were mankind's hope of stopping whatever power would consume the world so frightfully. The strongest males and females of the resulting order were bred until the number of available bloodlines ticked quickly down to one, Marcus's. He is the culmination of their work, and he has quite a bit of expectation to fulfill.

"When I was younger and claimed my father's military institute was no longer challenging and quit, I was sent to Marcus. I was not sure how my father knew of him, but it did not surprise me that he did. Marcus attacked me as soon as I walked through his door. It was a futile struggle on my part, and I soon found myself on my back and lacking in dignity. He asked me if that was enough of a challenge or if I would quit.

"I trained under him for three exhausting years and I still do not know all of his secrets. His skill was well beyond mine, but my brawn and size soon allowed me to hold my own, though barely. I could never best him, and I respect him more than anyone for that.

"When I went to train under Marcus, I lost contact with Max, who still attended the military academy of New Charleston and was already lax in communication. It was shortly thereafter that our mutual friend Kylie disappeared completely. In that time frame, it seemed as though I had lost everyone that mattered to me, but the training always felt so much more pertinent than keeping in touch.

"After a month of fighting Marcus to a standstill, I decided to move on with my life. Marcus told me he had never encountered anyone with such spirit before, and he gave me the cross you see before you. He gave it to me as it was given to him. He called it the 'key to eternity,' and I believe it may be just that," the stranger said, lifting the artifact gently between two armored fingers.

"I sought out my mentor at his home. I expected a friendly fight at the door, but there was not one. His home was an ancestral temple, part living quarters and part fortress constructed by his order. The hall was empty, and the once lustrous wood was rotting. The floor was dust encrusted and the windows were filthy. It was clear the place had been deserted for quite some time. No candles flickered in the eaves and no incense rose from the burners. The art which had once lined the halls was now gone, the silhouettes of the portraits and paintings echoing their former presence on the walls.

"I was about to leave when an overwhelming force drew me to the stairs. I descended into the darkness. My metal footsteps on the aged stairs were the only sound until a voice echoed off of the walls. 'I knew you would come,' it rang.

"Light began to filter into the void, allowing me to see without infrared. Marcus sat in the center of the room with his feet resting on the thighs of the opposite legs. He sat motionless. I was about to speak when he waved his long, lean hand in front of his face, cautioning me to be silent. 'Calm yourself. I accept the position, but we are not alone here,' Marcus said coldly.

"This was something I had never before witnessed. Marcus was apparently reading my thoughts and my emotions. He knew not only what I was thinking but what I was feeling, as well. In that instant, I was both concerned at what he might find and also began to believe that maybe he was born to save the world.

"I felt a drop of liquid on my shoulder; actually, the sensors detected it. At the conclusion of that second, a brilliant white-hot light flickered overhead and an explosion followed it. My helmet slid over my face as bright fire spiraled down the melting stairs. The weary burning boards overhead began collapsing in on the earthen foundation, gasping into ash. The smoke prevented normal vision and the heat prevented infrared. The often unreliable sonar became my only option for witnessing the event. I detected the outline of a figure in the center of the room. It was not buried but standing and it was definitely not Marcus. More surprising was the figure thrown over its shoulder. It was Marcus. The smoke seemed to glow around the standing silhouette. According to my armor's display, the figure radiated a purple aura, an aura in the visible spectrum.

"I had no idea how much time passed staring at each other across the debris-laden divide before I could see with normal vision. My oxygen reserves began running low and I had to evacuate the building. The upper house was nearly gone, but enough of the wood remained to keep the fire going. The figure's gauntlet reflected the blaze as it indicated a tunnel I had never seen in my time here. When I turned back around from inspecting the passageway, the man and the limp body of Marcus he was holding were gone. I followed them down the tunnel.

"Sunlight greeted my face as I cleared the egress. Before me stood the man swathed in volumes of deep purple fabric. He was armored but not to my own extent; nothing of his appeared modern or enhanced by electronics. His shoulder, arms, calves, and waist were armored in a layered fashion of brass and steel common to the mythical knights of old. His cape and hood hid his features in conjunction with the cloth covering his neck and mouth. The scratched, gilded etchings on the metal of his armor shone brilliantly in the warm sun.

"The limp figure slung across his shoulder was still breathing but it was shallow. My mentor's light blond hair was soiled with ashes and matted with blood at his forehead. His pale skin was scratched sporadically down to his black uniform. I was about to use my suit to run a remote check him on him for the effects of smoke inhalation, but the massive robed figure turned and stalked away.

"I drew my bladed staff and charged to what I expected to be a battle. 'Worry not. I know your home,' the figure's voice said directly into my mind, without my ear as a middleman. In a daze, I followed him to my home. It was a short walk, shorter than it should have been. We were ushered in by Jake at our arrival, and the mysterious man set Marcus on the cleared table. The dark featured figure placed his palm on Marcus's chest, and Marcus began to cough loudly.

"I was grateful to have my mentor alive, but I had no idea who this cloaked figure was or even what he was. It felt as though I had been functioning in a daze since the fire broke out, my clarity of mind as muddled as my vision. The liquid I detected had been combustible, and the arson was no coincidence. I could not allow myself to drop my defenses in front of this supposed savior. In fact, I firmly believed he was the one that started that fire."

CHAPTER 5

"I CANNOT EXPRESS how painful it was to see my oldest friend in such agony. Max was, by that time, able to sit up. The new chip was functioning adequately. I had since reinstalled all of his various wires and routing circuits, but I had not replaced his chest plate in order to monitor his condition.

"Jake wanted nothing to do with Max; that much was instinct I suppose. Jake instead sat silently in a corner, trying to get used to his scarred mirror image. There was something of myself I saw in his solitude.

"I turned to see Marcus recovering on the couch. The color had returned to his body, and his deep blue eyes were darting around in bewilderment. His senses were just returning, but he looked no less confused at my approach. 'What happened?' Marcus struggled to speak at all. I could honestly tell him I had no idea. The man in the cloak said nothing. When Marcus sat up, I pointed towards the stranger." The irony struck the reporter that the stranger before him was calling another man the same.

"Marcus strained to focus," Stone continued. "He seemed as though he were coming out of sedation. As that thought occurred to me, I turned on the dark figure and asked him his name. The answer of 'Robert' rang in my skull as though it was my own internal voice. At least he complied that far. He also said 'I will join you.' It was once more voiced inside my own head as though it was my own suggestion. Despite my deep caution, I found myself accepting that as natural and including him in my plan without further argument." Stone still wondered how Robert had managed that particular trick.

"I sighed as I looked once more around the room and decided to tell my assorted soldiers just what loomed ahead of them. It was strange to see people in my home; I had half expected to be forced to create my army by artificial means. Beyond the people before me, the only task I foresaw as a problem was finding a queen.

"'I want you all to realize what we are about to do. Robert, you may leave if you wish. I do not expect the rest of you to follow. We are going to compete in a game of chess; we are the pieces, and I am the strategist. There are two possibilities for the outcome of this competition. We can bring down my father and perhaps cripple this nightmare he calls government, or we will die. No matter what, this is our chance to weaken this dominion and crush its ruler. This is my father we face, an evil you all know too well, and I will have no dissension. If you wish to leave, do so now,' I ordered, looking at each of them in turn.

"To my surprise, Robert spoke out, actually forming the words. 'You need another bishop. I will join your cause,' he said.

"I suspected his motives, but I allowed him the opportunity to prove himself. 'Our army is nearly complete. When Max recovers fully, we shall begin constructing the rooks. My father will most likely use people as his pawns. I will not. No offense to any here, but I place my trust in technology,' I was careful to look at Robert at that. 'I need only a queen, and I do not foresee having one.' I noticed Max curiously mouthing the name Kylie, which had been my reluctant idea all along. His look was quite discouraging.

"'I am certain my father will accept my challenge, if for no other reason than the fact that his ego will not allow him to pass up an opportunity to prove his might, not to mention that he increasingly seeks my end. In this instance, though, we have him at a disadvantage; we have his greatest genetic engineer and his most prevalent source for technology. Tomorrow, I will go to make my formal challenge.'"

CHAPTER 6

DARKNESS WAS APPROACHING in both times. In the future, Stone was surveying his home. In the present, he was surprised by learning how quickly the events to that point had been recapped. He decided not to tell the reporter about the remainder of the evening. He felt as though he had revealed too much entirely, but it was cathartic to speak with the reporter listening so intently. Vowing to reveal only the relevant facts from that point on, he continued talking. However, he was torn with a desire to share his feelings with someone, anyone who would listen, even a carefully chosen, promising, young, upstart reporter he barely knew.

In the future, the darkness crept in much faster. Stone had shown each of his guests to his respective room. The guest wing had never been used before. He often wondered late at night why he had bothered to add it to the mansion's blueprints. He always told himself he had it constructed because of wishful thinking, wishing for a family. He shook off the thought with some effort. The end result of such thinking was always the same for him; it just drove him further into depression. He soon regained his stoic composure, and he turned his musings to strategy.

He thought of Robert. He was placed in a guest room, but it served as a prison. Stone wondered if his actions had been overhasty. Perhaps it was indeed warranted. Robert's room was comfortable. It had all of the necessary facilities. The only object separating Robert's chamber from any other in that regard was the signature lock that confined him within the room until Stone deactivated the device personally.

Jake was in the second of the two guest rooms. Max was in Stone's own chambers, and Marcus was still recuperating on the sofa. The excessive company made Stone uneasy. For all the courage and strength he could summon in public, he was uncomfortable with people. Something inside told him it was not his place by any means.

Stone decided to test himself. He went to the basement as he had done every night since his residence was completed. He placed his palm on the wall. His armored hand reflected the intense glow from within the wall circuitry. He pressed in a code on the keypad that replaced the light. At the cool burst of air, he walked through the door that was hidden until then.

He shed his armor in the dimly lit chamber beyond. In its place, he donned thick and stiff black combat pants similar to the ones Marcus perpetually wore. The only other object on his lithe form was the wooden cross that hung perennially around his neck. He chose his workout program: two combat drones, maximum setting, and partially resolved dojang. He had faced these drones almost every night since he constructed the testing chamber, but he had never faced two at once on the maximum setting. They would bring all of the combat skills he had been able to put into programming against him with lethal force. This was his test; if he could not pass this, then he was not worthy of his challenge and it would die unspoken along with him.

Stone walked down the pitch black hallway that opened before him. There was no light through the corridor. The darkness was meant to disorient him. He walked perfectly straight down the walkway and stepped into the holographic chamber. The door whispered shut behind him, and the dojang reared into three-dimensional life. The walls contained panels that would slide out to form solid geometric shapes, but the rest of the room was formed with sensitive projections. This was another test for the combatant. Because holographic projections sprayed the entire room, knowing which objects were bent light and which were backed by solid panels was half of the challenge. It also taught a person not to rely too heavily on sight. Other sources of light were barred from the chamber because they could reveal the lifeless gray projective walls.

He stood in the open area of the room, surrounded by various artificial objects and workout artifacts. He had ten seconds before the robots of his own design would attempt to kill him. Stone pushed his hand through a nearby boxing bag. It made him feel like a ghost whenever he did that. He clutched his cross in his other palm and waited.

The first of the robots stepped through the pseudo door in front of its maker. The drones were huge bipedal killing machines covered in a lightweight, durable alloy. The robot caught Stone around the neck even as he jumped away. He saw the robot's familiar green, oval eye sockets glow. The construct's forefinger and thumb squeezed him tighter. Using his honed agility and flexibility, he swung and landed a kick to the metal midsection of the robot. The robot loosened its grip and threw him through an artificial bench. His face grazed the cool, smooth floor. He expected to impact with wood, but that was the point: sight can be deceptive.

The merciless purple behemoth was on him again. Stone had twenty seconds before his attacker had company. The robot's hulking frame had him again in its wiry grip. This time, it held his sides. He saw the scanning green eyes, imagining the construct's expression if he would have installed a mouth. He was slammed down into a bench with mass behind it. The wind gushed from his lungs, and his ribs began to ache. He had ten seconds left. His familiar disappointment in himself turned to more familiar rage. Eight seconds.

He pushed past the pain, gasped for air, and charged. Six seconds. The mammoth being fell with the impact, taking Stone with it. Three seconds. Stone dug his bony fingers into the creation's eye slots and pulled with all of the strength he possessed. The countless hours of training served him well, but his muscles still screamed with the effort. One second. The metal figure's neck gave way. Wires stretched and broke. Tempered metal bent and weakened. Stone was out of time.

He had one chance; he delivered a powerful kick to the side of the now fragile neck. The sensors of the skull had not yet realigned, and the head went forward, swung, and fell. The first robot lost its balance but proceeded with its arms groping aimlessly as the second approached.

The second robot's thick tripod of a foot slammed through the chest of the first, spraying purple shards and sparks from the new opening in the damaged construct. Catching his breath, Stone realized he had not programmed the robots to work together. They saw each other as targets. As the new construct stomped its predecessor to the ground, he vowed to change that program even if his aching chest did not support him on the idea.

He looked up to see the second robot hoisting the headless wreckage of the first over its own head. It flexed the cylindrical conglomerations of its arms, and he ducked behind the bench he had been thrown into moments ago. The headless wreckage slammed into the bench, barely missing its intended destination of his body. The lifeless form launched sparks in its wake and exploded into shrapnel and smoke at the impact, the three fingered right hand landing beside him in a crumpled heap.

The new adversary ripped Stone from his crouched position and held him by the shoulders. He knew well enough what came next. His head was hard, but it was no match for the metallic head butt his creation could deliver. He forced his knees between his chest and the behemoth. He pushed with all the might he had, even as the metal of his adversary cut into his shins. Something gave out. He was not sure whether it was the plating or his back.

He felt the three fingers on both sides of him relax. He was free for the moment. At this, he resolved to strengthen the circuit integrity of the next batch to eliminate using the same procedure again. If the robots were designed any better, they would most likely destroy their maker as they had been designed to do.

Stone reached up into the whirring guts of his creation. It was a move only the robot's designer could have made. He felt for the hum of the fist-sized generator, and it burned him as he wrapped his hands around the device. He pulled his clutched fist straight down through the chest of the robot, and the glow faded from the construct's eyes. The metallic shell collapsed on the floor, and the holograms of the room wavered. He dropped the humming generator as the pain of the heat overwhelmed his grip.

After another ripple, the colors of the room faded away into the antiseptic, sickly gray. Twelve out of the twenty objects in the room were backed by the solid panels. The geometric shapes folded back into the walls, and Stone removed his necklace and knelt amidst the purple debris, holding his cross in prayer.

CHAPTER 7

HE HAD NO idea how long he stayed there. He never did. Fighting exhausted his anger. Only then did he feel fit to pray, and only when he prayed was he comfortable enough to sleep. When he had said his thanks to God and begged for forgiveness he did not believe he would get, he walked back out through the hallway, which now had illumination. He had beaten his own challenge again. He had survived another time.

The steady stream of sweat had slowed to a trickle down his aching chest, and Stone had replaced the cross at his heart. He gazed at his armor. From where he stood, it looked as though it was still occupied except for the hollow neck. It seemed to regard him as something lesser but it would accept him anyway.

Piece by piece, he reluctantly put the armor back on his person. After long consideration, he decided he would rest easier with it that night. He was not used to company, and he did not want to expose weakness before his guests. Even with the cushioning, however small, his bloodied shins and bruised chest throbbed. He desperately wanted to shed the bulk of the full armor he now wore and walk his grounds unencumbered. He was disturbed by a stray thought; he felt like an outcast in his own home. He had worked so hard to make a place for himself where he felt free of his father's cage and now that sanctuary had been freely handed over to others.

Marcus was awake on the couch. "I could never sleep on that thing, either," Stone offered. "Would you like something else?"

"No, your battle woke me," Marcus responded.

Stone was dumbfounded. "The walls are soundproof. That's impossible."

"Nothing is impossible. You're right, though, that I didn't hear the sound. I heard your rage, your desperation, your pain, and your sadness." Marcus's gaze fastened on Stone's eyes. "I heard the conflict in your soul, even louder than usual."

Wishing his helmet would slide over his face, Stone swallowed. "I didn't know you could."

"There is much you don't know about me. I never could do such things before a few months ago, though. Even now, I can only do them, unpredictably, at close range. Still, I felt your control as well. You never lost it. You have gone beyond what I have taught you," Marcus elaborated, beaming with pride and then disappointment, "though you have never learned peace."

"I have trained myself since I left your care."

"I see you still keep that at your heart," Marcus said, pointing at the wooden cross. "It is merely an icon, remember well what it represents. I don't know if you will ever be at peace, but the forgiveness you seek is not impossible. These are dark times, darker even than any in my order could have predicted. I'm the only one left now, you know, but I think I did well enough in training you."

Stone held the cross gently in his cold metal grasp. "I will always remember," he said quietly, staring at the fine grain that still stood out through the age of the preserved wood. It reflected slightly in his gauntlet and he looked again at Marcus sitting wearily on the couch. "Walk with me?"

"Yes, I think some air may be exactly what I need," Marcus agreed as he steadied himself on his feet. There was an age in him that did not show except in small moments like that one. The two of them walked silently through the upper balcony doors out onto the large porch on the third story of the manor. Marcus touched the black curtains as they passed through them. Stone's mansion was vast and empty. The walls were barren, the hallways clear. It was shades of gray from the entrance to the end, more akin to a mausoleum than a home. The night air greeted them with a chill. Marcus shivered slightly but a look of serenity crossed his face and it passed. Stone merely looked through the tree line to the waxing moon.

Stone turned to his mentor, his eyes reluctant to leave the lunar light. "Now then, who is that cloaked man?"

"He seems familiar, but my memory is failing me in this case. If I remember anything, I shall certainly share it with you."

"There's something else, too." Stone swallowed hard and his mouth set in its familiar scowl. "Will you come with me tomorrow, when I make my challenge? I trust you heard my little speech. Max and, unless I miss my guess, Jake belong to my father. He would simply enslave or slaughter them, and truly there is no guarantee we will not meet the same fate. I can't trust Robert, so that leaves you."

"Very well, but why not go alone?"

"My father would never take me seriously if I showed up by myself," Stone sighed. "He never takes me seriously anyway. He would think it is just one more foolish game, but he fears you. He'll never admit it, but he doesn't know what to make of you. I think he would take this challenge seriously if you went with me." Stone looked back at the moon as though mesmerized. In reality, the face he wore was no more expressive than the helmet that usually covered it. There was an inhumanity to his movements that had been trained there, eliminating any softness he had ever found in his own visage. "I need to make a stop first, too. I would like to walk if it's all the same to you."

"Walking will be fine. That stop you mentioned, you seek a queen." Marcus did not look at him, but he did not really need to do so. Looking at Stone's face would reveal nothing more than staring at the moon. "This will not go well for you."

"Goodnight, Marcus." Stone turned and walked back inside, his metallic footsteps ringing with light tinny echoes in the empty hallways.

"Sleep well, warrior Stone." Marcus looked out over the grounds. He watched the nocturnal stirrings in the forest below, reading instinct and primal needs in the multitude of creatures that stirred below him. He envied his predecessors for a moment, knowing a time that lacked such paranoia and violence. It felt so long ago that people visited things called zoos and wildlife was something that could be enjoyed rather than feared. His memory faded back to his childhood for a moment and unwanted tears of regret welled in his eyes.

Still disturbed and distracted by how quickly Marcus had assessed him, Stone went to his room to retrieve a blanket and a pillow. It was an act of habit. His armor controlled his temperature and comfort, and he would probably sleep standing up anyhow. He dropped the bedding back into the closet. In any case, Stone had bolstered his confidence, at least temporarily, thanks to Marcus. That was something he sorely needed, though he would need more than that to steady himself for what awaited him in the morning. For as much as he hated emotions, he could never really master them.

Stone soon found that he could not sleep. Nerves kept him awake. His armor quietly took him through the halls. Max was sleeping soundly, a small, oscillating red light above his head lending assurance that the chip in his chest was working properly. Jake was also asleep. With his arms folded over his chest, he had the appearance of a mummy in a black wrap. Robert's door had not been opened, which was quite reassuring. Stone pretended not to notice the signature lock laying in pieces outside the door. The motion sensors were operational, and they reported no movement. Tomorrow promised to be a very long day indeed.

Morning came slowly. As he expected, Stone had been awake all night. His heavy eyelids lost out to the dread of the meeting to come, though it was not the meeting with his father that concerned him. Daylight lent him some comfort, and Marcus was awake by the time he came in from watching the sunrise.

"Would you like breakfast first, or shall we go? It is going to be a long walk," Stone said hastily.

"My stomach can wait. We should go. I can tell you are desperate to leave, yet your anxiety overwhelms you."

"That it does." He looked at Marcus then, the slightest trace of age showing in his posture and he thought better of making his mentor hike for ten miles it would take to reach their destination. "I'm sorry for the way I'm acting. We don't have to walk. You're still weakened. ," Stone said nervously. He had forgotten that his armor allowed him to keep pace with most vehicles, a luxury Marcus did not have.

"Think nothing of it, young one. I will manage," Marcus ceded.

The words 'young one' struck Stone rather deeply. He forgot sometimes that Marcus was twice his own age. Marcus still looked younger than Stone himself. "It wouldn't take long to fashion accelerated boots with the abilities of mine. I can rig a kinetic field generator strong enough to keep you from breaking your legs when you walk in them."

"That might make them more usable," Marcus said dryly.

"It'll also keep bugs from acting like bullets." Stone continued undaunted. "Ten minutes tops. It would get my mind off of things for a little while at least."

"If you wish," Marcus said smiling. Stone had never seen Marcus this way. He seemed almost otherworldly.

"That will give you a chance to eat, too. You need strength after your ordeal."

"I won't trouble you," Marcus insisted.

"You volunteer to fight for me, and you think I will be troubled by feeding you?"

Marcus said nothing. Stone felt as though the conversation had taken on an awkward feeling, yet everything to him felt awkward of late. Stone warmed a plate of pasta and added strong seasoning. He remembered that it was one of Marcus's favorite dishes though one he rarely enjoyed. Stone assumed the taste had to be acquired until he tried it himself. He handed the plate to Marcus and added "I know it's odd for breakfast, but I don't have much else right now."

Without awaiting a response, Stone walked to a nearby closet, one of the many cluttered with pieces of technological debris. He began wiring various circuits through various pieces and ignited the soldering laser in his gauntlet without even bothering to move to a more open space. Quicker than expected, he had constructed two sleek, silver layered boots. Despite the near-perfect fit, Marcus still found them uncomfortable. The rounded rims fell just short of his knees and conformed to his feet with enough flexibility to launch a kick without affecting his technique. Two indentations on either side of his ankle marked the hydraulic joint and the emission point of the energy field. They were strange and remarkable, uniquely crafted by hand and appearing machined.

After finishing the rest of his meal without conversation, Marcus set out with Stone. They covered a mile in less than two minutes. The boots were working, and the kinetic disruption field was holding, yet to the two men it felt as if they were moving at a snail's pace over the sun dried terrain. They both basked in the quiet, knowing what was to come would change the little bit of peace that they had forever. This was their calm before the storm, waiting as the world churned darkly around them for their moment to have some effect.

CHAPTER 8

STONE BEGAN TO relax slightly after leaving Robert behind. He had run every possible scenario, and he could not understand how that lock was destroyed. He wanted answers, and Marcus had none to give him, at least not yet. Stone kept silent with his thoughts for nearly half an hour before speaking about the inevitable subject.

"I don't like Robert," Stone pronounced without realizing it.

"You have no reason to, though by the same token, you have no solid reason to dislike him, either," Marcus said passively.

"Yes, but he's just so mysterious and not exactly forthcoming. That distinctive rasp in his voice is from disuse."

"I fit that 'mysterious' category if you will remember," Marcus said defensively. "I don't think that makes me evil, and if it does, I've taken my life in the wrong direction. I chose to allow you into my confidence; that is something I rarely do with people. You are the only person other than those from my order that I have ever told about my proposed destiny. Does that make me a bad person for not being forthcoming to others?"

"No, no, not at all. By your destiny, I guess you mean the part about-"

"Defeating a force that will consume the world as we know it with an unparalleled army," Marcus recited.

"Yeah, look, I may have been wrong in making the whole 'mysterious' comment, but don't you find it strange that he can speak with his mind? Before he spoke aloud, he broadcast his thoughts straight into my head."

"That is an ability I have found that I possess as well. Sometimes, young Stone, you have to have faith in people. I am unsure of this

Robert, but, if he offered to join you, knowing what is at stake, he may be sincere."

"When you gave me this cross, you told me never to lose faith in people or in myself. I have done my best with that, but you know it's the hardest thing I have to face, and it doesn't help that he knew where the training grounds were, where my home was, and he won't even reveal his face."

"Wait a minute," Marcus said, pausing. He weighed the evidence in his mind: the man would not reveal his face, and he showed up at the training grounds calling himself Robert. Marcus did not see this as happenstance anymore. The expression on Marcus's face turned more solemn with a revelation Stone did not see. Stone, however, was simply glad to have finally inspired doubt in his mentor about the intentions of the stranger. "Not many people," added Marcus thoughtfully, "really do know where that is."

They were entering the dark side of the metropolis then. They had been treading through the quiet woods of Stone's protected estate to that point; here the rare forest gave way first to decayed desolation and then to abundant skyscrapers. Most of the towering structures, though once bustling with free people in a thriving economy, had, under the new regime, become little more than glorified concentration camps and breeding pens. Stone's father wanted the cheapest labor possible, meaning forced.

The streets of the city itself were lifeless. Even though New Charleston was the capital, it was no different than most of the other major cities under the dictator's rule. In general, the only people that were allowed to roam freely were military personnel. The rest were either trapped inside the walls or wisely kept to the few neutral districts left to corporate ownership. Since what would have been the whole of the lower class and the near-extinct middle class occupied the prison cells filling the enormous skyscrapers, the streets had very few guests.

"This changes things now," Marcus said gravely. For the first time since leaving Marcus's care, Stone saw his mentor upset. If Marcus was perturbed, something was very wrong indeed. "Robert. Huh, that takes me back. It has to do with my mentor. His name was Edmund Drake. Many of the skills he taught me are the ones I passed on to you. I guess the best word to describe him is 'unique.' Drake is the only name

I ever knew him by, even though I basically grew up under his care. Like Robert, he would not remove the cowl he wore before anyone but me. He was afraid of revealing any potential weakness to his enemies, claiming the face tells everything. It seems you two have something in common."

Stone was taken aback by that last statement. It was utterly correct, but it was just not something he ever talked about. He did not think it was quite that obvious, even to the man who probably knew him better than he realized or wanted.

"I trained under him for ten long years. I had to learn everything about my ancestry, and there was quite a bit to learn. Something that strikes me is that he looked the same when I left as he did when I first arrived," Marcus continued. Stone could understand Marcus's last revelation quite easily. Since he had been acquainted with his mentor, Marcus had not gained a wrinkle.

The most memorable time Marcus could recall of being under Drake's tutelage was his stay in Drake's American home. Before that time, Marcus had always boarded at the training grounds. Marcus was awed by the design of Drake's complex. All of the various towers and rooms were oriented around a wide central area filled with racks of weapons from around the world and mats that were only slightly softer than the rocky ground. The orientation of the residence reminded the young Marcus of a medieval castle. The insides were elaborately decorated in old English style, ornate and gilded tapestries and paintings lined every crevice into which they could fit. For as drab and foreboding as the outside looked, the inside was warm and inviting and beautiful beyond words.

Inside his home, Drake kept an ancient book. It was something like a journal of the order of monks into which Marcus was born. It was the basis for Marcus's existence. Marcus was shown only one page of the yellowed paper. It read that the best must train the young to be the best. Marcus only truly understood what that meant when Stone walked through his doors. Marcus was the best, and he had to train a protégé to replace him when he himself could no longer be the best. Marcus had fallen silent in his recollection along the road.

"Forgive me my lapse into memory," Marcus finally said. "Drake had a painting inside his foyer that intrigued me. It was ancient for certain. The canvas was aged, and the edges were worn away. The colors were faded and hardly looked like colors anymore. From what I could discern of it, the man in the painting looked just like Drake. Inscribed on the plate attached to the bottom of the frame blazed the words 'Sir Robert of York.'" A chill ran down Stone's spine. "I really didn't pay much attention to that fact until now. Drake told me it was from the time of the original Holy Wars, the Crusades," Marcus finished.

"A person several generations from an ancestor can bear a strong resemblance to that person's forefather. I am also concerned with the ancient practice that springs to mind of alternating names between subsequent generations. That makes it a real possibility that the Robert who saved us could in fact be related to your master," Stone surmised. "Could it be Drake's son?"

"I doubt it. If Drake had a son, I surely would have seen some evidence of the boy's existence in his father's home. Drake never mentioned any children, either."

"You said he was a man of mystery," Stone added questioningly. "Could Robert be Drake?"

Marcus flushed with a tremor of rage. "That cannot be. Even if my mentor was alive, he would be about seventy-five now. Besides," he paused, "my only peer killed my master. I don't think I've ever told you this before. His name was Erik. He arrived only three years before I left, and he hated the fact that Drake favored me. He felt that his lineage should have been the one to fulfill the prophecy, but mine was chosen by the seers. He suffered in silence until I was gone because I was a better fighter, and I never would have let him harm our master. A week after I departed the training grounds, he decided he had waited long enough.

"Drake was training him in the use of a war staff. Erik put a retractable blade in the tip of his weapon. Drake must have been showing him a basic move, probably the one where the staff swings over the opponent's head to force them down and then the other end connects between the lower ribs at the enemy's side, which sets up several further techniques. Just before impact, he must have unsheathed the blade. I'm sure the surprise delayed Drake's reaction. Of course I had to piece all of this together when I found my mentor lying on the ground in a fresh pool of blood. The blade's path traced from between

Drake's ribs clear to his heart. The incriminating weapon sat bloodied beside the body. Erik had signed the wall in blood with the message "True Born" and fled. The blood was still wet when I got there. I must have been only moments too late to do anything about it. I tried to find the murderer, but to no avail."

"Could Robert be Erik?" The shiver got worse.

"For his sake, pray that he is not," Marcus growled.

"That's a terrible burden to bear. You could have told me."

"It was never relevant or necessary. Every man has burdens. Now, tell me about your queen."

"She is not my queen yet. I truly doubt she will be, but I have to try. Her name is Kylie Freedwell. She and Max were my closest friends all the way through school. They were my only friends really; not too many other people would speak to me. I lost track of her around the time I came to train under you."

"Then how did you find her again?"

"It took me two years of tapping into my father's data networks, corporate contracts, and foreign exchange documents to even get close to her again. She has a list of aliases at least ten pages long. She did not want to be found," Stone suddenly appeared even more restless than before.

"Why?"

"For one, she became an assassin. No one seems to know just when or why. I found her through her last employer."

"Have you talked with her since then?"

"No," Stone said honestly, his discomfort overwhelming him. "I figured I would just drop in and say, 'Hey, it's been a while, want to risk your life, and I don't know, maybe die for me?'" Stone's pain was close to the surface. Humor helped with his isolation, though it too had grown cold and unfeeling within him.

"I hope it works," Marcus said with an expression of disappointment crossing his face.

Stone recognized the disapproval on his mentor's visage, and he felt bad for avoiding a necessary topic. He wanted desperately to make up for the insult. "So, do you dress like that in the winter now?" Marcus looked down at his borrowed sleeveless shirt and recently crisped, thin, black workout pants. Marcus took it well, and the little emotion that surfaced left Stone's voice for the remainder of the walk.

CHAPTER 9

THE PAIR APPROACHED the proper address: 18 Broad Street, West Columbia Sector. It was one of the last residential areas left around the downtown area of New Charleston, which still did not save it from military patrol. Kylie's home was plain, blending in nicely with the other compatible prefab houses on the street. It would warrant little attention unless someone knew what he was looking for. Fortunately, Stone did. It was a simple word emblazoned on the address box that caught his attention: StoneCorps. Any address that was occupied was corporately owned and sponsored. His father had provided this place for Kylie. If she was still working for him, things were about to go very wrong.

As Stone approached the building, he awakened the door's motion sensor. There was no sound response like that which was expected. Just as he began to turn back toward Marcus, he noticed that there was a gun pressed to his head. She was good. Of course, there was not much business for a noisy assassin. Stone's helmet slid over his face before the weapon could fire. Protected, he looked straight up the barrel.

The weapon pressed against his optic sensor was an ELF pulse pistol. It created an enormously magnified version of the extremely low frequency field surrounding most appliances. In such a concentrated form, it could poison and disrupt a person's brain before a standard projectile could leave the chamber. The ELF was a popular model among assassins who did not favor excessive gore, and it offered the added bonus of untraceable ammunition.

"Nice to see you, Kylie," Stone's voice rang through the helmet's projection system.

"Get in here before anyone sees me," she ordered.

Stone heard Marcus's voice ringing through his mind, saying, "I'll wait here. The tension is overwhelming. Be cautious." In response, Stone nodded at no one in particular and followed Kylie inside.

Her home was simple. It held a holographic/video screen, a bed, a table, a chair, and an arsenal. Her weapons outnumbered her furniture at least eight to one. The walls were unpainted, and the waxed metal floor lacked carpeting. There were only two doors, one leading outside and the other leading to a private chamber. The room was lit by a single overhead light that had a light blue cover over it, spreading an ethereal feeling throughout the sparse interior.

Kylie herself was as beautiful as ever, especially in Stone's eyes. Her flowing black hair enticed him. Her face was perfect, her features beckoningly sweet. Her green eyes were captivating, entrancing. He wondered just how often he had imagined her in his arms, but he always punished himself for such thoughts, severely. He would never allow her to be an object of lust for him. He knew that what he felt for Kylie was as close to love as he would ever get. She wore a tight navy blue jumpsuit with small leather belts on her arms, legs, and waist that held weapons and ammunition compartments. She turned on him.

"Why did you come here?" She tossed the sleek silver gun from her hand and looked straight at his helmet.

"I'm so glad you're happy to see me," Stone said sardonically as his helmet retracted.

"Answer me."

He studied her stern expression, her features harder than he remembered. "What happened to you, Kylie?"

"Three seconds," she said, pulling a blocky pistol from a holster at her upper arm. Her glare tore at Stone's trepid heart.

"Fine." He removed the helmet to look at her with his own eyes, dark as the sensors but deeper and revealing less. He had to make this quick or he would never be able to say it. "I am placing a formal challenge to my father. It is a game of chess with live pieces. I desire you as my queen. Kylie, at one time you were my most cherished friend, and you are an exceptional warrior. Will you either accept or promise to stay out of it completely?"

"Was that so hard?"

"Kylie, will you? He will use you against me, at least stay out of it. Hide, I know you can."

Her gaze was his only answer. It was the only answer he needed. As much as he had prepared himself for this eventuality, he had always hoped she would choose to side with him. She did not. With that wordless exchange, she had taken Stone's calloused heart and ripped it out of him. She could not have hurt him as badly if she had pulled the trigger on the concussive .45 she now brandished. He felt as though there was a numb void where the remnants of his heart had been, and he was getting sick to his stomach.

♟

In the past, Stone continued his story without pause. Evening had firmly asserted itself. He was still pained at tearing open the wound he would receive years from that point in time. "Kylie was the only one I ever had a chance with, the only one I ever wanted. I cannot recall another girl even returning my gaze in a long, long time. I was nothing to them, but she was different. She had my heart in its fullest. I was probably mistaken in tracking her down in the first place," he continued, once more abandoning his vow to stick to facts alone. He could not keep the emotions contained as well as he should or as well as he had in his own time.

Stone thought back to the last time she ever really smiled at him. They were in high school. His father had gathered the might of his main forces and he was poised to strike the first note in a symphony of destruction. Stone had no idea what was happening, but he took full advantage of the respite offered by his father's neglect.

Kylie, Max, and Stone had been playing paintball at the boardwalk near Folly Beach. Kylie was a better shot than either of them, so she usually let them team up against her. They won about a quarter of the time. After the sound defeat, Max had taken his leave, punching Stone encouragingly in the shoulder when Kylie was turned away from them. Stone's jumpsuit was covered in violent splotches of dark blue paint and Kylie's jumpsuit was paint free. They rambled about nothing and he bought her cotton candy from an incandescent clown cart. Eventually, they ran out of boardwalk and ended up on dry white sand, sitting down on the cement pylons from a pier that had been destroyed years ago.

As the waves crashed and the light faded, they stopped talking.

She just looked at him with those piercing eyes. Those sharp green eyes seemed to catch everything and reveal nothing. When he saw her staring, he backed away but she just kept looking at him. "You're a funny little boy," she said slowly and quietly. Stone felt his heart pounding, certain she could hear it, could see it with those shining green eyes. His cotton candy fell to the sand forgotten. He said nothing, just sitting there, looking into her eyes. She smiled so warmly, he would have sworn it was daylight all over again. He felt the heat of that smile all the way through him. The wind shifted and her hair blew across her face.

She whisked her hair back and set her hand unknowingly down on his. He froze. She looked up at him again, her face showing surprise, but she left her hand where it was. Stone knew with certainty that he was going to die of a heart attack in the next few moments. She moved two of her fingers beneath his on the rock, staring at him again. Stone's mind was screaming at him to say something or do something. The only voice that came to him was his father's voice. *You're worthless*, he heard. *Your friends make fun of you when you aren't around. Pathetic. Pitiful. Worthless, worthless, worthless.* Stone fought hard against the tears. He fought so hard, but he just could not hold them back. He was a little boy without a suit of armor. "Worthless," he whispered, tears forming in his eyes.

Kylie gripped his hand and held it. "Stop," she said forcefully. "Don't listen to him. Your father is a great man, but he's not a good father." Her tone was firm but not unkind.

"No, he's not a great man," Stone shouted as he stood, breaking her hold on his hand. She sat quietly for a long moment.

"Okay," she said sadly, looking down at the sand for the first time, kicking it with her tennis shoe.

"Sorry," he said, slumping down in the sand facing the water.

"It's okay," she said, carelessly picking up a swirled sea shell. She threw it at a crab that had just emerged for its evening meal, sending it flying at the impact.

"Why's he so great?" Stone asked quietly.

"Dad says he is going to change the country. He said he is the best hope we have to get the country moving forward again."

"My father?"

"You live in your head too much. You should pay more attention to what's around you," she said, standing and brushing the sand off of her clothes. "Come on, let's go dig up sand dollars," she said, running into the waves and not looking back at him. She never looked at him like that again and Stone thought of that look every day. It would take years to construct the stoic dam against his emotions and it was weakening as he continued his tale. As he began to speak again, he closed his eyes and remembered her looking at him again.

CHAPTER 10

IN THE FUTURE. Kylie sat alone in her barren room. She was contemplating choices that required a swift decision. Stone and his companion had departed half an hour ago. After weighing her options, she decided she had a call to make.

She opened a small bag that was concealed under her bed.

Inside were two video disks and a cash card. She had played the first disk moments before Stone had arrived. It offered twice her standard fee for the termination of a very tough mark. She inserted the second disk.

The holo/video screen clicked to life. A blanket of electronic snow covered the screen until blazing green letters spelling out "SECURE" appeared. The screen went blank until the same jade letters appeared again, this time saying "LINK ESTABLISHED".

She stared at death itself. Before her stood the image that haunted children's dreams, with a massive body swirled in dark garb and a face in pale illumination. A mark, perhaps a scar, the color of lava, burned below his right eye. Shadows seemed to come alive within his eyes. For a fleeting instant, Kylie wondered if she had died and her soul was about to be collected. "Will you accept my offer?" The voice was as powerful, resounding, and ethereal as the image.

"Yes, consider the mark terminated," Kylie assured.

"And my other offer?"

"Yes as well." Blade Stone was not a man to be refused.

"Excellent. You will not be sorry," his voice said as if from beyond the grave.

"I already am," she said to herself after the link faded to black.

CHAPTER 11

A MONITOR FLICKERED on in the vast combat arena. A disk began revealing its contents upon the screen. The disk had been rendered obsolete almost as soon as it had been recorded. In theory, the disk should not exist. It did.

The recording that burst into two-dimensional life brought an eerie glow to the immediate area. The contents were from an archaic security camera at a period of transition years ago when Stone had perfected holographic technology and adapted it to surveillance. The security cameras were in the process of being overturned. This particular device should not even have been operational. It was.

The image of Maximus Fitzgerald appeared. He held a small vial in his gloved hand. Since the backs of his hands were as hairy as his arms, he often preferred to cover them when he was working. Jokes had passed among his underlings that he was trying to give himself leather hands.

Max plugged the vial into an elbow jointed injection tube. He rechecked the equations on the screen and brought up the completed model of his latest virus. It had been hastily designed to meet a deadline set by Blade.

"Here goes everything," his voice cracked over the monitor. He took the injection tube and pressed it into his shoulder. He barely had time to set the plastic instrument down before every muscle in his back and arm tightened. Even through the flat screen with lines of age and color distortion, it was obvious Max was in pain.

With his functional hand, he had time to open a communications channel before collapsing, convulsing on the floor. The message was inaudible. He could only hope it would be traced quickly, before the select few of his cells that were called upon to replicate the virus could complete their mission.

Unseen by the camera, the call had reached Stone's residence. He played the brief call twice, having to turn the volume up to its maximum setting the second time. At that level, normal conversation became deafening. He barely heard his name called through the background noise. Luckily, Stone's private line automatically traced every call that came through. It was Max.

Stone had a horrible feeling in his stomach, and he knew he had a limited time frame. He already wore the lower half of his armor, and he grabbed the nearest shirt he could find. He clicked his boots to maximum setting and left. He arrived faster than he had hoped, but he could not simply stop when he neared the laboratory.

He had never calculated the exact speed he could reach with his phenomenal armor. He only knew that if he came to a sudden stop, he would shatter every bone in his legs and quite possibly crack his spine like a whip as well. He began to slow down just in time to avoid lethal impact with the sliding doors. The kinetic field generated by his armor would protect him for a few seconds, but it would break down quickly against anything more than air resistance.

A stray thought brought Stone's mind to focus on just how close scientists and engineers a few decades ago had been to that particular technology. They, however, did not even know it existed. Objects developed a shield of sorts out of the acceleration of the surrounding air particles from atomic collisions at extremely high speeds. Stone found a way to induce and magnify such a field. He lost track of that particular thought upon finding his ailing friend.

The fur on Max's left arm was visibly coarser than that on his right; it was bristling straight up. His skin was breaking down and returning as scar tissue right before Stone's eyes. Stone's gaze fastened on the source of his friend's pain. He saw the empty injection tube and vacant vial on the table top. He knew that messing with the actual chemicals would be like banging his head against a wall. Fortunately, Max had left his work open on his the computer. The computer was different. Once it was on that screen, it was simple data manipulation.

Max was getting worse. Cycling through the various screens, Stone saw the problem quickly. The external oxygen calculations were out of balance, meaning that the air was literally killing the geneticist. Stone accessed the isolation chambers and set the filter to screen out oxygen. Max was heavy to carry without his upper armor. He propped Max against the wall of the chamber, connected him to the breathing apparatus, and sealed him inside.

The image wavered as the watcher flashed the recording one hour ahead. Stone had been working unsuccessfully to create an antivirus or at least a blueprint for one. Max had stabilized; however, the damage was already done. At least it was not getting any worse. "I told you there was no such thing as a positive virus," Stone chided. He was half cursing Max for not testing the virus first and half cursing himself for his failure to find a solution. "But did you believe me? Of course not. This is your field, not mine. I could sure use your help."

"Then," a wheeze came from the isolation chamber's intercom, "you shall have it." A strained cough and a long silence came across the communications device, followed by a long puff on the respirator.

"I see you made it. I only have half of a cure so far."

A wheeze and static were the first reply. "Well, I only have half a body at this point, so that works." He coughed a laugh. "Must I do everything?"

Stone laughed at that. He was glad to hear his friend again. He then cursed only his own inadequacy. "Maybe you should do this yourself. The problem is that if you leave that chamber, your cells will start producing the virus again. You will die in less than two minutes at the rate it was going when I began suspension." Stone's usual emotionless demeanor took Max by surprise for once.

"How did you stop it in the first place?"

"I didn't. It requires oxygen to infect and perpetuate itself. I arrested its development by removing the oxygen."

"Well, what have you got so far?"

"Your skin has about an hour left in isolation before it suffocates. There is an all-purpose antiviral file here that would kill off all producing cells in your body, but it would kill the altered cells with it."

"How bad would that be?"

"You would lose about forty-three percent of your body by the time the injected solution could counteract the damage to your system. You may not survive at all. Your body would attempt repair, which would overwork your system, exposing you to every ailment that was not self-induced in the process."

"Well, you have to try it."

"Not in its present form. If I could mix it with micro-bionics, I could fool your cells into thinking they were healthy. They might even function with a specific electric current. It's definitely going to take a lot of reconstruction. I don't know how the virus missed every vital organ but your left lung. You are one lucky man, Maximus."

"I thought you needed help. You seem to have this all figured out."

"I had some time to think about it while you were conveniently unconscious. I need to find a way to get the micro-bionics to enter the new cells your body creates from now on, though, or this episode will repeat every few years."

"So get busy, then," Max advised playfully.

"I have to admit, chemicals are not my strong suit."

Another half hour slid by while Max explained exactly what Stone had to do. Stone found a small production unit that would accommodate the micro-bionic devices of his specification. When the solution was prepared, it was time for a field test.

Stone opened the door to the isolation chamber, and the virus immediately reactivated. The filter struggled to purify the influx of the atmosphere as he administered the contents of the vial. He pressed the injection tube firmly against Max's shoulder. Max passed out from the pain. The skin around the injection site developed a glossy gray appearance. The original virus began spreading down Max's leg too quickly, so Stone was forced to cut open the seam of Max's left pant leg and inject him with a second dose of the substance.

Max was soon conscious and resting again. His left side was numb and tingling. It would not respond to his mind's commands. Stone had gone to the electronics storage room to gather what would soon be a part of his friend. Since the virus had affected Max clear through the muscle and bone, Stone set to work fashioning a partial exoskeleton that would aid his movements. Max also required the containment of his unaffected organs and a boundary in his chest to contain the spread of the self-replicating micro-bionics.

When the outer plating network was completed, Stone began wiring circuits throughout Max's body, connecting them to his newly altered nervous system. He intentionally left an exposed wire running the length of Max's rebuilt body. When the plates were fastened, Max could slide them apart to expose it in case he ever needed access to his internal messaging system. He put a central chip next to Max's heart, which had been encased for protection. The chip pulled in energy from the wireless power grid, monitored its flow through Max's circuits, and directed the micro-bionic additions to his dividing cells. It also acted as an interface between Max's circuits and his brain. Unbeknownst to Stone, this same chip would later be augmented to act as Max's slaver. Once Stone sealed the plates, Max was whole again.

Stone kept vigil as Max slept soundly. The monitors served as assurance that his new robotics were functioning properly. "I can't believe I almost lost you again today. I don't know what I would have done. Since Kylie disappeared, you're all I have for company. You know, I've been thinking about her more and more. I haven't stopped thinking about her actually. For all I know of it, I'm in love with her, Max. Can you believe it? Me. I vow to you, old friend, I will find her." The hours passed slowly from there. Stone found it hard to believe it had only been a single day when Max awoke that evening. "Welcome back, old Mr. Fitzgerald," he said with as much inflection as he was capable.

"It's good to be back."

"Hmm."

"What?"

"You know, you have quite the literary name," Stone determined.

"Glad you're so concerned with my health. Thanks, I guess."

"Oh, yes, time for you to stand up."

Max complied with Stone's order and found to his surprise that he could do so after only a few tries. In time, he would learn to use his new semi-organic side as fluently as he had used his original body. He would also quickly learn to breathe with a single lung. "You saved my life today, and I truly do want to thank you for that. No more self-experimentation," Max groaned, "that much is for sure, at least, unless it is really, really necessary."

Stone walked up to the camera, and the video ended. Stone believed that he had erased the camera's contents. By all rights, he was certainly capable of doing just that, but he was unaware of the secondary feed Blade had running to prevent any tampering. In theory, that recording never should have been seen. It was.

"My arrogant son," the watcher's haunting laughter echoed throughout the chamber. His revelry was interrupted by an unexpected call.

"Sir, an unscannable presence has entered the premises."

"Good," Blade resonated. "He has finally arrived, and I have an exquisite new weapon to use against him."

The video had taken a week to find. It was one among ten thousand identical brethren. Being found at all was unlikely. The job had been assigned to one man, who worked straight through the week with no sleep. Anyone else would have rewarded him, but, as it stood, the man was two minutes away from receiving a death sentence for taking too long.

CHAPTER 12

"MARCUS AND I approached my father's colossal estate," Stone told the reporter. "He had a personal wing added to the Neo-Colosseum so that he could rule his empire from his personal gladiatorial arena. I knew my presence would be known immediately because my armor deflected the invisible beam from the Neo-Colosseum's scanning equipment. Marcus would soon register on the scan, too. Either way, the element of surprise was lacking, but it was unnecessary."

As Stone arrived, Blade descended from his throne silently. He appeared to simply be a very impressive specter. In equally ethereal silence, he walked down the halls of the building. He was soon at the main gate where his son awaited. "Let me guess," Blade said to the nearby guard, "his companion is Marcus, his mentor."

"Correct, sir," the guard saluted.

A smile found its way onto the face of a nearby agent. A cloak hid his face from the light, but by the person's very posture, it was obvious he was smiling all over. A warm red glow radiated from the center of his right eye.

"I trust you will be coming along then," Blade said to the agent.

"I wouldn't dream of missing it," the agent said, the restrained mad giddiness in his voice lost on Blade.

"The Council Room is to be ready," Blade demanded into the intercom, knowing for certain it would be prepared, especially since there was no council anymore. It was used only for meetings like the one that would follow, few in number as they were. Blade grabbed a complex mechanical weapon and slid it into the sheath on his leg.

The massive gates slid back into the walls holding them in place. The figures of his son and his son's mentor came into focus, silhouetted from the bright light of the outdoors. The two entered the dimly lit corridor and Blade silently led the way to the Council Room. Even though Stone had the massive form of his armor, Blade stood taller. The agent made it a point to keep in the shadows while the red glow of his eye penetrated Marcus. The various workers in the halls scattered as the two most powerful men in the dominion approached with thundering steps.

Stone entered the room first, his shadow eclipsing the ornate furniture that once entertained strategic planning sessions and the occasional report from an alphabet agency to the highest circle of trust in the nation. The chamber seemed to shudder at his presence. When Blade approached behind his son, his oppressive shadow consumed that of his son. It was, as Stone reasoned, an intimidation move, but an effective one nonetheless. Marcus and the unknown agent followed behind the two armor-clad men.

"Hello, father," Stone said flatly.

"Oh, spare me." Blade had already gained the upper hand. He always managed to crush his son's will power expediently, but that would not be such an easy task on this occasion. The agent stepped forth into the light. His face was unrevealed, and his eye glowed red. "Allow me to introduce an acquaintance of mine. If you would kindly remove your hood," Blade said unemotionally in an effective imitation of his son. Stone began to wonder if it was deliberate.

The cloak fell slowly away. The agent's eye was visibly brighter. The bionics adjusted to the light. Except for the fiery illumination, the eye appeared normal. Even the glow could be hidden, but it was obviously desired.

Stone had to physically restrain his mentor. "Erik," Marcus gutturally roared. Stone barely held his teacher back from ending the murderer's breathing permanently.

"I see you two know each other," Blade said darkly with a wide, illuminated grin. He had played this out expertly. Then again, he was flawless at manipulation.

"Calm yourself, Marcus; you can settle this in honorable combat.

Remember why we are here," Stone whispered. "Let's make this brief, shall we?" Stone allowed his voice to boom through the chamber. "I have come to issue a challenge, father."

"Is that all? What will it be this time, boy?"

"Chess, where you and I are the kings. You may choose your pieces otherwise."

"Okay, you've piqued my interest. Chess. I'll take black as always. The only game of value is a chess game with live pieces. It has promise. If a piece is taken, how is the person to be executed?" Blade leaned forward in anticipation of the amount of blood he could shed.

"That's the catch. Places are decided by hand-to-hand combat in your precious Neo-Colosseum. It will be a fight to the death."

"You've thought this out well, but since you're already bending rules, I'll bend some of my own. Pawns are a waste of time. Everyone else in the game will have to fight them first; it guarantees that everyone involved has an equal chance to die," he smiled darkly, "and it assures that everyone involved gets blood on his hands."

"Games can be won or lost with pawns. They should not be dismissed so easily," Stone protested.

"The game can still be won or lost with them; you just have to find a pawn that can defeat me."

"This isn't chess if the pawns are eliminated first."

"It could conceivably occur in the course of a game, let's just start in the middle of that scenario. We'll just assume all other pieces were moved back strategically to their starting positions, assuming your people survive. Who takes the position if a draw should occur?"

"Coin toss," Stone suggested. He had not anticipated that.

"Fine, the loser will be executed."

"The remaining pieces must at least move accordingly," Stone demanded as consolation. Marcus found it unnerving how these two men were toying with lives, including their own, so callously. Blade did it for amusement and Stone did it for purpose but coldly nonetheless.

"Those are the terms then. You have two days to prepare. The contest begins at 9:00 AM."

"I thought this was negotiation," Stone questioned.

"I could refuse your challenge and execute you both for treason right now."

"That will not be necessary. Goodbye, father," the anger in Stone's voice was plainly audible.

"No. Marcus and Erik will leave, but you will remain a moment." Blade did not continue until the two other men departed. Then, he had only a warning for his son. "This is a foolish gesture, boy. Now, you and your friends will die by my hands."

"You could never kill me before, and you don't know my friends."

"This will be war. I will find ways in war. I always find ways in war."

Stone was completely and rightly unnerved as he left. For one, he could not understand what had kept Marcus from killing Erik in the interim. He presumed it was Marcus's sense of honor, but then again, what did Stone really know of mankind? He caught up to Marcus outside the room.

"That was a quick acceptance," Marcus stated.

"He was expecting it. That's why Erik was there. He wanted to undermine our confidence."

"Two days. I hope you know what you've done."

Marcus and Stone stepped out into the sunlight. It was like waking from a very real nightmare. More accurately, it was like leaving an ancient mausoleum. The air felt fresher outside. At that moment, the two felt a freedom they had never known, an awareness of being alive that only comes from the very real possibility of death.

CHAPTER 13

"THE RULES WERE simple. Places were decided by combat to the death. Draws were decided by a coin toss, though I did not anticipate that occurrence. Pawns were fought first, and all other pieces had to move accordingly." The reporter once again changed the small tape amidst Stone's words.

In the future, the next two days were a mass of chaos and confusion. The short time they had grew shorter. Some trained, some created, and some tried to find peace within themselves.

Marcus and Stone had reached the mansion just before noon. Stone gathered the rest of his fellow combatants and explained the situation. "Then we haven't a moment to lose," Max spoke out. "You asked for my help in creating the rooks. I suggest we get started."

"If you will excuse me, I wish to train for the coming battle," Jake requested.

"Please allow me to offer you the use of my facilities. I will be helping Max, but feel free to wander the grounds," Stone offered. He was not fond of the idea of Robert wandering through his house. To that end, he whispered to Marcus, "Keep track of Robert."

Robert suddenly spoke up. "I would like to train as well," he said in a gravelly voice.

"As would I," Marcus added. Whether that was in response to Stone's request or a genuine desire was irrelevant to Stone as long as the mystery man was watched.

"If you will all follow me then. Max, the lab is down those stairs, second door on the right. I will meet you there," Stone concluded. He led the party down to the hidden holographic chamber. He opened it just as he had every night. This time, though, it was not he who would enter. He looked at the warriors behind him and set the challenge: five combat drones, maximum setting, Neo-Colosseum. If they could not handle that, then they had no hope in the coming battle.

He guided them to the darkened hallway. "The training room is just through there. Walk straight ahead through this hall and you will not have a problem. Don't touch the walls, though. They carry an electric shock, nonlethal, but painful. Once you get inside, any outside light will disrupt the program. A door panel will lock you inside until the robots are defeated. If any of you are critically wounded, you can use this," Stone said, handing a cylinder to Marcus. "Aim it at the robot's head. It will pause the construct's programming, allowing you a chance to destroy it. I haven't used it before, but it should work. Good luck." Stone turned and exited as the three warriors who had accompanied him entered the dark hallway. Neither he nor they looked back.

Max was astonished by the laboratory that greeted him. It held some of the most advanced technology available, some of which the world had not yet seen. A selection disk, complete with holographic projectors hovered steadily towards him. "Designate: Maximus Fitzgerald," the machine metallically chirped, pausing as it momentarily checked its memory. "Clearance: recent update; alpha as of 12:10 P.M. today"

Max found a new respect for his friend. Just because of one amazing laboratory set ablaze with technological schematics and holographic projections, Max's pessimistic opinion on the outcome of the upcoming challenge began to change. Max wanted very little from life; he was of the opinion that the less he expected, the less he would be let down. However, complete freedom was something that he desired above all else, and that very desire now looked upon its own fruition.

Max selected the rook file on the fifteen inch, round keypad. A small holographic projection came to life above the selection monitor as a much larger version materialized in the working bay below the railing from which Max looked down. He was startled by the image before him. He stepped back with his initial glance at it. The image looked almost like a hairless version of him where the image's right side was the same as its left. On closer inspection, the hands and face were different, and some of the other proportions were not those of the geneticist. The similarities still measured curiosity, though.

Stone's hand waved in front of Max's face, breaking the geneticist's concentration. His bewilderment was obvious. Stone decided to answer Max's question before Max even knew what he wanted to ask. "The model I have designed is basically an automated version of my armor covered in a reproduction of your virally affected tissue. I have been studying both the virus you created and the virus that stopped it. With a different micro-bionic component, it is much more adaptable than either of us anticipated. I need your help in recreating that tissue."

The three combatants entered the seemingly endless space of the Neo-Colosseum arena, or at least the holographic representation thereof. This particular image was unique among Stone's files. Because of the sheer expanse of the actual arena and the limited size of the room Stone had constructed, projecting the combat area required the wall panels to slide out to their farthest distance apart. Even with that, the room was still much smaller than the true arena. To that end, Stone replaced the flooring with panels that could scroll along the major directions without the room's occupant realizing the change. For a single occupant, it allowed the freedom of the entire expanse of the Neo-Colosseum's true dimensions. However, three occupants would complicate matters.

Three of the battle robots stood in triangle formation. The latest models had the same sleek, wiry appearance, but they were the deadliest versions that had been created to that point. During his insomnia the night before, Stone had corrected all of the design flaws he had encountered, and the robots were programmed not to see each other as adversaries any longer. On the smooth plate atop the drones' heads, a red brand carved out the Roman numeral MMXVI.

The hallway door slid shut, and a bright green glow lit up the constructs' scanning eyes. The first of the spidery drones stepped toward Jake with the tripod of its left foot. Its jawless, toothless metal skull of a face looked down at him as the machine hunched to the boy's height. The remaining two machines proceeded to their respective targets.

Jake easily avoided the robot's initial strike. He ducked under the metallic fist and slid between the creature's legs. He rose and delivered a forceful punch to what looked like the thing's spine. The pain Jake expected to burn through his knuckles never came. The drone seemed to cringe for a moment before it pivoted on its waist to face the youth again. A hand far stronger than Jake's gripped the boy by the neck, hoping to choke the life out of him.

Marcus fared no better. He leapt to avoid a wide leg sweep from the machine only to be caught by a metallic slap across the face. Marcus landed several feet from his former position, his vision blurring from both impacts. He thought of Stone facing these creations every night.

Jake raised his hands to the creature's grip. He held it as tightly as he could. A sizzle of blue-white electricity rippled up the creature's arm. The drone's grip loosened enough for Jake to free himself. The floor and ceiling wavered at the smallest bit of light emitted by the electric burst. A clean roundhouse kick to the creation's face knocked it off balance. Jake hammered at the robot's chest until it cracked open. Another blast of electricity put the drone out of commission. A fourth robot entered the room.

Marcus reached deep within himself. As he inhaled, he almost drank up the energy of the room. He seized the years of disciplined training he had grown up learning. As he touched down to his warrior spirit, his instincts began to take over. Marcus flipped forward, landing a kick to the robot's head. While it did not succeed in unbalancing the being, Marcus landed undaunted on his feet and punched twice. Marcus stepped back as the robot's forward jab attempted contact. A straight kick with Marcus's metallic boot to the side of the robot's leg caused its collapse. The drone's large right hand grabbed Marcus as the creature shifted its balance to its remaining leg. The fist holding the warrior slammed him to the ground and pinned him at the collar. The other fist fell quickly towards Marcus's face.

Jake had the fourth robot around the neck from behind it. Keeping his position, he wrapped his legs around the front of the drone. Successfully holding his position on the creation's back, Jake tried to unleash a jolt of electricity through the construct's skull. Nothing happened. Jake had exhausted the charge in the generator that replaced the radius and ulna in his arm, and he did not have time for it to build up another. Suddenly, the creature's green eyes grew brighter, and its head pivoted on its small neck. The jade eyes fired an equally jade bolt of energy towards the ceiling away from Jake. The bolt hit and bounced back straight into Jake's body. The light left an odd gray stain in the middle of space since the holographic ceiling was much higher than the actual one. Jake's body fell limply to the ground. Even though the wrist generator absorbed a fraction of the energy, it was barely enough to keep the boy conscious. He could not move.

Marcus arched his back, defying his physical limits with an adrenaline rush. It was just enough to shift the hand pinning him. The falling fist altered course, but the momentum was too great for the machine to overcome. The one-legged drone toppled to its side. Marcus broke the machine's cylindrical neck with an angry stomp. At that moment the fifth robot emerged.

Stone was doing well. The skeletons of the soon-to-be rooks were completed. While Max worked at improving the synthetically grown, virally enhanced tissue, he began construction of the pawns. By design, the pawns were basically reinforced metal skeletons filled with sensitive equipment. The shield he had developed for them that would serve as their main defense and offense. It absorbed heavy impact by displacing it and turning it back more efficiently on the opponent. Holographic projections would cover the fields and belie the pawns' true forms. The machines would look entirely human, three females, five males, each with its own distinct features. It would serve as a distraction to their opponents for a brief time at least. They would be well programmed to fight, but Stone doubted the ability of any of his automatons to best the warriors his father was likely to bring to the field. The pawns, however, would gather valuable combat data on each of his father's pieces. In truth, he expected only Marcus and himself to stand any chance at defeating his father's forces and asserting that the combat was one-on-one meant they stood a fair chance at winning. He would keep Max out of battle as much as he could but would need his strength and strategy.

Marcus and Jake were fortunate that they did not have the luxury of observing Robert. They would have been very disconcerted by what they saw. Robert had blocked every attack the drone had made. He then stood perfectly still. The purple behemoth stood before him, already winding up for another series of attacks. Its eyes suddenly blinked off and on. A series of small explosions rocked the figure, and a central explosion finished off the drone, spraying the area with dark debris. For several minutes, a pale splash of real wall would remain visible in the area.

Marcus closed his eyes. He forced himself to believe that his hand was solid metal, stronger than the drone. He found his target without vision. He punched straight through the dense metallic chest. He opened his eyes and extracted his hand from the unmoving form. Marcus saw that his hand was bloody and his knuckles were burned where he touched the blistering heat of the overworked and improved generator.

Stone plugged the final frame into the computer. The pawns would soon be ready. Max had found what he believed to be the correct base sequence to place inside the viral carrier to recreate the semi-bionic flesh. The two would know as soon as Max finished his snack break. Then, it would be time to test the constructs.

The final robot in the arena had not readjusted its sensors after the blast. Apparently, the energy response was only an emergency function. Marcus wanted to offer his help, but his knuckles were bleeding too badly to be used. His other hand was occupied in controlling that bleeding. Jake was running out of time. Feeling was not returning to his body fast enough. The robot stepped backwards, attempting to compensate for the sensor overload its own systems had caused. Using all the strength he could find from every muscle he was aware of having, Jake moved closer. More accurately, he inched closer. He gave the generator a few more seconds. Feeling the base of his palm connect with the metal, he emptied the energy contents of the cell in his arm. The bolt writhed up the creature's leg. The true floor grew briefly exposed. The mechanical monster fell to its artificial knees. It struggled to stand as hard as Jake did. Robert watched silently without moving. The drone's head abruptly exploded into tiny fragments.

The walls unveiled themselves as the hologram disappeared. The door slid open, and the hall brightened. Jake lost consciousness.

The boy awoke several hours later. Marcus offered the youth dinner. Robert said nothing. "Where's Stone?" Jake turned tired eyes toward Marcus as the boy asked the question.

"He and Max have just gone to test their new creations. Stone said the stun laser would not do any permanent damage. You have already weathered the worst of it," Marcus answered.

"Tell him ... he built ... one hell of a machine," Jake requested as he fell asleep again.

CHAPTER 14

THE ROOKS, CONTROLLED by Stone's armor, followed closely behind their puppeteer. Max carried two of the inoperative pawns on his shoulders. Stone set the program at the arena: four independent drone uploads, nonlethal setting, Neo-Colosseum. A small hole appeared in the wall below the control panel for the arena. Stone plugged a cable into the outlet and connected it to each of the four creations in succession. The cable downloaded all of the combat programs contained within the computer into the constructs. In exchange, the computer uploaded the energy signatures it would need to supply in order to operate the rooks and pawns.

The nonlethal setting gave Max a false sense of security. The setting was actually identical to the maximum setting, of which Stone was quite fond, in all respects except for the lethal attacks, which were toned down only slightly. He decided to use the setting for several reasons. He was not sure how well he had constructed the various artificial combatants and there was always the chance that they could malfunction. He was also unsure of how much Max's training at the academy had been maintained since his graduation. While his aid in strategy would be invaluable, Stone wondered about his prowess in actual combat.

The technological beings were sent down the hallway ahead of the two combatants. Once they crossed the doorway at the opposite end, they ceased to be allies. Max and Stone stood in the small chamber where Stone usually removed his armor. This time, he removed only the upper portion. Max had not realized just how massive his old friend truly was until then. The armor protruded approximately two to three inches from his body in various sections, meaning that the majority of Stone's bulk was actually his own.

"The pawns and rooks are set on defensive only. Our job is to attack them and survive. The timer is set for twenty minutes. If we live and cannot destroy them, our job is done. I should warn you, though, that the constructs are set to switch over to offensive mode if we do not attack them quickly," Stone said as coldly as ever.

What Max failed to realize as they prepared for the fight was that, in all things, Stone was, in essence, chained passion. By nature, he had unparalleled heart and enthusiasm, but with no outlet in affection of any kind, he turned that passion on everything he did without even realizing it. The restraints, both internal and external, placed on the intensity served only to make him stronger. These constructs were an external manifestation of that nature and they would express themselves violently.

The two somewhat human warriors walked down the darkened hallway. Stone's muscles rippled as he walked straight ahead. Despite warnings, Max reached his semi-organic hand forward. He came in contact with the wall, and a jade bolt of electricity writhed up his arm. His left arm engaged in a short, unnatural spasm, but he was otherwise unaffected.

"Had to do it, didn't you?" Stone did not even turn around to ask.

"You know me," Max responded with a laugh.

As they entered the holographic chamber, the door slid shut behind them. A countdown appeared in the center of the room. It displayed on a triangular prism hovering in space. Each side displayed the same numbers, but, although it was nothing new, it caught Stone's attention.

Stone was absorbed by the thought that hit him, and his surroundings faded away. Man's greatest invention, he thought. The numbers, the languages, and the physics had all been seen before. Nature employed the numbers and the physics in the everyday process known as life, and the languages just gave man something to call what was already there. Even the zero just gave a name to the concept of nothing. For all the reverence given to man's complexities, mankind's simplest invention was its greatest: a triangle. It is strong and versatile. However, its true importance came from its newness. Nature does not make perfect structural triangles by itself. Stone's thoughts went deeper until the sharp sting of a laser grazed his shoulder. It was not deep and it cauterized itself, but it angered him nonetheless.

He looked over in time to see Max land a hard punch to a pawn. He regretted the pride he felt when his oldest friend was thrown through the air with the amplified energy of his own attack directed straight back through him. Max hit a wall much sooner than Stone expected. The moving floor could keep a person from walking into a wall, but being thrown into one was another matter entirely.

Max quickly, and literally, bounded back into the battle. Stone was too busy to notice. He was engaging in a battle with a rook that had switched to offensive because of his thought-invoked inaction. His armored foot landed in the creation's stomach. Regaining his foot was a more difficult task than he had expected. When he was finally able to extract his appendage from the moving semi-organic tissue, a spray of organics and cybernetics spattered the floor. The mess was soon recollected back into the rook. Stone then realized how glad he would be when the creations were on his side once more.

Max tried a more direct approach. He punched the rook square in the face with his massive right fist. The face splashed away and reformed around his wrist. A smile crept over its previously impassive face. "Tell me you programmed that," Max said nervously.

"That I did. Intimidating, isn't it?" Stone managed a response as his own rook was spreading its outer layer over him.

"I'll say. Any other tricks I should know about?" Max pulled furiously at his arm, but the rook was unwilling to release him. The clock was running, though not fast enough for the geneticist.

"Only that they can spread themselves over you, kind of like this one is doing," Stone grunted. He struggled free as the laser protruded from the rook's palm. A sheet of the strange skin tore away as Stone broke its grasp. Before the skin was recalled, the headless skeletal interior was visible. The bolt stung him in the back, and he hit the floor before the shoulder mounted flamethrower could ignite. His back burned, and the impact pained his already sore chest. For a split second all he really desired was sleep and then he was furious. Stone felt he was failing, and the pain only fueled his anger. He pulled out the retractable bladed staff hidden in the thigh panel of his armor.

Max had wrested his arm free. The crevice left in the rook's head pulled quickly back together, but the haunting smile was still present on the construct's face. "All right, prick," Max cursed.

Stone unfolded the staff and swung it hard in a full circle. Debris from the rook was strewn about the circumference of the weapon's arc. The rook's interior once more sat barren as the skin meshed itself back around the frame. Stone had split one of the panels that served only for external defense and attachment of the skin-like substance.

Remembering the result of tremendous force, Max gently grabbed the pawn that had sent him reeling. He threw it into the rook, and, as he had planned, the strange flesh began to wrap around the holographic figure of a woman. The mesh began tightening its grip. When the force was great enough to be redirected, the strange skin was sprayed throughout the room. The skeleton stood exposed.

Stone grabbed the exposed spine of the rook he faced. He brought the creature to the floor as the skin began to meld once more. The tiny augmented cells were intimately linked with the core and, as long as they had power, would return to it regardless of circumstance. Stone lodged his staff in the construct's chest. He thrust the blade of his weapon deeper, but he could not penetrate the core of the machine. The skin began to swirl up the staff.

Max pounded at the core as the rook's skin began recollecting itself. The clock was nearly out. Max's own semi-organic fist pounded relentlessly against the frame. For all his genius, his attack was savage. The core, though, would not break. Metallic skin clanged on metallic ore, but nothing broke.

Stone swung his staff in a vertical arc. The swing slit the skin down the center, the blade scraping on the core. He did not notice the pawn behind him switch to offensive. Since it had not been attacked, the holographic visage of the female suddenly turned angry.

One of the female pawns grabbed Max around the neck; her artificial fingernails dug deep into his skin. Blood dripped from the wounds, and Max involuntarily grabbed the female's wrist. When he realized what he was about to do, he slowed the speed with which he applied the pressure so it would not be reversed and break his hand. The fur on his hand and forearm stood on end with the static of the energy matrix.

The other deadly female reached out to claw Stone. He faced away from the pawn and thrust the staff behind him into what would have been the lady's flesh. Though the point of the blade had great force behind it, the matrix could not reapply the energy to the tip of the weapon. The projection wavered and the buffer field collapsed with the reverberating impact energy. He raised his fist high above his head to crush the pawn's more fragile, exposed frame.

Max squeezed the arm slowly tighter. The clock hit zero. Stone's fist did not fall. All four of the constructs had survived the test, though one of them had barely done so. The rooks collected themselves, and Stone repaired the pawn's matrix. He made a mental note to tighten the energy bandwidth of the projection. Without the energy pouring into them, the technological creatures collapsed. Once Stone reacquired the upper half of his armor, he and Max carried the constructs out of the testing area.

CHAPTER 15

DUSK WAS IN its prime when Stone had finished the adjustments to the pawns. He needed to relax and settle his mind. When he went outside, he noticed the fading red hue in the sky. The real world held refreshing aspects after the long day he had spent surrounded by holograms. He realized how long it had been since he had truly appreciated the fresh air.

Marcus sat outside, lost in meditation. He sensed Stone's approach and brought himself back around to full consciousness. He could not gather the strength to move, and Stone sat down beside him.

"How's your hand?"

"Much better, thanks. The sealant salve is working fine. How was the testing?" Marcus spoke quietly in the breeze.

"Well enough, I suppose. I have mixed feelings about the results, though. I'm satisfied with the rooks and even the pawns, but I'm disappointed in my own performance. I'm proud that my creations passed their test, though I think I failed mine."

"It is hard for a creator to destroy his creation. Why do you think we're still here after everything man has wrought against this planet? So, were you committed to that end?" Marcus was genuinely interested in an answer.

"I really don't know. I do my best to succeed with everything. I know I fall far short of my goal, but at the same time, my goal is perfection. On the other hand, they were my creations. They weren't the carbon copies of the drones controlled by compiled battle programs; they were something more than that. I guess it comes down to why I even bother to create. I want a legacy. I don't want to die forgotten," Stone paused.

"So you would like for us to die with you?" Stone was shocked by Marcus's question.

"That's not what I mean at all. This campaign is not suicide. I just mean, well, I'm going to die without a wife and without a family. Maybe it's better since my mother died when I was born and my father may be the cause of my death. I don't know what a stable home life is, so how could I ever provide one? The point is that I am going to die alone. I know I sound pathetic, but at least when I create, my life accomplishes something, has some meaning even though it isn't the meaning I really want. I'll at least have something to be remembered by to posterity." Marcus did not have a response. "You know, tomorrow is the end," Stone said dispassionately.

"What do you mean?" Marcus was caught off guard by the sudden shift.

"After tomorrow, one way or another, our lives are going to be changed forever. If we win, we have a government to construct. Even then, there is no guarantee that we will all survive. If we lose, it is the end of our lives. Tomorrow is the last day of life as we know it."

"You need rest. You're getting distracted," Marcus advised.

"I've noticed that lately. Where's Robert?"

Marcus closed his eyes and inhaled deeply, focusing a part of his mind he did not yet understand. "He's asleep in the guest room. He hasn't moved."

"When did this all happen, with these sudden powers? I have to admit it freaks me out sometimes."

"I don't know when it began, but now that I have them, it feels like they have always been there. It freaks me out sometimes too. You have to remember, though, this is a world where everything is possible."

"That's what I'm afraid of. I have to train."

"Haven't you done enough for tonight?"

Walking away, Stone stopped and turned his head. "No."

"I hope you know that you don't have to prove yourself before you pray. Speak to Him in any condition. He will listen."

"Thanks," Stone said, holding his cross and continuing on his way, "but it can't hurt."

Stone decided to check on the occupants of his home. He walked quietly through the halls. Jake was sleeping; he had recovered from the effects of having the electrolytes in his body temporarily bound. Max was playing with holograms. Stone wondered if his friend would ever grow up; somehow, though, the childishness suited him well. He knew that Max was alone as well, yet somehow it did not seem to tear at the scientist the way it tore at Stone. Robert was in the guest room. Stone contemplated putting another signature lock on the door, but why have it broken? He knew Marcus was fine, so he decided not to check any further. He instead ventured back outdoors.

He descended the earthen stairs to his uncut grounds. When he had the house constructed shortly after he left Marcus's care, he vowed not to destroy any more of the forest that surprisingly surrounded the land than was necessary. It gave his house seclusion, and he felt a certain peace in nature. Peace was something he sorely needed at that moment.

Stone walked silently through the woods, his steps muffling even the soft crunch of pine needles. The forest extended for miles. He disengaged the boot enhancements, and he walked as any other man would walk. Wildlife surrounded him. This area was perhaps the only unrestricted ground left for wild animals. He had ordered the area preserved and sponsored the addition of all compatible forest species. In fact, the bear that tangled with Jake was his doing as well.

Stone needed to be as free as his surroundings. He lost himself in the analysis of why he had been so distracted of late. Deep within, he knew the answer quite well. He sought to focus on anything he could to keep his mind off of Kylie. She had wounded him gravely, and he always got contemplative when he was hurt.

His thoughts were interrupted, though, when he came upon a resting pack of gray wolves. They were startled at his presence but did not run. They merely watched him to see what he would do. Without anyone there to see him, Stone cut loose. What crossed his face was not a smile; it was something far more wild. He indulged a whim. He pulled his helmet back into his armor and threw his head back. He let loose a howl from deep within. Instead of running, the beautiful, usually timid creatures lent their voices to his in the eerie song. The sound that filled the forest was hauntingly sweet.

Stone lowered his head and leaned his weary body against a sturdy tree. The alpha male stared at him and took a cautious step forward, followed by another slow step. Stone ungloved his hand and extended his palm towards the wolf. The white snouted male flexed its paw and drew closer. Finally, it nestled itself between Stone's armored hip and arm. The rest of the pack encircled the newcomer to their territory. "If only I could attract women this way," Stone whispered to his new companion. He felt comfort among the creatures and some semblance of happiness came over him. Stroking the fur of the alpha, he closed his eyes and, exhausted, fell into a much needed slumber.

Golden daylight greeted his eyes when he awoke. He squinted in the sun and looked for his furry companions. They had gone. He could discern one of the females looking back at him from the visible distance. She ran when their eyes met, but it no longer mattered. They had served a purpose for Stone. Whether they knew it or not, they temporarily filled a void in him, and he realized that no matter how unbearable the scorns of man became, he was at least accepted in nature.

He was in no hurry to return to his home. He suddenly did not want to face the next dawn. The weight of the world truly rested on his shoulders. It was nearly one in the afternoon when he finally returned. The inevitability of the next day crept upon him with utter despair. He could escape it, he could find a way, but that was not even a consideration.

CHAPTER 16

IN A FAR darker part of the city, Blade strode ominously through the halls of his complex. In attendance was Alex Herring, Blade's first knight and unnecessary personal guard. He had acquired the position over a long, bloody time. By coincidence or fate, Blade had observed Alex's first kill. The utter fact that he was eleven years old at the time was impressive enough, yet the skill required in slaughtering a deer with a spear and a knife was even more astonishing. Blade had never seen anything quite like it, and he never would again in anyone except Alex. The boy had taught himself the art of hunting and stealth from books and practice without a mentor. He had a natural inclination to killing. The deer fell before the small hunter, and Alex all but bathed himself in the poor creature's blood. Blade watched the boy closely after that and guided his course in life.

"Is the weapon ready yet?"

"I shall see, my ruler," Alex bowed.

"As long as you never cross me, you will rule this dominion one day."

"What of your son, my liege?"

"He will die tomorrow," Blade promised. The darkness in his voice permeated the room. No man alive could be more commanding than Blade Stone, and, with that, Alex departed.

Alex's gold covered armor glistened even in the dim light. He strode briskly to his destination. He placed his sword to the throat of a nearby attendant and grabbed the unwitting man's hair with his free hand. "Is he prepared?" Alex had learned his tact from Blade.

"He, well, he's b-b-being p-prepared e-even now, s-s-sir."

"Not good enough." Alex's blade burned red hot as an altered electric current passed through it from the hilt. The reflection made his face look as though it would be comfortable engulfed in unholy flame. The attendant fell to the ground, lifeless. He dipped his fingers into the deep laceration on the cooling body. The blood was warm through his glove. Alex promptly streaked it across the gold chest plate he wore. A wicked smile crossed his face.

Behind him was a very dark corridor. The light had ceased completely by the time the other end was reached. A heavily reinforced cell stood at the end of the hallway. A low snarl and deep growl came from within. It was followed by the screech of metal on metal and the grating of metal on stone.

Stone was at the training room again. He did not want to risk injury, so he chose to lift weights. The holographic gymnasium was empty except for Stone and the machines. The wall panels had shifted and disengaged themselves to form free weights. He stayed there for hours, losing himself in the effort and repetition. Evening came and went. He retired himself to an outdoor slumber. His life, however gifted and miserable, was about to change.

Nine in the morning came far sooner than it was desired. Nonetheless, Stone and his army were present. Stone pounded on the large metal doors of the Neo-Colosseum. After several comparatively light knocks, the doors were withdrawn before he knocked them off of their hinges.

"By royal authority and presented challenge, I demand entrance!" Stone's voice boomed in the echoing entrance chamber.

"By presented challenge, your access is granted, but your royal authority has been revoked by our ruler," the guard said smugly.

Jake was puzzled. "What does that mean?" Stone was royalty by blood. "How can he take away your blood?"

"He will not, but it means that we are less than peasants in their eyes now, albeit dangerous peasants," Stone rumbled, increasing his volume for the emphasis of the last comment.

Stone found his lifelong hatred of authority growing as he treaded down the walkways leading to the arena. Every guard the warriors passed could not help but make a snide comment about their fallen commander. Stone felt the weight of falling from power. He saw the misuse and abuse of status around him. He was a target like no other. The soldiers and officials had been deathly afraid of him just yesterday; with only a word, he could have had every one of them executed. Today was different. The tides had been turned, and everyone was gunning for him now.

"If you make a move, we have authority to put you down with armed resistance," their usher grunted.

"If I make a move, none of you will be left alive to put me down with anything," Stone uttered cruelly.

"Bold words," the guard challenged.

"Shall I back them?" Stone's anger boiled within, and the usher backed away from the response.

They were sent to the upper level of the arena. The vast chamber of the Neo-Colosseum could seat one hundred thousand spectators quite comfortably among its steel and concrete levels. The materials that held the place together were simple yet quite effective. In the eight years of its existence, nothing had managed to inflict damage to any of its architecture. The group stood at one of sixteen observation decks in the circular layout. The lower fighting pit was vast, far more so than Stone's program would suggest. The tiered seats stood ready for an audience, but there would be none this day. Blade could not risk this being a spectator event regardless of outcome. While he believed wholeheartedly in his own victory, his son was cunning and able. There were bound to be surprises and definitely deaths. As Stone gripped the railing, a light whispered on in the deck directly across from him.

The image of Blade stood before the warriors. The hologram greeted them coldly. Stone looked to the throne upon which the real Blade sat. The shadows had not all left their ruler when the light had awakened. The image of a chessboard appeared before the mismatched band. Its setup was identical to the one in the room with the reporter twenty years in the past. Stone observed the absence of both queens just as the reporter had. He chose to reserve his psychological weapons by keeping his mouth shut about it.

The real and holographic Blades waved their hands in unison, and a row of black pawns invaded the rear line of white pieces. Stone had anticipated his father turning the contest into a mockery, so neglecting to let white go first was no surprise. "This is my world, and I make its rules," the hologram stated flatly.

Stone escorted his army down to the arena once his gauntlet had finished downloading the chess board into its projection banks. "Travel games," he mused as the small hologram rose from the panel on his arm.

"So it begins," Blade commanded from atop the deck of his ominous throne.

CHAPTER 17

"AND SO IT had begun," Stone said, sweeping his hand past the reporter across the board before them. A wave of black pawns crashed forward toward the rear line of white. "The floor contorted under a projection of my own creation. Giant alternating squares of black and white lined the arena. A translucent laser perimeter separated the squares and kept us from employing teamwork. Once the pawns filed in, the perimeter closed and my father gave the order to fight."

"Well, son, what do you think?" The holographic vision of Blade materialized in the center of Stone's square. The holographic rigging in the arena was one of Blade's favorite toys. It gave him a close view of the chaos he enjoyed without requiring him to leave his throne. The reference was directed at the pawn in front of Stone. At first glance, she looked just like Kylie. The face was convincing, but the figure was off. Stone did not have to match her to a video file in his armor to realize she was an impostor. He had shyly studied Kylie's figure enough that he could not be deceived. "I call her Medusa. Too bad you're already Stone," the hologram venomously spat. As it finished the sentence, Stone noticed the long hair moving of its own volition. It braided itself into a long tendril, recoiled, and lunged at him.

"Max, it's so good to see you alive. I thought for sure shutting down your chip would do you in. Alas, here's your replacement; the resemblance is scary, isn't it? Mirror, mirror, on the wall..." Max would have given anything at that moment to obliterate the intangible form in the midst of its commentary. He realized, though, that Blade desired that very response. Max did see the resemblance between himself and the pawn, though. The entire left side of the man before him was replaced with metallic substitutions for flesh.

"But you see, my former employer, my bionics are forged of flesh over mineral," Max said coolly before effectively tearing a handful of wiring from the man-machine he faced even as the man was about to take a swing.

The pawn that Robert faced lay dead at his feet, impaled on shards of its own altered hands. Robert looked as though he had not even drawn a heavy breath. His opponent was forever incapable of breathing again.

"As I faced the pawn my father called Medusa, I noticed something crucial to her defeat and the defeat of them all. When she attacked with the metal braid, I noticed how tight her face got. That meant that the alterations were relatively new. My guess was that none of the pawns had adjusted to their new bodies yet," Stone explained to the reporter.

The mesh of metallic hair flew at Stone like a spear. Instead of absorbing the blow, he grabbed the tangled tentacle. He felt the tiny component strands writhe in his armored palm as they ineffectually tried to bore through the gauntlet he wore. A slight tug was all he really needed and a clump of the thin wire was pulled free. Blood flowed down the woman's beautiful face as the remaining portion of the unnatural hair flailed about Medusa.

"She fell easily once I realized the implanted bionics had not been completely accepted. Her screams were haunting, but quite short lived. I mercifully slit her throat. After all, this was war. War is death." Stone tried to be as callous as he could in front of the reporter. He picked up the small black pawn sharing a space with the white king, effortlessly crushing it and cursing the woman's resemblance to Kylie.

Stone reassured himself that it had to be done, that it was him or her, but he felt as though he had killed her because of her mockery of Kylie. He had been forced to kill many times before that. Most people who had managed to survive in his era had. This felt so much worse.

The pawns were outfitted identically, a fact of which Stone was not aware until he had laid Medusa to rest upon the floor. They each wore a plain black shirt and pants. The metal armor lining their shoulders was the color of fresh blood. Looking away from his sensor readouts, he studied the rest of the costume from the body felled before him. The scarlet metal belt reflected blue from the laser walls, just as the metallic boots did. The cloth angling from waist to thigh on the woman hid a glinting weapon. As he studied his companions in the adjoining chambers, he noticed that none of the pawns were getting a chance to use those weapons.

"I had seen Max take first blood in his match, and I realized why my father was insistent on breaking the established rules of the game. He wanted to torment every one of my hierarchy and assure that they saw difficult combat regardless of the way the match was played. It was a simple matter to test the progress of the rooks. I brought up the sensor input from the white rook to my left on the small projector in my gauntlet. I watched as my creation distended the skin on its face, the familiar unnerving smile growing across what would have been its lips. The tactic must have held some merit because the metal legged pawn stopped attacking. It was only a momentary distraction, but it was enough. The rook forced a mass of its distended skin down the pawn's throat.

"The pawn had no time to react. More and more of the skin was forced into the man until the frame of the rook looked emaciated. The flow suddenly stopped and the rook withdrew its skin. The manmade flesh was covered in foreign blood. The pawn fell lifelessly to the ground, his vacant eyes frozen forever in dead fear.

"The other rook fared just as well. I watched as the flesh of its midsection withdrew in a horizontal spiral to expose a weapon I had not had the time to test. A glow formed a ring on the inner frame. It grew until the inner frame spiraled away just as the flesh had. The glow intensified and gathered focus. The pawn reached for the concealed weapon at his side only too late.

"The glow shot forward. It burned a perfectly circular hole through the pawn. The heat cauterized the wound, but nothing could keep life in the mortal vessel. The inner frame and outer skin returned to their former positions as the rook stood over the empty shell of the lifeless pawn. The laser wall still sizzled in an effort to contain the blast. The floor was visible through the pawn's midriff." Stone tossed two more black pawns to the floor from the board in front of him.

"All I could do was hope and wait for the holographic representations of the black pawns to fade from existence along with the people they represented."

In the future past of the stranger recalling of the tale, the battle in the arena continued as ferociously as his tale would indicate. "You seek to mock me with your very existence, yet your augmentation was voluntary," Max chided. "Does this look like it was voluntary?" He continued furiously, "I've done my best to gut you, but you're still standing, a testament to your creator. Just remember, the mightiest fall as well. Only, I will not fall today."

The sound of metal scraping metal rang out as Max dodged another swing from the pawn and tore more of the wires and chips from the once hulking frame. The pawn's bionic segments were getting smaller and smaller with every attack. Its left side was little more than a barely functioning metal skeleton.

"I see your metal elements have not quite adapted yet. You must have realized by now you are so much slower than I am. That it is pathetic. Here, I'll give you a sporting chance, one shot. Make it good." Max was beginning to enjoy this. He had been trained at the same academy that churned out Blade's ruthless soldiers, but he had graduated at the top of the class. He was a skilled fighter, though he rarely got a chance to prove it. The one thing Max was never found lacking was confidence.

The pawn should not have been able to move, let alone attack. He swung with his human hand. The attack was aimed at his opponent's head. At the last second, Max moved just enough to avoid a hit to the face. "I didn't say in the face, did I? I'm afraid you're going to have to pay for that little mishap." Max clutched the pawn's flesh and blood wrist with his own human hand. Max forced the nearly unmoving pawn's hand behind the man's back. He then grabbed the frame of the metal arm at the center. Using every bit of artificial might his bionics could muster, Max bent the metal arm at the elbow. He bent it backwards and broke it off completely.

The black pawn spasmed in pain and the jagged metal on the intact upper metallic arm jerked backwards. It scraped along Max's left eye in its arc. As fluid leaked from the wound, Max tightened his grip, and it was no longer a game. Max had truly been hurt, and he realized that the pawn had to die before he did. The semi-organic fingers wrapped around the pawn's neck; Max clenched them furiously. The black pawn's spinal column was severed completely by the band of semi-organic flesh that stretched between Max's thumb and forefinger. The body fell into the veritable sea of wires and artificial entrails. Max cradled the left side of his face with both hands.

The hologram of Blade appeared before Marcus. Marcus's battle with the pawn had thus far been simply a contest of basic hits and blocks. The pain lingering in Marcus's hand kept him from truly concentrating all of his strength on the attack. "Marcus. Marcus, Marcus, Marcus. You are the one wild card in this game. You made yourself known to me when my son needed to be taught a lesson. Aside from that, you have eluded my soldiers and spies, unknowingly I'm sure. Erik has told me everything he knows about your heritage, but your prowess remains to be seen." The proximity of the hologram and the tone of the voice gave Marcus the disturbing sense that Blade was trying to be personable. "You've been born to save the world, huh? That puts a little pressure on you, doesn't it? Unfortunately for you, I put very little faith in prophecy and you stand in my way. For that, I've saved the deadliest pawn for you; it's nothing personal, although you should be flattered." The image faded away with Blade's haunting laughter echoing in the enclosed quadrant.

Marcus flashed his gaze back to the being before him. Moments before chaos erupted around him, Marcus noticed that the man's chest and arms were constructed of metal bands. The bands unwrapped and extended towards Marcus, exposing internal, presumably living, organs covered in metallic casings. Just before he was caught, Marcus saw his only chance.

The bands were about the size of ordinary garden snakes. They were composed much like Medusa's writhing locks of hair. Thin wires, conductors, microchips, and integrated circuits were held within the coils. Unlike the other pawns, though, this man was used to his. More than likely he was the prototype for the technology comprising the rest of the black pawns.

Marcus was held by the wrists and waist. One of the pawn's arms was completely unraveled, but the other retained enough of its shape to grab the gun at its waist. Like the few guns in mainstream circulation, the model was outdated yet deadly enough. Though there had been a slow return to some sense of honor in fighting, projectile weapons still meant the fastest solution to combat.

Just as the gun was leveled at his head, Marcus took his one chance; he was wearing the boots that Stone had constructed for him. He balanced himself on one leg and delivered a kick to the pawn's exposed inner chest at ninety miles per hour. The pawn recoiled and dropped the weapon, dragging Marcus with him. The pawn gasped for air; his right metal lung casing had been punctured along with the lung inside of it. The lung was exposed to the air he was attempting to breathe. Even with one fully functional lung, he could not generate pressure to fill his air sacs. He then became the one with only one chance.

The pawn trembled and shook as he brought his own snakelike coil up and into the punctured lung. As the sickening feeling washed over him, he bored it through the lung and clogged the bronchial tube. The pawn silently vowed to take Marcus with him, unable to waste breath or effort on vocalizing the threat. Even with the bronchial tube blocked, air was seeping into the wound, causing blood to bubble from the opening.

The coils tightened. Marcus was caught around the throat. The bands constricted. Marcus backpedaled quickly with the aid of the boots. Marcus was very grateful to his protégé at that moment. The coils pulled Marcus to a halt. The pawn reluctantly fell; the coils slackened.

Stone stood up, astonished to find that the pawns had already disappeared from the squares occupied by Max and Marcus. He had not even realized he had allowed himself to sit down until that moment. The only remaining enemies were the pawn Jake was fighting and the one in the chamber that should be occupied by the queen. Stone wondered how the latter situation would resolve itself.

Jake was relentless in his attack. His barrage of fists had backed the pawn away. From his shoulders to his fingertips, the black pawn was covered in or replaced with metal. The pawn took advantage of Jake's momentary pause, leaping forward and brandishing a metallic fist. He pounded Jake below the ribs. Nothing happened: no wince, no pain, no response, nothing.

Jake kicked the pawn in the face. Blood spurted from the pawn's nose and mouth. The pawn went for the gun at his hip; he rolled and aimed through involuntary tears. Jake pressed his wrist quickly to the barrel, lancing a bolt of electricity through the tip of the weapon. The pawn jumped and backed away from the jolt in pain.

The pawn had apparently forgotten his proximity to the laser enclosure. He backed into the corner of two of the insubstantial walls. Jake was about to stop him, but then he remembered that the point of this combat was to kill his foe. In the adjoining chamber, Robert had a very good look at the inside of the man as he was burned away by the corner of the walls.

Jake walked to where the man had dropped his gun. *Just in case*, he thought. He made sure that the gun was still charged and undamaged by the electricity he had applied to its barrel. He tucked the weapon between his belt and the banded garment that covered him.

"Max, Marcus, and Jake had defeated the pawns they faced," Stone stated to the reporter. He swept his hand once more across the board. The remaining ebony pawns fell to the floor, all save one. "That left the one to my immediate left, the space that should rightfully have been occupied by my queen. The laser walls all dropped except where the ones that contained the area of the last pawn. I surveyed the damage, and it was quite extensive. None of my players had been critically wounded, but I noticed Max's eye.

"He cradled his face, and I saw the caked fluid on his glove. I took his hand away from the wound. The sight was ghastly, though at least most of his eye was still there. Max was shaking slightly. I had very little to work with, but I could not afford to lose Max this early in the battle.

"Luckily, I had the foresight to install provisions in a compartment in the wall. I had known since the Neo-Colosseum was constructed that I would end up fighting in its pit one way or another. I broke down the panel and entered the code on the box. It contained only limited bandages and contraband weaponry. I gave Max the cloth to wipe away the fluid."

Stone remembered trying to make a joke of it with Max when it happened. "You're just determined to lose your entire left half, aren't you?" Max's features lightened slightly, but for once Max had not been joking around. It was a wound early in the contest that would cost him, and Stone, as the combat unfolded.

"I dissected everything I had hidden in the wall panel. I had not planned on making an artificial eye out of the materials, but I did not have much choice. The medical supplies included a plastic gel that could seal wounds just as Marcus had used on his hand. I had no idea whether it could work on an eye or not. All I had at my disposal were fiber optic cables, a few wires, an infrared scope, and a spare helmet. Then I saw how fortunate the circumstances were. The helmet was baseline, yet it still had sensors. After using the equipment in my armor for a little welding and configuring, I fit the sensors and circuits inside the scope and attached the whole conglomeration to the fiber optic wires. The soldered scope was cut down to roughly the size of an eye socket, and all that remained was to connect the fiber optics to the retina.

"When I had finished, Max had an eye to match the rest of his left side. The flat end of the cylindrical scope protruded slightly from the surface of his cheek. The contraption was held on by the attachments to the real eye. It was unsteady, but at least Max could see, even if he could never blink again. I could only hope the eye would heal around my device," Stone said, wishing he had been able to do more for his friend.

"So you forfeit?" The hologram of Blade materialized before his son once more.

"What are you talking about? We beat your pawns. The one that rests in the space of the queen has succeeded; it can become any piece you desire now, not like it matters what you choose," Stone countered.

"There was no combat. The combat was the reason I accepted your challenge. Do you really think I care about your precious rules of chess?"

"But I had assumed it could simply carry over into the match you have already designed," Stone questioned.

"You know what always happens when you assume," Max said, breaking the silence. "You make an-"

"I know, I know," Stone cut him off. "What do you think of the eye?"

"Well, it couldn't be any more uncomfortable," Max said smiling as he grabbed the sealant gel from Stone. He smoothly smeared the substance around the base of the site. He looked around with his right eye shut. "This is going to suck when I try to sleep."

"It was the best I could do, Mr. Picky," Stone shot.

"I guess I can overlook it this time, but don't let it happen again. If it happens again, I won't really be able to overlook anything, will I?" Max did not notice the four-way gun pods descending from the heights of the ceiling. Each found a target and locked onto a second.

"You have one minute to act," the hologram interrupted.

"You have no queen," Stone spat.

"My queen died when you were born. The love of my life, the only love of my life, and you took her from me. You caused problems even then. Now you shall pay for her death with your own," Blade rang, audibly angered.

"How can you still blame me for that? I would give anything to know my mother."

"Then say hello to her for me before you go down the other way. Twenty seconds," Blade issued coldly.

"It's all fun and games until someone loses an eye," Max chimed.

Stone stormed through the hologram to the enclosed chamber. He projected a beam that would block the laser walls, and, as he approached, the walls disappeared. The energy barriers first dissolved in an arc and faded completely as Stone got closer. When he saw the pawn inside, he turned off the beam. He turned instantly to the image of his father. "What is this? What the hell is this?" Stone radiated anger. "You expect me to kill a child? You want me to destroy an innocent child?"

"No, I expected your queen to kill a child. After all, you've been doing me a great service in eliminating problem workers for me." The hologram imitated Blade's cold smile.

"You mean we've been killing citizens? Not even military personnel? Look at this," Stone roared to his companions. He tapped a button on his chest and a hologram of the chamber's contents burst intentionally over the place where Blade's image stood, leaving him as merely a simple green tinge in space.

Each of the living members of Stone's army saw the child sitting inside the compartment. His arms, legs, and chest shone with the same metallic reflection that the other pawns exhibited with their replacements. He sat in the center with his arms wrapped around his shins. He looked frightened.

Marcus closed his eyes. Stone knew he was trying to reach the boy and hoped he would succeed. Max studied the child, staring at the projection and getting accustomed to his new manner of seeing.

"He is in pain and extremely frightened. It is all too much for his mind to take at this age," Marcus said sadly as he lifted his eyelids.

"Too much of his body has been augmented too quickly. He lacks the organic element I possess to ease the adjustment of the mind to the new systems, not to mention the feeling that every part of his body that was replaced itches and tingles excessively right now. His brain is going to overload in a few days unless we end his suffering now. Trust me when I tell you it is about the most painful way to die you could imagine," Max assessed.

Stone would not accept that. These deaths were inevitable since the issuing of his challenge, but this was not the combat he had expected. This violated his honor. His father was forcing him to choose between killing an innocent boy and dying himself. Stone's own weak survival instinct and logic prevailed in the thought that Marcus, Max, and Jake were more important than a dying innocent. If Stone did not follow through with the action, he would be responsible for his companions dying in vain. He would never allow that; they had all come too far, even if they had not yet faced any of the greatest warriors Blade had at his disposal. Morally, though, it felt like cowardice and murder, which was exactly the reaction Blade was hoping to get. This contest was as much about psychological strategy as it was about physical prowess.

Stone felt the knot in his stomach tighten as he began to speak. "Is there anything we can do to make it painless?"

"I'll be back in a moment," Max offered.

Solemn moments did not sit well with Stone. He was unequipped to deal with them. Max returned with the bundle he had taken from his lab. He unfolded the tattered jeans to reveal several of the elbow jointed injection tubes he so often used on himself. He searched through the pile for the one that would deliver euthanasia.

"My father forced me to kill the last pawn. He knew all along that I was the only one who could even enter that chamber. It was a child, a child who did not deserve to die. Max made it painless for the boy, but it still served as one of the worst things I have ever been forced to do. He asked me if I was there to help him. I tried to talk to him but I choked on the words. The boy had not yet seen his teens. He looked into my eyes as he died. I watched unmoving as his spirit left him," Stone recalled through gritted teeth. The weight of his heart was heavy, and the reporter could see the pain in his face.

Stone left the chamber, and the laser walls came down just as the others had. The gun mounts were already retracted. He realized then that his father had not truly intended to fire upon him and his companions. Blade knew that such a gesture would not have even fazed Stone, but he also knew his son's concern for his allies. It was a weakness Blade had exploited before now and would do so again. Stone was completely aware of the fact that he had gone well beyond the minute he was given. However, he also knew that his father would freely blast away at him and his assemblage upon provocation. For now at least, Blade was content to play different factions off against one another, no doubt amused by the drama. Stone's anger for his father intensified, and it threatened to consume him.

CHAPTER 18

"YOUR TURN," STONE roared across the arena. The white pawns filed into their spaces, and Blade's men followed. Blade himself left the throne. The light whispered off behind him. The ruler walked into the square as regally as ever. This time, the laser walls did not spring to life when the combatants were in place; Stone was not about to let his father get away with that.

Stone tapped into the Neo-Colosseum's main computer network. He found the proper directory and activated the program it held. The blue lasers glowed and shot upwards to form walls around the squares; one of which burned the edge of Blade's cape off at the floor. "I'm going to pay for that one," Stone said quietly, with a miniscule smirk, from the observation deck.

Stone monitored each of the pawns via the link between his armor and their recorders. He gave each of them a cursory glance. The black rooks looked impressive enough. Alex was a knight, Erik was a bishop, and Blade was of course the dark king. The other knight was unknown to Stone; he was a bestial looking man who wore restraint clasps on his wrist, ankle, waist, and neck. He was obviously dangerous and evidently disobedient. The thing had enormous spikes grafted to its right side. The queen's chamber was empty, and much to Stone's disappointment, the other pawn's recording device was not responding to the commands his armor gave to it.

He began a closer inspection of the chambers. His father had not yet given the order to fight. Blade was waiting to see if his son would be so bold. He anxiously monitored the chambers.

Erik was wearing a black suit and hood. A golden shoulder pad blazed on his left side. A blood red cloth was draped up through his belt and over his right shoulder as a cape. His gauntlets and boots were layered in golden steel with plates extending over his wrists and knees. His belt also shone gold, and a small sword sheath was sewn into the right thigh of his pants, concealed though it was by the scarlet cloth. His eye glowed red.

Blade waited no longer. He gave the order to fight. Stone switched the image to his father; he knew his father would defeat the pawn he sent against him. In minute reciprocation for being forced to fight a woman and child, Blade was given one of the female pawns to fight; Stone recalibrated it to look like his mother, crafting the image from the only picture of her he had ever seen. Blade had shed his dark cape. Beneath it was armor very similar to Stone's.

"My father and his men now faced the white pawns as we had faced the black," Stone said as he pushed the line of white pawns straight into the remaining black pieces. It was the same wave of white the computer had moved in the future. The structure of the game was increasingly falling apart.

Blade outfitted himself in black armor. It made him look far larger than he actually was. His armor, though, merely enhanced his strength and speed; it lacked the electronic proficiency of Stone's attire. A hologram projected by the armor perpetually hid Blade's real face, replacing the human features with a grim, pale illumination with a flaming, churning scar beneath one eye. A piece of black cloth formed a large collar extending slightly above the top of his head, hiding the metallic reinforcement that shielded him from attacks from behind. When coupled with the cape, it gave him the perfect image of death. His image would haunt a person forever, if that person should ever survive their encounter with Blade. The deep set eyes and glowing pupils were not soon abolished from anyone's memory. In place of the cape, Blade had taken up segmented, scarlet metal shoulder pads. His segmented gauntlets, gloves, and boots shone gold. A retracting sword was heavily chained to his gold belt with a large clasp. The black skull over a red longsword, the symbol of his regime, was stamped upon his chestplate. A sunken panel on his abdomen contained the holographic generator. Just as his son, Blade could move unrestricted in his versatile suit.

Stone tossed a white pawn to the ground. "My father unclipped the sword and chain from his belt. One side of the sword had been sharpened to extreme while the other side was hinged to allow it to fold back into its handle. Instead of extending the blade, he swung the chain at the seemingly human female in front of him. The chain snapped taught against the energy field, only to bound back at its wielder. Father quickly wrapped the chain around the white pawn's throat as it lunged for his waist and. He clipped the end of the chain around another link, securing his opponent at his mercy. He pulled, and, and the field around the pawn's frame could not deflect it. The pawn, thrown by the momentum, was hurled into the laser wall, but it did not incinerate as expected. The wall glowed bright blue, and the field crackled, yet somehow, the field held. The hydraulic blade of my father's sword shot forward into the pawn. The energy barrier finally collapsed from the strain. As Blade withdrew the chain, the pawn frame slumped to the ground, and the upper half burned away in the laser wall to the smoky puff of rapid fluid evaporation."

Blade quickly rotated several gauges on the panel added to his gauntlet. He closed his eyes as his glowing green image appeared in all of the enclosed fighting pits. Shutting his eyes prevented sensory overload from the simultaneous projections contained within the arena's rigging which contained feedback capabilities. "They are not real, as I assured you they would not be. Each of them must have some sort of buffer field. As my son lacks originality, I am certain they all have the same capacity. Interrupt the field enough, and you should get through without a problem," the ghostly voice reverberated as all of the projections shimmered out.

Soon after Stone witnessed his father's speech, the pawn registering in the unknown bishop's chamber blinked out of existence. Its data detail immediately downloaded to Stones armor in its final moments. When the final data from that pawn's malfunctioning equipment emblazoned itself on the readout screen, it registered several pinpoint concentrations of attacks that were unsuccessfully blocked. A central energy burst and two subsequent explosions from projectile bombs had completed the transaction. Stone had an uneasy feeling in the pit of his stomach, and pinpricks of anxiety suddenly ran through his mind.

Stone cycled through the other chambers. Erik, wielding two rectangular gripped hand hammers, was trading shots with the pawn he faced. The bestial creature in the other chamber was unfazed by the pawn's attacks. It simply stood there with a puzzled, unfocused rage showing on its face. Stone was amazed to see the creature absorb that kind of impact, especially with its asymmetrical proportions. A single punch from the bestial man leveled the field-protected machine. The impact was reversed as well as it could be, but the power was unimaginable. In a display Stone did not believe possible, the beast picked the machine up, energy crackling from the buffer field, and effectively threw it through the laser wall. Several of the spikes grafted to its left forearm were singed off at the tip as the creature experimented with its prison after that. The pawn's frame, bereft of its protective shield in the flight through the incinerating walls, cluttered to the outside floor in an unnatural slump, destroyed.

Stone flicked another white pawn from the field. "I saw only the final moments of the battle between Alex and his assigned pawn. His charged sword had finally severed the head completely off of the steel frame. The unfortunate fact is that, though the head is surprisingly useless to the machines, the field requires full integrity to function at all. Alex indulged in overkill. I believe his words were, 'My only regret is that you do not bleed.'

"The rooks were another matter. The only thing remotely human about them was the fact that they were bipedal and had two arms. A sensor panel in the center of the sleek torso functioned as a makeshift, though well-guarded, face. Spikes lined every seam and appeared to serve as the rivets. Four taloned fingers, attached directly to the tapered cylinders that were their forearms, functioned as the hands. Numerous tubes and outlets on their frames obviously held weapons, but just what kind remained to be seen. The sad fact is that a portion of the technology for these things came from my own laboratory. My father demanded a constant supply of upgraded weaponry, and, as long as the supply to him did not dry up, I was able to conceal some of the projects in which I immersed myself. Nevertheless, these constructs and my pawns exchanged hits for what would prove to be the longest matches in our bloody game." Two more pawns white tumbled to the floor, noisily hitting the ground and rolling.

With some scarring and the loss of a few shield panels, the black rooks succeeded. They had adapted frequencies simultaneously until they reached a wave that would disrupt the pawn's shields. The frames made a futile attempt at continued brawling, but a personal bomb in the stomach of one and a row of spikes through the spinal column of the other ended that idea. A chilling thought occurred to Stone; Blade had not fired off a transmission since his warning to his combatants, which meant that the rooks had come up with the strategy on their own. Stone's white pawns ran on battle programs, but the tactic he witnessed suggested a level of sentience.

Erik battered at the white pawn before him. It countered his attacks with rather low difficulty. Erik dropped the hammer in his right hand and bent low to the ground in apparent defeat. His cape fell over his free arm, and in a blinding flash no less than ten pinpoint flechettes flew from his hand into the frame. With its shell pierced, the frame lurched, struggling to regain its standing position after its metallic knees had been skewered. The motors would not respond, and Erik leisurely pounded the frame into slag with his hammers.

"That was it. The laser walls fell again. This time, though, the losses were on our side, which I had truly expected. I had apparently not been as adept at constructing the pawns as I would have believed. The only chamber left belonged to the absent queen. However, the more pressing issue was the unknown bishop that had eluded my pawn from a system malfunction. From head to toe, the figure was cloaked. I knew it would be quite unpleasant to see who it was with my heart pounding in anticipation. However, shock does not encompass the spectrum of emotion," Stone shivered with the memory.

Before Stone could comment about the chamber still surrounded by lasers, Blade announced an important introduction. The bishop reached beneath the encompassing cloak and slowly pulled the hood free. The slightest glint of illumination reflected off of the dark hair impaled Stone with the realization he dreaded. He watched without seeing as the cloak fell away completely. The tight black jumpsuit was accented by golden holsters and clip pockets on the wrists, legs, ankles, and waist. The trim, gorgeous figure cocked her hip and raised her eyes as though to meet Stone's gaze, but she did not. Kylie merely reloaded her handheld bomb cannon and hung it from her belt. The skull and sword of Blade's army were emblazoned on her glove.

Hoping it was not real, Stone nevertheless witnessed what felt like his heart dying. He nearly crushed Max's shoulder as he breathlessly grasped it. He opened his mouth as if to say her name, but the emotional stab of pain took the sound from the words. The evident mixture of love and despair flowed from him in breaking waves. Stone swallowed hard and forced the years of loneliness away. He experimentally worked his mouth to see if it was still a part of him. "Jake, give me the gun," he uttered.

"What about the other chamber, father? Do you forfeit?" Stone erupted in a voice that shocked even him. It was a feral roar that erupted from his throat. His anger surged and with unthinking precision, he fired a hailstorm of ion bullets around his father into the laser walls behind the ruler. As the shots sizzled out at the wall, a latent, minor realization struck Stone. He saw why his father chose to arm his pawns with the guns. The bullets, unconventional to say the least, introduced radioactive elements into the body where the bullet penetrated the skin, disrupting the activity of hundreds of cells without being expelled from the system or destroyed. One shot could have killed them immediately or days later. They would not have even suspected that they could still suffer death from the wound.

Stone recalibrated the last pawn's field. Blade had forced him to fight a child, and he would respond in kind. Though his would be an illusion, it was the best psychological weapon he had in reserve. He lowered one of the walls and left it down. Inside, the pawn radiated an image of his younger self. Blade did not even hesitate before cutting cleanly through the field, in the form of his own small son, and leaving the pawn's frame in halves at the floor. He stuck the point of his sword through the pawn's holographic projector. "My move," Blade announced. His hologram appeared directly before his son. If it were real, Blade's breath would be warm upon Stone's cheek. "That was a cute trick with your mom there, but I would cut you down any day. So, how fond are you of my bishop?"

"Erik doesn't really do anything for me."

"Ah, wit. That was a little too close to humor for you, wasn't it? I know you love Kylie. She knows it, too. You may already know that much, and, if you did, you must also know that it disgusts her, just like it disgusts everyone else."

"Why?"

"Why Kylie, you mean? Or why am I bringing all of this up? The answer to the first question should be obvious enough. She is an assassin, and you could never hurt her; hence, she's the perfect one to kill you. As for the other matter, I just want you to learn how pathetic this is. Do you think destroying me could give you another chance at life? I know you. As horrible as it is, you are my son. Love is all you crave, which is why I will never allow you to have it. You deserve nothing." Without giving Stone a chance to respond, Blade's hologram disappeared. The haunting voice was still ringing in his ears.

On the holographic chessboard above his gauntlet, Stone saw Blade move the black knight from *b8* down two spaces and left one into the space labeled *a6* in the series of rows and columns. Stone parried to Blade's thrust. He moved his white knight, representing Max, in a similar fashion: forward two and left one into *f3*. Blade quickly moved the knight as far down as he could legally move and aligned it in its original column at *b4*. Seeing the pattern, Stone moved his left rook forward a single space on an intercept course to *a2*. Instead of pursuing the king, Blade gave in to Stone's scheme and moved his black knight into the rook's square.

The first real battle had begun in earnest. Alex strode down to meet the bionic/organic rook. Though the floor was still marked off in alternating black and white squares, the arena would not be sealed in by lasers this time. These battles were given the full scope of the arena as the combat zone. Blade silently ascended to his position on the shadowy throne.

CHAPTER 19

"WOULD YOU MIND telling me who that is?" Marcus's question startled Stone from his quiet focus.

"You must not get out too often. That is Alex Herring, personal bodyguard and second in command to my father. He was chosen for his ruthlessness. You may know him as Crimson. He got that nickname for the nasty little habit of streaking his armor with blood. I have witnessed the barbaric practice several times myself. I think it's a trophy to him. I've always thought he would be a great ad campaign for an asylum, but he's an extremely dangerous man by any standards," Stone answered, watching the pair circle each other in the vast arena.

"We must be alert in facing one such as him," Marcus responded.

"Yeah, but I can be a very dangerous man to deal with, too," Stone flatly stated.

"That can't be confidence uttered from those lips," Max gasped, feigning shock.

"Maybe, friend, just maybe," Stone said, distracted by Blade issuing the order to fight. Stone's gaze flashed to Kylie, who looked to everyone but him. Blade watched silently from his throne. Even the eerie glow of the image projected on his face was hidden in the shadows of the dim landing wherein the throne sat. He was intent on the battle before him between his greatest warrior and the construct of his son's design. There was a hint of distraction with him. It was as though this was not his most pressing concern, merely the one requiring his presence.

Alex hammered at the expressionless rook that was blocking his every move. Finally, he put all of his strength into an overhead sword strike at the rook's head. The rook blocked with a forearm, but one of the shield panels split under the impact of the weapon. The rook shed the plate as if it were a broken fingernail. The preprogrammed unnerving smile crossed the rook's face. Alex punched the being's face, marring its image temporarily, striking too quickly to be grabbed by the flesh. The automated bulky frame showed from under the temporary gap in the manmade flesh. Alex cleaved at the being again, his eyes flashing under the dark helmet. The sword struck against the bare frame as both of the rook's forearms launched jets of flame at the twisted knight.

Alex spun as fire lurched at his shining golden armor. Black streaks of consumed fuel marred his tempered golden steel plating and handcrafted helmet. Crimson's cape and body suit absorbed the heat, and Alex turned on the battery inside his blade. When he turned back to the rook, it was unfolding the energy weapon that had previously burned through the black pawn.

The glowing blade tore through the rook's arm. The inner frame was breached by the superheated, superconductive metal charged by the altered electric current which was generated by the battery in the hilt. The skin converged on the blade, and, releasing the severed appendage, gripped the hilt in a shapeless tendril. The manmade flesh was charred but operational. It wrenched the blade from Alex's grip while focusing the energy blast with a small laser point. Alex pounded his gauntlet completely through the creation's face without losing a second. The impact sprayed the strange flesh through the arena.

The energy burst gathered focus on Alex's heart. He leaped and turned away. The blast erupted and followed Alex as he ran the perimeter of the arena. The blast rocked the walls as it reverberated off of the reinforced arena's boundaries. Alex managed to evade the blast until the energy was exhausted. As a second flame burst erupted from the intact forearm, he lunged for the blade lodged in the remnants of the rook's arm. He wrested it free with the help of a kick to the rook's side as the ineffectual flames died away on the singed red cape. The skinless face seemed to glare at the man as it grew back together. Alex's foot was snared by the roving flesh.

Crimson charged the fiber optic, metal composite blade. The electron waves flowed through the weapon, as though they were shipping a signal to the point of the sword, and diffused angrily through the sharpened, conducting blade. The superheated metal glowed red in seconds, ready for the strike. Alex cut his leg free and slashed through the rook's right leg. The rook shifted its weight and recalled the skin to its lost forearm. The seared leg fell to the floor as sparks spewed from the opening. Thick pale blue hydraulic fluid dripped from a sliced hose.

"You bleed," Alex said gleefully as fire flashed in his bestial eyes. He spun the blade to slice through the various lashing tendrils reaching too close to him. In a blur of glowing red heat, he cut through the metal skull at an angle down through the waist. Explosions staggered the oddly balanced frame. The skin drew to the breach and covered the open area as the greatest part of the being's mass was uselessly shed. The skin continued performing surgery on the body's remaining portion as parts were either collected into a central mass or expelled with efficiency. The faceless mass of synthetic skin took on a more human shape as it left the last of its shielding behind.

"Not bad, eh, Max?" Stone looked away from the battle long enough to observe his friend's reaction to the occurrence. "It's just your skin and my armor." Stone appeared to be as awed by the resiliency of his creation as he was capable of showing.

The walking flesh extended several tentacles of itself towards Alex. Alex spun the blade to burn them off as two more gripped him solidly around his ankles and two grasped his waist and chest. Precision allowed him to snap them cleanly off and spray their components across the floor. A laser beam lanced from the chest area of the being towards Alex's helmet. The sword flew from his hand at the source of the beam as it arced closer to the T-shaped opening on his helmet. The laser exploded at its source in a fiery red. The skin splashed to the floor with no motivation left to move it. The flowing form spread out lifelessly. Alex approached and smeared the skin away from the heart area. Stone saw from the deck that the being had effectively retrieved all functional weaponry from its endoskeleton and quickly fused it to the calibrated magnetic core that constantly reshaped the skin.

Alex retrieved his blade from the mess. He placed another power battery in the hilt to replace the emptied one that had destroyed the rook. Without charging his weapon, he cut the main fluid cable next to the laser emplacement. He reached into the thick blue fluid that felt cool to his hand. He put a single streak across his chest plate and shook his glove to remove the excess. After all, it was not real blood. He removed the scorched helmet and lifted the blade aloft.

"The splattered mess formerly known as a rook," Max commented wryly. "We gave it a chance, and at least it was resourceful."

"I knew he would defeat it. I wanted to see if Alex, or Crimson or whatever you creatively call him, could cut through my armor with that sword. I did not sacrifice the rook on purpose, but Alex was coming for me. Father wanted this to end quickly," Stone responded with some distraction.

"It appears Crimson is a bit blue today," Max quirked.

"My father is planning something, Max. This is either a distraction or a real push to rid himself of me." Alex ascended the arena stairs as the laser walls erupted in dazzling blue to clear away the mess for the next battle. "Leaves nothing useful behind," Stone assessed, drifting his gaze to Kylie.

CHAPTER 20

STONE DUPLICATED THE moves that had already been played out in the future on the aged chessboard in the present. He casually dropped his own white rook to the floor. "Alex has struck me as extremely feral since I first met him. I did not realize quite how sadistic he was until I led a task force in which he was a prominent member. One of the more recently acquired Latin American nations resisted my father's rule not long after his major military campaign through South America began. You see, my father ruled every speck of land in the Americas and quite a substantial portion of Africa and Australia by the time my challenge came."

Stone's father expected resistance to his rule, but this particular insurrection had resulted in two assassination attempts. Though both attempts failed, such actions demanded personal punishment as an example to those who would be foolish enough to attempt such feats in the future. Of course personal punishment meant that Stone was in charge of the mission. He realized now the reasoning behind placing him at the head of such actions. Blade foresaw his son's rebelliousness, and placing him at the head of the vengeance missions would discourage any other disloyal factions from trusting Stone.

Stone gathered the memory and forced himself past the distractions that still plagued his thought process. He continued with the side story despite his own objections and the urgency of what he had to accomplish here, but the reporter was listening to him and wanted to hear what he had to say. "A carrier shuttle dropped us down on the rebel encampment. Crimson was the first out of the hatchway, rolling into a crouch position with his blade held ready. I followed closely behind. My armor had not been perfected at that time, but it was substantial enough for the task at hand. The army troops followed rigidly behind us. Their red armor and body suits were hidden by lightweight black cloaks. The skull and sword were emblazoned everywhere on the unit so there would be no confusion as to who had done this. The fighting was over quickly, and the entire camp of people was either captured or killed. One of my father's personal soldiers held the leader just as other soldiers held the lesser members of the organized revolt." Stone realized then that the fight there had been one of the bloodiest and most chaotic he had been unfortunate enough to witness.

The Latin American army had no chance whatsoever. The armor of Blades's soldiers far outclassed anything their weapons had hopes of piercing. Only one soldier died of his own misfortune, stepping in front of Alex Herring in a battle. Aside from that, the casualties were one sided.

The waning forces clung to their relics from the era driven by the forgotten "my gun is bigger than yours" syndrome. Stone was fortunate to witness the end of that mindset. When a person can fire fifteen rounds from a pen cap and everyone made a fashion choice tending toward bulletproof, that philosophy lost its mass appeal. Strategy became more important than firepower. What followed was the shift to energy research and the campaign to turn every technology into a weapon, ending merely in some of death's more inventive forms. That was when Blade appeared on the scale of global power, offering some of the most impressive pieces of the new line of weapons and the promise of protection. The inexplicable followed; people began to respect those with a skill in fighting rather than those with the ability to spray the most lead. Even though it began to decay before it fully returned, respect for the old techniques was forced out of its long hibernation.

Stone continued with his tale. "Crimson approached the leader of the *Insurrectos* and beckoned him to attack. The leader declined immediately, having at least marginal intelligence in the decision. Although I believe either choice would have seen him dead. Any other person may have let it go at that, but Alex handed the man, Prospero I think his name was, a loaded repeater rifle and let him go. The man made a fatal mistake in firing the weapon at Alex. Despite the man's accuracy and the fact that he had actually killed a number of my father's dedicated soldiers in the course of the campaign for his people's freedom, it was still a mistake to fire. Armed only with a blade, my father's favorite pet cut the man down before he could pull the trigger again. He was at point blank range straight to Crimson's chest and Crimson won. I got to witness Crimson's trademark habit of streaking his armor with a fallen enemy's blood. He reached deep into the cut across the man's stomach. He raised his glove, covered in the leader's blood, to his gleaming golden chest plate and streaked his fingers across his heart. His vicious, wild smile made me sick." Stone recalled the rest of the scene in vivid detail. That moment was perhaps the first time that the seed of doubt about his father's purpose was nourished and allowed to grow within him. It was the first major push of the snowballing mistrust and rebelliousness in him.

Alex ordered all of the soldiers to prepare the malcontents for their promised execution. Stone objected vehemently, arguing that the leader had been killed per orders and that the rest would submit after the spectacle Alex had created. Alex merely glared at him, and an evil smile crossed his lips as he gave the affirmative to his orders.

Stone interceded directly, though his action would later receive rebuke from his father for weakening the army's position to those who were witnessing the scene. "You will not execute these people in such a manner."

"The orders come directly from our ruler, Blade himself. All involved are to be killed," Alex said angrily in response. His fiery gaze burned at Stone.

"I am in charge of this mission. My orders are to be followed," Stone demanded coldly.

"Not above those of our supreme master," Alex countered.

"Our Supreme Master is not my earthly father," Stone growled.

Alex's spit on the ground was the only response he received. Crimson spun his bloodied blade and motioned for the soldiers to release their captives. The prisoners struggled with the chains binding their hands to the tent shafts while they fought to even stand. Alex stood roughly in the central spot of the camp and removed his helmet. He again engaged the wicked twist of his lips he called a smile. He pulled out a small electronic device from his belt. When he pressed the button, the pinpoint grenades that had been forced into the mouths of all of the captives exploded. The closer soldiers were spattered with blood. Stone was far enough away to avoid the same fate. He turned his head again at the warning click of detonation as Alex burned the camp.

Stone ran through the charred, bloody mess of the camp. He took refuge in the relative cover of the trees and removed his own helmet. He experienced his breakfast leaving the way it had entered. He replaced his helmet with the burning taste of bile in his throat. He had killed before, but he never felt bad about it. This had just been a sickening display of power.

Alex was dripping with the liquid that had once sustained life in the rebels. His teeth flashed white in the otherwise red spectrum. It was the vilest sight Stone had ever witnessed, and his father had ordered that very outcome. In all of the assignments he had been given, Stone had never seen anything as horrifying and shocking as a man who enjoyed mass murder as much as Alex.

Crimson proudly got his nickname that very day, from none other than Blade. He discarded his cape and rinsed the rest of his garb in a nearby stream the *Insurrectos* had used for drinking. He kept the liquid remnants of the battle only on his chest. His blond hair still held streaks of red when he returned to the shuttle. Most of the soldiers had shed their overcoats to reveal their serial issue military suits and shining red body armor. The example would long be remembered as the price for crossing Blade Stone in the land the shuttle left in its wake.

Stone stared at Alex the entire way back to New Charleston, where the Neo-Colosseum was just being constructed. Alex stared silently back until the shuttle had landed, unmarred by the enemy fire it had encountered at its target location. "You hate what I did, don't you?" Alex enjoyed the confrontation. He smelled of stale blood and fuel.

"Yes, it was unnecessary, and it was well beyond overkill," Stone said, meeting his gaze.

"Should they have been spared then?" Alex brought the cleaned blade up in front of Stone. He looked distractedly at the glazed reflection in the tempered metal.

"We were sent for punishment, not annihilation," Stone said, his stare unwavering.

"No. You were sent for punishment. I was sent for annihilation.

Those assassination attempts were closer to succeeding than any other. Go back to your technology and leave the military aspects to those with the stomach to handle it," Alex bit intently. Stone wanted nothing more than Alex's death at that very instant.

In the present past, Stone shook himself out of the vivid memory and forced himself away from the unimportant elaborations in which he was indulging far too much. He blocked the memory from his mind with a final realization that the events in the third world country impacted not only the people there but Stone as well.

As Stone reproduced the next move in the chess game, he wondered why he allowed himself to tell the journalist so much. The answer was simple. The reporter listened and cared about what was being said.

It was Stone's move in the twisted battle of strategies and warriors. As a simple delaying move, he angled the bishop at the king's side, Marcus, into *e2*, angled in front of the white king's piece. Blade again openly attacked, sending the black rook at the left of the board to *h3*, level with Max's knight piece.

"He's planning to take you out first, Max. If he can't get to me quickly, he's going to get you out of the game. It's my move. I can get you away from that thing for a few moves at least," Stone assured his friend.

"I came here out of loyalty, but I fully intended to fight. I don't believe any of us are taking this lightly despite the banter. Destiny and our own hearts have brought us here. If we don't win this, I'll be hunted down for betraying Blade, assuming I'll leave here alive. I'll take them all on for you if you want. I've committed myself to this, so use me against any of them you desire," Max responded genuinely.

"Even her?" Stone's eyes rested again on his beloved.

"Yes. It's better for me to do it than you. You'd quite literally cut your own heart out and gift wrap it for her before you died," Max answered with a smile.

Stone knew Max would not keep the serious tone of the conversation for long. "She already has my heart gift wrapped."

"Stop with the melancholy for once. Face it, friend, she's an assassin. Your father hired her, that's all. You know their code. Once they accept, they can't sell out on an employer for anything. She was my friend too, you know."

"She accepted an assignment to kill me, Max. How's that for compassion?" Stone knew the situation concerning Kylie was very bleak indeed.

"Maybe she's just playing hard to get."

Stone had to laugh at that. Max was a much respected man, but Stone cared more for the lighter side of him. Max was the only person that could make him laugh in any situation.

"Your move," Blade's hologram appeared swiftly behind them. The shimmering green image carried through the slightly hurried feeling of his posture. The darkness played over the hologram to sweep even that in shadows.

Stone looked at his best friend, who gave him a silent nod. He moved Max's knight piece, and, when it rested two spaces beyond in the extreme left column at *h4*, Blade's image flickered just as silently away. The black rook native to *h8* completed its trek to the white knight's square. Stone realized only too late that the rook had been specifically created to destroy his friend Maximus.

CHAPTER 21

STONE WATCHED HIS friend pocket a handful of the injection tubes he liberated from his destroyed lab. He strode down to the arena where his life was truly in jeopardy. "You gave me back my life, let's see if I can repay that debt," Max whispered under a deep breath.

Stone watched Kylie walk forward to the end of the observation deck opposite his side. Even if she wished his death, she at least had a cursory interest in her old friend Max. She glanced quickly at the pistol strapped to her ankle. Stone wanted desperately to confront her, but he knew he would not be able to do so, at least not without Max at his side. Although he believed Max's help would be required just to scrape the pieces back together later.

Blade stood at his throne with the hologram on his face the only light among the darkness. He issued the order to fight. His voice resounded in Stone's ears, which were already pounding with his nervous heart. He could only watch as the machine pounded on his oldest friend. As he looked quickly over his shoulder, he realized that Max had not left his side since Kylie's presence had been announced.

The massive, dull metal frame stood imposingly in front of Max. Using both hands, Max vaulted over the construct as two circular panels dilated on either side of the roughly triangular sensor plate located in the center of the giant torso. Max's leather gloves were torn by the small spikes lining the rook's seams. Two hovering globes, roughly palm size in diameter, rolled out of the open holes and halted in midair. The only disruptions on their smooth surfaces were the blinking eye lights and the seams separating the globes into hemispheres.

Behind the rook, Max wondered why the being had not turned around or followed him. Then he saw the sphere hovering in front of him. He recognized it immediately as a targeting globe. The other flying orb was spiraling towards him, creating a tunnel of its sensor wake for the volley of missiles launched by the rook to follow.

Max backhanded the revolving globe, using its momentum against it to slam the device into the wall he had unknowingly neared. Max leaped away, and the missiles, without a tunnel to follow, exploded without result against the reinforced arena boundary. The second targeting globe had tracked him, and the rook itself turned to face him. The strangely corrugated and curved triangle, with a single vertex closest to the floor, was as close to a face as the robot possessed. A lone sensor blinked red out from the panel's side. Two more globes rolled out, again pausing as they engaged their magnetic rebellion against Earth's gravity.

A battery of spikes launched from a central, open panel in the rook's taloned forearm. The spikes caught Max in the semiorganic leg. They caught but did not impede the leg's functionality. The twinge of feedback was not enough to cause him to lose vital time removing the metal thorns. Instead, he ran at the rook, aiming for the single sensor apart from the others. He hit it sideways with his robotically enhanced fist. A glancing blow was all he could manage since he was avoiding the rook's attacks at the same time. Something clicked in Max's mind that he had seen the body's movement pattern before, but he could not place it. The globes swarmed at Max as he rolled away. He grabbed one in his gloved human hand, only to receive the sharp sting of an electric prod. The globes had defensive capability, though not much. Two more rolled from the rook just the same.

Still holding the sphere despite the pain he felt in his arm, Max again rushed the rook. As he anticipated, another pair of missiles launched from the hydraulic launch tubes in the rook's shoulders. He jammed the globe he was clutching into the hole it had come from. The orb's light blinked furiously, but the missiles still followed the target and slammed into the rook. The explosions rocked its frame as sparks showered the floor.

Smoke billowed from the stretched and torn metal hole. The ruination of one of the orb launching ports was the extent of the damage, though. Max took advantage of the momentary confusion and pried at the slightly raised sensor panel. It began to come loose in Max's semiorganic hand as a purple glow focused on him from the center of the bent sensor plate.

Max suddenly felt his left half slowing down in response time. Then he remembered the counter-electronic signal the rooks had used to disable the pawns. What was left of Max's original cells was all that kept that half of him working. He grabbed the dangling sensor in his right hand and pulled sharply on it. It snapped off in his hand, and, in his weakened state, he toppled to the floor. He watched the rook reach for him with its four talons held in a clawlike position. Max scrambled away and regained his footing. He backed only a few feet away when the rook launched four of the targeting globes in succession from its remaining launch port. The orbs no longer followed Max. Instead, they encircled the rook in fixed positions halfway between the rook and the walls.

Max quickly examined the cable in his hand. He needed one more test to be sure, but it was beginning to fall into place for him. Suddenly, the hemispheres of the globes separated several centimeters from each other. Then a laser wall erupted from the center of each one, cutting the arena size to a quarter of its area. Stone keyed rapidly into the computer only to find that the walls were being emitted from the globes and not the arena itself, so there was nothing he could do covertly to stop them at this range.

Max had dropped the sensor and struggled to remain equidistant from the rook and the deadly walls. Max watched a bomb roll down the forearm chamber into the taloned grip. Seeing a tiny ignition flicker in the shoulder missile tubes, Max again rushed the creation. More dragging than using his left side, Max reached towards the right missile tube with his left hand. He knew that without any more targeting globes, the left missile turret would not fire because of target proximity, but the right would fire because of a target lock straight ahead. He covered the launcher and pounded at the sensor panel in what appeared to be an awkward attempt to push the rook over.

Max was aware of the ache in his human hand an instant before the missile exploded in the other. The shoulder frame burst outward in the blast, disabling the right arm that was already reaching to attach the bomb to Max's semiorganics. Max was thrown to the ground when the missile exploded. He looked up to see the gaping hole in the frame's top pouring smoke and spitting sparks. His gaze drifted back down to his own robotic hand, which was now missing its charred center. The pinkie and index finger were unnaturally mangled around the blackened palm, and he smelled charred flesh in his nostrils. Max realized it was not bad by comparison.

Struggling again to his feet, he wrenched the bomb out of the creature's motionless but still intact grip. He placed it carefully on the nearest globe vertex of the hexagon caging him with the rook. Thumbing the locking switch, he stumbled again towards the still reeling robot. The disabling energy wave had ceased. However, the return of control was a less abrupt process. A barrage of spikes shot at Max from the working forearm. They caught Max glancingly in the human arm and scraped more severely on his shoulder. The tough reptilian scales took most of the hit, but several chipped off and bled.

Meanwhile, the bomb went off on the small globe. Contrary to what Max had predicted, the wall did not fall. Instead, it contracted, leaving the vacant position out of its perimeter. The rook leapt to avoid the closing wall, agile for its bulk and quick to react for a machine. Max heard the sound he was hoping and dreading to hear. Then he placed the pattern in a discomforting realization.

"You just *slooshed*," Max said, much to Stone's surprise. Stone passed the comment off as merely part of Max's typical banter. "Machines don't *sloosh*," he continued, being well aware of the whir of motors and the hum of live wires in his own body, not to mention the time he spent in laboratories.

The machine swung absently, as though it were puzzled at being addressed. Struggling with actual pain and mechanical feedback, Max walked closer in the tight pentagon of incinerating walls. "Jameson, is that you in there?" Max was almost friendly with the curious question. The machine stepped back, igniting the second and only working missile tube. "Yes, I think it is. That was trans-synthetic cable, the kind used in scanning organic tissue. Then there's the fact that you *slooshed*. Even the attack pattern feels familiar. Jameson, if that's you, shut this thing down. When it's over, we'll get you back in a real body. You know what I'm capable of doing." Max was cautious, and Stone was enraptured by the revelations his friend had just bestowed. Kylie watched Max approvingly. The rook did not attack or respond.

The rook slowly pointed to the orb at the tip of the pentagon. It exploded in a shower of blue sparks. "I understand," Max said solemnly. He made what remnants of a fist he could muster from his left hand and punched the sensor plate as hard as he could. It clanged and dented away just enough to open a gap wide enough for Max to fit his hand inside. The purple glow shorted in and out quickly. The missile tube did not fire, but the six remaining weapons emplacements opened up with rounds of standard antiquated projectile bullets. Max was caught in the lower robotic chest by one. The others burned harmlessly away in the rectangular prison. Using everything he could put into the effort, Max pried the plate away enough to put a fist through it. He ripped several wires free in his human hand, spilling them from the opening. The storm of bullets ceased from every port except for one on the lower left that kept firing.

The rook gently gripped Max's wounded arm, but the talons tightened enough to cause pain. Apparently the rook, Jameson, wanted to live yet could not do so by shutting itself down for the duration of the battle. Max twisted painfully to deliver a kick to the open area. A second kick and some lost blood from his wound left Max with the desired result. Fluid was spilling from inside the sparking frame. Emergency systems sprang to life, keeping an electric arc from reaching the fluid's source. The rook released its grip and almost clawed at the wound the way a person would.

Max fumbled for a suitable injection tube, spilling several in the process. When he found it, he clenched it lightly in his teeth and adjusted the injection angle to one hundred and eighty degrees. Forcing it through Jameson's automated guts, he found the fluid source. The hiss of injection followed. The frame quivered, and the remaining globes fell to the floor; three of them exploded as they hit. The rook was motionless. Max pushed it over just to be certain. The last missile tube exploded, leaving little for the lasers to remove. A battered but ever-smiling Max ascended to the observation platform. He carried the lifeless globe and a few trailing wires.

"He *slooshed.*"

"So I heard," Stone said absently.

"Think I'm fixable?" Max stood before his friend with a glimmer in his right eye and a reflected glint in the other. His scaly shoulder was bleeding, his arm was covered in blood, his lower chest held a slug, his ankle of the same side was ridden with spikes, and his left hand was completely twisted.

"I don't know if it's worth it," Stone said playfully. "How did the eye work?"

"I'll say it's perfect if it gets you to fix me up," Max answered.

"Fix you up with whom? Kylie doesn't seem interested and I killed the only other pretty one here." This was Stone's way of expressing his relief at having Max back, and Max knew it.

"When I find her, I'll let you know. Since I'm not a fan of military women, that could take a while. Would you like to rewire my circuits instead, smartass?" Max handed Stone the extra parts he salvaged from the broken rook with a grin on his face.

Max applied the smooth sealant to his wounds. Stone had pried the spikes from his leg and was involved in repairing the main leg support shaft that allowed Max to stand more easily with the welding torch in his gauntlet. Stone mused on just how many devices he had incorporated into his armor.

"So what did you finally do to stop it?" Stone had lost most of Max's later commentary to the static of the laser wall.

"Not it, him. His name was Jameson," Max said absently, picking at his broken hand.

"How cute, you named it," Stone said, concentrating on minimizing the damage to Max's semiorganic tissue.

"No. It was one of my underlings from the glorious days of service under your father. I've sparred against him before. It was how we occupied our very limited free time. He won then, but that was before either of us had a metal content," Max explained.

"So you mean my father finally found a way to download a person's brain into a machine?" Stone looked up from his work with a grim expression on his face.

"I resemble that remark, but, no, not exactly. It was an organ casing like the one that keeps my heart out of my circuits."

"The '*sloosh*'?"

"Yes, the organ casing had his brain in it. The sensors used wire developed in our lab specifically designed for mechanical to organic signal transfer. So, when I found the source of the wire, I cracked the casing and injected his brain with a very nasty replicating virus," Max concluded.

"Leg's done. So, any thoughts on this Jameson?" Stone was carefully removing the expired bullet from Max's lower chest with a calibrated magnetic pull.

"Have you checked your status lately?" Blade's smiling green hologram appeared at Max's side. "I thought I would give you a little time to chat, but that's over now. Check your board," he demanded.

Stone flared the hologram of the chess board to life from his gauntlet. He quickly noticed that one of his bishops was missing. "Robert has deserted us," he said half accusingly and half questioningly. Blade's hologram spread its cape as if death were about to encompass them all.

"Surprise," Blade uttered. A specialized scan readout appeared on Stone's monitor. "He escaped unimpeded, though I would have liked otherwise."

"The scan says that he is nowhere in the arena or the surrounding grounds," Stone said, looking at the readout for something he missed. "So you planted him among us?"

"Sadly no," Blade said through the shadowy image. "But you would be surprised to find that he's rather close, relatively speaking."

"You sought him out then?" Stone was cycling through the various scenarios his mind could construct.

"Wouldn't you be quite astonished to find that it was the other way around?" With that, Blade's image seemed more to give in to the shadows than to disappear.

Marcus approached. Jake still sat propped against a wall. "I remember him leaving now. It's all so hazy, though. It was almost as if it was something remembered from a dream," Marcus added. "You were right, Stone."

"No, Marcus, you were right. I have to learn to trust people, to take chances on them. I just picked a bad time to start listening," Stone assured.

"So what now?" Max was still prodding at the hole in his hand.

"Now we continue with the strategy. Robert was never a part of it from the beginning. I trust the two of you with everything, and I trust Jake. I just have a good feeling about him, but I never trusted

Robert," Stone said, rolling the removed bullet between his thumb and forefinger. "I expected him to disappear, though I expected my father to gloat a little more or at least have his body. Now, Max, what about this Jameson?"

"Your move by the way," Blade interrupted. "I'll even make an exception and give you some time. Go ahead and talk to Kylie. You can even have your privacy. I know I'm being too generous. Don't worry; I'll decimate a city you like to make up for it after you're dead." Blade's hologram vanished again as abruptly as it had appeared.

"It doesn't look like he wants us to talk about the rooks," Max suggested.

"No, he doesn't care what we talk about. He's just trying to distract us," Stone said, creasing his brow in thought.

"This time, though, I suggest you obey him. Go talk to Kylie," Max encouraged.

"I can't. I'm not done repairing you. What would you do without me, hire a mechanic?"

"Oh no, levity won't get you out of this one, my friend. Go," Max prodded.

"Don't you see? This is what he wants. She doesn't care about me at all, Max. You know that. She's just going to hurt me even more, and we cannot afford that right now." Stone was close to yelling in confused frustration. Kylie, though, noticed both as she watched him from the observation deck.

"There is pain in her. It is a desperate pain, and you may not get another chance to talk to her," Marcus added, breaking the tension between an encouraging Max and an unwilling Stone.

"That's something I'll have to risk then. Max, please tell me about the rooks," Stone said with a definite undertone of demand in his voice.

"Well, you are certainly as stubborn as stone. Jameson had a little pet project that he worked on with two other bionic engineers, Frederick and Raymond I think. Their ultimate goal was to create a body for a scientist to do research in uninhabitable areas. Radiation, heat, and pressure have less effect on the mechanical. Technically, the project was under my supervision, but I had very little to do with the actual testing involved. They tried several different methods of getting the consciousness into the machine. It looks like it worked this time. My guess is that the other one is Frederick."

"Why not Raymond?" Stone resumed his work on Max, sealing the skin with light welding and stimulating a current with electric pulses.

"When they settled on the organ casing method, Raymond volunteered to be the test subject. The test failed miserably. All of the scanning and sensor equipment plus the strain of the output relays overloaded his brain pretty quickly," Max answered.

"Well, that explains the dulled reaction time and difficulty operating more than one system at a time. The scanner relays must be mainly automated. It also explains their reliance on these," Stone said, holding up the targeting globe and cracking it open like an egg. Internal antennae. The globe was relaying back to the main body. Consistent with all else we've found, I'll bet the relay was time-delayed."

"Our benevolent ruler must have gently persuaded them to finish their research and become a lovely little part of it," Max said sarcastically. "Looks like Frederick held out for the better model. Jameson must have been the prototype of this particular design."

"The other model does appear to be of better quality. The sensor panel has been condensed into a sharper triangle with no scanning lights out to the side. The body frames are almost an exact match. The rivets are still tipped in spikes, but the weapon emplacements on this one are entirely symmetrical," Stone said, skimming the readouts under the holographic model comparison on the monitor Blade had overridden. "I don't get it. Why not send the better one after you? The move was entirely feasible."

"Jameson is the only one to ever beat me in the sparring ring. I guess it was a case of choosing a weapon to fit the target," Max guessed. He had not stopped working his damaged hand. The black leather glove on that hand was gone, and the other was in tatters.

Marcus again walked silently back to Jake. It was quite obvious Stone wanted to talk with Max alone. There were certain things that he could not comfortably discuss in front of his former fighting instructor. It was more a matter of respect than a matter of trust.

"I know you think I'm being stubborn, and I suppose I am in some regard. My father knows how I feel about Kylie, though. He's trying to weaken me with it. The distractions are far too frequent as it is; I don't need any more. I feel like I am losing myself already. Everything is a weapon to him. Even if he gets the two of us to fight over this issue, he wins a small victory. Frankly, Max, I'm afraid of what she'll say either way," Stone said, holding the cross close to his lips.

"Point taken. So what will you do?" Max disagreed, but he resolved himself to keep his position to himself.

"I'll do the exact opposite of what he expects. I'm sending the last rook after her, and may I be forgiven for it," Stone said, again torn apart inside. The helmet rushed quickly over his face to keep any emotion from showing. In a rare display, Max reached out and embraced his armored friend. In an even less common display, Max seemed to be sad as well.

"As Marcus would so eloquently say, 'Unite your heart and mind. That is the only way to succeed.'" Max stepped back, and the smile had returned to his face.

"You have a long way to go, but that isn't bad advice considering the source," Stone said, composing himself and retracting his helmet.

"Let's change the subject. How about that traitor, huh?" Max reclaimed his wry grin.

"You know, I've noticed that I haven't been the only one who is distracted as of late. There appeared to be a bit of rush in my father's demeanor, but it vanished along with Robert."

"So are you suggesting Blade was afraid of him?" Max was curious as to how those words even came to mind.

"I was curious about that myself. However, he hinted at Robert approaching him. Any threat to his rule would have resulted in Robert's immediate termination right then and there regardless of the amount of force required."

"That leaves the possibility that Blade planted him, but Blade denies that. Do you think he was lying to us?"

"No, my father wouldn't twist the truth if the reality was much more fun. In case you haven't noticed, he enjoys his power and his abuse. In that regard, he has very little reason to lie to us. My guess is that it was a mutual deal," Stone said, resuming his work on Max. Max placed his hand flat on the observation railing as Stone relocated the fingers to their proper socket connections.

"Does this mean Robert ruined our little surprise party?"

"I'm quite impressed. Could it be that my friend Maximus Fitzgerald has a mind capable of something other than wreaking havoc on his own body systems?" Stone used several wires to fuse the broken circuits in Max's burnt hand. "I think that's exactly what happened, though. I assume he agreed to infiltrate us in exchange for something to do with position. Robert didn't seem like the kind to worry about his own neck, though. I don't think it ends there. My father is considerably more relaxed, now enjoying the challenge at hand."

"So Robert relays Blade's orders while you're occupied here, preventing your untimely intervention in something," Max guessed with a pessimistic opinion on the outcome of those orders.

"Blade probably planned to have him killed after the orders were relayed or whatever he was sent to do is accomplished. That way my father gets out of paying him or fulfilling the deal that was made," Stone continued. Max was able to work all of his fingers again, but Stone noticed the two that were twisted were grinding badly in their sockets.

"Why not give the orders himself and have them carried out while we are in here?" Max felt an insignificant amount of feedback from his palm.

"Blade is still not entirely sure who is loyal to me. I'm still connected enough to have influence. There was a chance I would find out what his plan was before he got away with it. This makes it a double victory for him, too. We lose a member of our team and he gets to keep his plans hidden." Stone was unaware of what secret was being kept from him, but his suspicions pounded in his head.

Even Robert was unaware of the true importance of what he was helping to further. The static Stone had picked up during Max's battle was not from the laser wall, it was broadcast specifically to mask his scanning equipment and transmission crackers. Stone would have picked up a signal sent outside of the arena because of his connection to the main computer network, and the intercom was the only broadcasting device that functioned inside the main arena. A transmission inside the arena, or even a personal message depending on the level of paranoia involved, could only be secured by the static burst. It did not help Stone that he was distracted at the time, either.

Marcus barely remembered Robert leaving, and Stone was not sure exactly what Robert's capabilities were. Marcus had shown a surge of strange powers lately, so there was no doubt in Stone's mind that Robert could tap that same source. Stone himself had felt the effects of the disorientation Robert could cause, and it was certainly possible that the strange man increased that effect to encompass everyone in the arena aside from Blade.

"Well, I say we forget about that and concentrate a little more on staying alive. You know, between the two of us, we actually have a single mind capable of logical, deductive reasoning. I think we've let my father wait long enough. Surely he thinks I'm considering his double-edged offer. You ready?" Stone received a nod from his companions as he looked at each of them. "Why don't we see what my father has planned?"

CHAPTER 22

STONE RECALLED MAX'S piece to *g2*. Blade moved Alex's piece to *c3* aggressively. Stone assumed correctly that Blade would not test Alex against Marcus lightly. Stone moved the remaining white rook forward to the row where the black pawns would have started in any normal chess game, *h7*. Blade moved his remaining black rook forward to defend the row at *a7*. Stone moved the knight representing Jake out to the far left column at *a3*. He knew his father would send his mechanical death machine to attack. This would be a test of Max's engineering against Blade's engineering. Jake stood and walked over to Stone.

"Good luck," Stone said encouragingly.

"I will not fail you," Jake promised.

"I know," Stone said with a smile tugging at his face. Jake stalked confidently down to the arena. Stone had rarely seen him otherwise.

"The funny thing is, his real name is Jake. I thought I had wiped that clean," Max admitted. Stone expected his friend to elaborate, but Max ceased the commentary at that.

Stone looked at Blade's shadowed face. He did not move immediately. Stone looked at Kylie, though her face did not rise to meet his. He wondered how often he had dreamed of merely having her in his company. In his dreams, he always awoke when she tried to embrace him. It always felt empty. He had never held her, or any woman, in his arms that way, and that made his heart cold all over again. Bits of those dreams flickered into his mind even in the midst of the war game. Then the memory of the other dream surfaced, but that one could not be allowed back into his head.

The black rook thundered forward at a pace far exceeding the other. Its multicolored sensors blinking and swirling in their sockets, the rook roared to a stop in the center of the combat arena. Jake bowed, and Blade ordered the fight to begin. A single targeting globe rolled from the familiar launch port. The rook's missile tubes unfolded from its shoulders. The flicker of ignition increased an instant before the missile fired. Jake caught the floating orb in his hand; it fired a charge of electricity through Jake's hand. He responded in kind by frying its circuits with his own electrical battery.

The sphere sizzled and jerked out of control, flitting around the combat level. The missile found it and exploded in a shower of fire and smoke at the far end of the arena. The rook swung at Jake. The impact knocked him back and shook the rook's frame as well. Jake jabbed at the construct and followed it with a denting right hook. The metallic being stepped back and rolled bombs down its forearm chutes into its talons. The bombs were set to lock on impact, and the rook threw them with pinpoint accuracy.

Jake blocked one with his palm, and, much to his surprise, it held. The other locked onto his chest. The first bomb exploded in his fist. The resulting force threw him to the ground. His hand was unharmed, but the top layer of the wrapped-band clothing was burned and blistered. Jake attempted to pry the remaining bomb off of his chest, inadvertently shocking himself with his own electricity. The latch still held until he simply crushed it with his tensed fingers. The bomb still exploded, though the resulting flame was mostly directed away from him. The clasps of the bomb remained on his strange garb. Bits of the metal shell from the bomb clung painfully in his face.

Jake pounded at the black rook with three powerful hits, one of which was blocked by the rook's forearm, denting it. Targeting globes rolled from both launch ports. Jake again grabbed the floating spheres and threw them back at their origin with all of the strength he could find. Both of them squealed to a halt inches from impact with their source. The orbs could not reverse their momentum, and they remained almost stationary in front of the metal construct. A purple glow flashed momentarily, and the globes clinked lifelessly to the ground.

One of the vacant spheres was crushed under the thick, flaring, prismatic lower leg extending from the rook's plated knee. The other rolled lifelessly behind its launcher and destroyer. The rook pounded again at the white knight. He fell at the impact, but rolled to avoid being crushed under an enormous metal foot. The rook erupted with six barrels spraying projectile bullets. Jake blocked his face from being shot as bullets ricocheted against the walls he was sprinting around. Only two shots connected. One bullet went into his forearm and the other went into his ankle. Neither got through the mesh of his clothing, yet the sting of high speed impact was worthy of notice.

The rook rushed him with its arms locked out as a battering ram. Jake scrambled to his feet and slammed into the rook's side to offset its acceleration. The tactic worked to a degree, but the hit took more out of Jake. Though basically unhurt, his head was spinning.

The rook fell on its front. Jake shook his head and leapt onto the creature's back with a reverberating clang. Another dent resulted, and the rook was getting quickly back to its feet. Jake, off of the creations back and at its side, kicked the lurching rook. As it fell on its side, six targeting globes buzzed from the rooks ports along with the projectile cover fire.

Jake avoided the shots with the only effect being the increased pain from his headache. The globes began circling around to set up a laser perimeter to cage the white knight with the deadly machine. Knowing he would only further limit his space for mobility by destroying any of the globes, he instead charged between them. The laser walls flared to life with Jake outside of them.

"That's my boy," Max whispered. "Just keep it up, kid."

Max's attention had been riveted on this match since Jake walked down from the observation area. His look was one of curious concern, much like the look Stone had when testing one of his creations.

Jake picked up the lifeless globe the rook had previously left in its wake and threw the object at one of the hexagon vertices of burning laser beams. The projectile nicked the active sphere enough to tilt it, burning away its generating mechanism. The hexagon was reduced to a pentagon extending from the floor to the ceiling. The rook inside was upright again, scanning for a frequency to move the laser cage with it. Jake was again aware of the stinging pain left by the bullets and the burning in his hands. His head spun. He lost his balance momentarily and fell precariously close to the incinerating wall. His eyes finally focused the spinning room in front of him. Jake stumbled to his feet, holding his head to contain the slowly spreading burn from his minor injuries. He knew that such wounds should not have that kind of effect on his head. Besides, he had endured much greater impacts in the past.

While Jake was recovering, the rook had placed a bomb on its apparently unchangeably programmed globe. It placed two more of the explosives on the neighboring devices. A sensor blinked, and all three bombs and the globes they held exploded into a shower of blue sparks. The pentagon collapsed instantly into an unrestricting, upright rectangle. Jake ran quickly behind the cover of the remaining laser wall. Spikes chased his heels as he went, firing from both of the rook's forearm launchers. The firing stopped, giving Jake a strong urge to peer around the corner of his cover.

Spikes suddenly pierced and skewered the active globes unknowingly protecting Jake from their controller. The globe to his left erupted in blue sparks and exploded. The other globe sputtered and crashed to the floor. The six projectile gun emplacements let out a volley of chase fire until each clicked empty. Jake felt the stinging in his foot and calf at the recent shots. He fought to keep his consciousness from fading.

The rook approached Jake who spun and pounded the creature's sensor panel with both fists coupled together. Repeated hammering finally yielded results as the rook reeled from the force of the attacks. A complete sensor blackout cut the rook off from its surroundings. Jake's leg was on fire with the same sickening pain from which he had been trying to recover. He relinquished his attack and gripped his head. Missiles launched unguided from the battered rook in front of him. His head was swimming, but Jake dodged the impending impact. Instead, the stubby, sharp cones of the explosives slammed into the floor behind the boy.

Lights began slowly returning to the crushed panel as emergency systems realigned damaged connections and circuits. The rook's left arm jerked as it relearned control of its systems. The open weapon turrets retracted and slammed closed into the hulking frame.

"Just avoid the spikes," Max urged nervously. He palmed an injection tube as if in anticipation of what was to follow. Stone saw Max load the content vial into the injector. The next few moments seemed to pass outside of time.

The rook locked its finger talons into a claw position. Jake was trying futilely to fight the pain numbing his mind to thought and reflex. The sharpened blades on the rook's fingertips quickly slid over the restraining garment, cutting it into broad ribbons up Jake's arm. The tightly wound garment slackened from its severed side. Less than a heartbeat later, Jake was collapsed in pain, clutching desperately to his exposed arm. The rook stopped as though to observe the writhing young man.

"Jake!" Max shouted to get through the boy's impending shock. He threw the injection tube high into the air to fall where Jake could catch it. Blade raised two fingers and a laser burst arcing from the ceiling to the floor caught the healing projectile.

"I don't think so," Blade said over the speaker system. "He has to win on his own or die on his own. No help." Stone grudgingly ceded that he would have done the same in his father's position. The injection tube flashed and evaporated in the washed-out blue incinerator laser.

The knowledge that help existed must have sparked life back into the ravaged boy. He ground his teeth hard in agony but forced himself to his feet. The cloth hung loosely on his shoulder and chest, kept from completely unraveling by the tight under-layers and crisscrossing pattern of the cloth band. Jake's fingernails became marred and began scarring.

"Max," Stone began and trailed off as he focused on the youth.

Through obvious pain and unheralded strength, Jake grabbed the rook's forearm with his scarred hand and twisted it loose with a single effort. The other arm, which had cut open his protective bandaging, was even less fortunate. In the midst of retaliation, the rook's arm was ripped completely off at the shoulder. The tear was not clean and the wires spewed from the hole.

A bomb rolled down from the chute in what was left of the rook's dangling forearm. Jake did not pause to plan, he merely acted. He tore the dented sensor panel completely off, sending it clattering to the floor. He reached into the sparking, smoking center of the construct.

Jake ripped the metal-encased cylinder out of its frame. Numerous input ports tore out with the casing. The rest dangled from the location of the sensor plate's violent removal. The remaining output connections broke off as Jake pulled again.

He slammed the cylinder to the ground with a louder liquid sound than Max had heard. Fluid was seeping out of the mangled wreckage of the brain casing. Jake pried the last bomb from the rook's dead forearm and gripped it in his scarred palm. He locked it onto the dented metal casing and stepped far enough away before crumpling to the floor.

The bomb went off only a short time later, leaving a mess for the cleaning lasers. When Stone had confirmed that the rook's piece had been removed, Max ran to the arena floor. He quickly gathered Jake in his powerful arms and raced him to safety ahead of the blue incinerator lines.

Max carefully laid Jake down on the observation deck floor, cursing at the feedback from his still unfinished hand. He quickly gave the boy an injection in the arm and chest. Another in each leg followed. A quick burst of the contents into Jake's hand finished the second and final vial of that particular substance.

A second substance was injected into Jake's forehead, leaving with it a curious monitor and tiny feed through his skull. Max placed his human palm on his own head and pushed his shaggy hair back. Max shook his other hand and cursed the response it gave him.

"Give him time to recover. It's all we can do. I've given him the potential antidote which should counter the damage that hasn't been done yet and fight what is already affected. I've eased the pressure in his head and numbed only his pain receptors," Max said in the most clinical voice Stone had ever heard from his friend. "I really don't know if it was given in time."

"You did your best. He's a fighter. I'm sure he'll give everything he can to live," Stone said coldly.

Marcus kept watch over the boy to be sure his pain was at a bearable level. Jake's skin had turned a strange, glimmering shade of gray in the exposed areas below his neck. The scarring, which had compounded itself even after Jake was unconscious, had ceased. It too was turning that same shimmering shade.

Jake's eyes slowly gathered themselves from the back of his head. His mind had lost the uncertain nervousness that had bothered him since the bomb went off in his hand. The burning pain he had felt had also smoldered into embers. His hand was rough over the flesh of his face. A glimpse of it was all he saw before his world swirled around him in his vision.

When the black void of unconsciousness no longer threatened him,

Jake stood with a little help from Marcus. His body felt strange and unused. Jake recalled the last few moments of his battle.

"Just like I promised," he said, supporting himself entirely on Marcus's willing shoulders.

"Yeah, so much for Frederick," Max added as the laser walls cleared the arena below.

"Are you sure it was him? This one didn't use hand to hand combat enough to get a fighting signature, did it?" Stone watched blindly as the last metal remnants burned away.

"That's how I know it was Frederick. He hated being personally involved in physical brutality. Unfortunately, in your father's reign, that is one of many necessary evils. He grudgingly learned to fight, as is a prerequisite, but he wasn't too sure of those skills. He liked guns, though. That rook used every weapon at its disposal to avoid prolonged periods of fisticuffs," Max reasoned.

"That makes sense," Stone said, impressed by his friend's grasp of subtle observance.

"How's Jake doing?" Max had taken up a genuine concern.

"I'm doing better. Whatever you gave seems to have worked, at least in part. I still don't feel too good, though." Jake was able to support himself. The chemicals Max had introduced into the boy's system appeared to be doing an adequate job of keeping the scarring in check. Beads of sweat glistened off of the boy's forehead, but his brain was numb to the true extent of the pain ravaging his system.

Jake's face was still a pale skin tone, kept from the scarring and injections somehow by the thick band around his neck. Similar bands on his waist and upper thighs facilitated the ability to answer when nature called. The rest of his body was coursing with gray, glistening skin that functioned with concentration. The once tightly wrapped, multi-layered band hung loosely now on his shoulder and chest. One arm was completely exposed, but the other retained its tight restraints. Jake's torso and legs were still covered, though the seal was no longer air tight.

"I can fight, and I'm probably the strongest one here right now with the effects of whatever this is. Get me to as many of the others as you can. I don't know if this is going to last," Jake resolved.

Stone was about to ask the boy if he was sure about this, but the look in Jake's eyes confirmed that he was. Stone moved the knight resting at the far end of the chessboard forward two spaces and one to the right into *b5*. Blade moved the other black knight piece in the knight's distinctive "L" pattern to the end of the board at *h6*. Stone moved Jake's representative piece only one space up and two more right to *d6*. Blade angled the right black bishop, Erik's representative piece, to enter the white knight's new square. Jake took a deep breath and looked at Stone.

CHAPTER 23

"I KNOW," STONE said before Jake could speak. The young man smiled with considerable effort. He began descending to the arena below when Max grabbed his arm. Without a word, Max handed the boy a vial of painkiller for the direct feed into the boy's brain. Jake nodded his thanks and continued down to the lower level. The confidence remained in his step, but there was more effort with it now.

Erik walked to the center of the arena gripping the thick hand hammers. The glow still shone through his otherwise unnoticeable artificial eye. Jake met his mixed gaze with a projected air of certainty. Stone for an instant feared that Blade would sense Jake's deteriorating state and prolong the fight until it was too late for him to contend. He did not, however, and allayed Stone's fears by standing and beginning the match at once.

"Marcus, if Jake wins-" Stone turned to his mentor.

"Then my mentor will finally be avenged. Erik must die this day, by any hands willing. I have no personal bloodlust. Emotion has gotten the better of me before, but I will find his death acceptable by any means," Marcus finished before Stone could add to his unvoiced query. Stone nodded and turned back to the battle. "If Jake fails, I kill him myself." Stone decided not to look back at his trainer.

"You're not Marcus, but I guess you'll do," Erik jibed. He was circling Jake, who merely pivoted where he stood with an unchanging expression. Erik's hood hid his face except for the circular red ring of the glowing eye that was otherwise deceptively human.

Wordlessly, Jake slammed his exposed palm into Erik's chest, silencing him quickly enough. Erik gasped for air and slammed a hammer blow into Jake's shoulder. Jake barely moved. Still gasping,

Erik jumped away from Jake's uppercut. Erik held his hammers together and swung them in a sideways arc. Jake twisted and allowed them to hit his scarred forearm.

Erik stepped away and fingered a small trigger in the center of the open grip of the hand hammer. The tempered steel of the hammer top fired off an impact shot from the magazine in the front part of the handle. The shot hit Jake in the chest. He doubled over momentarily and sweat began to bead on his tight face. Erik's hammer top exploded in recoil from his attempt at firing a second shot.

Jake intercepted a swing of Erik's remaining hammer and lifted the traitorous monk off of the ground. A twinge of strain rippled through Jake's expression as he sent electricity writhing through Erik from the generator in his wrist. Some of the energy conducted back through his grayish skin, but Erik was engulfed in the jolting force. Jake had emptied his entire battery. Erik's eye sparked and blinked out. Burns were visible around the eye socket where the metal element in the eye had been fused to slag.

Jake hurled Erik to the ground with the strength remaining in his scar-covered arm. The serum Max had injected into him covered the results of the contact with the air, but it had not reversed it. The glimmering gray skin was smooth where the scars appeared rough. Jake felt a wave of agony and tapped the monitor on his forehead to stimulate more of the dose of painkiller. Calmed slightly, he continued approaching Erik.

Erik's face was bloodied from hitting and skidding on the floor. He was slouched over with his thick cape over his arm and boot. Through his own pain, Erik swept his arm away towards Jake. The young man looked down to see six needlelike blades in various parts of him. Two rested in the scarred arm, pinning the loose remaining strand of plastic- textured cloth to him. One point stuck in his lower rib, again not bleeding. The last three were stuck in his leg. Two of which stuck through his calf, bleeding over his thick soled boot. The other pierced his thigh. His wounds were painless, but the strain of motion was increased by the attack.

Jake went forward with a limp favoring the bloody leg. Erik spit blood in Jake's direction and backed away. Jake stumbled and pulled the spikes from his bleeding lower leg. The blood was already clotting.

"He's bleeding," Max said, holding another vial in his hand.

"How bad is it?" Stone questioned his friend without taking his eyes off of the fight.

"Well, it's in his bloodstream now. You can see the blood is already clotting in the wound," Max said gravely.

"It's the same virus, isn't it, Max?"

"Yes, my friend, it is. His bones will start to calcify soon. His muscles will tighten and scar after that. Beyond that, I thankfully do not know from experience," Max answered frankly. "The virus spreads throughout the skin by continuous contact with air. That's how I stopped it from reaching his face and skin; everything else is infected, though. The skin scars most unusually and creates a barrier that blocks everything, just as you've seen. It becomes incredibly dense and durable like metal. The problem is that when it is left to run wild, it has a similar effect on every other kind of tissue. The virus doesn't quit, either; it goes as deep as the oxygen feed will allow. It begins to scar the scar tissue. That much I have experienced. It is quite fatal unless you put it in check as I did with the wrappings, and it all stems from a simple unbalanced chemical equation." Max felt thoroughly helpless in the situation.

Stone knew of his friend's experiments, and he had already guessed at a similar scenario when he witnessed Jake's arm becoming exposed. He thought no less of Max; it was his job. Stone would have done the same thing if his field of expertise had been genetic engineering and research.

Erik regained his standing position, spit blood on the ground again, and slammed the hammer in his hand at Jake's face. He ducked and punched Erik straight in the stomach. Erik coughed again and fell once more. Jake pulled the remaining blades from his body and dropped them to the floor. He was forced to key the monitor on his forehead up several notches to stop himself from passing out.

Jake approached Erik. Both battered warriors were reeling. Jake lifted Erik up with both hands. Erik's hood was gone, and his cropped black hair fell in his face, mussed. His living eye looked at Jake without seeing him. Erik's nose was split and broken. He attempted to fight the grip, but it was a futile effort. Jake rested him on his feet where he was unlikely to stay. Jake looked strangely at him and then broke Erik's neck with both hands. Erik's body crumpled to the floor.

"At last," Marcus said, sighing audible relief and releasing the vendetta he had carried so long within him. Peace washed over him.

The room around Jake spun in the encompassing pain. The floor came up all too quickly to meet his face. He felt his muscles tighten, and darkness overcame him. He awoke again sometime later with Max leaning over him. Jake was dimly aware of being flat on his back in the observation area. Pain wanted to pull him back into warm unconsciousness. Max keyed the painkiller output to maximum. Injections over the boy's body were yielding little in the way of results.

"I knew you before, Jake. I couldn't bring myself to tell you earlier, but you have every right to know. You were given to me as a test subject. Apparently you aided four people in an escape from the cages into which Blade has placed the lower class workers. You were the one that was caught, but you led them away, and your companions escaped. That's where you got that," Max said, pointing to the only natural scar on the boy's body, the one beside his eye. "One of the soldiers gave it to you. I'm sorry to say that I'm responsible for the rest.

"You see, I injected you with a sequence of my own DNA, the one that was affected when the scarring virus infected me. Your DNA was already a close match, so the substitute sequence didn't alter too much. Your legs, chest, and arms were infected; the rest of your body was spared the effect by those airtight bands. That virus is what cost me my left half. It wasn't intended for that purpose, but it induces great strength and resistance if it is stopped early. You were given the injections in an isolation chamber free of the oxygen that feeds the virus. A minute amount of oxygen was added and filtered out again, allowing the virus to progress enough to give you its benefits without the side effects. We wrapped you in this. The soldier who delivered you gave me orders to wipe your memory. I had you released when you recovered and turned the report in as a failure. That's when you met Stone, and that is as much as I know of it.

"I've done everything I can to help you now. You are strangely the closest thing I've ever had to a son. Really, you have a part of my genetic makeup in you. I can't ask you to forgive me, but I do want you to know that I truly regret what I put you through," Max said, trying to keep his voice calm.

"It's … okay. You … gave me … the … strength … let me be …

part of ... something good," Jake struggled with his reluctant throat, forming words through intolerable pain.

"Thank you. You've done more than I ever could have asked. I am very proud to know you," Stone added.

"The Lord is with you, Jake," Marcus said, looking through the dismal ceiling to the heavens above.

The life faded from Jake's eyes with obvious reluctance. Max closed the boy's eyes. Despite all he had accomplished, Max felt as though he had failed in some important test. The injections, modified from what recreated his left half, simply were not enough. The futile effort of the tissue softener was wasted. The metallic additions did not save Jake as they had saved Max, and now a boy closer to Max in body and spirit than any of his other subjects had ever been lie dead by his hands.

Stone placed his hand on Max's shoulder. He had removed the gauntlet, and Max felt his friend tremble and grip him hard. Stone slowly returned to the monitor where he keyed for an incinerator box in the observation deck wall. It slid out to specifications at the size of the formerly used coffins.

Max carried his lost experiment, a lost part of himself, in his arms to where Stone and Marcus stood solemnly. His eye went slightly glassy as he lay the youth in the black abyss. Each said his final goodbye, and the lid lowered shut. None of the onlookers watched as the edges and joints flashed in a brilliant light as Jake's soul was truly set free to soar into another realm.

The box folded back into the wall, and silence hung in the air for several tense moments. Marcus finally spoke. "He is free of his suffering, just as you should be, Max. He died a warrior's death. There is tremendous honor in that. You tried your best to save him, but it was his time."

Stone saw a flicker of the old Max ignite again with those words. Whatever Marcus had projected with them had worked miraculously. The seriousness was cooled to its previous level, caused only by the intense contest.

Stone knew then just how important these people had become to him. He could not fail them at any cost. He searched Kylie's gaze across the arena. She had watched in silent mourning as well, though no trace of that was showing any longer. She had killed many times before this. It was rare for a person with residential status not to have killed, and she was, after all, a professional assassin. However, she had never been faced with killing good people like Jake, and it stirred regret inside of her she never knew existed.

CHAPTER 24

MARCUS HAD WATCHED with silent approval as Erik's remains were scoured away by the lasers in the arena floor. Satisfaction washed over him in spite of the tremendous price that had been paid for the murderer's death. He did not need the aid of his recently acquired mental insight to see that Stone was on the verge of a breakdown from watching Kylie. He had done his best to heal Max, and he was confident that the man would recover well enough in time. The hardest person to forgive is often oneself. Max was standing with Stone, both of their backs turned to the incineration chamber that had just retracted itself.

"Tell me, Max, do you regret what I did to you?" Stone looked his friend in the eye.

"You mean this," Max said as he held up his left hand. "Of course not. It was all you could do to save me. Maybe it was the only thing that could have saved me. The injections I gave Jake didn't work. I tried to improve upon the substances you injected me with, and I failed. You worked a miracle, friend."

"Then why did you inject Jake with the virus?" Stone felt as though it was his judgment day, when everything he had done in his life was gathered before him to be questioned. Max winced slightly at the memory of putting the boy through the horrific procedure.

"Curiosity. Part of it was the hope that I could give Jake what I almost had. I told you, the virus gives great strength as a temporary side effect. I wanted to give that to the boy. I wanted him to be able to live the life I couldn't because of my carelessness. We here are all gods among men, my friend. You surely must realize that. On both sides, this arena is a voluntary test for us all, and Jake did not fail his. Virtues and sins, here we are all laid bare in the finest and possibly final moments of ourselves. You saw the way those bombs went off in his hands. He was almost invulnerable. He was free, too. I have some strength, but I am most certainly not free," Max answered sadly.

"Not yet," Stone reassured. Max smiled at his friend's uncharacteristic shift to optimism. Max thought it to be a part of what he had dubbed Stone's "leadership mode" in which inherent but dormant traits of his friend tended to appear in place of melancholy.

"Talk to her, Stone. It's the only way," Max said, seeing through Stone's resolved front. Stone looked back at him with pained eyes.

"I can't do it, Max. I'll just be hurt, and I will look like a fool," Stone said, sighing away a little more of his hope. Max smiled with mixed feelings.

"Well, in that armor-"

"Funny. I'm glad to see you joking again, but I'm serious," Stone continued. "Besides, you're one to talk about appearance."

"I'm serious, too. It can't be as bad as you think. I know you. You make the worst of things."

"You didn't see her face," Stone said, eying the ground.

"No, but you were also wearing a suit of three inch thick armor at the time," Max argued. "Has Jake's death taught you nothing? This is no game, my friend. People are dying here. While it is certainly a worthwhile cause, you can't dispute that fact. She could die here, Stone. Think about that."

"No, she will not die here, not while I am here," Stone defended, his glare shifting back to Max.

Marcus approached amidst the mounting tension of the situation. "Go to her, Stone. Now is the time. It is your last chance. She is in pain and you can help her. I am your master, and I can still order you to do this. I hope it won't come to that," the monk demanded softly.

"You were there, Marcus," Stone pleaded.

"Yes, I was there when the pain and the regret started in her."

"Very well," Stone uttered, defeated, "but I want you both to know this is a mistake," he whispered. Stone knew a face-to-face confrontation would be futile. However, he could easily tap into his father's holographic network. It would not be easy to confront her in any case, but a part of him wanted to do it.

Stone knew his body intensely well. He knew every muscle, every stance, and every moderated expression. He even knew his gestures and nervous ticks, though he would suppress them permanently if they were brought to his attention. This suppression of his natural tendencies gave Stone an inhuman quality when one was faced with the man. Then again, his feelings dictated his actions on that part. Though he had never mapped his synapses, he knew roughly what sections of his brain functioned in his physical activities. This knowledge combined to produce the very system he was about to utilize and the very armor that housed it.

Stone was reluctant enough to engage in this activity, and eavesdropping would make it impossible for him to continue, especially interference from his father. Therefore, he used the armor's internal pressure points to simulate gestures in a remote unit. An electrolyte scan of his mind helped to pinpoint the exact movement for the remote and duplicate it with Stone's personal stifled flare. The remote in this case was a simple hologram shoved through his father's arena projection system.

When the feed from the armor system, isolated to prevent hacking into his armor's other systems, was connected to the monitor he had used to access the network, Stone said a silent prayer and let the helmet slide over his head. His armor stood rigid from that point to all who would observe him when in actuality he was living through a hologram.

A monitor near Kylie blinked out a message in green letters reading "You've got mail." She touched the corner to open the file. The message blinked again.

"Cute." As the screen turned black, she realized with a certain degree of uneasiness who was contacting her. Blade expected it far sooner, even advised it. Kylie just could not bring herself to do as he asked, not yet at least.

To her surprise, a blue hologram blazed to life in front of her. It was standing closer than she would have liked, but she voiced no objections. "Hello again, Kylie," Stone said unemotionally through the brilliant blue hologram. He was being projected without his armor. He instead wore simply the pants and shirt he used in unarmed training and the cross hanging around his heart. His long hair hung behind him with random wisps playing at his forehead, all glowing with the same ethereal tint of blue.

"What do you want now?" She was harsh, but, inexplicably, she was wavering.

"Aside from the fact that my father seems all powerful, I cannot possibly see why you are doing this. Notice my use of the word 'seems.'" No emotion had touched the holographic face. "I do not even know why you disappeared for all of those years. It was obviously when you became an assassin, but does an assassin not require companionship at times?"

"Companions get killed," Kylie said coldly, struggling to meet his continued gaze.

"So you believe me to be so weak that I would be a liability? Max, too, for that matter?" Stone's face softened slightly. "We have both faced far worse than assassins."

"What if I was your assassin?" Kylie let her guard down for a second. That second was enough for Stone.

"You still need friends, Kylie," Stone eyed the ground as his voice came through.

"That's just it. You don't want to be friends. As if that alone wouldn't be," Kylie bit back, hesitating a moment, "bad enough."

"The word you were looking for is 'difficult.'" Stone turned his head to follow her as she walked to the railing overlooking the arena. He did not see the tears she fought back. "You do not have to be an assassin. Stay with me, or stay with Max. We have the entire country's resources at our disposal. You would not need to do this anymore."

"You seem so confident that you are going to win. Notice the word 'seem,'" she said with her previous hostility.

"If I knew you would be at my side when this is finished, I would guarantee that I will win," Stone promised.

"You still don't get it. I don't care about you, Stone," Kylie said, still not facing him.

It was Stone's turn to fight off his emotions. "I know," he said softly. "I know I'm the reason you left."

No longer feeling his eyes upon her, Kylie chanced a look back at the illuminated form of the equally brilliant man. "In part," she ceded.

"You do not care about me, but that does not change the fact that I care about you." Stone looked at her again. "I won't let you die here."

"It doesn't matter," Kylie said, unconvincing to anyone except Stone.

"Little matters to me except for you," Stone said, swallowing through the sting of unrequited love. "There are few people for whom I would, but I would die for you, Kylie."

She straightened a bit, turning to the side though not looking over at him. "I know you would." Her voice was almost a whisper.

"Kylie, get out of this. I know you can't desert my father, but you can allow yourself to be defeated. You have to know that I would keep you safe. You have to trust me. Kylie, I could never hurt you," Stone offered, holding his cross at his chin.

"I can't do that. As long as Blade is alive, I have far too much at stake. You can't get to him yourself, either. Why do you think he has me positioned at his side on the board? It is because the king can move only one space at a time; if you decide to bend the rules and make a push against him yourself, I have you. Anywhere you go, you cross my range of motion before you can get away or reach your father."

"Kylie, do you hate me?" Stone looked at her directly. This time, he did not receive the look he expected. To his surprise, she walked over to where she had been when the confrontation began. She looked helplessly into his eyes. She covered her mouth with her knuckles as her eyes glazed over with tears.

Stone could not stop himself from reaching out to touch her cheek with the back of his fingers. She closed her eyes at the intangible touch, barely keeping herself from leaning into it. Tears ran unstoppably from her eyes. Stone felt his heart as he had never felt it before.

He was denied the feel of her cheek through the hologram. He was suddenly very sorry that he did not go to see her in person. When Stone's eyes were shut with emotion, she reached slowly with her own hand to where his glowing hand still rested. The silent moments ticked on to eternity for both of them before another word was spoken.

"Tell me how you feel about me," Kylie said quietly. She had withdrawn her hand before Stone again saw through the hologram's estimated line of sight recording.

"I love you," he said slowly, looking deep in her eyes. She closed her eyes again to stop what was happening to her.

This was one point at which she could not carry out the contract Blade had made with her. She could not repeat the words she had been ordered to say. "Go. Please go. Please, just, please go," she uttered through increasing tears. Her soft lips were twisted in indecision.

Stone had withdrawn his hand, but again held it out to hers. She started to reach for it, and then she caught herself. She had given herself too much already. The loneliness would inevitably hurt again.

"Trust me," Stone said, dropping his hand back to his side. He closed his eyes as the hologram began to fade. Kylie slid down against the wall. Tears were still trickling down her face, and the more she recalled everything that had transpired, the more she cried. Her silky hair fell in her face, and she pushed it away, seeing one of her weapons for the first time in what felt like forever. She had fought against the desire for company since the time she left New Charleston, and the fight was lost to a man who truly loved her. *I'm an assassin*, she reminded herself without feeling the thought. *I trust no one.*

Stone disconnected the monitor and walked out of the platform's light. The helmet slid off as he disengaged the system. His eyes were red and his hands were shaking.

"You have helped her, my boy. Her pain has lessened now at the expense of yours," Marcus said after his silent approach.

"That's the first time I've ever heard you talk in real terms, Marcus. Don't tell me you're getting less vague." He paused. "I love her so much," Stone said looking away.

"I know. I knew on our first trip to see her," Marcus reminded him.

"She doesn't trust me, Marcus," Stone said with sadness in his voice.

"She doesn't trust anyone right now, in time, perhaps."

"Feel better now?" Max was again at his oldest friend's side.

"Yeah, thank you," Stone said, grabbing his friend's shoulders. "I still don't know, Max. All she said was that I was part of the reason she left. She didn't say how she really felt, one way or the other."

"I think the fact that she's still crying answers that one," Max said sincerely. "We'll get through this, my friend. Even though coercing you is like trying to sink a Waterstrider tank with a ping pong ball."

Stone patted his friend on the back. "I still have to do this, Max, if she can only trust me."

Stone moved the rook to the space marked *c7* directly in front of the remaining black bishop. Blade tapped his fingers on the arm of the throne, realizing his son's ploy. He was amused for a moment by the fact that his son was attempting to play chicken with a fearless man. Blade merely toggled his piece to the left into *d8*.

"God forgive me," Stone asked, holding his cross as he moved his rook into the remaining ebony bishop's square.

Kylie walked silently down the stairs to the combat zone. The rook did likewise, though not as silently. Kylie began to approach the center. The rook reached its place first and stood stiffly as the monolith of power it was. Kylie looked up at Stone. She met his gaze, but her expression was unreadable. Something, however small, had changed between them, and that much was clear.

"If she will only trust that I cannot hurt her," Stone said to no one in particular. He began involuntarily reaching towards her with an open hand, but he clenched it into a fist at his side just as quickly upon the realization of it and slammed it down on the console in front of him.

Blade's hologram sprung to life beside him. "I'm quite impressed, son. However little, you're starting to show potential. I really didn't think you capable of doing this, especially after your little reunion. Oh, yes, I heard. Doesn't she give a remarkable performance? If there were still enough free people to make up an audience, I think she would be a terrific actress." The green figure disappeared in amused laughter.

"He was lying, Stone. She was probably instructed on how to respond, but she was genuine. You cannot doubt that," Marcus added honestly upon seeing Stone's confidence crumble. Marcus grabbed his former student's wrist in his hand and held it up beside his own face. "Look at me, Stone. Read the truth in my eyes when I tell you her heart was speaking over there."

Stone obeyed and saw clearly that his mentor was right. His father had nearly won that time. Stone was at his most vulnerable, and Blade knew that well. The exploitation of Stone's weakness remained inevitable.

Blade stood and ordered the fight to begin. Kylie stayed a cautious distance away. She had taken the impact gun from her hip and the augmented sting rifle from her side. She steadied both in her hands. The rook circled slowly with her, awaiting attack.

"So how badly is it going to be destroyed?" Max had come up beside his friend again, looking with considerable curiosity at the battle below.

"It's not going to be destroyed. I've altered its program, but left its adaptability," Stone said absently.

"So, in other words, I stay in the dark," Max said knowingly.

"Not for long. Just watch," Stone responded.

Kylie shot the rook with the impact gun, each shot spraying synthetic flesh to the ground. The frame beneath was visible in expanding circles, but the cells were being quickly recalled. Kylie rolled to the ground, unleashing two more shots as she went down. Only when she was safely to the ground did the rook launch twin jets of flame at her former shoulder height.

From her low stance, Kylie launched a series of the pronged disks that loaded the sting rifle. The disks, individual electroshock weapons with far more power than a handheld stun gun, stuck to the rook's frame in the open areas. Purple energy writhed from each projectile with little result except for rippling off another wave of the flowing skin.

Kylie quickly holstered the ineffectual weapon and sprang to her feet. Her sleek, honed body was a blur of motion around the rook. She pulled the bomb cannon from her belt. Low on its particular ammunition, she fired conservatively to yield two massive explosions relieving the rook of its forearm flame throwers. The skin reformed as tentacles in place of the forearms with scraps of the former structures protruding out through the flesh.

The laser emplacements of the rook targeted the weapon and sent a concentrated pulse at it, rending the barrel into a charred and shredded mess. The accuracy of the rook inspired both a tinge of fear and awe in the assassin. She quickly moved from the spot, dropping the useless weapon.

Three of the seven heavy artillery weapons she had on her person had done little to stop the creation. Two of the remaining choices were geared towards a living target. The rook finally made a serious attempt at catching its quarry in launching several tendrils at various points on Kylie's body. Laser sighted pulse shots burned them off at their source, though she knew the skin would not be permanently lost from the kinetic impact of the minuscule ammunition.

"She doesn't trust me, and she's not going to," Stone said audibly over the armored hand rubbing his chin. His tension visibly increased.

"So, what happens now?" Max was very nervous about his friend's unrevealed plan. That was mainly because it put his other longtime friend in danger.

"Now, we make it look convincing," Stone said again towards his cupped hand, covering his lower lip.

"How? You can't send a transmission," Max said, not at all comfortable about being left out of the planning.

"Why not? I just did," Stone said with a look in his eye that both reassured and perplexed Max, though the latter was short lived.

"A voice signal. It triggered a change in programming I take it," Max whispered.

"Exactly. I installed the receiver code with the quick program overhaul," Stone said, whispering as well. A glimmer of pride came to him when he saw that his quick work on the rook's main computer module had succeeded.

The rook's skin receded around the circular weapon housing in the inner chest frame. A glow began to expand in a widening circle from that area. As planned, Kylie fired both of the pulse weapons with literally laser accuracy. When the glow began to sharpen and focus, several impacts hit it with amplified kinetic force.

The skin receded as expediently as it could, and the upper frame exploded in a shower of sparking debris and manmade flesh. The remaining frame crashed to the ground as the skin converged upon it. Kylie had been thrown without injury to the ground, partially of her own volition.

She stood to find the rook's remnants approaching her in an exaggerated human form. A succession of shots tore holes through the mass, but that did not impede its pace. The arms shot out as an intertwining mesh of tentacles. She severed a few with shots, though the number was far too great. The tendrils caught her loosely at the wrists and ankles, and they let her go rather than allow her to fall harshly in the struggle.

Kylie appeared to recall Stone's request just then. Somehow, though, she just could not trust him as completely as he wished. The tendrils had found her again, attaching only to her arms. She pulled with quite some effort, but they did not relinquish their hold this time.

Kylie ceased the true struggle and settled into the entwining grip. She reloaded the gun closest to her arm, no small trick using only one hand. Slowly stretching her arm above her head, she jerked her elbow down and fired a single shot straight through the construct's head.

She grabbed as much distance as she could manage in the rook's momentary confusion. The head reformed with relative ease, though the unnerving smile preprogrammed for that event did not cross its face. It remained expressionless as it sent more of itself to reinforce the thinning restraints.

Kylie struggled and put several more holes in the creation, only to have them close as quickly as they were made. The rook eventually wrapped itself completely around Kylie in an oddly human combination of the two. The rook elongated its midsection slightly to facilitate walking without the assassin's agreement. The rest of the flesh surrounding her tightened only slightly. The spaces between the artificial cells had been altered to allow enough air to flow for breathing, to no one's knowledge except for Stone.

The rook struggled to contain her for several seconds. It then meshed the skin in as close to a solid structure as it was capable, giving the appearance that Kylie had stopped fighting. It would clearly not be perceived as a conscious decision, especially with the rook's triumphant whine, a static noise like an electronic screech. Stone then knew Kylie was safe.

The rook, disproportionate throughout its torso, stood in the center of the arena. Dumbfounded, Blade removed the black bishop from the playing field. The rook began lumbering back to the observation deck with its unwilling passenger inside its open center.

"Tell me she isn't ... She can't be ..." Max could not bring himself to finish the statement.

"Of course not, Max. It looks that way, but I'm in love with her, lest you forget. Do you honestly think a creation of mine would kill her?" Stone said passionately, "We just keep the rook out of further combat, and Kylie is safely liberated from my father's grasp."

The rook took a step onto the stairs back to the platform. Suddenly, an explosion blew the synthetic face away. The eruption paralyzed Stone with fear for its passenger. Then, the rest of the flesh collapsed to the floor, sending Kylie tumbling back to the arena. She stood slowly and wiped the debris off of her and examined the wreckage of the magnetic controller.

She holstered the gun that had liberated her from her roving chance at escape. She did not turn to look at Stone. Instead, she simply walked to the other set of stairs from the arena and reclaimed her place on the perimeter of Blade's observation platform.

"That's my girl," Blade said, comprehending what had happened. He replaced the bishop's piece and removed the rook.

"Why couldn't she just trust me?" Stone looked at Max when his heart began beating again. Stone was more upset and hurt than angry. "Had she cooperated in the first place, the rook would have looked normal hiding her."

"A valiant effort, son. You came a little too close to bending the rules there. For a moment, I actually thought you had the courage to kill the love of your life like you killed the love of mine. Needless to say, the pride I felt in that is gone." Blade's hologram had quickly delivered the message and disappeared.

Kylie stood at the rail watching the debris clearing from the battlefield. She knew she had failed her former friend from long ago, the one who genuinely, sincerely loved her. She also knew he would interpret the situation as her personal support of Blade, but there was little she could do to change that at the moment. Had she looked into Stone's eyes again, perhaps she would have seen the love for her that touched his actions.

Stone sighed, sure that any returned emotion that had been built by the moment he and Kylie had shared was lost in her. He believed that she had seen this as a serious attack. He felt sure that she would never trust him at all. Marcus felt the despair in both of them, but he had far too little control of his recently surfaced abilities to get past the strength of that raw emotion. He could tell, though, that Stone's despair was coupled with sadness and Kylie's was coupled with regret. Beyond that, he had nothing to offer his student, his veritable son.

Even Max did not break the oppressive silence. Blade allowed it to linger on both sides, the tension playing a glorious symphony in his ears. He did not even utter a sound in planning his next move. The distraction he had encountered was gone, and he was enjoying this moment.

CHAPTER 25

WHEN BLADE GREW tired of savoring the pain around him, he made his next move. He shifted the position of his right black knight down two spaces in the extreme right column and one to the left to *g4*. Marcus's piece was now vulnerable to one of the black knights and in a position to challenge the other. Blade was goading his son into attacking his monstrous right knight with his son's remaining bishop, which, Blade assumed, was a victory from the outset.

"He has me at a standoff. He wants to pit Marcus against whatever that thing is, so, Max, any idea what that thing is?" Stone tapped the projector in his chest plate. An image of the wild slavering beast sprang to full color life from the decimated pawn's recording.

"That, my friend, is a gigantic package full of trouble," Max answered in his usual tone.

"Well, I know I never could have guessed that on my own. What would I ever do without your incredible sense of the obvious?" Stone always somehow managed to add sarcasm to his otherwise unemotional voice.

"If you're going to have an attitude about it, I might not explain," Max said, acting hurt at the friendly jibe. "I guess you want me to start at the beginning for this one. This is as much as I've been able to ascertain."

"Not to interrupt your delicate train of thought on its way to something profound, but you really know quite a bit about our opposition. I'm starting to be grateful you're on our side," Stone said wryly.

"I am the leading geneticist and bio-engineer in the hemisphere," Max added. "Now then, if I may finish without further distraction," he continued, raising his eyebrow at Stone. "His name is Adam. It took quite a lot of prying to find out what he really is. He was nowhere near as large when he was turned over to me six months ago. As was the case with an increasing number of my subjects, I had no idea where he came from. He was horribly disfigured and extremely underdeveloped on his left side, especially at the extremities. Notice he only has three fingers on that hand, each with only a single knuckle," the geneticist spouted, pointing to the frozen projection. "He had no foot on that side, either. Even with those unnatural malformations, he put up quite an enthusiastic fight against his captors.

"I was told to make him a weapon for utter destruction, which was not a surprising thing. I gave him that robotic leg extension for balance. I know it looks like a weak point, but it has been welded directly to his deceptively strong bone structure. The same is true of the spikes protruding from that side, even the ones on his face. If they could be broken off, I doubt it would hurt him significantly," Max continued. "As for the proportionate, normal right side, I used the most powerful muscle enhancement chemical I could find. I was told to ignore any adverse effects on his mind. Apparently, his mind was as underdeveloped as the rest of his left side, guiding him to feed and fight and little else. It took about a week for everything to react and heal. Then, the soldiers came back for him."

"Let me thank you for doing such a wonderful and thorough job of creating a mindless engine of destruction," Stone said with sympathetic sarcasm. Since Blade had placed the relay chip in Max's chest, the one that could shut off his connection to the power grid, Max had been subject to Blade's every order and whim. He had very little choice but to obey unquestioningly. "So, does he have any vulnerability?"

"His mind is his only weakness, and it isn't even a real possibility. His mental capacity is severely limited, but he doesn't need quick response time. His hide is so thick I don't think it even bruises. It's not like you can go down there and confuse him with algebraic equations, either. You know, sometime later, I found out that the Vault, your father's personal think tank, flooded his tiny brain with thoughts of violence and bloodlust. Now, even they can't control him. He has been kept in a cage in the adjoining complex since then," Max answered. "They feed him delinquent workers, sometimes alive."

"That explains the permanent restraint bands around his neck, waist, wrist, and ankle. Can he break the chains holding him to that wall up there?"

"I doubt it, but at the same time it wouldn't surprise me too much. Though the muscle mass on his left side is relatively low, his right side is little else," Max commented.

"What about heart rate? Can that be exploited?" Stone was searching for any opportunity to defeat this seemingly unstoppable opponent.

"His heart rate is high, but his blood pressure is normal. His heart is extremely strong. It was even before the changes. Even electricity has minimal effect on him as far as that goes. On that subject, the metal is conductive though not to any extremes."

"Great," Stone muttered, tapping the projector off.

"There's one more thing, and this is the real kicker here," Max warned. "I told you his name is Adam, in reference to the first man. Only this time, it's the first clone."

Stone looked shocked and puzzled, to those who could read his expressions at least. "The technology for cloning has been available for quite some time. The moral repercussions forced an abandonment of that technology and kept it in check. You think someone created him in that era and lost track of him?"

"No, I'm saying he is an adult clone. The Vault found a way to create an adult clone. I never did get a chance to see the equipment, but there were plenty of rumors and a small amount of indisputable proof. Adam's genetic signature registered as another person in the database. I had to fight with the thing for half an hour before I could log it as a new subject. The similarities were striking, except the brain and left limbs registered as a critical change." Max paused. "Apparently, despite the success of the right side, something malfunctioned, or didn't function at all, on the left," Max continued. "The patient whose genetic signature map came up as the match had come in only once before. An assassin's knife had been lodged in his spine. No doctor available could reconstruct the severed vertebrae and realign the spine as exactly as I was capable of doing. They cloned-" Max had no chance to finish the sentence.

"My father," Stone finished, finally placing the familiarity of part of Adam's face.

"I'm afraid so. They got an extensive DNA sample, but they didn't get anywhere near his brain. The best they had in that area was a genetic scan much like the one in my own files. It appears that was insufficient by far," Max confirmed.

"So, did they make any more clones?"

"No, the project was abandoned after this grievous failure. I'm surprised you didn't already know this. The Vault was beyond my reach without some serious security violations, but it is certainly not beyond your knowledge," Max searched.

"I know it exists. I know its only mission is to create the ultimate soldier for my father's use. It is an elite team of experts that use pirated and confiscated technology to achieve my father's goals. It was established several years ago, before my father impounded most of the populace. Beyond that, my information on them is almost nothing. I don't even see their failures," Stone said.

"Luckily that is all they have had, at least to my knowledge. There are six members at all times. No one retires. It isn't like the military, where retired soldiers are given residential status and left to wander. If you leave the Vault, you do so deceased. It is a position I am happy not to have," Max informed his friend. Max's versatility had saved him from the isolated fate. He could do much more in practice than in research.

"So Adam is only six months old?" Stone looked across to the darkened place where sparks of scraping metals and stifled roars disrupted the shadowy silence hiding the chained beast, the first attempt at duplicating an adult.

"He's big for his age," Max said smiling.

"What about light? He tends to remain in the dark an awful lot," Stone speculated.

"No, if you blind him, he'll just start swinging madly. Rage is something you don't want to combine with that thing," Max said, defeated. "I've seen it fight before. No one ever got close to hurting him, and they tried just about everything. It was quite a gruesome thing to watch. Most of them ended up eaten, at least in part."

Stone saw in his friend's eyes that Max had his own share of demons and memories to wrestle in the dark, and his father had done a very good job of collecting them in his hierarchy for what was just a simple game to Blade. Max had managed to overcome all of those hardships with humor. Sometimes he made what seemed to others to be a very inappropriate comment, but it never meant that he had no feelings. He was just dealing with it in the only way he could that would keep him sane. Somehow, Stone found that side of him comforting.

Marcus approached calmly. "He has laid a trap for me. That creature is supposedly invulnerable."

"I can go after it myself," Stone said.

"No, that is what he wants," Max realized. "Look at the positioning." Stone ignited the holographic image of the chess set. "If you go after Adam yourself, you would be completely at Blade's mercy. If you defeated Adam, which is not an unlikely occurrence, you are within range of his bishop. Since it would require your move to get there, he could attack you again before you could get away. He wants to force you into fighting Kylie."

"I will fight him, Stone. Chances are that he would not use Kylie against me," Marcus volunteered. "If this creature has any weaknesses, I will find them and destroy him."

Reluctantly, Stone moved his only remaining white bishop diagonally into Adam's square at *g4*. Marcus walked calmly to the center of the Neo-Colosseum arena. His hand, cut in training, had begun to heal. Whether that would be allowed to continue remained to be seen. As a precautionary measure, he had rewrapped his hand in the cloth he had worn to the chess match.

He was met by no opponent at first. Stone was about to aggravate his father with a comment about that fact, but he was not given the opportunity. Blade stood and ordered the fight to begin before having Adam released from the chains connecting him to the wall. Alex stood with his charged blade glowing, herding Adam into the arena. The creature complied with low persuasion. He more leapt than descended the stairs leading to the fighting arena, landing on all fours and continuing to walk that way. Stone was curious as to how exactly they had gotten him chained in the first place.

Blade did not interrupt the fighting with his usual smug comments. He simply watched with casual interest. He had underestimated his son in believing him unable to send his mentor to his execution. This would yet turn out to be a day for surprises.

Adam looked at Marcus with a puzzled, animal expression. Adam pawed at Marcus with his bladed left fingers. Marcus flinched away, and Adam, responding to the evasive tactic, erupted in a mindless roar. Adam swung his hand in a wide arc. Marcus turned with astonishing speed and cracked Adam in the right side of his face.

Adam's backlash threw Marcus to a literally screeching halt against the floor. Marcus scrambled back through several of the black and white spaces lining the arena. He shook the disorientation from his head only to discover, from the mineral scent of blood, that his wound had opened again.

Adam leapt the distance separating them and roared in Marcus's face. He reacted only by kicking the beast in the ribs with a speed enhanced boot. Adam did not even back away; he simply stabbed down at Marcus with outstretched claw blades. Marcus rolled just enough and scrambled away on his hands and knees.

Marcus's shoulder had been caught on one of the numerous spikes protruding from Adam's left side. Adam's lip, stretched low from a spike protruding through the skin beneath, curled in a snarl. He ran to Marcus as much on his hands as on his feet. The coppery smell of the fresh blood caught Adam's nostrils. He paused and sniffed deeper. Marcus ran as quickly as he could. He reached the opposite side of the arena and faced Adam with failing vitality.

Adam hunched low. The shadows playing on his face showed his left eye socket to be wider than the right. It was rimmed with tiny spikes around the edge. His eyes shone blue and bloodshot in the lighting. His blond hair hung low on the right side, pulled back in a single metal clamp. That appeared to be a much better option than having someone torn apart as he or she attempted to cut the locks.

In a growling, gravelly tone, the word "Marcus" came from Adam's throat. Marcus was shocked at witnessing the creature speak anything intelligible. The distraction kept him from avoiding the finger spike through his bicep. Marcus reeled from the pain, but pulled backwards and sideways nonetheless to prevent being entirely skewered. Marcus had three open wounds, and he knew that he would receive more if he spent any time nursing them. He had to find a way to actually get into the fight before he lost his life. The rage he felt from Adam was rubbing off on him from the sheer intensity of it gathered by his senses.

Marcus forced himself to regain calm, knowing rage combined with weakness meant certain defeat. His extraneous senses abruptly shut off, as they had done before. For an instant, he feared he had lost them for good. He strenuously focused his mind on the hand to hand combat he had been extensively taught.

A hit that would shatter concrete landed in Adam's throat. Adam swallowed with difficulty, but again voiced Marcus's name. Adam backhanded him loosely and knocked Marcus to the ground. Marcus wondered if it was worth trying to get up.

Adam stood over the weakening monk in a bestial stance. "Marcus … kill," Adam snarled, drool dripping from his sagging lip. Marcus felt the hot breath as Adam sniffed his face and wounds. Marcus fancied him as something rabid in need of mercy. "Eat," the creature growled.

Adam gripped Marcus's bloody upper arm with his cloned human hand. He squeezed slightly. Marcus struggled to keep himself from flinching lest he inspire the clone to tear him apart.

"Kill him, Adam," Alex said, spinning the charged blade in his hand. "Kill him," Alex demanded, aiming the blade at Adam with both hands. The charged weapon was clearly Adam's most feared jailer, and he responded quite obediently to its wielder's commands.

Marcus, abandoned by his powers, was unable to read the eyes of the monster staring down at him or even the monster behind them. Adam raised a clenched fist to bring death down upon Marcus as ordered.

Max could watch no longer. "I warned you, Stone. He is unbeatable. No weapon in this arena can take that thing on."

"Have faith, Max. Marcus would," Stone responded, holding the cross his mentor had passed on to him. He examined its simple but perfect design painstakingly etched in ancient wood. Stone had lost himself in its design countless times, yet, this time, it was the symbol to which he held. "Besides, Alex's blade seems to affect him, so he isn't completely indestructible."

Marcus violated noble tactics and landed a knee to the universal weak spot among men. Apparently, Adam was no different in that respect. Blade found the spectacle comical, but he did not indulge laughter. Adam reared up, and a ripple of pain and fury coursed through him. Marcus ran away, again reaching the opposite edge of the arena. This time, however, he did not face his opponent.

Marcus circled the arena, assuming correctly that Adam was in quick pursuit. Were it not for the boots he had been reluctantly equipped with, Marcus felt sure victory would have been sealed for Adam by now. Adam gained enough ground to catch Marcus's upper leg with one of his spikes. Fortunately, the spike that caught the monk had its end burned off in the laser wall. Unfortunately, the diamond hard blade sliced into Marcus's hamstring anyway.

Marcus fell immediately. Adam was moving too fast to simply stop and pounce. Instead, he continued around the perimeter, cutting it short to circle back. He quickly approached Marcus's fallen, bloody form. He stopped. Then, the unexplainable happened.

Against all odds, against all probabilities, against all possibilities, and against all reason, knowledge fell apart. Against everything but the faith in the hearts of Stone and Marcus, Marcus stood. He did not even waver as he rose to his feet, poised and supported on his functioning leg. The air around him appeared to ripple. Standing over a pool of his own blood, he wiped more of the substance from his split lip. His mind roared with the searing pain tearing at almost every cell in his ravaged body. He struggled to focus his eyes on Adam, who stood motionless.

Like a fading echo hitting his ears, Marcus's powers flashed back in a flicker. Though he fought them before, he embraced them now. He stared, bleeding, straight at Adam. Adam reared up and growled. In that very instant, that flash of time, Marcus held complete focus. The air shuddered around Marcus and Adam fell to the ground.

Marcus had tapped an extension of his powers he had never known before. The energy had flowed from his mind in a cascade. The unearthly gift of standing left him. He fell first to his knees with a whimper and then a scream. He fell to the floor and rolled onto his back. A smile of triumph crossed his face, and his eyes rolled back in his head.

Adam still lay motionless on the floor. All mental activity had ceased. Marcus had shut down every last neuron in Adam's brain. Adam's body died simply because his brain stopped telling it to function.

Marcus was still breathing, barely. He had lost a great deal of blood. His heart still worked, but the hamstring was far beyond his body's immediate capacity to repair. His body had entered severe shock.

"You take care of Marcus. I'll handle my father," Stone ordered to Max from the observation deck.

"Right away," Max said, already on his way with crude suturing instruments he gathered from the remnants of Stone's technological dissections.

"What was that handy little trick?" Blade's hologram appeared again, curious at the fate of his clone.

"That was the ultimate failure of the Vault," Stone said, turning to look at the dark image.

"So, you know about that, do you?" Blade's image tensed.

"Yes."

"No, you don't. You want me to tell you something you haven't figured out yet, and I won't bite. I guess you'll have to go fishing elsewhere," Blade said with dismissal as his image vanished.

CHAPTER 26

MAX HAD STITCHED the worst of Marcus's wounds to the point where the bleeding stopped but they were still on the arena floor. The lasers began clearing the arena of Adam's corpse and Marcus's blood. Max struggled to carry the ailing holy man with his damaged left hand still not functioning properly. Max barely made it to the stairs of their deck when the laser cleansing intensified and caught up with them.

Marcus was sprawled out on the deck with Max and Stone hovering over him. Max injected him with the closest thing to an anti-shock chemical he had left and hastily stitched his hamstring back together lest it tear completely. Marcus's awareness came back slowly. He felt his eyes and his mind first. The rest felt numb. He could move all but his leg with effort. In time, he had himself propped up against the far wall. He felt impossibly confined yet somehow more free than he had ever been. Marcus was alive, and his mind was more alive than he ever believed possible.

Blade, apparently waiting to see what his son had planned, seemingly wasted his next move by placing his own king piece one space forward and one space to the right into *e7*. Stone moved Max's piece to the outer edge of the board at *h4*. Blade put his last black bishop into play, moving Kylie to *d7*. Stone watched as both the main board projection and the smaller simulation on his wrist gauntlet responded to his father's move. He stood motionless, examining the diminishing pieces on the scattered board. He glanced at Marcus, mentally crossing him off of the active duty list. He wondered for an instant whether Blade would send Alex after the reeling monk but figured Marcus's trick of taking Adam down without a hit would ward off any such plans.

He calculated his chances. His mind raced as he stared through the board to Kylie's face across the arena. Max was in position. He could challenge Blade in two moves, but his chances were another matter. Stone himself had little chance of reaching his father without a forced battle with Kylie or without being evaded and lured into another trap.

Were the board and pieces real, he would have thrown them to the ground and crushed the black king under his metal boot. Frustrated, he decided to speak with his mentor, though he was dubious of getting a response. Stone walked over and eased himself against the dark wall where Marcus rested. He slid down to sit against the wall, propping his elbows on his knees.

"How are you feeling, Marcus?" Stone spoke quietly, loud enough for only Marcus to hear. He doubted Marcus would respond but he was interrupted by a feeling. It was a peaceful sensation, an unspoken voice in the back of his mind telling him Marcus would be fine. With that reassurance, he was comfortable going on in his confession.

"I've been having this dream again. It went away for a time, but since we went to see Kylie, I've dreamt it every night. It starts out where I'm in a field, a vast, green field. I'm alone with no armor. I'm poised and ready, even confident," Stone said hastily. "I feel nothing of the world around me. I know what is inside me, and I see what is happening. It ends there, though, with emotion and sight. For some reason, I run.

"I know I've been in the field before, and I know that I failed before. I run for some goal, something I think I can reach. I'm deluding myself, though. I fool myself into believing that I'm faster and stronger this time. As I run, I see ghosts of the past before me. Like a mirage, they fade at my approach. Then there is the blade, a reaper's scythe with no wielder. It swings over and over, sometimes close and sometimes far away. Every time I see it, I run faster. I convince myself this time is different," Stone shook his head at the recognition of what came next.

Stone continued, "Then, I see it again. This time, it doesn't disappear. I see what it is swinging for next. Of all things, it is a flower. I don't know why I run towards it, but I cannot stop myself from the act. The reaper swings. I run faster, push harder, yet still the reaper swings. Then, I see the flower's beauty, its awe-inspiring magnificence. I'm close, closer this time, and then the blade begins to fall. I'm so very close, almost able to touch the petals, but the blade is faster. In that instant, the very second the scythe breaks the stem, I fall. The flood of loss washes over me, the knowledge that all the confidence was a delusion. The blade looms over me, taunting me." Stone shuddered visibly. "I don't know what it means. It gives me a chill every time I think about it. Now it won't get out of my head." Stone looked at the ceiling of their enclosed platform but saw only the dream. He saw himself alone, vulnerable. Max broke through the memory, standing directly in front of Stone. The master strategist looked at his oldest friend.

"Welcome back. It's your move," Max said with a look of concern.

"I know, but what can I do? I can't get to Blade, and Marcus is out of it," Stone said, not getting up.

"What about me?" Max looked down at the diminishing chemical vials. "Don't you trust me?"

"Of course, Max, but do you honestly think you can beat my father?" Stone met his gaze. "Or what about Alex or Kylie?"

"I can get to him, Stone. One clean shot is all I need," Max offered, holding out an injection tube filled with organic-corrosive acid.

"You're forgetting Kylie. He'll use her on you, too. You were just as good a friend to her as I was, probably better. You meant more," Stone added, free of jealousy but not regret.

"I have her covered, too. Only I don't think it's really necessary. She is our ruthless dictator's insurance against you, not me."

"Tell me you aren't going to use that," Stone questioned, pointing at the vial.

"No, I have one injection tube of anesthetic. It will knock her out cold. When she comes to, she'll be safe," Max assured.

"You still need a clean shot." Stone looked at the ground, pushing himself up with his legs. "I don't think you'll get it, unless she lets you get it."

"I won't take that as an insult, but it really feels like you don't think me capable of this," Max said, less angry than hurt.

"I don't want you to die, Max. Jake is already dead and Marcus came close. If it wasn't for whatever it is he did, he would be a ghost right now. This is a battle of the survivors, Max. There are six pieces left. Cross off Marcus and there are five. I still don't know if any of us will actually leave here alive."

"You can't protect her forever, Stone. You can't protect me forever, either. We're adults now. Kylie and I were out of your life for years. We have all grown stronger in that time, and we've all changed. I'm glad we found each other again, but life changes us. It's never going to be like it was. We've all chosen sides now, Stone," Max said, seeing past Stone's words.

"I know, Max, but I can't sentence you to death. Putting me on the line is one thing. I don't matter, but you do."

"You call this not mattering?" Max held up his patched left hand.

"What do you suggest?"

"I suggest you let me go after Blade, and hope he toys with me long enough for me to take him down."

"Can you do this?"

"I hope," Max inhaled, looking at the board. "There are two ways to do this. Each requires two moves and the hope that he takes the bait."

"I see them. It stems from the pattern of the first move. From that, it is a matter of Blade's options."

"He has a chance to either move himself or use Kylie on me. I say we make this move count," Max assessed.

"Fine, we opt for the right edge, past the range of the bishop," Stone said.

"No, it's not your decision anymore," Max apologized as he took the liberty of moving his piece up one and two left to $f5$.

"Max," Stone sighed, staring, betrayed but knowing, at his friend.

"Now you're committed. Help me."

"If he takes the passive approach, you have no chance. One space ruins everything. It's done now, though," he breathed in deeply. "Fine, I'll help. What do you need?"

Max lowered his voice to a whisper. "I need to switch vial labels. My database was networked. I'm willing to bet he has the codes scanned and he knows just what chemicals I'm carrying. If he discovers what I'm actually using, our plan is ruined."

"You're becoming as paranoid as I am. Okay, a wide frequency wave of static should throw out any cameras for a second as well as any remote readers, but you will only have a second. Get them ready. We'll do it right when he moves," Stone whispered. "I must say, that is quite a nice touch. If you fight my father with a sedative, he'll let his guard down, and he won't suspect anything if you fight Kylie with an acid vial."

The move came, the decisive factor in the way the rest of the game would play out. Max switched the vial labels quickly, and Stone barely remembered to trigger the static wave before his head and heart swirled sickly. Max was about to face Kylie in a battle to the death.

CHAPTER 27

THE CONVERSATION HAD left a bad taste in Max's mouth. He knew that Stone was not dealing well with Kylie's response to their conversation, not well at all. Max had never before questioned his friend's judgment, but he found himself doing just that. Stone often suffered from his own pessimistic interpretations of the world and the people in it, but he had always accepted that and kept going. Now, he just didn't seem to want to keep going. Max had been forced to take action lest Stone capitulate.

Stone stood over the board, watching his beloved enter the arena. He knew he was not performing as the capable leader he should be. He was not confident in many things, but his leadership, technology, and power were his pride. He had to force himself back into this fight. He held his cross in his fingers and wished that he could redo his last conversation with Max. He forced the dreams away, though not before he realized the true relationship that existed in them. Kylie was the beautiful flower. Stone saw that she was the latest of a long line of failures. The scythe was the end of his chances.

Kylie stood in the center, her eyes flashing to Stone in a look softer than he had ever seen in her. He vowed to himself he would not lose her again. Her glistening green eyes settled again on the arena level, locking her wholly on the battle. Max walked by Stone with the switched vial stuck in his scratched belt. Stone retracted his gauntlet and caught his friend's arm in an unarmored grip.

"Max, I'm sorry. I trust you. I trust you more than anyone. I just needed to really see what I have become," Stone wavered. "I can't explain it, but I am glad I can see it to change it," he finished.

"Maybe you can explain it," Max said, pointing to the cross in Stone's fingers. A smile threatened Stone's face, but he had not yet let go enough for that.

"You'd better get down there, and you both better come back." Stone released his friend's arm. He wanted to tell him he loved him, yet the words refused to form.

Max didn't reply with anything except a nod and a wave behind him. He walked down to the arena and faced Kylie with an uncertain expression. She looked emotionless, but her eyes flickered to Stone. Max mouthed the words for Kylie to trust him. Blade began the match.

Kylie fired two surgically precise shots before the word "fight" was finished. The first burned through the jury-rigged repairs to Max's left hand. Rendered useless, it unwillingly dropped the drawn vial from its sparking palm. The second kinetic bullet hit the vial. A spray of mist erupted from the shattered shell, and Max felt his face and chest tingle at the surface contact with the anesthetic.

"That was a big mistake," Max said, backing away with his hands forward. Kylie lowered the weapon. She holstered it as she pulled another without a serial number. "I hope that's a stun weapon." Kylie fired the gun, and the impact dissolved a small part of the holographic floor.

Stone recognized it as a focused electron magnet. It was a highly charged piece of unstable matter. The extreme positive ore is exposed in certain areas through the neutralizing frame that constantly drains off the excess buildup of electrons in the core. That particular shot drained enough from the floor and laser generators that Max should have been relatively unharmed. However, a single connecting shot could drop him instantly and permanently.

"Sorry, Max," she said, softened from earlier. She walked forward with the gun still steadied on Max. Max stepped back, his semiorganics reluctant to move.

"Not to argue with the lady holding the gun, but that was a little hasty before. I can't kill you, Kylie. I won't," Max said definitively, still looking into her eyes instead of the nearly spherical gun tip. She pressed the gun to his forehead. She wavered, yet her hand held steady.

Kylie cocked the weapon with her thumb. A quiver, a small brush of the trigger would fire the weapon. By a strange twist of fate, Max was very lucky to be facing someone with the cool hand of an assassin. Without even a perceptible movement, Kylie rolled the gauge to the fully open setting.

Max, previously motionless, hit the gun with his human hand and ducked the ensuing reaction fire. Two of the uncovered spheres of projected core material shot in a blackened blur past Max's shoulder. The shots hit the floor far beyond him. A circle spanning four black and white squares vanished from the holographic floor. An orb of darkness surrounded the charged globes themselves like two tiny black holes pulling every vestige of electron activity from the world until it touched on some semblance of equilibrium.

In a liquid flow of movement, Kylie had pulled new weapons while putting the electron magnet launcher away. The twin kinetic guns were aimed at Max's heart and head. She cocked them both, but again stopped there. As heartless as she professed to be, she could not shoot her friend from long ago. Then it truly sank in: Max was her friend. Stone was her friend, too, yet that felt somehow different now.

Blade's hologram appeared beside Stone, mocking his enrapt stance. "Looks like a draw to me," he said. "Kylie, shoot him and end this." Her eyes flicked to the hologram, but flicked back again in disobedience. "Max, this is your chance." Again, Max just looked at him, trusting Kylie not to shoot. "Yeah, it's a draw." Blade's hologram materialized a coin. "You said it, son, not me." It was a royal cent, minted with Blade's shadowed face on one side, encircled in his motto of "All is Power." The other side bore the nation's new borders and the skull and sword symbol.

"Here, let's let everyone see it. You can even call it," Blade offered. He waited for his son's response, but he got none. "Call it when it lands, then." He flipped the coin in the air. A giant hologram of it appeared above the arena. Its shimmering gold form began to spin in place while the actual coin rose through the air. Stone looked to his father's throne, making sure the coin was real. "Pennies from Hell, huh, son?"

Heads.

Kylie dropped the gun aimed at Max's heart.

Tails.

Max looked her in the eyes, unable to move against her.

Heads.

Kylie uncocked the remaining gun in her hand.

Tails.

Stone watched the golden hologram as it prepared to pass judgment on the lives of the two of the people that meant the most to him in the world.

Heads.

Kylie unclipped her golden holster belt, dropping the two weapons it held to the floor.

Tails.

Max turned to look at the coin's representation hanging over him.

Heads.

The familiar gun turrets lowered from the ceiling.

Tails.

Stone gripped the observation deck in impotent anxiety, dreading both sides of the unearthly weighted coin.

Heads.

Kylie wrapped the belt in her hand, holding the metal buckle outward.

Tails.

Max stumbled as a low impact shot pried the stabilizing panels of his leg apart.

Heads.

Kylie realized she had backed the wrong side. She knew then that she had turned her back on her own humanity, on her friends, and on her heart.

Tails.

Max stood again and looked, but the larger coin disappeared from the air.

Heads.

Kylie plunged the buckle into the electrical trip wire in Max's leg.

"Call it," Blade hissed acidly.

"Heads," Stone said through dry lips.

Kylie fell back from the initial sparking, but the belt around her wrist kept the current flowing into her. Her bones invisibly calcified; her heart invisibly raged. Her eyes rolled back in her head.

Stone impulsively leapt from the observation deck to the arena floor. The hologram of the chessboard shivered from the powerful impact. Even in his armor, Stone nearly fell from the impact of the floor hitting his boots. He screamed her name. "Kylie" resonated throughout the arena in a boom that would raise jealousy in thunder. He ran to her, dropping his gauntlets and pulling the helmet away from his face.

He ran to her fallen body, unable to see anything but her. Max stood still in shock. The belt still arced from its hold in his leg. He stumbled away with his mouth fallen open, clearing the way for Stone even as he stumbled from the feedback

Stone held Kylie in his arms, ripping the belt from Max's leg and causing his friend to fall over. Stone felt the heat radiating from her body. The static bristled the hair on his arms. He saw her burns, the blackened patches of flesh and her bloodied lips and face. Yet through that, her beauty was undiminished in his eyes.

"I was wrong," she said frantically in all the voice she could gather. "I backed the … wrong … side," she cried. "I'm sorry." Her voice faded in the tears.

"No, no. Don't you be sorry, you just survive. That's all,"

Stone begged through rising tears. Kylie tried to smile.

"If I … had only … known … before," Kylie struggled to focus. She was truly fighting to hang on a little longer.

"I should have found you earlier," Stone apologized.

"Maybe we'd have had … a … chance … but … Tell me how … you … feel," she gasped for air. "Just … once more."

"I love you, Kylie, with all my heart and everything I am." He looked deep in her eyes and saw something he never could have imagined truly possible.

"I … I called … it … I … I l-" Kylie looked at Stone one final time. She focused to make sure he was the last person she would ever see with those eyes.

"Kylie," Stone asked, shaking her in his arms. Her eyes closed and her labored breathing stopped. He said her name again, hoping to draw some response. She had sacrificed her life to save Max.

Stone removed his cape and wrapped her in it. The dark blue death shroud covered her burned jumpsuit. Her face was wrapped gently in the folds of the soft fabric. She was sent to eternal peace, where Stone vowed he would find out what he had seen in her eyes. Silently, he carried her back to the observation deck.

"Heads. I guess you won. Looks like she was done for anyhow," Blade smirked. "Honestly, I have wanted to kill her for a long time, but I had to save it for something special, like this." In that flash, that heartbeat, the torturous grief became focused rage purer than any emotion Stone had ever experienced. Everything he wanted revenge for in his life came from Blade. His eyes burned with fury. He spoke nothing, but his visage guaranteed that vindication would soon be at hand.

CHAPTER 28

MAX WAITED UNTIL Blade's image was gone. Then, stumbling to his friend's side, he asked, "Do you want me to take him out, Stone?"

"Never," Stone growled. "He's mine," Stone whispered. He kept his look focused on Kylie's shrouded body, which he rested on an extended wall panel. "He's mine," Stone repeated.

He wasted no time on his next move. He shifted his own piece a single space forward into Blade's column. He keyed the move on his gauntlet, not leaving Kylie's shrouded body. He chanced a look at Marcus, who had still not spoken since his battle. Marcus looked at him without turning his head.

Stone inexplicably felt justified in his quest at that point. He no longer wondered whether it was a wise choice or tactical solution; he just felt it had to be done. Max limped slightly as he walked to meet his reeling friend.

"How are you holding up?" Max looked as bad as Stone felt he himself did. Max was cautious in dealing with Stone right then. His eyes and cheeks were ringed in purple and he looked as pale as death.

"We'll be together again. Death isn't the end, just the end of our stint in this world. Until then, she'll be avenged," Stone said, still viewing the shroud, forever denied the warmth of Kylie's touch. "How about you?"

"I can't even crack a smile, and that is definitely saying something."

"So, how's the leg?"

"I'll be fine. It's just a power drain. I'll realign the intake soon enough naturally."

Stone forced himself to walk away from the wall he had kept vigil at since his loss. He walked to the main computer bank above which the board shone in a full color resolution hologram. Stone stood with his back to the display, a small amount of light playing over his shoulders.

He pulled a small pack from a panel hidden in his thigh compartment, much like the panel holding his compacted weapon. A tiny wire shot from his gauntlet into the box's side. He paused for several seconds and retracted the wire link. Max spotted the box with a puzzled look, but a flicker of Stone's gaze warned him to be silent.

When his armor was separated from the box, he placed it on the main system's intake drive. A soft whir was the only readable result. In actuality, the box was activating a back door program that Stone had worked into the main operating system when the computer was first fitted for placement. With a password, a software package would cycle a program known only to him. The password is the only part that can actually be viewed on the screen while the rest fulfills its designated task.

The box disconnected itself, and Stone crushed it under a boot heel. The added charge inside the casing caused sparks to shoot from under his foot. When he lifted his foot, a charred footprint against the ground was all that remained. Stone walked to Max and lowered his voice to a whisper. "Back door. Password is lost," he said, glancing back to the form wrapped in his cape. He could not yet bring himself to have her body incinerated. His glove registered that a move had been made. Blade was calling his bluff. He had also moved his king piece forward.

Stone again acted without hesitation. He made another single space advance. Blade acted much faster this time in responding, again moving himself forward.

"This is the slowest game of chicken in history," Max said without smiling.

Stone again followed suit in moving forward. He felt the emotion, the anger, flare within. His adrenaline roared like a river through willing veins. He looked at the board. A single space separated him from Blade. He cast what remaining valid rules were still in play aside and prepared for a battle with the other king, his own father.

He awaited the move, sure that Blade was intentionally building tension. Then, he moved. It was, however, not Blade's own piece. He had moved his last and only companion piece, his trusted black knight, into the space occupied by Stone. Stone had not even noticed the check.

Stone clenched his fist and cursed. His father had planned this all along. He had intended for Alex to intervene, but Stone would not allow it to cease his advance. This was the last roadblock his father could place in his path. He would not be defeated. He simply willed himself to win as though he could bend time and space with his very thoughts.

Stone nodded to Max, who wished him luck and nodded solemnly back. Stone walked without his cape and apparently unarmed into the arena with a brazen stride. A smug look twisted his lip at one corner. His anger was burning within him as it never before had. His thoughts of Kylie intensified it. To his own surprise, his grief did not crush him. He felt loss unquestionably, but at the same time, he knew she could not be hurt anymore. He knew that he would find her in his own death, and, with that, he could not be hurt anymore either.

Marcus was far holier than Stone ever was, so Stone held no fear for him in the eternal sense. Max was another case. He had never expressed belief one way or the other, but he believed in Stone. Stone focused on the anger, though. He was one of the rare few that did not lose composure in a rage.

Alex walked confidently down to meet Stone in the center of the arena. He smiled that proud, wicked, dark smile unique to his face. The spines of blond hair piercing his forehead with shadows only worsened the effect. He licked his sharpened fang and drew his blade.

Stone barely moved to pull his retracted staff from the panel on his leg. He held the grip in his hand and flicked his wrist to swing the doubled over staff into a single, thick rod. His eyes did not waver from Alex as he did so, and a hidden button sprung a blade three times the staff width from above the joint to the tip of the weapon. The glistening, diamond sharp blade with a shining silver finish contrasted against the blue metal of the staff.

Either king was able to start the fight, so Stone decided to exercise his right. "Fight," he snarled. Immediately, he spun the staff in both hands and cracked Alex stiffly in the jaw with the blunt end. Alex spun his own blade into the metal staff, which Stone twisted to unbalance his enemy. An armored fist clanged against Alex's helmet.

"I've been waiting so long for this," Alex hissed through a bloody smile, his ears still ringing as he swung his blade.

"I'd call that a death wish," Stone countered, knocking Alex's sword out of his face with the blade of his own weapon. A quick swing of the staff snapped the golden chain connecting Alex's rank insignia to his belt. In a swirl of cape and sword, Alex dropped behind Stone.

Stone turned his head as his helmet slid into place to block a swing of Alex's fist. "This really is quite pathetic," Stone added as his helmet slid away again. Alex growled behind him.

Stone turned calmly around to look at the point of Alex's blade. His helmet slid away again and Alex withdrew his sword. "Close," Alex mewed with a chuckle. Stone swung quickly and Alex's helmet clanged to the floor. "Nice," he admitted, "How's your sweetheart?"

His blond hair was visible now, and it seemed to shine in contrast with his cape and shoulder guards. Cloth covered his neck, and his muscles rippled beneath. Stone recalled what he knew of Alex. He remembered mostly that day he was forced to travel with him in the low altitude shuttle to the country where Alex stained a town with his bloodbath. He remembered, too, that Alex had killed assassins. It was not that Stone truly respected the profession, only the fact that Kylie was an assassin. It was a way to focus his hatred on the man he was fighting rather than the one pulling the strings.

Alex charged his blade to glowing red. Stone sent his own charge through the blade of his collapsible staff. Coronal discharge glowed around the blade from the raw voltage cycling through the staff. Alex swung, but Stone was faster. The arcing blue and violent purple reflected in both men's armor.

Stone shoved his bladed staff like a spear through Alex's chest plate, piercing it and its bearer. Alex gulped as Stone's weapon broke through his sternum. He gasped a final time as his heart exploded. Blood ran from the wound in all directions. This time, the blood streaking Alex's armor was his own.

Crimson's blade clattered to the floor, disrupting the holographic floor with its energy field, but the hum of its power ceased soon enough.

Stone stepped on his foe's body and pried his staff out of the limp carcass. "One down," he spat.

It was obvious to anyone that Alex was dead. Blade was shocked at actually feeling anything at the loss. Alex should have been better than that, he should have succeeded. He was trained to succeed. Somehow, a stray feeling of sadness and grief drilled into Blade's impossibly hardened heart. He sighed and awaited his only son's exit from the arena.

The lasers nearly burned Stone's heel off in springing suddenly to life. Alex "Crimson" Herring was no more. With equal shock, Stone felt a twinge of regret on some level, but he got over it quickly.

Blade was waiting for him on the observation deck. His hologram was in black and white this time, the perfect image of death. On seeing him, Stone realized the full significance of his dream. His father was the reaper, and he had not beaten him yet. "You have five minutes until the final move of this game. Enjoy the end of your life. You will get no such lucky shot from me." Blade's image vanished, and Stone had to remind himself it was only an illusion.

CHAPTER 29

MAX WAS WAITING for Stone. "Well?"

"Yes, it is time. Marcus, how are you?" Stone looked at his former mentor. Marcus only nodded. Stone walked to Kylie's shrouded body. "Goodbye, my love. God willing, I will see you again, but I know not what will become of sinners like us," he said, opening the incineration box from the wall. Carefully, he unshrouded Kylie's body and retook his cape. He carefully lifted her from the slab and lowered her into the coffin box.

Stone looked one final time at her face, burned and serene, and lowered the cover. He hesitated, not pressing the final incineration sequence. He instead walked to where Marcus sat.

"No doubts about this, right Marcus?" Stone held up his cross. "I'm not saying I have doubts, but I just want a little reassurance here. I want to know for sure that I will find her again."

Marcus responded in a raspy tone, trying to use his voice again. "Yes, it's real. I have no doubts, Stone. Some find answers only after truly questioning. My stint in that is done," he paused. "Find what you believe and believe it. I want to reassure you, but your beliefs are indeed your own. With everything I am, I think you will find her again. Don't go getting yourself killed, though." Marcus smiled before continuing. "You are like a son to me and I hurt so badly for you right now," Marcus finished, looking at Stone and clearing his rasped throat.

Stone actually smiled at his mentor. "And you are like a father to me. I've always felt that way. Thank you. You always know what to say. I have to do this, Marcus, no matter what. I don't have long, but I'll see you soon. Thanks again, Father." Stone was washed in strength and certainty, and he knew it was Marcus.

"Be prepared for anything," Marcus advised, "and for something you don't want to hear." Stone nodded yet did not stop.

"Max, remember what I told you. I don't plan to fail, but just in case, right?"

"You come back, okay?"

"This isn't goodbye, Max. Not yet," Stone assured.

Stone's time was going by quickly. He had one more thing on which to follow through. He pulled on his cape, realizing it was all that would remain of her for him. He initiated the incinerator and forced himself to watch Kylie's cremation.

No anger lasted for her opposition to them. Marcus watched as well. If not for his leg, he would have been at his surrogate son's side. Marcus decided against any mental obtrusion, even if he could offer comfort, some experiences needed to be had as they were intended.

"I will win this," Stone said solemnly. "I will win this for her and for Jake."

Max had to smile at his friend's sudden burst of confidence. "At this rate, you might just drop the armor and wander around the neutral district."

"Maybe, but I have to say, I'm not wearing anything under it," Stone quirked with exaggerated consideration. Max's smile widened.

"It's good to see you this way, so don't listen to him, okay? Whatever he says, it's just a ploy. He is a skilled liar and he knows your weaknesses."

"Agreed," Stone offered his friend.

Blade's hologram flared to life, again in the gray scale. "Your time is up. You wanted this, so I am calling your bluff. It ends here. You'll get no mercy from me. Remember that clichéd and overused phrase about being careful what you wish for? You should have listened." He vanished again, blending into the shadows once again.

Stone watched the white king move illegally into the black king's space. This time, he would accept the destruction of the rules, especially after the violations he had suffered already. Blade's throne went dark, no trace of light shone within. Stone walked again to the arena's checkered floor. Blade met him silently in the center, looking down at him from his slightly greater height. Blade spread his hands from beneath the black cape and issued the command that would begin the end. "Fight" echoed throughout the massive arena and its various, empty decks.

CHAPTER 30

BLADE UNCLIPPED THE heavily chained sword as Stone raised his assembled staff. Both capes, black and blue alike, swirled with the quick current of air raised by the weapons' first clash. Blade smiled and swung again. His cape, singed off at the end, followed.

Stone countered and struck again with speed impressive even to Blade. A strike above Stone's head and one below his knees followed in quick, clattering succession as the weapons struck and sparked against each other with a force that could rend mountains. The parrying continued for some time. Blade backed off while Stone was in mid-swing. The blade of the staff scraped noisily into the ground.

Blade retracted the hydraulic sword and worked the hilt between his fingers. He lashed out with the chained end and caught Stone's extended wrist. He yanked the handle, but his son braced himself and neither moved. Stone arched his own blade back in his uncaught hand and swung for the chain.

The force was strong enough in the staff to break the chain's grip, but it did not get the chance to be tested at impact. Blade quickly sent a ripple through the chain that uncoiled it. With that, he swung it around again in the direction of its previous course and hooked Stone's staff in midair. The pull and velocity of both ripped the staff from Stone's grip and sent it to the far side of the arena.

"Well, what else have you got?" Blade's words rang as he shot the sword out again and spun the hilt in his hand. He spun it in front of his son's face. Stone did the last thing his father expected; he hunched himself over and rushed Blade. Blade was offset by the impact and nearly fell.

Stone halted his momentum as Blade stumbled back. In a quick turn, Stone ran for his staff before his father recovered. Blade clipped the sword back on his belt and withdrew an elasticord mace. He clipped the thin device to his wrist gauntlet and attached the spiked mace ball to the durable clip.

Blade swung his wrist to his opposite side, thumbed the release, and threw his hand in a gesture toward the wall beside him. The cord spun from its spool and hit the wall, bounding at Stone across the arena. The woven elastic, nylon, and thin metal strands pulled tight and traveled further; it would easily reach Stone, even at that distance.

Stone neared his staff and dove to the ground as the mace rushed over his head. He rolled away as it hit the wall and again bounded back. Blade saw that it would not impact and pulled sharply from his wrist. The cord spun back into its chamber, never touching the floor.

Not an easy weapon to use, or avoid, Stone thought. In truth, only a master at its subtleties would even attempt to use it in a controlled battle such as this. The nature of the device lent itself to inaccuracy and randomness, the kind of chaos Blade enjoyed.

Stone quickly palmed his staff and ran the perimeter before his father made another attempt at using the device. This time, Blade swung at the ground, releasing the mace at full impact to arch across into Stone's path.

Wary of losing his staff again, Stone stabbed downward with the blade to sever the cord. His father responded faster and withdrew the assault. The pull was enough to re-clip the mace, and Blade did not swing again.

"You are just as pathetic as always. You know, I really don't know how you managed to best Alex. Now he had promise and potential," Blade said.

"He didn't have the heart for it," Stone said smartly.

Blade gave him a waning smile. "There you go again. That humor shows confidence. That's what makes it so funny, you see," Blade said, drawing his sword as Stone got closer. "You have always been a murderer, but boldness is something quite new to you. You are the worst kind of sinner. You already started killing your family, so I guess I just have to stop that."

"I didn't kill my mother," Stone shouted angrily.

"Maybe not intentionally, but you certainly did. You were difficult even then." Abruptly, all trace of humor vanished from Blade's tone. "You were a difficult birth. Even the Caesarean wasn't enough. The doctors couldn't save my dearest Kristen, but they certainly saved you," Blade nearly spat on the last word, "murderer."

"No," Stone said, more to himself. "No, it was not my fault."

"Just keep telling yourself that. After all I've done for you."

"You've done nothing for me, except crush my emotions and abuse me. You never beat me, but maybe it would have been easier if you had. Don't you see? This confidence comes from defying you. I'm being what I truly am for once," Stone countered, wavering.

"And just what is that, pathetic? Well, I'm sorry I didn't beat you. Fortunately, I can correct that now." Blade's swing nearly took Stone's head off of his shoulders. His helmet was scraped by the blade's tip. Stone stood firm and cracked the staff against Blade's grip. The sword loosened, and Blade released the mace in his son's direction. Stone swung back and caught the cord on his staff's end.

Blade pulled the mace back, but the cord was slit on Stone's blade. Blade eyed him curiously and fastened another mace head to the broken wire. Stone took his warrior's stance and prepared, too far out of range to open himself up with an attack.

"You know, it isn't just your mother you killed in this family," Blade said, poising himself.

"Don't lecture me again about how you died with her. This isn't grief, it is just megalomania."

"Not me. You ready for this? You killed your brother, too." The look on Stone's face showed his uncertain interest. "He was your younger brother at that, well, half-brother. You made sure it couldn't be any more than that. Can you guess who it was?"

"No, not Alex. That's impossible."

"You said it, not me. It is extraordinary, though, since you two were nothing alike."

"That's why you decided to face me yourself. That's why you didn't just call your guards in to herd us into the laser walls. I killed your precious pet, your preferred son."

"Exactly. I guess you aren't that dumb after all," Blade said with a sneer of disgust. "You killed your own brother, Alex 'Crimson' Herring. That isn't his real name of course. He was my real son."

"So, who did you have an affair with?" Stone's anger redoubled at the thought of his mother being betrayed, though he only knew her from a picture.

"Rest assured it was no such thing. Now, is this a battle or gossip hour?" Blade swung, barely missing Stone's side. Stone flew at his father with blinding speed. His shoulders ground into his father's chest with the unique sound of clacking metal. Blade managed to step back and balance himself before Stone caught him with the staff, knocking Blade's knee from under his weight.

Blade actually fell, though he easily batted the staff away with his own lengthy sword. He arched his back and leapt to his feet. "Not bad, but, again, I say it is pure luck," Blade growled.

"I'll take that as a compliment," Stone hissed back through gritted teeth. He thought of his brother, his unknown brother. He didn't realize how the truth could have been hidden from him for so long, but, with his father, their father, involved, it did not surprise him too greatly. No grief accompanied Stone's regret, though. Alex was no brother to him.

The blades continued to grind and spark against each other. Either Blade was toying with his son or Stone was better than he had given himself credit for being. Without anticipation, the mace cracked off of Stone's helmet, knocking his armored head sideways. His helmet prevented the impact from being lethal, but it jarred him just the same.

The helmet again receded, and Stone shook himself from the dizziness. His head was reeling and swirling from everything that had hit him all too quickly, and the physical pain was only that much more. He looked at the hologram covering his father's face.

He made himself focus before he spoke. "How could you let me do it? How could you let me kill my own brother?"

"It was your move. I didn't force you to do anything. This whole game was your idea. It isn't my responsibility," Blade said arrogantly.

"You never did take responsibility for me, did you?" As expected, Stone received no reply. That just made it worse. If a man did something wrong and admitted it was wrong, it was always better than knowing it was wrong and saying nothing. Blade was famous for the latter, though he was never the kind of man to care.

Stone hadn't realized that his ears were ringing until they stopped.

He also realized then that everything hurt, but there was very little to be done about it then. The duel had not paused for the interjected conversation. It appeared that this, the greatest match of all, may end in a draw.

Silently, Stone admitted that he was weakening. Blade did not appear phased in the least, though. He fought with the animal agility that Alex had inherited and a wealth of endurance.

One shot, Stone thought. This was the confrontation that had been inevitable since he was a child. In fact, his youth was not gone. It struck him as odd, then, that he was the one tiring in a fight with a man literally twice his age. Stone seemed to take strength with that, willing himself to triumph as he had in all of those little battles he had fought with himself as of late. The fact that he was fighting in the Neo-Colosseum resulted from one such battle.

Then, he realized he could end it all right then. He had designed the armor Blade wore. Though Blade had ordered it scanned for improper subroutines or hidden, locked, or intertwined programs in the operating system, Stone knew its frequency. He could shut down the armor or even make his father destroy himself.

However, he could not bring himself to do any such thing. Even if his father had no honor or integrity, he did. He would not allow himself to go through with it. Instead, he went into a fury of perfectly executed attacks, pummeling his father's armor with fists, kicks, and hits from his staff. Some, his father blocked, others had connected with negligible effect.

In the last series of moves, Stone delivered a forearm to his father's throat. Blade fell flat on his back. Soon, he was propped up on his elbow, about to retaliate. Stone did not give him the chance. He prodded Blade's chest with his staff and inadvertently forced Blade to crawl backward, away from his son. Then, Stone struck. The blade fell like a hammer of judgment. If it had been his aim, a clean decapitation would have been the result.

Instead, the blade shattered the holographic component projecting the pale image onto Blade's face. The projector burst into smoke and sparks. Stone began to move his focus from the burnt mess to his father's face, only to find it was not there.

CHAPTER 31

A COLD, LIFELESS metal image rested there in its place. A thousand questions and possibilities ran through Stone's mind in the ensuing moments. His concentration was broken only when his father's hand gripped the knee guard of Stone's boot.

Stone ruled out the possibility of armor and pounded a metallic fist square into the dull cast of the face. It dented and changed far easier than Stone had thought it would. With clean access to the shoulder joint of the armor from his vantage point, he severed the groping appendage completely, relieving his father of that limb.

Instead of blood, blue hydraulic fluid seeped from the cut, coupled with burned and sparking wires. It was not possible, though. Stone had never known a robot to fight outside strict battle programming. He had never known one to speak, to act, as this one had.

Then, he knew what had transpired. He put it all together in his mind. His father had been so careless with the clues, but Stone had been oblivious. The rooks and Adam were the keys to unlocking the answers to his extensive questions.

He charged his staff blade and made an incision down the relatively malleable face. What he found was an organ casing with thousands of thread-thin wires connected to it. It was a brain casing. Stone ripped it free.

He had his own guess, but he decided to indulge the logic. "So, this is what's left of my father," he said, tossing the palmed casing to the arena floor. He crushed it with an armored boot. "So much for that."

Suddenly, a loud, disdainful clapping filled the arena. Then, the throne chamber lit up, fully this time. There stood Blade, unscathed. Stone noticed that his cape was not singed.

"A robot with your cloned brain? That's what I fought?" Stone ascended his father's side of the arena, walking to the edge of the separate throne room.

"Correct," Blade said. "You didn't think I'd actually stick my neck out, did you? I mean you could have programmed that pawn to go concentrated nuclear. Even your armor wouldn't survive that. I thought that the substitution was rather kind of me. It had my brains after all, close enough, right?" Blade gave Stone an acid smile.

"So, do we finish this now?" Stone's rage went cold right along with his heart.

"No. Let's chat first, shall we? I know you have questions, and I think you've earned the right to be utterly crushed and humiliated by the answers. No, no. That's far enough for you to walk. Guards! Kill the traitors."

A hoard of soldiers filed into the chamber. Each of them was armed with a laser prod capable of cutting the foundation out from under a building. Stone froze in his approach, and cautiously eyed the laser walls springing to life.

"No questions? Well, here's a good one. Who was Alex's mother? I knew you were going to ask that. I swear you are so troublesome. Her name was Jessica Heron. She was always willing, but while I had your mother, I was not. When your wretched little soul was put into flesh, I lost my wife. My grief overwhelmed me, and I gave in. Nine months later, you had a little half-brother I could manipulate."

Stone fought his way through the first seven guards and threw the eighth into the laser wall. Blade eyed his son curiously and motioned for more soldiers to enter. Stone shot a look at his father and questioned, "So would you like me to kill them all, or are you going to be civilized?"

The soldiers ignited their cutting rods and filed into position. They allowed Stone to pass within a foot of his father. Then, his father vanished. The guards closed in around the son of their ruler but none of them advanced to attack. Then, Stone vanished.

When he realized his father was not truly there, he had sent a hologram in his place the rest of the way up the stairs. Simultaneously, Stone had masked himself with a hologram as he backed down to the arena floor. Stone's form reappeared at the end of the walkway. A tap on his gauntlet locked the ceiling guns on his father's observation platform.

Each of the turrets erupted in kinetic bullets that threw the guards off of their feet.

Stone diverted power to deflecting the laser walls and charged into the center of the arena. "Bravo, but I'm still not impressed. You aren't the only one who can plan a trap, though. I've done quite well at just that," Blade's message broke as a heavy electron magnet fired from the ceiling. Stone's cycling armor power was siphoned off. The laser walls began drawing closer as the energy diverting them was drawn away.

Stone began getting queasy, and he entered a command to drop the laser walls with his barely functioning armor. The energy of the floor generators was added to the draw of the electron magnet. With less of a burden directly on him, he found the energy to stand. "You can never defeat me … I … deny you … as … my father." Stone resorted to the last vestige of hope he had for survival. His father had planned the trap well. He looked at Max and Marcus with considerable effort. Max merely nodded. "For Kylie," Stone whispered through the pain. He activated the only independently shielded system he had. It had never really been tested and only recently developed. At the time, he contemplated abandoning it. He was happy to have decided otherwise. He manually engaged the four switches and nearly passed out.

His world spun. The colors mixed, and motion became a blur. A green glow began touching everything in Stone's sight. The same brilliant green erupted from every crevice in his armor and expanded to encompass the whole of his entire being. A final flash of brilliant light erased Stone from the chamber, and, for the first time in history, time went negative.

Max watched the last traces of his best friend disappear in the sharp green haze. With the laser walls down, he saw the guards on the opposite walkway drop their laser prods, and, for a brief moment, Max thought they were free. He was quite wrong. Each of the guards unholstered a serial issue R-17 Rioter rifle common to the military elite. They were common enough that the holster was built into the front leg panel of the guards' armor to eliminate superfluous belts and catches and to avoid extra drawing time. As Max readily saw, the guns had a powerful impact as well.

The hail of fire was short. Marcus wondered why. When the bullets struck the wall, he got his answer. Each bullet/missile exploded into two hundred percent seismic efficiency. The walls behind Marcus vibrated with a force that strained the walkway's integrity. The computer terminal shook itself free and crashed to the ground. Max fell with it.

Max opened his eye, quite surprised that he was not deceased. He rolled to the keyboard. By some strange twist of fate, it was still functional. Half of the computer screen was even active.

"How are we still alive?" Marcus picked himself up in a crouch.

"They dropped the laser prods. For once, Blade's ego is working for us. He loves this arena," Max responded, doing his best to decipher the half of the screen prompt he could read. As near as he could tell, the back door Stone promised was a one shot deal. The wrong password would probably delete the entire file. Stone told him the password was "lost." They had all lost quite a bit; it could refer to anything or everything. It could also literally be the password, though Max doubted that to be the case when Stone was involved. Then, it made sense to him.

"M-A-T-E," Max voiced as he carefully typed. Max could not read the screen, but he would know soon enough whether he had followed his friend's line of logic. Stone had a flare for the subtle. The chess match was lost, and so was Kylie.

The screen went black. The visible half displayed gibberish followed by a message: they had an unknown amount of time to leave or something very unpleasant was going to befall them all. Another explosion rocked the wall behind the surviving combatants.

The blast had not come from the R-17's. It was the program. The wall fell apart, and a hallway appeared behind the hole it left. Max rushed to pull Marcus out of the way and back near the corridor. Max redoubled his efforts when every gun turret in the arena ceiling descended. A hailstorm of bullets, missiles, and impulse bursts rained down throughout the arena. The guards fell, firing. One of them was struck with the momentum inducing impulse scatter, which landed him against a wall at the far side of the arena. Marcus was struck in the calf of his sliced leg with two standard shots.

Max hurried Marcus and himself behind the previous line of the wall. Another wave of guards entered from the door closest to the two fleeing allies. The new line was cut down just as the first had been. A laser wall erupted where the detonated wall had been, and two reinforced panels slid into place behind it.

Behind them, Max saw a locker. Upon opening it, he found an emergency kit and three Wayward uniforms complete with cloaks and pyre-staves. Max pulled out the plaster tape and slit the appropriate length on the locker door to make a cast for Marcus. He diligently sealed Marcus's leg after pulling the expired rounds through the holes they had created using the tiny reception antennae embedded in one of the Wayward face masks. Max pulled out two of the uniforms and all of the weapons. He dropped the clothing in Marcus's lap and began draping himself in the retired officer garb.

The Wayward were the recipients of the best retirement plans available in Blade's government. Most of the military became a part of estimated casualty exercises since Blade wanted an accurate picture of how truly destructive his forces were. The Wayward, though, were the exceptions to this. They were all given the same dark cloaks, filter cloth masks, low grade infrared goggles, their military jumpsuits, and meager pyre-staves. They were then allowed to pursue any career they wished as long as it supported Blade. Of course, the Wayward were simply the lucky few who lived to retire. It took talent and devotion to earn the title Wayward, but they were regarded as vermin by most of the free populace.

Max helped Marcus as he struggled to brace himself with the staff. As the tunnel outside narrowed before them, Max saw a computer screen cycling on a countdown. Before it went dark, it cycled only one name: Desyree.

"So, my place or yours?" Max smiled at the weary warrior beside him.

"How about Stone's," Marcus answered.

"Yeah, I guess he's not using it. Lots of guards," Max added.

"The guards will be everywhere now. We'll just have to get by them somehow."

"Should I even ask how you are able to stand?"

"Probably not, but my leg is no worse than your hand. Do you think we could fight off anything between us?"

"Maybe a bunny, but that's pushing it. I saw some pretty mean rabbits when I was little," Max said, mocking contemplation. The vast urban decay stretched out in front of them. The dark night had only begun.

CHAPTER 32

A RUINED ROAD ran behind the immediate line of trees. Various mosses and an assortment of weeds had found it to be a comfortable place to grow. Marcus stepped on that very vegetation as he tested the strength of his makeshift cast. The blood of the wounds had soaked most of it, but he was forced to spit on the corners lest it weaken as he walked. The wet cloth hardened into a substantial plaster-like substance from the reaction with water.

"That's sanitary," Max whispered.

"It's not your leg. Besides, I don't want it flimsy anywhere. We've got a long walk ahead," Marcus countered.

"So, what do you know about this Desyree?"

"I say we go to her, or it, first. Stone has planned for everything here," Marcus said proudly.

"Then we go his way."

Marcus leaned against his staff as they traveled onward.

Max wound the tape from the third mask around his semiorganic arm to hide it from detection. Max had done his best to collapse the third pyre-staff, and it now only slightly offset his pace as he walked with the weapon strapped to his back.

"Wait. Wait. Shhh," Max beckoned, stopping Marcus. "That's the sound of a Landskimmer tank. You can hear the click of the stabilizer spring on the main gyro wheel. It's an incredible machine. It weighs five tons and rides perfectly on a three inch wide wheel."

"How high is it?"

"You're about to see."

An enormous metal destroyer rolled within four yards of the weary travelers, and stopped in an instant. It had the appearance of an twenty-eight foot scorpion with four-barrel gun turrets for claws on both sides, a flat deck on top, a wrecker missile battery at its rear, and a cycloptic view window in the front center.

Inside, Deck Officer Garrison paced the main level. A buzz at the man's side called him back to the main console. He looked out the main view window and reflexively swiveled the slot guns at both sides to face the center of the deep set shadows.

"Do you see them, sir?" The man at the scanner center asked his superior.

"Of course, they look like Wayward to me. This shouldn't take long," Garrison grunted.

A soldier came up behind the commander. "Card them or kill them?"

"Kill them of course. Use the big guns, I'm bored."

Garrison watched as the left side turret swiveled and locked. The click of the chamber warned the Wayward, and one traveler pushed the other into the underbrush. The familiar weapon of the military retirees ignited and lanced through the air, bouncing harmlessly against the hull of the vehicle.

"What did he think that would accomplish?" The soldier at the rear turret station watched and almost pitied the people below for being so helpless against the Landskimmer.

"No! He could not possibly know." Garrison gripped the console and braced himself just as the entire craft rocked around him. He pulled himself off of the floor and went to the window. "No current Wayward knows that we switched to heat-seekers. Call in to the patrol unit and run a check on them. Send out a ground troop. I don't want that trick repeated."

"Are you saying we shot ourselves?"

"Yes, soldier, I am," Garrison said with enough venom to poison an elephant.

"Sir, team is away. Communications are open," another officer yelled.

Garrison was becoming very annoyed. He promised himself that the next person to speak was going to get shot. He grabbed one of the slot gun controls and sprayed timed shots in a semicircle in front of the vehicle.

"Sir-" The officer did not get the chance to finish the sentence before a bullet shot through his throat. Garrison's handgun had barely left its back holster. No one else spoke a word.

Max grabbed one of the descending soldiers and used the man's own gun against him. Absconding the weapon, he positioned the dead man's gun and cut down two of the other soldiers. Marcus held both remaining pyre-staves and launched a jet of flame from both. The underbrush ignited in a V before him. The last soldier ignited along with the vegetation, and Max shot him as he flailed.

Garrison growled and shot another officer approaching him. He spat with his own words, "Call the station. We have a situation." He was infuriated by the fact that his Landskimmer was losing a battle against two lone Wayward. "Send an unarmed team to card them and bring them aboard. I want hands up and no more shooting."

Max rounded the tree to the sound of the external speaker. "Deck Officer Garrison wishes to verify your identification. If you pass, you are free to go along your way," an anonymous voice boomed.

The ramp lowered again slowly. Max pressed the R-17 to his shoulder. He angled it to decapitate any hostile soldiers that may emerge. Max was certain this was a trap, and he had very little chance of defeating the Landskimmer with a single round of Rioter ammunition and a broken pyre-staff.

When the four troops emerged, Max hid his weapon. It was not easy to conceal, but he operated on the assumption that the soldiers already knew he had it. The four troops formed an honor guard around him.

"Where is the other one, Wayward?" One of the soldiers got so close to Max that flecks of saliva hit Max's mask.

"Your man shot him. His body is over there," Max said gruffly through his breath filter.

"Cooperate and your infraction may yet be excused," another soldier said unconvincingly.

Max was soon face to face with Garrison. "Now, who are you?" Garrison paced imposingly in front of him. Garrison was a big man in upper rank uniform, lacking significant armor and masking an increasing gut. He grabbed Max's cloak sleeve and withdrew a scanner disk from the pocket.

Max exhaled slowly. Stone thought of everything, Max thought.

"Decorated veteran, traitor to the original Constitution. So, you helped Blade in the Second American Revolution?" Garrison eyed him cautiously. "Who is your companion?"

"My gun," Max said as he whisked his cloak back and unloaded the last round of Rioter ammunition in the weapon. He split another guard's helmet with a blow from the butt of the gun. Garrison's handgun made an effective relief weapon as he picked off three more soldiers. When the fire fight had ended, Max found that he had an extra hole in his left shoulder. His thumb no longer functioned, either. He went to Garrison's crumpled body and withdrew the deck officer's identification tag. Only then did he notice the blood coming from his own abdomen. He tore Garrison's jacket off and bound the wound. He went to the last functioning console that lacked bullet holes and impact scars.

"We had a weapon's malfunction here. Who is your mechanic anyway?" Max deepened his voice as he yelled into the intercom. He set the wrecker missiles to fire ninety degrees in the air, shot the console, and ran down the ramp.

Max stumbled outside in just enough time to watch the wrecker missiles fire. They had been designed to level buildings for construction companies, but Blade found them too useful to remain solely in that application. Two of the tiny spherical rockets soared straight up into the air until they were out of the onlookers' sight range. The fuel gave out, and the beauty began. As the orbs fell, they encountered greater and greater friction, and, the more friction they encountered, the more charged the surrounding air became until it formed an impressive static hammer around the projectiles. The moonlight glimmered wonderfully off of the air fields as they smashed through the Landskimmer.

Every portion of every window shattered. Every bit of broken wire sparked. Every electronic device exploded in impotent smoke. The giant metal scorpion had been crushed. It lurched again on what remained of its wheel but fell flat forward as the hydraulics gave out on the gyro.

Max heard a small preemptive click in the ensuing silence. He saw a flame erupt in the shape of a man behind him. "Thanks, Marcus," Max whispered. "We should be okay for another half an hour, longer if we find a city path."

The burning guard fell. The Landskimmer was a hollow, crushed shell that was still smoking when they left. Max had the handgun and his staff, as well as the belt he had stolen from one of the soldiers outside. Marcus, at Max's persuasion, was wearing soldier armor beneath his cloak as they traveled further, carrying the R-17 from the very same soldier. Max made sure that Marcus's stitched hamstring had not been further torn from Max pushing him out of the line of fire.

They were uncomfortable, wounded, and weary. Somehow, though, they kept walking. They trampled over the brambles, leaves, and mossy ground. They walked on for two more hours. There, by a lonely stream, they fell in exhaustion and slept.

When they awoke, it was dawn. They barely perceived the sun rising over the trees. They realized then that they had lost their cover.

CHAPTER 33

EVERY COLOR IN the visible spectrum swirled back into its proper alignment. For a moment, Stone thought he was dead. When he tried to stand, he wished for a second that he was dead. His knees gave out and he thumped his head off of a tree. Then, the thought hit him: *Why didn't my helmet react?*

Stone punched every manual gauge and override on his suit. Absolutely nothing happened. His suit was entirely drained of power. The electron magnet had sucked every last bit of it that the armor had.

Stone disengaged his gauntlets, unlocked his helmet, and unclasped his chest plate. He swung the outer layer of armor off and threw it to the dirt. The gauntlets dropped on top of the pile. The neck ring unhooked and clattered onto the mass. He walked bare-chested into the sunlight. He spread his arms and looked up at the sky. His cross glinted with a certain shine that reassured him.

Stone saw how bright the sky was. He watched the brilliant hue of the heavens as the glowing clouds churned by before him. Several minutes passed there in the sunlight. Suddenly, his leg panel shifted open. He reached down to close it, but the power was gone. Every few minutes, a light would flicker on and away.

He dragged all of his armor beneath the rays of the shimmering sun. He opened the back panel manually and exposed the solar array. The solar power would not last as long as the power supply available in his time, but it would have to suffice. The "time capsule" as he had dubbed it was still pulsating green in longer and longer periods. Stone decided to lie in the sun while his armor recharged.

His head rested on the soft ground, and his vision swirled again. His body did not respond quite right for a while, and he fell asleep again. He was in little danger of being disturbed as he was deep in the woods. He had little say in the matter anyway.

When he awoke again, he saw only black from his left eye, black with a blazing red center. Each of his limbs fell asleep in succession and awoke in a different order. The green pulse of the time capsule ceased, and Stone's vision returned. He stood more slowly this time, and his knees agreed with him. He had no idea how long he had been out cold. The light on his boots indicated that they were ready.

The rest of his armor was not so fortunate. The glove that had fallen beside his head was usable, and he was anxious to move. He set the targeter on his belt to lock down the armor's location and detached the spare hologlobe. A snap recording of the uncovered ground worked suitably. When the orb was in place, the grass did not quite match up, but it was better than him hauling an extra hundred pounds of dead weight with him.

The breeze was cool on his chest, and, as time went on, the sun charged his gauntlet fully. He activated his civilian program, and his lower armor glimmered into a pair of jeans, his arm showed through the gauntlet, and a tight shirt appeared on his chest. His cross was the only visible piece of his real attire.

He was closer to a city than he imagined, and he soon found himself on the outskirts. He began to encounter people. They were not the elite, and they were free. No matter how wretched and poor they were, they were free. They failed to notice that fact, though.

Stone was entirely self-conscious as he entered downtown Charleston. He felt the eyes of strangers, and they were seeing him without his suit of armor, his protection. He felt entirely vulnerable and had no idea where he would find the building he sought.

As he searched for some vague stroke of recognition, he glanced at the people. Their clothes were so frail and offered no protection at all. Still they were free. The women he saw were nearly indecent. He fancied for an instant what Kylie might look like in such attire, but he dismissed the thought quickly. Such outfits were not allowed under his father's rule lest a soldier would trade the rigidity of his training for the rigidity of something else. They were denied and they were controlled. The essence of loyalty to Blade Stone meant control.

He walked for a time through the streets and alleys before realizing he had no currency on his person. He was quickly seeing that food and drink were no mere luxury. He knew enough of the age he was in from growing up in it, but he knew that even he would not find work so quickly.

He also knew the capabilities of his technology, and a holographic dollar forged of the air would look as accurate as any other. However, he could not ethically allow himself to use that kind of trickery for theft.

As a seemingly divine reward for passing by the seediest and cheapest places where his needs would be temporarily purged, he found a leaflet posted to a window advertising a strength contest. Stone found time to be on his side for once, and he decided to at least investigate the prospect of semi-honest cash. After all, his agenda was his own in this era.

After inquiring directions, Stone encountered a neon-lit nightclub full of the night life most of the free people so richly missed in his era. It was surrounded by a pavilion placed twice as high as he stood. It was apart from the twin alleys of stores that were otherwise closed. Evening had set in by the time he reached the place, and he was easily granted his entrance.

Stone found the inside filled with the young generation of the era amidst their personal rebellions. The inside was smoky, and he was hardly noticed, much to his relief. Several tables were filled with drunken college students drafting freely of their spending money, glowing under the black light. The bar was lined with twenty-something chimneys. The odor of burning tobacco bit Stone's lungs, but he held his cough.

He instead waded through the crowd gathered around the pit in the floor. Below, he saw the reason he had journeyed there. Two men were at the neon-lined table below. Their hands were locked, sweating, with their elbows held firm on the table. Although he knew the contest to be unfair, he asked if he could enter. The man leading the battle of all but wits allowed him to do so for free with the idea that he would owe double for a loss. Soon enough, Stone's turn came about.

The substantial man opposite him chalked his sweaty palm and reflexively flexed his bicep and forearm. A grim smile crossed his face at Stone's appearance. "Next? Oh, you're so scrawny I didn't see you there. Hope I didn't hurt your feelings, Tiny," the gruff man grunted.

Fortunately, Stone was seated in a position to use his gauntlet in the contest.

"Not as badly as I'm going to hurt your hand, you inferior waste. Will you still be able to count when I break your fingers off?" Stone met the man's eyes and observed his opposition nearly foaming at the mouth. Stone had been raised to feel inferior, but he had recently taught himself otherwise. More accurately, he taught himself the appearance of confidence. Regardless, an insult from a smug and seedy stranger meant very little.

"Why you arrogant piece o' shit! I'll enjoy breaking your arm now," the gruff beast snarled.

"We shall see who is broken," said Stone, finding the battle to be as much internally psychological as anything else. He saw sufficient anger in the man's eyes to promote recklessness, yet he restrained enough to keep the victory sound.

The man cracked his knuckles and slammed his elbow down on the table, rocking it under the impact. Stone easily rested his elbow opposite the man's and lifted his own hand. Their eyes were still locked. "That must have hurt," Stone quipped. The man snorted but said nothing.

The man attempted to crush Stone's hand, unknowingly trying to break steel with his unaided grip. Stone did not even flinch; he simply stared through his competitor. The man with the money squinted and agreed that both men's hands were locked soundly, positioned at the center of their range of motion. The scrawny money man in the green suit began the match by waving two fingers down. The man with the larger bulk made no immediate move. Stone pulled his own hand backward until it hung three inches above the table.

The gruff man then applied the full force of his own strength. Stone slowly forced his hand back to the center and slightly beyond. When he was satisfied with the strength he possessed alone, he decided to crush the competitor's ego as well. He engaged his gauntlet.

The force applied to the gruff man's arm was far more than enough to throw him for several yards, and all of it was directed at his hand. The bully's arm crashed into the table and cracked the neon-lit surface at the center. The man's arm was broken and immobile; every knuckle was snapped and splintered.

The bewildered, defeated man simply looked at Stone. Stone just shrugged in response and unseated himself to a round of applause. The man with the money just handed him a twenty dollar bill and gaped at Stone's handiwork.

Stone exited the smoky club and stood in the light of the neon blue exterior. He looked down at the twenty dollar bill and afforded himself a smirk. He stored the cash in his belt and continued his travels. He still needed sustenance and rest.

CHAPTER 34

MAX AND MARCUS walked through the brush along the failing road for the rest of the day. They did not encounter anyone else, and they were grateful for it. Finally, they came upon a section of civilization, and something in both of their cloaks let out a soft, electronic whine.

Marcus swirled his cloak off and removed the hard object embedded in a hidden pocket inside the neck cover. Marcus held the chip cautiously in his palm. A small light vibration monitor read "You Are Here."

Max could not repress his smile. Marcus merely nodded and dropped the chip with his cloak. He handed Max his pyre-staff. He withdrew the Rioter and shot the small chip.

"It wasn't that bad of a joke," Max smirked.

"Just destroying the evidence. I actually thought it was pretty funny," Marcus admitted, donning the soldier's helmet and unwrapping his mouth. "I advise you to burn that cloak and hide your new belt."

"Indeed," Max responded, puffing his cheek as he collapsed the other pyre-staff and ignited his own. "Do we just ask around now?"

"We would, but we are not far. I know where we must go." Marcus went slowly forward, adopting a soldier's gate as best his leg would allow. Max did not question, he simply followed behind. Max hunched himself down and kept his head low.

Once they had completely left the woods, Max recognized the area as the neutral district. This was the home of the wealthy, the lucky few to whom Blade owed a favor, and the corporate people allowed to remain on their own agendas. Most lived comfortably there, at least until a soldier wandered into the place. Any living outside the military was modest, and the wealthy only found their way there by providing an extremely generous offer to the current residents, persuading them to become vagrants or leave the country entirely so that the affluent may be untouched.

Once Blade quarantined the population at large as military and corporate labor, the neutral districts were the only untouched places with any real semblance of freedom. At this, no amount of money could displace the occupants of the comparatively scant residential streets in the district. Of course, soldiers could still cause problems and every freedom hung by a spider's thread.

The travelers found themselves inside a familiar bar and grill. The appearance of a soldier and his Wayward companion disrupted the bar's patrons into silence. Max was careful to hide his left side. The man behind the bar stood unflinching. Marcus examined the room with mock caution from the doorway and suddenly jerked Max into the bar with a force that surprised the geneticist. Max made a mental note to ask Marcus just how bad his injuries were.

"This Wayward is a licensed mercenary," Marcus said harshly. "He informed me of a bounty of particular interest to the administration. I wish to speak with Desyree."

The man at the bar searched over them both, and, finding himself in a subordinate position, submitted. "If you will but allow me to get her, Sir. I am in full cooperation."

"Here, take this foul shell of an officer with you," Marcus said, throwing Max through the counter's half door. Max had to smile beneath his wrapped mask.

"Agreed, Sir, if I may address you simply as sir?" The bartender was stalling.

"Get on with it," Marcus commanded, placing an armored hand on the butt of his Rioter.

The bartender and Max went back into the kitchen area, where Max caught a glimpse of the girl he thought to be Desyree. She was dressed in a plain, tight black jumpsuit with a vest and apron over it complemented by armor on one shoulder. She had neck-length blond hair tipped in black at the ends.

When she turned, Max saw that she had a beautiful face, scarred though it was. Three thin scars ran down her right cheek. He also saw her artificial right arm. It was poorly constructed but functioning, bulky in places and consisting of only a single pipeline in others. In it, she held a very large weapon.

"Are you Desyree?" Max braced himself on his staff.

"There is a soldier with him, Madam. I only obeyed him to warn you," the bartender said.

"Thank you. Stranger, you will go out first," the woman said, her voice flowing sweet from her lips.

Max said nothing. He simply obeyed. Max walked out behind the bar and glanced at Marcus, who was still standing strong in his soldier's attire. The bartender followed, and the woman in dark attire appeared last.

At the same instant, both the woman and Marcus drew their respective weapons. The woman's large gun was steadied with both hands at Marcus's stomach while she herself had the tip of an R-17 in the V neck of her jumpsuit.

"We are at a standoff I see," Marcus said calmly.

"Not really. My gun has a firing time exactly zero point five seconds less than yours. Even if you shoot, you die." The woman's harsh, singsong voice was captivating to Max.

"Sorry to disarm you, quite literally, but I must object," Max apologized, placing his confiscated handgun at the thin portion of her prosthetic arm. "If I shoot, you can't. It was rather a mistake to place your missing appendage at the firing position. See, I know bionics, too. Besides, that's my friend you're aiming at. Gorgeous as you are, I would kill you." Max smiled yet kept his hand steady on the gun.

"You are no Wayward. A Wayward would not care about a soldier. A Wayward knows nothing of elegant speech and certainly nothing of flattery," the woman said, still staring ahead. "Besides, a Wayward would have killed me by now."

"And that, my lady, is no soldier," Max said, stepping closer to her yet keeping the gun on her joint. "If you would kindly ease the gun down, we could sort this out without destroying the place or any of the customers. Please don't let me shoot someone possessed of such beauty. How could I stand to wake up in the morning?"

The woman lowered the gun, but Marcus did not drop his as quickly. The lady backed into the kitchen and bid that Max and Marcus follow. When they were all in the recessed kitchen, Max and Marcus lowered their weapons and breathed a sigh of relief.

The woman with the singsong voice led the soldier and the Wayward out the back door after dropping the EL-10 Grenade Spiker in the storage bin. She told the bartender to close early. They soon entered the forest again along the same path the travelers had previously followed. No one spoke until they had passed the clearing.

"So, you're Desyree," Max stated.

"No, I'm not," the woman answered frankly. "We are far enough away. Who are you?"

"My lady, I am Maximus Fitzgerald, preeminent genetic engineer, and this is just Marcus," Max answered easily.

"So you are Max?" The woman softened at that. "Prove your identity and tell me how you came to my place."

"We happened upon it by accident in our escape from the fight at the Neo-Colosseum." Max ripped the sewn pocket from his cloak and withdrew the same chip Marcus had found. "The name Desyree was on the wall in a countdown sequence, and these went off in our cloaks when we reached you."

When she read the chip, she laughed aloud. "I believe you," she said. She opened a compartment in her arm. "Reactionary receiver. It doesn't transmit, but those lock onto it. I have been instructed to take you to the back door."

"Stone would have planned that, too, wouldn't he?" Max kept the wraps about his face though his tension had considerably lessened.

"He spoke of you both often. I knew the plan, but I wasn't expecting soldier armor," the woman's sweet voice rang.

"He didn't mention the beautiful backup plan, either," Max said. The woman could not restrain her smile, hidden from the two by having her back to them. "The armor wasn't provided. We had company, and Marcus needed stronger support for his leg than plaster tape."

"I see," she said, closing a panel on her arm. "Is Stone dead?"

"He is no longer with us, but dead is too final a word for Stone," Max said with a plain tone of sorrow. The woman's eyes grew moist. "So what is your name then, and who is Desyree?"

"My name is Leona. Desyree is Stone's Siberian husky, my husky, well, our husky. It's a long story."

"We have time," Max said eagerly. She did not fail to notice.

CHAPTER 35

BLADE SAT IN the center of the Earth, or at least the holographic representation thereof. The spherical chamber was in the lowest level of the complex attached to the Neo-Colosseum. He had briefly left the complex until it was confirmed that his son was truly gone. Then, he descended to the lowest area, his holosphere. The throne in the center and the surrounding walls were the only real objects. From the throne, he could contact any point on the planet instantly.

The world around him was inverted. Every point on the globe was in its exact position, only Blade was looking at the underside of those places in vivid blues and greens, all carefully labeled with a digital screen that would display any available scene from any one of them. So, Blade was very truly at the center of the Earth.

Blade sighed and leaned back in the chair. He had lost two sons that day, and he did not grieve over either of them. He was highly disappointed in Alex and mildly curious as to how his first son had gone. Suicide, elaborate though it would have been, was not truly an option. Well, as he had said, he had more pressing matters.

Under the light of the world, Blade eyed the arm of his throne. He pressed one key and the world separated into his territory and the collective unconquered. His territory appeared in red, and he remembered how long it had been since he had made a real push against Eurasia. He knew well enough that he was secure in the Americas. He also knew he had to make a serious assault soon, or the United Armies under Britain might revolt and attempt to whittle him down abroad. He balled his fist amidst his prompt vow to crush them.

Blade tapped another button on his throne. The world shifted slightly in front of him. A violet shaft of light shot from beside him to the point in question. A man's face appeared on the digital screen before the world.

"How may I serve you, my liege?"

"Commander Shureman, have my Harbingers been successfully launched?" The voice of grim death echoed in the dark room.

If Alex had been Blade's right hand, Shureman was his left. Blade knew enough of modesty that one should fortify his strength while not placing his entire elite in the same position regardless of certainty. Shureman was assigned to a very special project the Vault had been preparing. Alex's iron fist had been restrained on the project because Blade was hoping to pit one of his sons against the other. He got his wish, though it did not turn out as he would have liked or expected. Until that moment in the competition, Alex Herring's true lineage was known only to Blade Stone and Alex's late mother, but that mattered no longer.

"The Harbingers have been sent as per your orders, relayed through our courier, my liege. They are now moving towards their destinations. Their speeds are being closely regulated for a simultaneous arrival and attack. The coordinates are being transmitted now. Estimated time of arrival: two hours and thirty-two minutes," the commander concluded.

"Excellent, Commander. You serve me well again," the visage of the reaper spoke. Blue dots appeared shining on Blade's world, marking the positions of the fortified carriers. He terminated the link with Shureman, thinking the vast land would still be in good hands if Blade himself should actually perish, though he cared less and less for his legacy.

He then sent a laser shaft of light to the lead carrier dot. The vehicle's blue prints scrolled across one holographic screen while its pilot appeared on another. Blade looked at the schematics of his son's design. They were the merging of a jet engine and a helicopter with an electromagnetic stabilizer engine. They were sleek, light, and fast with the ability to undergo strictly vertical or no movement. The ones used in this mission also carried fifty tons of metal in each cargo bay.

"Captain, how fares your mission?" Blade kept the venom in his voice as he asked.

"My liege? The Horseman One is perfectly on course and

synchronized. Cargo is secure. My sister vessels fared likewise at the last check," the pilot answered.

"How long ago was that, Captain?" Blade's question sparked harshly, and his eyes flashed at its asking.

"Exactly thirty-seven seconds, Sir," the captain answered nervously.

"Good. You seem to be performing your routines adequately. Do not fail, especially at this mission. Your troop would next be assigned to a reconnaissance mission at the testing islands. That would not do you credit, Captain," Blade purred.

"Indeed, my lord," the captain gulped.

Blade terminated the link and the schematics display. He keyed for a projection of the estimated territorial status if the attack was entirely successful. Half of the Eurasian continent turned red, including a hearty portion of the former Soviet Union. Siberia and its harsh tundras would finally be broken and conquered, though he had little interest in the actual land.

Blade typed in a series of five numbers, and the screen before him focused on the members of the Vault. No beam of light lanced out to show its location. He knew where it was, but his son had not inherited his paranoia from nothing.

"So, Devron, how is Genesis doing?" Blade eyed them all, but spoke to the most senior member among them.

"Genesis is doing well. No handheld weapons of any sort have damaged it, even repeated blasts of an electron magnet. Sheer force of size and momentum has stalled it, but only momentarily. It has no weaknesses. While it is running, it is indestructible."

"I should hope it is, Devron, because I sent four hundred of them out against the United Armies. This was based on the success of a single prototype. It seems you are the one with the most riding on this. It would be unfortunate for you to resign from the Vault. You mentioned handheld weapons, but what about automated heavy artillery?" Blade shifted back in his throne, lending a gruesome line of shadow to his face.

This time, the only female in the Vault's numbers spoke. She was plain even in her military garb, but she was given superior intelligence as compensation. "We are not given the greatest artillery with which to test our projects. It easily defeated a Landskimmer and a Waterstrider tank if that qualifies," she said sternly.

"Do not risk making me angry, woman. You are not irreplaceable, either. Besting a Landskimmer means nothing. I lost one just yesterday on a weapon's malfunction. The wrecker missiles misfired, crushed the vehicle, and set the surrounding area ablaze," Blade said, though in saying he was no more convinced of the ruling.

"Then what would you have it destroy, my lord?" Devron resumed his speaking role.

"Itself. Use its weaknesses. You built it, and everything you build has weaknesses. Exploit them against it. Attack its joints, attack its bolts, and attack its operating weapon's systems. I watched my rooks destroyed by just that process," Blade said scathingly.

This time, the aging Dakker spoke. "We have already done this. On my reputation, Sir, it cannot be defeated by any known weapon the United Armies may possess."

"You made two grave errors in your statement, Dakker. First, you said 'on your reputation.' The Vault has failed before with you as a member. As far as I am concerned, you have no reputation aside from that which got you the position. You have done little to further yourself. Second, you said 'known' weaponry. Anticipate the unknown; that is the point of this council lest you had forgotten. That is why I let you eat every day. The Vault is mine to disband, and rest assured I shall if you fail me in this. You would all do well to remember that. This conference is terminated," Blade seethed.

The screens went dark. The world reappeared fully, still projecting the prospective range of Blade's rule if the front succeeded. Blade smiled and laughed grimly as he examined his potential territory. He had already corrected the mistakes of previous dictators. He had been climbing to his present position for roughly eighteen years, facing little opposition until his true agenda came to fruition. He had chosen surprise and the secret buildup of strength as his true weapons.

It had taken him exactly seven months to dismantle the states after the federal government fell before him. His strength had accumulated in small towns that went unnoticed both domestically and abroad, fostered by the unrest and dissatisfaction with the presiding government and an ever-rising climate of fear. Blade had proven by force that a pyramid sometimes falls best when you knock it down from the top.

Blade keyed the lighting back along the walkway to the door. He shut down the world, and the dark gray walls appeared in its stead. Blade strode into the upper halls. He grabbed the nearest officer. "Find me a sparring partner," he demanded and continued. The officer began searching for an unlucky person about to fight death himself.

CHAPTER 36

LEONA LED THE way through the twisting terrain leading to Stone's elaborate, hidden home. She was armed with one of the Wayward pyre-staves Max had taken, and she used it quite efficiently. The crackling of the crisp brush underneath the feet of the three was muffled through Marcus's powers. Max broke the silence.

"So, were you really going to spike a grenade into my friend's stomach?" Max continued his pace as he spoke.

"I was told to expect Wayward only, not an arrogant soldier. Yes, I would have blown him all over that diner," she said, twisting the edge of the last statement harshly.

"I see. You certainly seem to know your way around a staff," Max commented.

"Stone taught me. He gave me private lessons," the woman remembered pleasantly. Marcus smiled.

"So, you and Stone …?" Max's jaw nearly fell out of the wrapping.

"Of course not. The body belongs with the heart, and Stone did not give me either, though I gladly would have accepted his heart," the woman said.

"When did Stone get a dog? More importantly, when did he get you?" Max was genuinely curious concerning the last question.

"The dog was a stray, and, really, I was, too. Eight years ago I was in an orphanage where I was beaten pretty severely. They called it testing. I knew what came next, especially since they were recruiting for Blade's army: I was to become a casualty in war weapon testing or a pet for the soldiers. I ran away before that could happen. I lived on the streets for as long as I could. Blade started enslaving the lower classes then. He spared the rich if they funded his war. Stone happened to find me before the soldiers did. He offered me shelter. I was skeptical but desperate. That was the best thing that ever happened to me," Leona remembered, reflexively clenching her artificial hand.

Marcus questioned her this time. "How did you get the bar and grill if you were destitute? Does the bartender own it?"

"Stone gave it to me for being his backup plan. He had those beacons planted all through the highest security areas throughout the capital, just in case. The only one who can activate any of the back door programs is Stone, and he has to load in a password before the program can read one, which means hacking the code is impossible. He never meant to save himself, only those that would fight with him.

"I am the bartender's patron just as Stone is mine. I still remember the night Stone found me. He was wearing thick soldier armor. As soon as he saw me, he approached. I had nowhere to go, but for some reason I really wasn't afraid. He asked me my name, and, when I gave it to him, he apologized and told me I reminded him of someone.

"He began walking past and stopped. He asked me to a meal for my trouble, and, nervous as I was, I accepted. We talked over dinner in a place much like the Halo Tavern, where you met me. I casually commented that I would like to own a place like that someday. He offered me shelter just from this first impression. The next day, he gave me the Tavern and a home in the neutral district on the condition that I look after his dog, Desyree, and take any Wayward that asked for Desyree to the back door of his mansion," the woman said smiling.

Marcus asked curiously, "When did you see him last?"

"It was only a few days ago. He came to check on his 'puppy.' He left after he talked with a young man wrapped in a band of black cloth, another stray for his collection I guess. I still remember when that poor kid screamed at the sight of his own face. Anyhow, Stone was offering his generosity once more. I had no idea that I would never see him again," Leona added.

"What happened to your arm? If it isn't too personal," Max inquired.

"It was a fight with a soldier. He wanted more than a drink. He shot my arm before my bartender knocked him out and his friend drug him back on duty. Stone was my benefactor, but I bought this myself. It was all I could afford," she offered.

"That is a very old model. There are a wide variety of adaptations now, especially with Stone as your benefactor. He could have done much better himself, would have in fact," Max said sympathetically.

At this, Leona spun on Max, cracking his chest with the end of the staff and knocking him off balance. When he was on his back, she spun the staff and landed the burning tip a few scant inches from Max's face. She planted her foot on his waist.

"What do you know of it? So you installed these things yourself. Maybe you even made some or caused people to need them. Do you think this was a fashion decision? It works, and it is mine. That is all that matters," Leona hissed. "Like you know anything about losing a part of who you are, not feeling it there anymore, not seeing it. It's not easy."

"It is not wise to kill your allies, dear girl," Marcus said, calming her as well as he could.

Leona pulled back the pyre-staff. Max rose wearily to his feet. As he did so, he remembered just how sore and hungry he was. He decided how he could best soothe the situation. He began removing his cloak and wraps. Leona was looking away from him, working her artificial arm as a reminder.

When his left side was again bare and his eye was no longer hidden by the mask, he began speaking softly to her. "No idea? No idea of what it is to lose a part of yourself. Apparently Stone did not tell you everything about me. While my sparkling personality tends to compensate, my dear, I know very well what it is to be incomplete."

Leona turned slowly back around. When she saw first Max's eye and then his upper left half, she stepped quickly back. "I didn't know. I'm sorry. I … I really didn't know … I … he … I … I'm sorry," she stammered.

"It was not your doing, and neither was that," Max said, pointing at the dull metal limb. "All I meant is that it does not have to be a limitation. There are worse things for which you can punish yourself. Accept what you can get."

Leona looked sympathetically at the damage Max had taken to his semiorganic side. "Does that hurt?" They continued walking as they spoke.

"I assume by your question that your arm has not been damaged since it was attached. Broken circuits send feedback. It itches and the phantom pieces tingle. There's nothing you can do but fix it and wait. Scratching doesn't do any good at all. Even if Stone were here to fix the damage this very minute, I would still have a long day's wait until the current realigned and my body left me alone."

"Again, I'm sorry, but we need to shut up now. We're too close. There are a whole lot of soldiers guarding Stone's house. Whispers can get us killed quickly," she said softly in her sweet voice.

A small key jutted out of her artificial wrist. She ceremoniously cleared the ground until a tiny hint of metal emerged. She flicked a tiny switch inside another compartment of her arm and her finger involuntarily pointed to a nearby spot in the ground. She smiled softly and went to it.

She found a small crevice and lifted the hatch. She fitted the key inside, and the ground itself began to separate in a whisper. A tube wide enough for two people opened in the ground. Leona fell on her side in the grass as the key was harshly expelled. A glowing one minute countdown appeared inside the darkness of the tunnel.

"I see Stone had his way with your arm after all," Max whispered.

"Step away from there," a soldier demanded with a hail of suppression fire. He had spotted them on his patrol of the grounds.

Max launched his staff into the man's stomach and fired a single shot through the soldier's throat from the handgun in his right palm. The soldier did not make a sound as he fell clutching his bleeding neck. Max looked at Leona and then at Marcus.

"Marcus, go out there and tell them it was a false alarm, and get back quickly. Knowing Stone, this tunnel isn't going to open again once it shuts," Max implored.

Marcus nodded and drew his Rioter. Leona dropped into the tunnel, and Max followed. The downward fall was only six feet. They braced themselves further knowing Stone's penchant for holograms. Max began inspecting the walls for controls of any sort while Leona continued down the narrowing tunnel.

Marcus walked back around to the front of the estate, where the soldiers were stationed, emptying the cartridge of the gun in his hand. "False alarm. I could have sworn I saw someone. I wish to continue my patrol," Marcus announced brazenly.

"Agreed, but I'm sending reinforcements to investigate," the officer said, motioning for two other guards.

The guards withdrew their weapons and followed with Marcus in the lead. Marcus made a dangerous gamble. They soon reached the opening of the tunnel.

"Look. There in the ground!" Marcus pointed to the place of refuge. The guards went ahead, leveling their weapons. Though he was in immense pain, Marcus hit one guard in the nape of the neck with his palm. The other guard turned straight into his rising knee. The impact knocked both the startled guard and Marcus into the shaft.

When the tunnel had closed completely, Max broke the fallen guard's neck to be sure he was dead. The three proceeded down the tunnel into the base of another vertical shaft. They each climbed cautiously to the top. When they opened the cap of the shaft, they saw Stone himself in full armor under a single artificial light.

"You will proceed no further," Stone insisted. His helmet locked in place and he brought the blade of his staff up to face them.

CHAPTER 37

STONE DID NOT even notice the music and the rumble of conversation until they had left his ears in silence. He walked on from the nightclub. The crisp chill of the summer night had arrived to claim its place. He decided to sleep under the stars nonetheless.

Unfortunately, he was not yet meant to find food and rest in the forgotten era of his childhood. As he walked towards a cafe that did not close its doors for the night, a man bumped carelessly into Stone from the side. Stone turned to the man as he was walking away.

"I have no money on me," Stone said emphatically.

The man froze and glared at his intended prey. The shady man in loose dress retreated to an alley hidden by the cafe. He emerged again with five very seedy companions. Stone decided to play. He began to run, and three of them followed on foot.

As he ran, Stone realized he was vulnerable to their primitive guns for lack of the upper part of his armor. He chanced a glance back at his pursuers and found that the two that did not run were pursuing him on combustion engine motorbikes.

Stone abruptly halted and thrust his armored arm straight out as the bike to his left continued. It effectively removed the man from the bike, knocking the wind out of him as he fell. Stone stood on the man's arm as the other biker came back around.

The other man drew a gun on him, which Stone ripped from the man's hand as he struck a glancing blow to the bike's handlebars. It tipped the bike enough that it fell on its side, sparking as it skidded on the pavement.

The others ran to their fallen comrades. One was apparently assigned the task of removing the wounded. Once the biker that wrecked was scraped off of the asphalt, Stone targeted his next opponent. He casually glanced at the blood trail just before a chain struck him across his back.

Stone had acclimated himself to pain, and the hit merely caused him to back-kick the person holding the incriminating weapon. The man with the chain and the dread locks fell hard against the light pole. In the arcing of the tearing electric circuit, Stone saw flashes of the brilliant green that removed him from his own era. Two accidents would be reported before the light would be fixed.

The only woman amidst the gang fired a pistol at Stone's heart. His gauntlet intercepted the bullet's course and the shot ricocheted into a nearby store window. Stone's vision blurred; a robbery would be reported that night in the store. A second shot was palmed in the same gauntlet. His armor retained its programming even when it was dismantled. The primary function of it was to protect Stone's vital organs against lethal attack, even if he would act otherwise. It was Stone's protection against himself and his own self-destructive tendencies.

Stone produced the bullet from his palm, much to the surprise of the female. He feigned a puzzled expression. "Were you looking for this?" Stone dropped the bullet and ripped the man with the crushed ribs and the chain from the sidewalk. "Or this?" Stone threw the wounded man at the woman impotently holding the gun. They both fell heavily.

"Then there was one: you," Stone resonated. He turned slowly to the last man standing. Stone unceremoniously ripped the knife from the man's hand. "None of you get it, do you? You go through every single day, complaining about how tough your lives are." Stone caught the man's panicked fist on its way to Stone's jaw. "Are you beaten? No." Stone threw him back. "Are you oppressed? No, you're free." The conscious biker swung at him with some semblance of brass knuckles. "All you can do is war with each other and spit on the greatest gift you were ever given: life!" Stone twisted the new assailant's leg behind his body, pulling the muscles it contained. "You drink, you smoke, and you party. You don't see freedom." Stone threw the biker into a garbage bin nearby. "You band together in criminal gangs, wasting every second you have." Stone broke another assailant's arm as he collected himself from the last round and swung again. "Until, boom, one day it's all gone. Then, you have nothing but regrets."

The broken attacker fell on his knees at Stone's feet. Stone reflexively grabbed behind him as the woman attempted to stab him. He pulled her around to his front. He glanced at her and twisted the knife out of her grip. He held it in front of her and threw it into the newspaper dispenser. His left eye relayed only black through his retina; all of the papers would be stolen by morning.

Stone raised her off the ground, holding her by the wrist. He grabbed the man at his feet by the collar. He carried the woman and dragged the man to the garbage bin where their fellow gang member lied unconscious. He casually threw them both over the side and slammed the lid on them. "Stay with your own kind," he bid.

Stone carried the rest of the human garbage to the side of the receptacle. When he was sure they were alive, he left. He crushed the remains of the bikes, and the wreckage was strewn about the street. He did not encounter them again, and he did not recognize any of them from his future.

Stone decided that his stomach could wait until daylight. He returned to the tree where his armor waited. As expected, it had not been bothered. For safe measure, he donned the rest of it and leaned wearily against the tree. The padding felt cool against the stinging pain of his bruised and bloodied back.

He looked through the leaves at the stars. He picked out as many of the timeless constellations as he could, taking comfort in some stability of the universe. He enveloped himself in a hologram of foliage against the ground. He spent the night in an era in which he did not belong.

He did not dream that night. Instead, he remembered. The time stream sparked around him. He was weak. He was barely conscious. Brilliant green and brilliant purple swirled around him in the vast current. He saw friends, relatives, and Kylie. He saw strangers, famous and unknown. People that were alive and dead alike in his mind were plainly animated at different ages all around him. They were echoes, ghosts. He saw his world and the personal worlds of others spin around him. He had no concept of how long a duration he was in the time stream, just as a point has no concept of where it is in a mile. Abruptly, Stone witnessed a hand, a real hand, not an echo, reach through a green orb as though through liquid and pull back empty. Behind it was the face of the prophet Nostradamus, glimpsing the events untold to the rest of humanity.

He was aware that he could not move. He could not breathe, either. Then, he ascertained the situation. The vibrant green was the expanse of history that had indeed come to pass. The twirling lights of purple were the various possible turns of events. Every point of decision swirled out more purple bands. Visions of various times and timelines would appear at random out of the brilliance. At the center, Stone saw an endless column of blue light. It shone brighter than the rest.

He theorized that the blue pillar was the axis of time, and speculated that it originated from the Divine. He also began realizing why he was unable to move. He was traveling purely through the fourth dimension. That was why he could not even breathe, which was the most unsettling fact of all. The air around him that had been captured by his machine remained hauntingly still.

He then witnessed the appearance of a second green orb. It opened onto a scene that was very familiar to him. He saw himself working in the lab he had built himself. His echo turned, spat an expletive, and approached the unintentionally active time machine. Perfect, he thought later, this is my impact on the time stream, a curse. He tried to smile at that, but he was unable to do so and a fresh wave of panic washed over him.

As he again reflexively gasped without any physical result, Stone approached a swirl of green. He saw within it the world of his youth. A spark of brilliant blue grew steadily above a forest in the winding band of green. When the forest was directly beneath him, a shaft of light sprang from the vibrant point and pierced him. Purple bands swirled around Stone as the shaft of blue light drew him closer to the stationary, vibrant world below him. He had just enough time to realize that his brain responded to the energy of the time stream and fed the information into his memory, overloading with perception in its stillness and causing him to see the scenario simply in a visually remembered dream state.

The purple bands struck him first, passing into and through him. The blue light drew the green around him into a bubble. He saw himself pass into the forest below. He remained still in the green orb until it burst. He gasped as the air of the future mixed with the air of the past.

Every image of every time he saw hit him at once now that he was free of the time frozen passage, and his mind went black.

Stone awoke with a violent shudder. Vision in his right eye went black. Exactly twenty people had sat in the very spot Stone slept on in the woods. He felt warmth in his mouth, and he tasted metallic salt. He drew his armored palm to his nose. Only five hundred people would ever lean against that tree. The gauntlet determined it was his own blood running from his nose. Four hundred eighty-one people had wandered into these woods alone. Stone's heart rate must have increased to the point of rupturing the capillaries in his nose. The twenty dollar bill in his belt had passed through exactly seventy-four hands before reaching him. Stone lost vision in his other eye. His mind shut down again.

He awoke at noon. The hologram around him had changed accordingly. His brain reconciled itself to normal functioning. Both of Stone's eyes cleared, and the day around him became visible. The past and future that had become an unnatural part of his memory unburdened him through repression. His thoughts were clear again. He raised his hand to his face. The caked, dried blood he found there unsettled him. He had a very long way to go and he was not sure how much time he had to get there.

CHAPTER 38

HE PACED. HIS was the youngest face in the room, and it was more obvious when gauged by the stern expressions gracing the other leaders of the nations of the United Armies. He saw worry beyond words in each such face, so he paced. His name was Cessil J. Chirac, and he was the most charismatic leader France had seen since Charles de Gaulle. He was of mixed French and German descent, but he was entirely French at heart. He spoke with the force to motivate men, and the council did not appreciate it.

"We must employ our macro-nuclear arsenal. It is the only chance we have," Cessil demanded in his native language. Each leader had a translator apparatus attached to his ear and his throat. A turn of the dial in the ear piece would access an automated translation of every uttered word in the listener's language of choice.

"How many times must we tell you that is not even a consideration? The quest for the nuclear arsenal is what turned the Siberian steppes into an uninhabitable, glowing chunk of nuclear winter and made the Arab nations into a collectively charred sand crater," John Rowan reminded.

At this, the German representative stood and offered his part. "President Chirac, Prime Minister Rowan is correct. Our combined arsenal could destroy the American continents, but what about the network he has running throughout Australia and Africa? He may not even be in the Americas anymore. I offer you Germany's arsenal for any purpose designed to stop President Stone, but I will not encourage employing a nuclear weapon. There are better ways."

"Indeed, President Verndestag, there are better ways. I am also sure we are all committing our respective weapons caches to stopping the impending invasion. This council is the last hope. You should all be aware of that. From what I have heard, President Stone's son has failed in his attempt at internal usurpation of power," Rowan added.

"All the more reason to strike with the most powerful weapons we have," Cessil interjected.

"I am forced to agree," the Russian representative added. "President Blade Stone has developed automated space weaponry. Our satellites will be little more than debris now. We must strike every major city under Blade's control."

"That is hardly a surprising suggestion coming from Yarishnachov. The Soviet state has only its population of proletariat laborers and its rusting nuclear weapons," Verndestag spat.

"Enough. Bickering solves nothing. The question is whether or not we employ a nuclear strike. It has nothing to do with personal qualms," Cessil reminded.

"We cannot. The only precedent Blade has respected is the nuclear standoff. He has already abandoned our silent agreement on conventional arms. If we strike with even a deactivated warhead, we will be destroyed," Rowan defended. "Besides, it gets worse. Helmut?"

"Our new GroundScan system has detected a fleet of air vehicles departing from both coasts of North America. They could be carrying anything, but it is certain this is the next wave of attack we will face," Verndestag continued.

Cessil stopped pacing. He abruptly looked around the room. The charcoal colored walls in the large circular room cast a shadow of gloom over the assembled group. He glanced at the tired bodies in the four filled chairs around the circular, silver-lined table. The screen at the far end from the door displayed the German GroundScan readout. "Why did you not tell us this before? We are debating about how we should strike when we have to mobilize our defenses? Whatever your decision, France is going to be at the head of this counteroffensive."

"You know, infighting is the first sign of collapse." At the new voice, the five people present turned to the screen before them. Blade's pale image burned over the screen. "I should know. I have seen it myself. Honestly now, did you really think you could meet in secret?"

"You will fall eventually, Blade," Rowan asserted.

"To whom? Nazis and Commies and Brits. Oh, my! Go ahead, fight with everything you have. You can watch as I dismantle Eurasia piece by piece, country by country, just like I have every other.

"You know, I am quite disappointed in you, Ho Xi Ming. For the man who overturned the CCP in China and founded the world's largest free democracy, I expected more rhetoric. John Rowan, how goes the collectivist government? I am surprise you lasted this long. Helmut Verndestag, how long before the swastika in you comes out of hiding?

"We cannot forget dear Mikaelis Yarishnachov, can we? Use those self-serving interests of yours and surrender now. I would hate for the rest of your country to end up like your steppes. How did the CPSU recover from that?

"Oh, and finally we have Cessil, the upstart ruler of the Sixth Republic. How many governments does it take to stabilize France? The world may never know."

Cessil quietly withdrew his hammerstaff from its resting place against his leg. He quickly smashed the screen into a shower of sparks and crystal. "Charge my account for it. I could not listen to another word."

A spidery black box with four antennae and a projection tube jutting from its sides became visible. Cessil removed his cloak, ripped the device from its perch, threw it to the ground, and abruptly pounded it into its component pieces. Cessil put his cloak back on his shoulders and left the older men behind. Only Rowan followed. The older British noble caught up with Cessil several yards away.

"Excellent. I believe we convinced him," Rowan beamed.

"Yes, even Mr. Ming did his part by keeping his position silent, keeping the nuclear vote uncertain to Blade. I think it is safe to say that Blade is entirely unaware of our planned counter invasion. He must still believe that we are considering a nuclear strike because we have no better weapons," Cessil returned, smiling as well.

"Then we are successful in keeping Project Arctic Fire secret," Rowan sighed.

"Yes. I assume we actually have a much better picture of the incoming forces?" Cessil cocked his eyebrow.

"Of course. The German GroundScan system has detected two fleets of airborne carriers consisting of twenty-five carriers each. The engine trail indicates sonic-based drive systems and primary weapon power. Each carrier has eight dark spots, not lead, either. The material is just too dense for the scan. If Arctic Fire fails, we may have an enormous battle on our hands," Rowan said soberly.

"Four hundred attackers in unknown armor are approaching alone. Blade must be pretty confident about this. His last force consisted of thousands, backed by tanks and at least four times the air strike team this wave has," Cessil said, losing all traces of the former triumphant smile.

"We were lucky to beat those Waterstrider tanks, submersible arsenals that can fire underwater. Fortunately their turtle shell design retained the soft underbelly. I hate to think of the submarines and surface ships we lost to even one of those monstrosities," Rowan remembered with a visible shudder running down his spine.

"When President Verndestag leaves, have him send the dummy image to my National Assembly. Have him transmit the true result and a probability read for the site of engagement to my Prime Minister. I will be in the field. Send the prototypes to my coordinates as soon as possible," Cessil ordered. Rowan simply nodded and returned to the circular assembly room.

Cessil walked across the lawn to his armored transport. He listened closely as he opened the door. "Get out now," he told the guard and the driver. When they complied, he shut the door, and the transport exploded around him. The guard and the driver rolled to the ground. Cessil threw the door off of himself and withdrew a miniature cigar. He popped the end of the casing which automatically lit the tobacco, and he proceeded to a side street. A duplicate transport appeared.

Cessil listened as he opened the door. He sat calmly inside and finished his cigar. He snapped the filter and dropped the remains to the ground, where they quickly incinerated into nothing. Cessil drew his hammerstaff into the car and knocked the guard unconscious before the man could fire the weapon in his hand. Cessil shut the window and motioned for the driver to proceed.

"I am getting very tired of these assassination attempts. There is not going to be a Seventh Republic, especially while we are at war. Even if they kill me, there will be another election." At that, Cessil opened the car door and tossed the unconscious guard through the opening.

At the command/conference center, Verndestag received a call. He pushed Rowan outside quickly. "The first series is ready. It will be shipped within the quarter hour."

CHAPTER 39

"STONE?" MAX NEARLY fell back down the shaft in shock. Marcus felt as though he were losing his powers again when he could not sense the nature of the confrontation. Leona just froze, letting her jaw fall open.

"Hello, Max. Marcus. Leona. Surprised to see me, are you? After all, I did have a rather unceremonious disappearance the last time, did I not? Come in, slowly," Stone ordered.

The three stepped slowly from the hatch to the unlit ground. Stone turned around and walked away in a straight line. Leona stepped forward and walked cautiously behind him. Max and Marcus stopped and eyed each other, wondering if they could defeat Stone if that scenario arose.

Stone spread his hands slightly apart on the staff. A narrow hallway lit up from the darkened room. "If you wish to survive, go through that hallway in the next eight seconds. Begin now," Stone prompted, turning back to face Leona. A swipe of the bladed staff convinced her to go. Max followed, nearly pushing Leona through the doorway. Marcus entered and stopped just inside the entry to the hall.

In the shadow of a glowing green light, Marcus recognized a staggered arrangement of training robots lining the side wall. He guessed the same arrangement was held along the wall he stood behind when he saw that same glow immediately around the doorway. A nearly blinding burst of jade energy lanced out into an intricate lattice work that spared only the positions of the robots and Stone himself. The energy was close enough that it sparked against the frame of the hallway.

The jade energy ceased, and a single drone trudged to the vertical shaft. It leaned over and fired another wave of the same energy down the shaft. Marcus guessed it destroyed the rungs allowing ascent, or descent.

Max squeezed past Leona in the hallway and peered curiously outside. He saw the familiar entrance chamber to the holographic arena. Marcus appeared behind Leona. Stone followed him closely. "Go upstairs, now," Stone ordered.

Max led the way, almost pulling Leona behind him. Leona was unsure of the situation, but she still resented the offer of help. Marcus proceeded apace and began to center himself within to recapture his abilities. Stone, still helmeted, walked solemnly behind them all.

The lights rose in the living room. Max pulled Leona to the side and forced her out of the way. Marcus reached the top of the stairs and sidestepped quickly. Max spun into a kick he aimed at Stone's substantial chest. To Max's great surprise, Stone turned away precisely as Max was about to connect. Max stumbled, but he caught himself easily enough on the banister.

Stone lowered the point of the staff to Max's throat. The armored figure drew the weapon back in a preparatory manner for spearing. "I will destroy you if you force my hand," Stone cautioned.

"What is wrong with you? You couldn't have been playing us for fools this long. Answer me," Max demanded.

"There is nothing wrong with me. Now that security parameters have been reestablished, status has returned to standby. This facade is best ended," Stone said.

"Why do you have to be so paranoid?" Max lifted himself from the stairwell and limped to Leona's side.

"I am incapable of paranoia," Stone responded. Marcus fell into a nearby chair, relaxing to a degree.

"You don't think you're paranoid? You?" Max cocked his eyebrow curiously, allowing the flood of mixed emotions to finally wash over him.

"Of course. I must obey my programming. I have no free thought. I, as an entity, do not exist. I am a creation designed for human interaction. I cannot be paranoid." Stone said emphatically.

"It makes sense. I couldn't read any emotion because there was none to read. Stone created you, didn't he?" Marcus eyed the being curiously.

"Yes. My program specifies that I am to maintain the residence in the absence of my creator. I am to utilize all accessible files available to give the most complete portrayal of Stone to all who enter. I am able to recognize scans of known allies' electromagnetic body signatures. I am equipped to destroy all other intruders. The last transmission accessible to me is the signal sent from the Neo-Colosseum in which my creator informed me of the outcome of the conflict," the image of Stone stated. "I have used this information to compile a new persona. I am without personality."

"So is Stone," Max sighed, relieved. "Show us who you really are then. Why do you have a duplicate of Stone's armor?"

The image of Stone disappeared. In the space where the assembled company believed Stone's hands to be were two independently operating artificial hands with complete articulation. One of the hands held the very real staff. The free hand pointed upwards.

Directly above the hand's position was a hovering disk with a wide, thin screen on its bottom. A light began in the center of the disk and gradually expanded. As it did so, the image of Stone reformed in the air. When the image was fully reformed, the light went out and the disk itself faded into a transparent hologram.

"I am a computer designed to operate independently from the systems in this house while maintaining a symbiotic relationship of information with said systems. All languages used and gestures made have been programmed. I do not evolve, but I can access new files in the house as they are created.

"I operate on electromagnetic pulse. It retains the appropriate height at which the projection must hover. The projector in turn emits a pulse that mobilizes and stabilizes the hands of this construct in their proper alignment with the image. The staff can be operated independently within a radius limited by the power supply of this construct. However, I am able to locate it wherever it may end up going. I am EMPulse, so named by Stone. I refer to this construct as I by program specification alone," the construct recited.

"Electro Magnetic Pulse. That certainly is something Stone would do. Can you really use the staff?" Max began focusing on the place where the disk above Stone's image had become visible before.

"Yes. I operate the staff according to the programming of the combat drones in the holographic arena. The same attacks cannot be used twice successfully against this construct," EMPulse responded.

"I thought you couldn't evolve," Max said questioningly.

"He cannot, but the program he utilizes can while it is active," Marcus said with sudden understanding.

"That is correct, Marcus. It is the work of a genius," EMPulse stated.

"I thought you had no personality," Max said, finally relaxing. "Stone was certainly modest when he created you, wasn't he?"

"Yes, he was/is extremely modest. My statement is fact. Stone's intelligence quotient is far higher than the requirements for genius qualification," EMPulse responded. "I have been instructed to inform you that there is a nutrient pool off from the laboratory. From a previous entry, Max, I should caution you that my creator is unaware of any adverse effects on your biomechanical anatomy. Leona, you are given full clearance to use any facility in this residence upon your arrival."

"EMPulse, can you cook?" Max smiled at the prospect that he may get food out of this scenario.

"No, I am unable to participate in that activity for sanitary reasons," EMPulse advised.

Marcus approached the window and quickly walked back away from it. "Can the guards outside penetrate this house?"

"No, a laser perimeter has been activated for the immediate grounds. Stone's private access remains, but it cannot be opened without an electromagnetic scan and DNA confirmation. The residence is secure."

"We got in," Marcus reminded.

"Your arrival was anticipated," EMPulse flatly stated. At that, Marcus withdrew to the spare room where Robert had stayed. That left Leona and Max alone with the construct.

"EMPulse, take my hand please," Leona asked. EMPulse complied. Though his touch was cold, it was not harsh. The images of Stone's eyes were without expression. "I didn't get to say thank you, Max. I thanked him for everything at the time, but, now, when it means the most, I didn't get to thank him. I didn't even get a last goodbye." Leona's eyes glassed with tears.

Max put his human hand on her shoulder. "Neither did I, but that's the way life works."

"Why did he work so hard to create something like EMPulse without giving it adaptable intelligence?" Leona looked again into those artificial eyes which met hers yet stared beyond.

"That one I can answer. He wanted us to be the only people on the planet," Max said, drawing her closer easily.

"EMPulse, why were you created?" Leona averted her eyes from the construct's face.

"My creator was bored one evening," EMPulse said flatly.

CHAPTER 40

"DROP THE ALTITUDE of carrier wing seven. Send wings two, three, and five ahead. They can operate at full power and use all weapons at their disposal. I am not seeking maximum damage at this run," Blade said from control center that appeared to be the center of the world. "They are planning something over there, and I don't want to lose an entire fleet to that plan." Blade's eyes narrowed as he watched both his army and the entire shoreline on the display.

Carrier wings two, three, and five obeyed. Each pulled forward at precisely the time Blade calculated they would be coordinated to move. Mere moments passed before the four carriers of wing two reached sight of the mainland. They came upon the usual Guardsmouth tanks produced by the overturned automobile industry of Germany.

A front line of tanks rested on the water while two rows sat brazenly on the shore. Each member of carrier wing two fired a volley of infrasonic waves at the armored tanks below. It was not the carriers' strongest weapon, but it was best for surprise because it left the enemy weapons completely intact while it destroyed the operator's internal organs.

"Excellent, they're falling for it. Bring about the manned tanks. Have the weapons arrived yet?" Cessil turned to the nearby German officer for a response.

"Negative, Sir. They will be brought by land in approximately ten minutes. We have to hold them until then," the German commander responded unsurely.

"Then we take out as many of them as possible until it arrives," Cessil said sternly. "Bring the sonic shielded jets to the line. We should still have sixteen functional. Before you arm them, scan them. I only want aircraft with full vacuum shielding flying into this mess. Bring the third line of automated tanks full about, lock on targets, and fire. Be prepared, Blade never invades with this small of a number of vessels."

The third line of tanks sprang to life. The heavy artillery gun atop the base of each tank turned and rolled skyward in its socket. A volley of kinetic shells unleashed itself upon the carriers above the shoreline.

Upon impact, one of the carriers rocked far enough sideways that it began to fall. In overcompensation, it crashed itself upon the sparkling golden sands of the Atlantic shore. The others merely jumbled but continued flight. The three airborne carriers locked their main weapons arrays to each side of their vessels. The fourth, fallen carrier exploded in a loud, brilliant flash, spilling its unknown cargo onto the shoreline.

"I have it. The drive systems are modified from the Screamers he used a few years ago. These are more maneuverable, but if you upset them far enough, they cannot come back around," Cessil spouted through the translator. "Concentrate fire on the left underside. Are the jets ready yet? These carriers are about to have reinforcements very soon."

"Confirmation received. Nine of the sixteen jets are intact, loaded, and approaching as we speak."

"Good. Prepare for a second attack. Quickly, the main weapons pods are arming. Send a team to collect one of the unknown passengers. We have one carrier down, but these three are only the beginning. Fire now," Cessil demanded. "His invasion forces consist of hundreds of vessels, and now he trusts fifty to succeed?"

"Sir, the jets will arrive within the minute. Enemy carriers approaching. Eight vessels, similarly oriented, on attack vector," the French general shouted over the hum of the machinery surrounding the coordination team.

The second volley of tank fire erupted, toppling another carrier. The two remaining outmaneuvered the tracking tank guns and retaliated with explosive sonic weaponry. The third line of tanks was severed at the end as the ground-based machines shook themselves to pieces.

"Sir, wings approaching. Enemy vessels will arrive within two minutes," an officer said over the intercom. "Their weapons arrays are already locked. The enemy is about to hit the shore firing."

"Time to blow our cover. Engage all Guardsmouth tanks and jets. Target left undersides and main weapon systems. Destroy any and all carriers. Bring out the manned tanks. They will have abandoned subtlety by now," Cessil commanded, gritting his teeth and staring at the screen before him. He whispered, "Hurry up, Verndestag." Pounding his fist on the controls, he aimed the front line of tanks to fire on the incoming attack wings.

The jets tore silently into battle. Each was equipped with a strong cutting laser and full immunity to sonic attack, at least for some duration. A single shot from the cutting laser of the lead fighter ripped the sonic array from one of Blade's carriers. The carrier rocked and fired a full shot from its right array.

The outer covering of the jet ripped away. The rest of the fighter jets rolled away as the covering plates flew back through the air. The burst shattered the outer vacuum shielding, but stopped in the absence of a medium. "My outer shielding is shot. Secondary shielding is holding. Rear jet remains intact. I am going to rip that carrier through its center," the British pilot insisted. A laser burst lanced straight through the carrier's hull. The pilot was quite surprised when the same shot came straight back at him. The pilot had turned away, but the shot tore his right wing from its base. "I am hit. The best we can do is tear open their weapon systems. I can strafe the carrier one more time with the emergency systems, but I have to pull out while I still have stabilizing thrust."

"Understood, Captain," Cessil said. "Do your best without dying on us." Cessil turned to the two commanders at his side. "The carriers cannot possibly have the capacity to repel a high energy laser. Even if they did have such shielding, why would it be placed behind the cockpit? That earlier shot went through the side. Whatever is in that cargo bay is impervious to the best weapon we have at our immediate disposal. We must decimate it. Position tanks. Topple that carrier for our friend up there."

The tanks obeyed. The British pilot tore the main weapon off of the right side of the damaged carrier. The tanks fired staggered volleys that effectively pushed the carrier over onto its side. The fighter pilot backed off from the fight and signed off from the communications channel.

"Punch it sideways. I want two craft to rip off the main weapons. When that is accomplished, I want a third vessel to fire straight through the side of the cockpit. Rip them apart, but do not hit the cargo bay," Cessil ordered over the speaker.

"Sir, the enemy reinforcements have arrived," the commander to Cessil's left cautioned.

Cessil fired the volleys of the first line of tanks. Three of the carriers toppled, but five of the tanks were destroyed in their fall. "Knock them out, people, and we have half of the fleet out of the way. We appear to be four short of twenty-five," Cessil assessed. "Wait, he is dividing his forces. Okay, he has two wings staying course and one wing dropping back. Then, there is a lone, armed air freighter," said Cessil, pointing to the screens before him. "No. I want four fighter jets to break off from the attack, two to a carrier wing. Intercept and flank the two wings staying course. They are not headed for this shore. The four lagging behind are just backup artillery. We deal with them as necessary." Cessil could not, however, determine the purpose of the lone freighter.

Two fighters peeled off from their entanglements at each end of the melee. Their sleek forms sprayed a laser burst across the carriers' fore sections, and flashed in the sun as they flew off toward their new targets. Five carriers remained flying. Two were still firing their weapons at the ground forces. The tanks were dwindling in numbers with each carrier they toppled.

"Air strike team, remove the artillery. *Screamershield Six*, roll back past your carrier and move out as you fire a shot straight through the drive engine. You have until the shot hits the cargo bay and bounces back harder," Cessil commanded.

The pilot of *Screamershield Six* complied. The shot ripped open the drive engine, impacted inside the cargo bay, and punched a hole back through the vessel on its return trip. The shot tore a hole through the fighter jet, which had not evaded in time. The carrier burst open and exploded. The electromagnetic core stabilizing the ship's movement fired straight into the sky without the added weight.

The cargo fell, clearly visible, to the ground. "They are robots, enormous biosuit robots. I want every one of their air units destroyed but do not hit the cargo. I repeat, air strike unit, do not fire on the cargo. That is what has the shielding. Those unknowns are lined have spherical mirrors housed in intensifying lenses. I have never seen a practical application for it," Cessil puzzled, "but they have it."

"The wing behind is heading for the coast. The altitude remains constant. Weapons systems locking," the commander warned. "Sir, the report confirms it. The weapon has arrived. President Verndestag sends his blessings."

"Well, it is certainly about time. Prepare the launch vessel. I will command it myself. Load the prototypes. I want a status report, and how many times do I have to order one of those things picked up and ripped apart?" Cessil opened the door to the launch bay of the central command station near the battle scene.

"We have less than one-eighth of the tanks, four jets on an intercept course, and two jets in combat. Casualties total at twenty-eight. Enemy cargo is intact. One carrier remains but lacks functional weaponry. Tank artillery has been exhausted. Thirteen enemy carriers remain on approach vector. Twenty-five carriers launched from opposite shore have yet to engage," the German commander reported.

"That could be better, could it not? Have the two remaining jets repeat the stunt with the drive engine on the last active carrier. Make sure they are moving as they fire. Order one jet to rendezvous with each team I already sent to engage the enemy. Hopefully, we can destroy the incoming carriers with one shot. The time to strike is now," Cessil finished.

Across the globe, Blade smiled. "They think they are winning. All units escort and deploy quickly. Go in firing all weapons, including infrasonic," Blade snarled into the communications console of his throne, smiling at the prospect of complete victory.

CHAPTER 41

MARCUS WAS NAUSEOUS. He had been swimming in the fetid fluid for several hours. He was wearing a breathing mask with a tube connected to the side of the clear pool walls. He bobbed to the surface and raised his hand out of the viscous solution to watch it drain away. The liquid was discolored, but Marcus could not determine just how discolored. The small pool was cloudy, too. He rolled his eyes and submerged once more.

Max returned to the room. He brought with him a light tissue scanner that was based on ultrasound. He withdrew a tube of murky solution and an injection. Max lightly pinged the reinforced glass walls of the tank, and Marcus surfaced. Max asked, "Why do I feel like I should throw you a fish?"

"For the same I feel like splashing you with this nasty stuff," Marcus retorted.

"Cheer up. When this is over, you'll be healthier than ever. Your cholesterol may be pretty high, but it'll give you something to work on," Max encouraged. "How is your breathing?"

"Fine, a little accelerated. I feel like I'm going to vomit," Marcus responded through the breathing apparatus.

"Yet another reason why you're wearing a mask. Do you know how much it costs to fill one of these things? Now, if you would please step out of the pool onto the platform," Max asked.

"Leona isn't around is she?" Marcus braced his hands to pull himself onto the platform at the rear of the pool.

"No, she isn't. Even if she was, there's no need for modesty. I've already shown her the scans and pictures of you in here," Max said, smiling widely.

"Very funny. At least I won't turn into a prune in there. I have to get out enough just for tests," Marcus said casually.

"You're right. You can't turn into a prune. That solution is entirely isotonic. It is perfectly compatible with your cells, just the right mix of phospholipids, proteins, nucleic acids, calcium ions, growth hormones, sugars, amino acid subunits, and nutrients to keep your body supplied with the necessary materials for repairs. Oh, and how could I forget the leukocytes? Now, hold still," Max asked. He ran the scanner down Marcus's back. "Okay. Your hand is just fine. The antibiotics and antivirals in the water should prevent infection. Your leg still needs a little longer. All the scrapes and bruises are gone, though. I need to give you one last dose of adrenaline and adenosine triphosphate, almost pure energy to keep your defenses running and repairs going. When you get out of here, I want you to eat everything you can," Max advised.

"Why didn't you ever become a doctor, Max?" Marcus turned to him at this.

Max injected the mixture. "It just didn't interest me. I guess I'm better at building things than fixing them," Max mused. "Now, get back in there or you'll pass out. Just remember, you're going to have great hair when this is over."

"Terrific," Marcus said sardonically as he sank back into the muck once more.

Max left the room and headed for the laboratory. He walked into the darkness, and the lab lit up around him. Everything sprang to life. The familiar control disk hovered towards him. Unexpectedly, a hologram of Stone appeared above the disk.

"Hello, old friend. If you are seeing me, then I must be dead or gone. If so, at least I didn't get you killed with me. I know if the situation was reversed, I would miss you dreadfully. Unless things have changed in the time since I recorded this, say hello to Kylie for me if you ever see her again and tell her I love her, even if it is moot. Max, this lab is yours. Everything I have created here belongs to you now, except one thing," the hologram paused. A case in the lab below opened to reveal a large cylinder. "That," the recording continued, "belongs to Leona. I know she will never accept is as a gift, so she has to pay for it. She has to adopt my dog and maintain that these grounds remain a forest haven. She should not have a problem with that; this house is an arsenal. You are free, Max, but please look after her. She is as close to my heart as a daughter or a sister. She is strong, but she needs someone by her side, too. I have a present for you, too, Max. Let's just see if you can find it. If you cannot, ask EMPulse," Stone's image finished. The hologram faded, and Max saw a personal greeting to him on the main screen.

Max guessed what was inside the cylinder, but he had to see for himself. He opened the casing, and he rested his eyes upon the most beautiful machine he had ever seen. Despite the fact that it shone with a metallic luster, Max realized it was a perfect replica of Leona's lost appendage. It was even crafted to attach precisely where her real body ended.

Max then noticed that the disk had followed him. Max replaced the casing on the cylinder and keyed up a menu. He discovered a curious item called "Maxwire." He keyed for the read only text as a precursor to running the application.

Another hologram of Stone appeared. This image was in the same celestial blue, but this hologram wore full armor regalia. "This program contains a full-depth scan of the semiorganic sections of Maximus Fitzgerald. This program's operation requires Maximus to enter the production chamber, in which the original routes and appearance of his circuitry will be repaired providing damage has occurred. An addendum to this program has been enacted. An authorization code is required to activate the additional application," Stone's hologram faded again.

Max marveled to himself at all the planning and all the organization. Stone knew he would never see peace, but he kept planning and organizing. *It's almost easy to forget he's gone,* Max thought, proceeding to the production chamber to investigate. The shielded doors slid open on a fleet of transport crafts and countless automated tools filling the room. At a rough estimate of the house's geography, Max guessed that the entire chamber was underground.

A mechanical appendage lowered itself from the ceiling. A hologram sprung from the cylinder. Max saw an image of his own left side begin to overlay his true left half. As he instinctively turned, the image turned with him. Sections of the hologram began to outline themselves in green. Circuits in the depths of Max's injuries suddenly glowed red. Tiny prods and repair arms complete with circuit logic probes descended from the same port as the hologram.

"Max, this will go much smoother if you would remain still for a moment," the probe voiced. Max smirked and froze as best he could. Tiny sparks of pain shot through him as the tiny welder joints fixed his broken circuits, some undoing the emergency work Stone himself had done. The charred flesh was removed and replaced with a fresh layer of synthetically created tissue complete with mechanical receptors. Many of the arms withdrew as a second set of probing spikes descended to the green outlines. A glow warmed his unnatural flesh as flexible plates were cut and fitted to his broken body parts. The red and green lights stopped. Max noticed quickly that a single arm remained undescended from the main pod.

"Was that so difficult? You are as good as the day you remade yourself," the voice finished, locking the arms back into the pod.

"Very droll," Max added, flexing each of his semiorganic fingers in turn. He moved his shoulder, and found the sensation acceptable. The feedback remaining would take some time to stabilize. At least they all had a little time to relax without the world crashing down, at least not on them personally.

Max walked out of the lab. He found EMPulse out in the hallway. "How are things outside, Stone? Well, EMPulse? Sorry."

"I will answer to either designation if you wish. The troops outside are holding position. A partially overheard transmission suggests that heavy artillery is approaching. I am unable to determine a specific time," EMPulse answered.

"Can the weapons systems of this residence stop them?" Max glanced down the halls for Leona.

"I cannot determine that without specifications on the artillery. This residence is more than likely capable of stopping all attempts at intrusion," EMPulse speculated in his programming bounds.

"Can we get out if we need to?"

"Stone's private access is heavily secured. The main exit is inadvisable. A return through the tunnels is impossible. Scanning other potential exits. It is unlikely that you could leave at the present time," EMPulse stated.

"Great," Max huffed, returning to Marcus's treatment. He entered the room quickly and shut the door behind him. "EMPulse said the war wagons are on the way. We can't leave, either."

Marcus was sitting on the platform of the pool in the breathing mask. "Max, my mentor is alive, and he's coming for me."

CHAPTER 42

STONE WAS AGAIN going towards the dismal section of the city. This time, his mind was stable. No sudden, strange visions struck him as he walked. He did, however, seem to possess a new, clearer understanding of the era in which he resided at present. His personal experiences living in the time at such a tender age in history were insufficient alone.

He was aware of the chill more than anything, the smooth chill of a summer breeze. Weather, he thought, how fickle. Stone remembered the era he had left. Global cooling had eroded the seasons into a precarious balance of extremes. A long, dry, scorching summer followed a long, cold, bitter winter. He wondered briefly whether man had always been so blissfully ignorant of what his conglomerate role in the planet's course truly meant; no natural phenomena had decimated the seasons.

Stone quietly entered the grocery store, just as quietly silencing all of the surveillance equipment lest a face that does not belong in the era be caught on tape. He cautiously picked up a loaf of bread and a quart of milk. He went to the checkout counter, where he waited in line for the first time since his father took over the country.

"Is that all?" The checkout girl looked at Stone with deep blue eyes, smiling sweetly.

"Yes," Stone said lowly, meeting her gaze with his own cold eyes. Every trace of the young girl's smile faded from her face. In some other time, that may have bothered him, but it was no longer a concern. As he left the store, the only subject on Stone's mind was how sparsely he could eat to make the money last.

Stone walked to the park, and quietly seated himself on a bench. He tore open the milk carton and drank deeply. The cold liquid felt soft to his dry throat. He almost smiled as he wiped away the residue on his upper lip. He paused to look at the area around him.

He saw the last vestige of forest remaining in the city, a few desperate trees reaching relentlessly upward that they may not be smothered. Grand statues lined the park. At one time, Stone knew the name of every person important enough to be carved in these stones. If he wanted to do so, he could remember again, but it was a wasted gesture. The grass and the weeds looked at the castings more than the people passing through the park. One day, the statues would all be broken. Stone did not need his recent prophetic visions to tell him that.

Stone brought a slice of the crumbling bread to his lips. The soft, sweet taste of the white bread filled his mouth. He surprised himself with the sudden Spartan nature of his meals. When once he ate in luxury, he now foraged in poverty. Stone sat on the bench, eating and drinking his fill. He tore the remaining slices of bread and tossed them to the ground, where hungry little birds began converging. He carried the milk with him.

Stone retreated deeper into the park. He leaned against a tree, sipping milk and staring at readouts he allowed to become visible on his glove. He was correct in his calculations; the journey through time after the attack by the electron magnet had shorted several of his systems. The main database, the defensive programming, the cooling system, and the operational programming were all that remained intact. Only two of the remaining holographic generators were functional. Stone knew, though, that even in its weakened state, the armor used against a person in this time would be the equivalent of using an atomic bomb to hunt a deer.

Stone attempted to remove his staff, only to find that the compartment was jammed by the burned hydraulics. He used an armored hand to pry the disagreeable compartment open. He took the collapsed staff from his side. He easily locked the pieces in place and finished his milk. He stood and tossed the empty carton into the air, activated the staff, and swung the weapon a single time through the space in front of him. Two neatly cut pieces of milk carton hit the ground in front of him.

Stone had one stop to make before he began affecting his last chance at victory. Then, he would decide how best to serve the rest of his life.

Perhaps, he thought, *I may yet have an impact on future resistance. Maybe I can see if history stays its course.*

He picked up the dripping remnants of the carton. He proceeded quickly towards the city, effortlessly tossing the carton into a receptacle on his swift course. He finally stopped at a playground he knew only too well. The unknowing children ran and jumped on their merry hour of freedom.

Three in particular caught Stone's eye. A little boy with tan hair in a bright blue shirt and jeans with the knees ripped open limped slightly beside a little girl with flowing hair in a pale red dress tending a skinned elbow. The second little boy stood quietly to the side in his black shirt and jeans, no smile graced his face as it did with the two others. He looked most intently at the last.

He could not hear them. He did not want to hear them. His memory would welcome the scene far better without childish banter. Stone remembered that child; Stone remembered being that child. He thought about the scene before him, pressing his fingers through the chain links of the fence that much harder. He thought about how impressionable that youth was, and how hardened he had become. His merciless father had tempered him into an unwilling, but driven, weapon of war.

That small boy, the only one on the playground not smiling, was losing his childhood. The adult clinging to the fence felt himself losing his own again. Stone knew that he would serve himself best by liberating the boy from his father's custody, but doing so would risk his place in this era and the valuable position in which it placed him.

Stone closed his eyes. The little boy he once was had just accidentally tripped the little boy in the tattered jeans, who in turn pulled the little girl in the red dress down with him. Reopening his eyes, Stone saw what he knew would come next.

The little boy in the tattered jeans, a young Maximus Fitzgerald, put his arm on Stone's tiny shoulder. A smile finally touched the face of the little boy in dark attire and the face of the grown man at the fence. The little girl had her back turned to them both. She would in time forgive the injury. Seven-year-old children had little capacity for hatred, and the young Kylie had not yet grown to despise Stone.

As the piercing bell rang to recall the children to their more studious pursuits, Kylie was already hurrying to reach the two boys. In the haste of returning, a ball was left bouncing behind the children's exodus. Stone released the fence and walked to the gate.

Some unknown force called him inward. He caught the ball in the air as it continued its path away from the school. Stone examined its crude construction, finding significant capacity for air loss and breakage. *Sometimes,* he thought, *you have to look further than the product.*

He bounced the ball experimentally on the asphalt. He caught it again on its return. *Significant energy loss,* Stone judged silently. By all means crude yet preferable to the sticks and rocks children in his era had as toys.

Stone heard the door to the school click behind him. He spun instinctively and placed his hand to the compartment at his side. To his surprise, it was only the small child in torn jeans. Stone smiled at the remembrance of his old friend, his best friend.

The boy looked curiously at the ball and slowly lifted his gaze skyward to peer unsurely at the man. The boy immediately put his hands behind his back and looked again at the ball, twisting his face into a look of concern. Stone relaxed his position. He lowered himself to the boy's height.

On his haunches, Stone turned his hand and extended the ball. The little boy reached forward but hesitated. Stone instead set the ball on the ground, holding it under one finger. "Is this yours?" He examined the little boy's dirt smudged face. The little boy nodded carefully.

Stone handed the ball to the child, smiling at the innocence before him. He usually despised children, but this was different. Stone, looking in near disbelief at the miniature Max, asked, "Thank you?" Max nodded and then walked back towards the school. Stone heard the door open again.

"You're welcome," Max yelled from the door and hurried inside. Stone laughed in spite of himself. He realized then that time was a commodity he could afford for once. He decided to go to the one place where he had been happiest.

CHAPTER 43

"HE'S COMING, MAX, and he's going to change everything we seek to accomplish," Marcus said through the filter mask, adjusted to his present, accelerated body conditions. Every trace of his former composure and knowing calm was gone. Apparently, even stoics had their limits.

"I thought that your powers faded in and out. Even real psychics and prophets aren't right all the time," Max said, hoping to lower the other's heart palpitations with reason over sedation. Marcus's body was spiking in blood pressure and heart rate. If the respective levels rose any more, Marcus would flatline.

"No. These visions, these concrete, real thoughts are just getting clearer and stronger," Marcus insisted.

"Calm down right now or have a heart attack," Max interrupted. Such a blunt statement towards anyone else would have bred a reaction opposite of what was intended. Marcus was another case. "These tanks and the necessary injections are intended for a calm person. Meditate or something. Any sudden fear, surprise, or anger while you're under that kind of duress is deadly. I'm not even going to scan you. Get back in the tank. You can get out in about ten minutes."

Marcus obeyed without question. He plunged back into the temperate, foul mixture. He took a heavy breath through the independent air filter, silently willing his body back into a relaxed state. He purged the horrible image that had inspired the panic in the first place. He tried to draw up his patience. Marcus was a finely tuned living machine. His emotions were filed away. A map of his own body always flashed on the screen of his mind. His will was the programmer. "At least now I know how I smell on the inside," he sighed. He concentrated his efforts on healing his leg above all else. Imperceptibly, his body obeyed, sending just that much more blood into his battered appendage.

When Max returned later, he found Marcus sitting still below the water's surface. The overhead monitor showed the return of normal vital signs. The adrenaline coursing through his veins had slacked off in its intensity. Most of it had been consumed by sheer force of will. The vital status of the patient soon read acceptable, and Max released him.

"I'm leaving," Marcus said flatly. "I have to find him before he finds us."

"If you don't?"

"Then we all die here in this house," Marcus said, entering the cleansing chamber within the room. "Then the world falls, hard."

"Your mentor is responsible for this stuff?" Max pressed the button for the polar solution wash.

"I don't know that yet."

"What are Leona and I supposed to do until you get back?" Max keyed for the non-polar cleansing.

"Live. I may not be coming back for a very long time, if at all," Marcus said unsurely, looking down at the floor below him.

"Oh." Silence filled the room then. Marcus left the chamber, collected his clothing, and dressed quickly. He then stormed out the door, leaving Max alone in the chamber. As the door hissed shut, Max wondered if Marcus had lost his mind.

Marcus found EMPulse almost immediately. "Unlock Stone's private entrance," Marcus demanded.

"I am unable to do that," EMPulse answered.

"Do it or I will turn your real parts into scrap," Marcus threatened through clenched teeth.

"I feel no emotion. Your threat means very little to me. Remember, though, that I do possess the capacity to destroy you."

"I forget myself, construct. Do you have access to Stone's private entrance?" Marcus visibly relaxed, but the tone of immediacy remained in his voice.

"No. Stone's private files are inaccessible to me at present."

"Max." Marcus turned and caught the geneticist as he left the chamber housing the nutrient pool. Max approached the solemn pair curiously. The look in Marcus's eyes was enough to merit caution at least. "You have to give EMPulse acccss to Stone's personal files."

"It'll take time. Can I ask why?"

"Time is something we cannot afford, and I already told you why," Marcus said sternly, turning an icy glare on Max. Pain flared inside Max's skull.

"Fine. I'll get started now, Master," Max said, feigning a submissive bow.

The soldiers outside were getting worried. They had been deployed to repel an attack on the home of their ruler's son. Aside from a minor disturbance, there was no indication that a force warranting such a battalion was arriving. As far as any of them knew, a lone agent had gone rogue, fired on his comrades, and disappeared. It was becoming ordinary in the ranks, especially as a soldier neared retirement.

The commander ordered a search of the surrounding woods. All of the patrols had returned except for one, and each had turned up empty handed. The missing patrol consisted of two men, one of whom had his head broken open against a tree. The other had found something promising: a tiny plate of metal visible beneath a rift in the dirt.

Unbeknownst to him, a tiny spider had crawled onto his boot. As its tiny metal legs clambered diligently towards the man's chest, a reaction was taking place in its soft abdomen. The soldier continued to clear away the dirt from that area. The only warning of what was to come was a barely visible light switching from green to red. The soldier casually swatted the arachnid clinging to his chest. At the instant of impact, a concentrated explosion reduced the soldier, and his passenger, to vapor and dust. In the place where the soldier had stood and cleared away the ground, a hologram of foliage grew over the burnt grass and exposed metal.

Max had deduced that the unlit corridor near the training room was the central processor for the vast operating system running throughout the house. He had already hotwired several of the connections through a small monitor to determine the transmission codes. As he was carefully disassembling another circuit, he saw an image of a spider appear on the output monitor. Reading the file on the Defense Plastique Arachnid, Max realized it was guarding an entrance, a private entrance. Tracing the connection back to its source, he disengaged several wires near the spider output line and ran them through the display. As he made the final connection, the power dimmed and came back. The lights in the holographic arena went out completely. In the center of the arena, he saw a glowing blue image of Stone. Max was at first frightened until he realized it was a recording.

"Today I have seen it," Stone's image said, "the worst scenario imaginable. The weapon my father now has in his possession is the realization of the nightmare everyone must at some point face: the decimation of our society. With only a handful of these remotely operated death machines, my father could kill the planet. That is why I must act soon, for this is the coming of my past sins to haunt me. After all, I designed them for him."

The recording abruptly terminated. A shiver ran down Max's spine, resulting from both the words of the recording and the fact that he had violated the inner world of one of the most introverted people in history, his best friend. Max sighed slowly before continuing. He knew the recording was never meant for him, but its contents struck him with a force that reverberated through everything he knew.

Max checked the log's date and dropped the monitor. It had been recorded only two days prior to the destruction of Max's lab. These weapons Stone had designed would be deployed soon, probably very soon. However, Marcus's growing animosity towards the group felt like the more pressing problem. These files merited at least reluctant viewing later, though.

Within the hour, Marcus was standing on the hydraulic platform that would lift him to the surface forty feet from the edge of the residence. Max had temporarily disengaged the spiders and the laser grids. The cover plate lifted and Marcus climbed out onto the dirt. As Marcus stood, the lift returned and the cover plate resealed the entrance. He had twenty seconds until the defenses re-engaged themselves.

The soldiers took notice immediately. Marcus was greeted with a volley of fire. Fortunately, he had enough adrenaline left to escape. Unfortunately, he did not get far enough away. A warrior from an era long past surfaced in his path. The soldiers behind Marcus suddenly stopped. Blood filled their helmets as their hearts exploded simultaneously.

"You," Marcus whispered, panting as he was forcibly halted. The unrobed figure before him just smiled, a strange glow coming over his black irises.

Marcus's eyes rolled to the back of his head, and he fell hard to the ground. He was unconscious. "They make it so easy. Marcus, I did expect more resistance out of you," the warrior smiled. He grabbed the monk by the arm and waist and dragged him off, leaving the eight dead soldiers where they fell.

CHAPTER 44

"TELL ME WHAT we have, general," Cessil said to the monitor in front of him on the bridge of the German *Rache*-class launch vehicle, the *Harpoon Runner*.

"Sir, as far as we can tell, these robots are a weapon from the inside out. We have only been able to penetrate the outer twenty-five percent of the one we have in possession. It took high impact weaponry at extremely close range to even crack the outer covering. We had to work it like a crab shell from there. The bad news is that this thing functions in levels. If you destroy one level, the next kicks in. We surmise that you have to keep hammering it until you destroy the innermost core. The worse news is that there is a new weapon at every level, and most of the old ones would probably still function. We are down to hammers and screwdrivers, Sir. It repels energy weapons, and each new level gets harder to break. We have one arm off and one additional, prehensile appendage disconnected," the officer reported.

"Interesting. What about a high incendiary between the levels? Could that blow it apart or at least stop the inner core from taking over?"

"Honestly, President Chirac, I do not know. We have not gone for destruction, only surgical disassembly. Do you want us to try it?"

Cessil paused a moment. "No, but plant an explosive deep in its core. These things will activate soon. When that one gets up, blow it to pieces."

Far above, just outside the boundaries of the life-giving atmosphere, another invasion began. A metallic cylinder with a dozen different antennae started to change. Its silvery wings spread to both sides as the tiny fingers of probes and signal receivers stretched forth. All around the object, identical changes were taking place in its counterparts, each held fast in the relentless grip of Earth's gravity.

Intermingled with the active objects were the remnants of a past era. Military payloads, ancient satellites, and two aging space stations were slowly decomposing under the continual bombardment of the lightless void. None of the relics functioned, Blade had seen to that, but they were in the way.

Each cylinder of the large intruders began to turn. On the nearest satellite, a single, glowing violet dot appeared. Within a second, an invisible, destructive laser had reduced the satellite to the slag it virtually was. The other intruders were doing the same. The silence of space saw only the muted explosions marking the end of all the useful benefits the Cold War had yielded. The broken space stations released their bottled atmosphere in unvoiced anguish. Once the rain of shrapnel exhausted itself in reentry, only the network of cylinders remained.

Blade smiled as he watched his glinting satellites come to life after two years of dormancy, waiting for this day. As the offensive military satellites aligned to form a solid network of relays, a slight touch of a button sent the same destructive laser force down on the heart of Moscow. Though the beam lost considerable energy punching through the atmosphere, the shot made an effective demonstration of reducing the Kremlin to rubble.

In the midst of the land battle, the *Harpoon Runner* roared forth under the watchful leadership of President Cessil Chirac. As it neared the shore where the battle was about to restart, Cessil called for a weapons report. He was satisfied with the craft's capabilities. He smiled grimly as he issued his orders. Arctic Fire was about to be deployed.

The four reinforcement carriers neared the beach, their weapons systems already brought to bear on the forces of resistance. Cessil stood from his console and uttered the single word that would do his bidding: "Now."

"Set detonation for proximity," Rowan ordered from the haven of the impromptu fortress outside the engagement zone. "And fire two shots in the center of their formation, one direct and the other leading."

Cessil nodded his approval at the hologram, and his subordinates responded immediately. The two imperfect spheres screamed from their separate launch tubes, venting external thrust. The first shot fell behind the target carrier wing, but the leading shot found its mark. In unison, tiny sparks broke through both spheres, and the energy being sucked inside was nearly visible. A growing ball of ice replaced the air and caught the four carriers in their individual attempts at escape. The blast radius was so large that it formed a temporary support of ice holding the frozen crafts above the sandy shore.

"Anyone feel like crushed ice?" Cessil turned to look at the commander that had spoken the question.

"Very much so. Give them a high impact where the sun does not shine," Cessil responded. The commander acknowledged and targeted the lead craft.

The blast was true, and the frozen pieces of molded metal fell away like sand. The lighter pieces caught and suspended themselves in the waves. The cargo, Cessil noticed, was still intact; however, he was sure no hydraulics would ever be activated within the machines again. Cessil was still not one to take unnecessary risks. "Send one after them, depth cued, to net our cargo."

The launch vessel complied. Then, *Harpoon Runner* shook from an impact. It was something like being punched in the jaw. The cylindrical satellites far above were now broadcasting a very dense signal to four hundred separate points on two coasts of Eurasia. Soldiers wired with expensive sensor packages immersed in remote translation tanks controlled that signal from across the globe. Thirty-two of those soldiers were about to find that their units were not responding. Their Deathunter drones rested at the bottom of a frozen stretch of sea. One of the soldiers had already taken the initiative to attack the weapon's launch vehicle.

Blade was furious. The leaders had fed him with false information in their most secret meeting place. A wing of his fleet and its invaluable cargo had been completely destroyed by an extreme scale chemical reaction like that in an ordinary cold pack. Blade had presumed incorrectly that he was the one with the superior weaponry.

"Sir," an officer next to Cessil shouted. "We have taken a massive hit. Our rear turrets are destroyed, and our reserve engines have gone offline." Out the viewport beside the diagnostics technician, the culprit was clearly visible: a twenty foot mechanical beast with a near featureless head mounted on its chest. Its forearm swung back on the double support pendulum of its upper arm, preparing for another punch. Cessil watched helplessly as the creature's forearm, dangling from those two support struts, rammed his vessel again.

"Weapons options," Cessil shouted over the nearly unbearable impact.

"Two forward cutting lasers and the Arctic Fire launch tubes are the only things I can bring up," someone yelled.

"Cut a path under its feet if you can. Trip it if possible. Put a high impact missile in one of the launch tubes. Set it for impact detonation, and fire immediately after that thing punches us again, any sooner and that thing goes off in the chute. Any later and we will not be around to fire it at all."

What felt like ages passed. A new voice shouted something unheard. Cessil heard another voice shout "ready." The crushing impact came. The shot fired and the hastily cut laser trench caught the mechanized attacker as it staggered, basically unhurt, from the shot. The behemoth fell, and it fired its main energy weapons in frustration as it struggled to get up.

Harpoon Runner was a lost cause. Cessil instructed the remaining crew to seek refuge, and, after he had covered their escape with the *Harpoon Runner*'s laser, he deployed the two man fighter craft above the front viewport. Its weapons were limited, but, without a gunner, that was a moot point. As the engines fired behind him, Cessil heard a sigh of relief expel from his own lungs.

The fighter roared above the battle, or, more accurately, the slaughter. All of the tanks, manned and unmanned alike, were mere wreckage. Cessil had no word on the Screamershield fighters, but he could guess a similar scenario had played over them, as well. For the first time, Cessil was fleeing a battle.

CHAPTER 45

MARCUS FELT THE unkind slap across his face before he heard the voice. "Wake up, Marcus." In his semi-conscious state, his mind played tricks on him. He at first believed it to be Max, rousing him from a hit to the head. Maybe it was EMPulse, who knew no other kindness, waking him from his slumber. Unfortunately, when Marcus opened his eyes, his nightmare got worse.

"About time. I thought you were stronger than that," Marcus heard in a voice that could best be described as rusty. "I taught you to be stronger than that."

As Marcus's eyes regained vision, he saw his mentor before him. "You." It was not a question or a mere statement. In his state, it was just a word. His mentor was stripped of his usual robes and cloaks. Marcus could see the man's muscled body through his tight black uniform. His usual shoulder adornment was present, but his jet black hair was visible then, ceremoniously pulled back into a ponytail. He had a set of metal knuckles overlaying his right hand. Both of his boots were constructed of a material resembling a slick, painted iron. A gold belt with several solid pouches completed the outfit. A longsword sat poised in its scabbard at his hip.

"Yes, and I taught you better manners for greeting your superiors." Another hard slap struck Marcus's face. This one mercifully came from the man's ungloved hand.

"Thought you would be," Marcus paused, "coming ... for me." Marcus struggled to speak. "How did ... you ... find me?"

"I know you" was the only response Marcus got.

As his thinking became clearer, Marcus found the reason for his labored breathing; iron bands held his hands, feet, and chest upright against the wall. "It was you ... in Stone's ... house ... and my ... house. You're Robert." This time, a gruesome smile was his only answer. Marcus became increasingly aware of the flickering golden light around him. The lights danced across his mentor, encircling him in an unnatural glow. "What do you ... want?" Marcus slumped to inhale sharply after his last word.

"Gratitude to begin with. I saved your life."

Marcus was about to lash out with a comment about the man abandoning him in battle, but Marcus was not in a position of strength. It served best to bide his time. He inhaled with increasing difficulty.

"I flushed you out of hiding and gave Blade everything I had on his son so that you would survive the encounter," Marcus's mentor said.

"I ... beat them ... on ... my ... own," Marcus coughed.

"Had you faced Blade, you would have died," his mentor asserted. "None of your pupil's parlor tricks from the sidelines could have saved you from an electron magnet. The whole challenge was a trap from the beginning."

"Stone didn't ... die."

"No, quite truly he didn't, but Stone is a very rare breed of man. More on that later. Any other questions, pup?"

"What ... do you ... want?" Another slap hit Marcus's face with the cold metal ringing in his ears. "What ... happened to you?"

"Nothing happened to me. I have always been this. Your mentor 'Drake' was one of a hundred personas I needed to adopt over these long years. Erik was corruptible. He was easily persuaded to play his part in my exit from that particular stage. What I want is for you to realize your true potential. The seed I have planted in you is on the verge of blossoming into a very powerful fruit, one of global importance."

"What ... seed?"

"You are not only my pupil, you are my son."

Marcus did not respond. He had never been told who his parents were; he was simply part of the order of monks, born and raised in community. It was also a good possibility that Marcus was too dazed to care at that point.

Marcus's father walked around to the side of him, forcing him to endure his neck muscles rippling against the metal clasps. "What do you know of magic?"

"In all senses ... it died ... long ago," Marcus wheezed.

"Yes, and I am its last product. You see, magic is a by-product of creation, Divine creation. Its wielders passed out of existence when the world found a new balance, but before it was completely gone, I was created."

With effort, Marcus snorted. "You are ... Divine?" Another ferocious slap tore open his cheek.

"Don't mock me; I'll show you," the man said, pulling the sword to Marcus's chest. He did not draw blood as Marcus expected, he instead cut his own forearm off at the elbow. It was a ghastly site with jagged tears through the visible bone and blood gushing forth as though from a red river. The man's sneer of pain did not go unnoticed.

"You're insane," Marcus said in revulsion.

Then, the impossible happened. The blood began collecting as mercury would. The lost limb melted in layers into the pool, and the entire mass turned the color of flesh. A single, thin tendril leapt from the pool to the previously bleeding elbow. The mass poured through the mystical channel, and the man's arm reformed. He flexed his fingers, and he was whole again.

Marcus knew he had to be dreaming. No one had such power. No mortal had any right to it.

"Immortal. Impervious and functional. Though I may tend to suffer the separation of anyone else, my limbs come back. Even from the guillotine, which is very painful I assure you. I have been alive since the first Crusades. Magic made me this way. I am blessed and cursed to walk as a mortal man until God ends time. There are of course other stipulations, but they are not important at the moment. Some of what I am is in you."

Marcus was forced to meet the man's eyes. Only then did Marcus notice his mentor's, his father's black irises. It appeared as though the pupils had engulfed the color. Suddenly, the restraints on all parts of Marcus broke, spraying rivets and clanking metal to the floor. Marcus fell with it.

As he heaved and sighed on the floor, his mentor paced circles around him. "Unfortunately," his mentor said, "you can die. Thank your mother for that one. You can still be of use to me, though. You see, never before have I been so close to a seat of power atop the world.

I tried to stay hidden before now, keeping to the shadows and watching. Call it old age, but I want my position of power."

"What is your real name?" Marcus gasped air into his weary lungs after the question finished.

"I am Sir Robert of York, knighted by the king himself. I even got to meet the Pope."

"Why do you need me?" The immortal's boot ground Marcus's chest to the floor.

"Every father should know his son. Besides, you have potential no one else in the world has."

Marcus rolled over, heaved his back from the floor, grabbed his father's boot, and twisted him to the floor alongside Marcus himself. Before he was even aware of what he was doing, Marcus had the sword at the immortal's throat.

"Good. Self-preservation has become its own entity in you. Foreseen, but very good. You know, that won't do a thing to me. I've lost my head before."

"Where are we?"

Robert grabbed the blade of the sword, slicing his palm wide open, and twisted it out of his son's grasp. With one fluid motion, he was up and pointing the sword at Marcus's heart. Marcus watched the cuts heal with the odd liquid flesh taking on its own life. "It is none of your concern, yet." Robert threw his son back to the ground and set his boot on his son's windpipe.

"Do you have any heart?"

"Yes, in some manner but the trouble, I have been told, is that my soul is gone, judged and sentenced all those years ago. Do you honestly think I would do all of this, though, if I were just going to kill you?"

Marcus watched the golden light swirl around the room from his place on the floor. "No."

"Now you're thinking, but make no mistake, I will take your life if necessary. Now, get up."

Marcus complied. He saw the source of the flickering lights. They were rays of the sun passing through the open spaces of the walls. From the pattern, Marcus reasoned that they were standing on a moving transport.

"Skyrail. Old but still useful," Robert responded at seeing his son read the situation. With that, Marcus kicked his father through the grating that had held him captive.

Marcus turned and pulled himself up to the driver's level. This particular train was following a prearranged course, and Marcus could not change that lest he strand himself skybound in a vessel at some unknown height. His sense of danger had lessened, and he lay facing the sky on the deck of the creaking cargo hauler.

Robert lied on the track, the bottom of the track. His legs and back were broken, and he had been cut thoroughly on the way down. Some of the injuries had come from his own sword. He smiled, thinking he would die again in a few minutes. He thought about how funny it was that pain never lost its intensity. He thought, as he always did before he died, of his wife so long ago. She was the only wife he had ever had, and he had lost her of his own arrogance. At least he had a son now, someone he could care about for a while at least. Fate had already decreed, though, that everyone he loved would grow to hate him. Then, his thoughts faded to black as he barely restrained his scream at the anguish of rebirth.

CHAPTER 46

"CRAP" WAS THE only word Max found appropriate to the situation. Stone's mansion was being pounded by a Barriercrusher tank. It was similar to a Landskimmer, but it was specially outfitted siege weapon for direct ramming. Wrecker missiles were slowly eating away at the face of the residence between straight assaults from the thundering ram's bombardment.

"You can say that again," Leona whispered from behind him.

"EMPulse, bring all weapons to bear on those four tanks," Max ordered.

Instead of giving a human nod, EMPulse recited the available weapons list. Instantly, a barrage of high incendiary drop missiles unloaded on the tanks. Five laser batteries joined the campaign, two targeting the tanks' wrecker missile salvos.

Suddenly, one of the windows before the trio exploded inward. A barrage of expended Rioter fire followed the supposedly shatterproof glass. Max pushed Leona out of the way. The lady rolled gracefully to the side, but Max hit hard from three shots to his back. One grazed his flesh with only surface damage. The other two went straight through his semiorganics, leaving two fist-sized holes at his thigh and side. Max was also dimly aware that his artificial eye was no longer functioning.

Leona's metal hand was locked in an unnatural position. Max was barely aware of an explosion on EMPulse. Its right hand sparked and pinged against the ground in a burning spatter of metal scraps. The clang of the staff followed.

Max yelled over the confusion, "EMPulse, you still there?"

"Yes, I am. My hand is unresponsive."

"Make a stand," Max spat. "Warn them not to mess with this place. Angle your projection so you can't be shot again."

EMPulse obeyed. He appeared brazenly in the broken window. "Desist. This struggle is futile. Cease or you will be destroyed." The answer offered by the soldiers came in the next round of fire and the battering of the door. Apparently, word had leaked about the events at the Neo-Colosseum. As warned, the house systems responded and the power went dim. The surgical laser batteries sprang to renewed, intensified life.

One shot gutted the Barriercrusher. Another dismembered an assemblage of soldiers. The third ripped open the local carrier hovering at the window height and leveling the sonic weapon that tore open the glass. The propeller pod of the latter lodged itself in the face of the complex as the vehicle exploded. The remaining soldiers fled from the lessening laser fire.

Max requested assistance in standing. EMPulse unceremoniously lifted Max to his feet using the hole in his torso. Max screamed in pain and stumbled on uncertain legs. He caught himself against the wall and limped over to Leona. He checked her for a pulse and the breath of life. Once satisfied, he hefted her to his shoulder, feeling the warmth of her against him.

Max struggled with the steps, attempting to reach the lab before the second wave of tanks arrived.

Max laid her down on the lab floor. He commanded EMPulse to continue the barrage against the soldiers. He saw that Leona's arm was crushed and sparking. Max grabbed the small box that Stone had added to the model, and he fell hard. "EMPulse," Max whispered through the feedback in his left arm, "heart." The construct came quickly and pulled Max away.

When Max awoke beneath the descending repair pod, EMPulse was standing over him. Leona was crouched at his side, her real arm supporting her on the other side of his waist. Her artificial arm had been removed to the base connection socket. Max began to sit up and noticed that his left eye was blinking in and out. The feedback still coursed through him.

"What's going on?" Max stammered, scraping dried blood from his lips.

"We are under bombardment once more. The power exertion is too great to continue the laser response. You both must leave. The compromise of this structure is inevitable. Terminal program engaged. Presence: Maximus Fitzgerald. Encrypted document code: you have items being prepared for you at present. Presence: Leona Ramses. You have a payment being prepared," the EMPulse construct proclaimed.

"Payment? I don't want payment," Leona began.

"Just go along with it. I'll explain later. I think we've lost the EMPulse program. We're on direct interface now," Max interrupted.

"This construct must engage in further defense. You may exit from the lab sublevel. This construct shall hold out for as long as possible. You are advised by the operating system of this residence to vacate immediately," EMPulse stated more flatly than usual.

"You'll die," Leona pleaded.

"This construct cannot die. It does not live. Destruction is inevitable; it has been inevitable since this construct was created. I must engage front line defense. Terminal program upload complete. Executing. Engaged."

"Goodbye," Leona whispered.

"Bye, EMPulse," Max added sorrowfully.

"Goodbye." The reply was simply that, a preprogrammed response at the base interface level where the lower level language was in charge. EMPulse spun his, its, staff and charged forward to the exit.

Max grabbed the cylinder he remembered from the lab. A box descended form a mobile arm in the ceiling. "Leona, if I don't live through all of this, I just want you to know … I just have to tell you … you are the most beautiful girl, woman, I have ever seen in my life," Max stammered. Leona did not say anything, and Max could not bring himself to look at her. He just grabbed the cylinder and the box and turned to leave.

"Max, I'm at a loss here. I can't fight at all like this. Where are we going?"

Max laughed lightly. "You know Stone. Who knows where we'll end up," Max said, still avoiding her eyes. The pair entered the lowest chamber of the lab. Holograms of everything Stone had ever designed lit the walls. A wireframe hologram of Stone's massive armor pervaded the center of the room. Eerily, it looked up at them and pointed down. "This way. Now," EMPulse demanded from the hologram. Beneath the hologram was a shaft with hand rungs. Max went first to catch Leona if she fell. He felt the pain of his stitched side as he lowered himself down the first few feet. Refreshingly, the tunnel was lit thoroughly, and the pair proceeded along a predetermined course.

The image of Stone walked brazenly out the front door. The two Barriercrusher tanks that arrived to reinforce the attack ceased their fire temporarily. Stone raised his bladed staff, and a full surge of laser fire ripped through the command pod of the left tank. The soldiers did not respond. Some were too confused. Some were waiting with their Rioters trained on Stone's helmeted head.

One soldier, the highest ranking officer present, approached Stone with his hand raised to stay any fire. Stone cut him in half the long way and was answered by an immediate barrage of expended ammunition from all sides. The gutted Barriercrusher exploded and vented debris from every pore in its frame. The other launched four wrecker missiles.

Stone planted his staff in the ground and kneeled down to it. The missiles struck. The explosion was deafening. When the smoke cleared, only the staff remained in the crater, surrounded by small metal shards. The soldiers approached slowly. The staff blade began to glow. The glow grew brighter until an uncertain, breaking wave of electromagnetic energy seared through the air. The soldiers were thrown lifelessly from their feet, burning from the fusing of their armor to their skin. The Barriercrusher died abruptly. The lights of the residence went dark.

The lights in the tunnel browned out several times. When they surged fully back into existence, Max guessed that EMPulse was gone, along with Stone's entire database. When they reached a branched chamber at the end of the tunnel, Max leaned against the wall and slid to rest at the floor. "Come here, and I'll take a look at that arm," he sighed.

"It won't do much good. EMPulse had to remove the bionic enhancement. The circuitry was burned out and broken at the elbow. It's not like we have a replacement, either."

"Yes," Max said grinning, "we do." Max popped open the outer casing of the cylinder containing the arm Stone had constructed. Max struggled to break the glass casing, and the hiss of air when he succeeded told him it was vacuum sealed. "Good sterile conditions," he whispered. Leona kneeled down to him. "This is for adopting Desyree. You aren't going to argue, are you?" Max eyed her curiously. Leona shook her head. "Good, now let's get started." Max cleaned the connection circuits on Leona's shoulder. "Wire splicer. Damn." Max searched the canister and the box, finding only a duplicate of the box Stone had placed on Leona's original arm. His left arm jerked suddenly, and he nearly fainted at the feedback when a rotating toolbar shot through his wrist.

CHAPTER 47

"WHY?" THE WORD was screamed. Piercing and thundering, the word was screamed over and over again. Stone ignited the blade of his staff and cut an enormous swath through the sand, burning and scarring the beach. His journey to this place had been swift by the standards of the age, less so by the standards of his own. He traveled in full armor, reading infrared at night. He had arrived five minutes ago, relying on the sleep he had before his departure only. The night was closer to dawn than dusk. He was alone with the waves.

Stone stepped into the surf and collapsed on his knees into the waves. "Why?" Tears streamed down his face. He clutched his cross with his armored palm. "Why, Lord, why?" Stone hefted himself with the staff and collapsed onto his rear. The tears came harder then.

"Why did you take her away from me? I loved her, Lord. I love her. God in Heaven, please, get me through this. You are timeless. You know what will transpire. If I can accomplish what I came here for, please take me to see her. When I am finished here, my life will be accomplished. Please, God I need her. I need her. Please, lest you force me to lose a battle with the tides, and I will, my God," Stone cried.

Stone blacked out from exhaustion. The flood of futures and pasts returned in his slumber. He knew this beach. This was his beach. It was not his in ownership, but it was his in belonging. The few happy times of his childhood were spent here at this beach. As soon as he could get away, he would come there. He would collapse, rest, on the beach. The surf would eventually reach his ankles, and the world was peaceful for those few scant hours.

He remembered the waves, the roaring ocean relentlessly pounding the shore. He took in every sunrise he could, as though he could possess it in witnessing enough of them. The brilliant colors blazing across the sky implanted their power in Stone's brain. To him, the beach was the fringe, where the world fought its most valiant war to stay above the seas. Stone knew the taxing fight to stay on top better than most, so he belonged here.

The swirl of time recollected into a nosebleed. Stone's helmet was off. He found himself still holding the cross and his staff. His vision was unsteady. The energy adjustments throughout his body were a tremendous strain. His left arm went numb as he moved it towards his nose. The pain in his head increased.

When Stone came back around, he rinsed his face in the surf. He backed away and shed the torso of his armor. He raised his arms to the sky and begged relief. The hours of the morning fled into sunlight. The sun burst out, in all of its brilliance, from the waves.

A broken heart found a reason to go on for one more day. Carefully constructed armor found a willing host. A weapon of destruction found an able master. A wooden cross found an ample bearer. The salty air found calmed lungs. The soft, moist sands found a new, determined set of footprints. Stone was whole again, and no one noticed the robed figure, who observed the entire scene, standing where the nearby air seemed to shimmer purple.

CHAPTER 48

THE LIGHTS IN the Neo-Colosseum combat arena were dim. Only the center had illumination. In that light stood an enslaved man holding a large sword and looking frantically around him. The doors slid closed and automated locks cried shut.

"The silence is nice, isn't it?" The voice was eerily pleasing to the ear. "Relax, you're free for the rest of your life. So, how do you like your accommodations? Be honest, I can take it."

With unexpected vitality and speed, the response flew forth in echoing resonance. "I hate them. You use us to build just because we are unfit to fill a higher corporate position, and then you discard us with the biggest weapon you are testing when we cannot work any longer. We live in cages. We starve and die and breed at your whim. I hate you," the lower class man spat.

"Good. You have spirit. I like spirit. It's so fun to break," Blade said. "I'll show you something. It's a sight most people never get to see." The lights above the throne rose to reveal Blade inside his impressive battle armor. The seams of his armor clicked, and every piece of it fell to the floor. Beneath the suit was a man with very impressive musculature wearing a deep red suit with a gold sash and a chest plate with several empty socket connections and a holographic generator. Blade knelt to the pile and rose with a large hydraulic sword, the one with the strong chain at the hilt.

Blade snapped his fingers, and all of the lights in the arena rose. It was empty except for the two men. "Just to show you it's fair."

"If I am free, I can leave."

"You're not that free," Blade said, leaping nimbly to the arena floor. The clang of his boots resounded. The lights died. "Are you afraid?"

The voice came from the deepest shadows of the room. "Do you want to live? You can, you know. Just defeat me." The lights flickered on and off again.

The enslaved citizen listened and looked, his senses giving him almost nothing. The man panicked, swung his weapon, and struck the ground uselessly. The attack seemed to come from three places at once. "That is why I am feared," he heard. Then his life passed out of existence.

"Now, I truly have better things to kill. If you will excuse me." Blade's echoing laughter and the clank of armor pieces being replaced were the only sounds in the room.

Twenty years prior, Stone stopped on his trek back along the roads. He felt dizzy, but it was not the same as before. He checked his nose for the telltale sign of a quick flash outside of time. This time there was no blood. Instead, a bright blue haze filled his vision, and he was not standing in that spot anymore. His mind was no longer confined, and it decided to take a field trip.

He heard shouts in a small room. There were two doctors frantically rummaging through containers and tools. Their gloves were bloodied. "The Caesarean got the child out, but she's hemorrhaging." One of the doctors left the room. A nurse bundled a newborn in her arms. The door shut behind the second doctor.

"Let me see him, please," the woman begged weakly. The nurse walked slowly to the woman's bedside. The woman, beautiful in spite of the pain twisting her face, reached out with two bloody hands for the tender bundle in the nurse's arms. The woman's cheeks were soaked in tears. Her forehead was smeared with the blood on her hands. Her deep-hued brown eyes were glassed over and red. Her flowing brown hair was somewhat matted to the pillow with sweat. Somehow, she still had a glow about her. Her arms were gentle in their embrace, and her cargo was quiet. The newborn's eyes met his mother's.

"I love you. Know that always. I love you, my son," she said, cradling the tiny boy at her shoulder, letting her tears soak the blanket that wrapped him. "I love you, Baby. I love you."

Then her embrace slackened, and the child began to cry. The glow left her then. Outside the door, a horror stricken man pressed himself against the glass window. His painful tears burned their way down his right cheek like fire. He pounded a fist against the frame in futility.

"Sir, there was nothing we could do," one of the doctors apologized.

"God, no," the man whispered. His face went very pale.

"At least we saved your son, Sir. You have a baby boy," the other doctor offered.

"But I had a wife," the man said.

Stone's mind returned to him then. The blue haze passed from his vision. This time, he did not even stumble. He just pressed his weight down against his staff and stepped forward with his right foot.

"I love you, too, Mom. Please take care of Kylie for me. I'll be seeing you both soon, one way or another," Stone said to the sky. "One way or another," he sighed and pressed forward.

"Well," Blade began twenty years from then, "how is it proceeding?"

"Sir, thirty-two of the Deathunter units are dead in the water, literally. Five are buried under a broken cliff on the opposite engagement site. Eight are trudging along the sea bed to shore. One is barely receiving a signal. Some of its systems are severely damaged. Sixteen have yet to engage the shore, but the rest are fully functional. We have already crippled the front line defenses on both coasts, though Chirac escaped as an oversight," the general reported.

"Forty-six units out of the fight already. Sixteen waiting. The Vault should be commended for this accomplishment. They did not fail completely within the first six hours as they usually do," Blade spat.

"Sir, this was waiting for you. You would have had it sooner, but you silenced communications," the lieutenant said, handing him a holographic generator.

"Good. I would have been here sooner, but I was checking my public approval rating," Blade said with a haunting smile.

CHAPTER 49

"THAT TINKERING BASTARD," Max laughed through the agony. "Like I didn't have enough circuits in my body already." He flexed the tools on his new wrist extension. "They override my fingers, too. Oh, well, I guess it serves the purpose now. I hope the feedback isn't permanent, though. Maybe I can fix my eye while I'm at it, huh?"

Max pulled the artificial arm out of its wrappings and set the temporary locks on Leona's empty shoulder socket. "This may hurt a little bit, but it'll get easier. I'm telling you from experience," Max said, perpetually smiling.

Max pensively tested his joint coupler against the wall. A quick flash of brilliant purple sparked from the device. "It seems to work okay. What do you say?"

"Go ahead. I need an arm," Leona said, smiling nervously.

"I'll be gentle, I promise," Max smirked.

"I know this isn't your first time," Leona said laughing.

"With this appendage it is." At this, they both allowed the tension to lighten in laughter. Max spliced the wires and sealed the joints of Leona's arm. He was only mildly frustrated when her thumb did not work and he had to redo twenty-three connections. The job was finally finished, and Max was proud of the near seamless integration to Leona's old grafting.

Max ordered Leona to keep her arm still while her body adjusted to the new circuitry. Max had to try twice to retract the rotating toolbar he had sticking out of his wrist, each time learning what movement impulses started which tools. Then he found the tiny control box dangling from the main column.

"This is going to hurt," he said as he pressed the three prongs of the control box into the back of his semiorganic hand. "Yeah, I was right," he yelled. Satisfied that it was connected, he pressed the extraction button, and he was pleasantly surprised when the tools emerged painlessly, expanding from their collapsed position where his ulna should be and locking into a usable setup. He retracted the device and walked up to Leona.

Max inquired, "How's the arm?"

"I could ask you the same question, but mine appears to be working fine. I'm nauseous, though."

"That's to be expected with circuit integration. It isn't natural, and your body wants to purge it. It'll get better, though. Your personal equilibrium just has to adjust. That's the only drawback of the new models."

"You're brilliant, Max. Why didn't you ever get away before? You could have," Leona said, looking into Max's eye.

"I had no reason to get away. I don't consider myself some idealistic crusader, but I tend to be friends with a bunch of them. Until Stone asked me to leave, I hadn't thought about it much. Unlimited resources and subjects hold a whole lot of promise to curiosity, so a lack of freedom can be tolerated for quite some time," Max said. "Now, I'm in it for Stone. I owe him this much at least. If it were entirely up to me, I'd be content with a nice place in the Australian outback."

"I don't know. What would the harsh sun do to that complexion?" Leona stroked his grayish left arm playfully.

"Oh no! I'm rubbing off on you," Max said in mock horror.

"No, not yet."

Max placed his human hand on her real shoulder. "Sit down and get some rest. I have a feeling no one will get to us here. Imagine that, a few minutes of peace." Leona complied, cradling her new arm. Max slid down beside her. "What a cheerful scene: two exhausted people suffering from electronic feedback in the midst of being hunted."

"It could be worse," Leona said.

"Yeah, I could be without you," Max whispered.

Leona put her hand on his face. She ran her fingers from his brow to his chin. "You know," she said sweetly, "you really need to shave." Max smiled, and Leona leaned up against him. Max shifted slightly so her head did not press against the scales on his shoulder. "So what was it like growing up with the magnificent Mr. Stone?" Leona looked up at him, nestling into his chest a little more.

"We had some great times. I can remember every prank we pulled on our teachers. There were some good ones, too. We actually ratcheted the principal out the window. I can still see his face, red as a beet staring up from that rope. We were awful. The war came not long after we graduated. Stone was never much for confidence, but it got worse then. Now I see why. Suddenly his father starts taking down the country without anyone truly realizing what is going on. Next thing you know, his father rules the continent, and there are soldiers escorting you into the military academy or the labor camps. With the kind of change I saw in Stone, I figure there was some serious emotional abuse going on in that house. I really miss him, you know."

"Yeah, me too."

"Are you still in love with him?"

"No. I'm not sure that it ever was love. I'm waiting for someone to teach me just what love is. Of course, in this world that sort of thing isn't too important, is it?" Leona did not look at Max.

"Oh, but you're wrong. Love is something we all need, whether we know it or not. Maybe if a few more people embraced it along the way, we wouldn't be in such a dismal situation. I know, all this from the man who professes indifference?"

"Max, what does love mean to you?"

"I don't know, Leona. I don't know."

They sat there silently for a while, neither looking at the other. Then, Leona shifted to stare up at Max's face. He leaned down until their foreheads and noses were pressed together. Max gently pulled her closer with his human arm.

Leona tilted her head ever so slightly. Max kissed her deeply, an experience he had not had in a very long time. She wrapped her arms around him, and they both lost all sense of the feedback coursing through their bodies. They lost track of everything except each other.

"Maybe we can find out together," Leona whispered, her face pressed into his cheek. Max smiled and held her tightly. They fell asleep together.

When they awoke, they moved on in the passageway. They decided to follow the brightest path, hoping it would end somewhere useful.

They encountered a shaft with rungs leading to an access hatch. Max climbed the distance first and cracked the hatch open.

Above was a man in a long black rider coat kneeling over him with a Maker's Call impact rifle slung over his right shoulder. There was a menacing look in his eyes and a broad smile on his face. Over the first man's shoulder stood a larger man in a spotless white suit aiming two tazer pistols straight down the hatchway.

"Allow me to introduce myself," the man with the dark coat and long sideburns said, "My name is Franklin James. My partner here is Saint. He doesn't say much. We're what you might call mercenaries, and I think you may want to take advantage of our services."

"I'm not in much of a position to argue," Max said, defeated.

"No, but you can refuse if you want. I should caution you that it is only a matter of time before our wonderful, esteemed, etcetera, ruler offers a contract on you. Being the good, upstanding citizens we are, we're bound by honor not to accept an assignment if it poses a conflict of interest with a client that got to us first. You have to reward expediency in a business like ours, and it is my understanding from observing your position that you are in need of transportation, you and your lovely companion." Max's expression turned quickly from defeat to anger at that. "Oh, don't worry. I myself am happily engaged, and Saint, well, Saint is Saint. Come out of your hole and we'll discuss this, okay? Saint and I just happen to be in a day and a half layover between jobs, so our services are yours, for a price of course."

Saint holstered his weapons once Max and Leona had exited the shaft. Franklin James stood back and adjusted his purple dress shirt, keeping the rifle slung over his shoulder amidst the flapping of his coat in the breeze. Saint sealed the hatch and stood ominously over it.

"How did you find us?" Leona was nervous and she was clinging close to Max.

"Well, Saint noticed the shift in the grass line where the lock seals the hatch from the inside. We've come by once or twice since then. We intercepted a military transmission, and, after the blackout and the massacre, we figured it was high time someone showed up," Franklin James said, spinning the rifle down to his ankle and back up over his shoulder with his gloved hand.

"So what exactly do you want?" Max had a harsh expression visible on his whole body.

"The question is 'what do you want?' We already have our price picked out. I think you'll find it agreeable since none of you have currency on you. Trust me, we scanned already so don't try to scam us. We provide any service you desire, and we get to loot young Mr. Stone's mansion. Deal?"

Max knew that the pulse that caused the blackout fried everything useful in the residence, and the soldiers would rummage through it anyway. "Deal."

"Good," Franklin James smiled.

"But there are bound to be soldiers going through the place," Max added apologetically.

"Well," Franklin James said, "that becomes our problem, doesn't it?" Franklin James somehow smiled wider, and something dark flashed in his eyes. He glanced at Saint, and Saint simply nodded.

CHAPTER 50

EXPLOSIONS ROCKED THE tower. The open wall that served as a makeshift launch bay was the only clear window to the scene of destruction beyond. The crew ran frantically between the jets and carriers.

"I am just glad you made it back alive," Rowan said, looking weary and grim.

"Un minute," Cessil demanded. His translator had fried in the crash. He pulled the tiny device from his throat and tossed it aside. Rowan called over one of the technicians. "Je nais spleake englis," Cessil apologized.

"Your translator has been magnetized. I will get you another one," Rowan said with exaggeration as though Cessil could understand him by sheer volume.

Cessil pulled the second piece of the translator from his ear. Without either piece, the contraption did not function. Even with both pieces functioning, the device was limited to translations of people with similar systems. Cessil pulled out a cigar and popped the end. The thick smoke furled around his head as he turned toward the approaching crew member. The Englishman fitted the French president with another set of the two-piece, small devices.

The technician stepped back and asked, "Can you understand me now, President Chirac?"

"Yes, thank you. Well, Rowan, I got a good look at those things. The shielding is all external. No energy weapon has a chance. I got lucky. They did not seem to notice me until I got close to the hanger. Then, I took a few glancing scrapes on my left wing. Then one of them caught sight of me. They have a prehensile whiplike appendage. It took off my right wing and magnetized my electronics. I barely got stabilizer thrust and manual control. This is bad, Rowan."

"I know, and now they tracked you to our staging area. We have lost six squadrons of jets and four *Stille*-class carriers with full shielding. We have no more tanks in the immediate area. Emergency evacuation is proceeding twenty miles ahead of the onslaught," Rowan assessed.

"Well, they are knocking over buildings out there. Nice touch picking a corporate headquarters, by the way. The corporate sabotage war a few years back led to armor reinforced structures like this," Cessil added. He stuck his finger distractedly through a fresh hole in his torn overcoat.

"Do not feel overly secure. We cut out that wall easily enough."

"Yes, I suppose so. I want to go back out there. What do we have as far as attackers?"

"I think I have the perfect craft: a refitted Abomination attack carrier. I will send two of my best pilots with you," Rowan offered, forcing a smile.

"Good enough. I know you can handle the tactical end from here," Chirac said confidently. They brought the craft, prepped and ready, far sooner than he expected.

Once seated inside the center cockpit, Cessil scanned the controls and twisted the stick experimentally. He punched up the thrust and clicked on the internal intercom. "Everyone set? Weapons check."

"Systems go. Weapons online," Kreer said.

"This thing is rusty, but it works. Good to go," Jacobin snapped.

"Damn American imports," Cessil returned.

"Amen to that, Sir," Kreer chuckled.

Rowan watched as the quad-wing thrust freighter barreled out of the open wall. "Godspeed, Cessil. Come back in one piece, all of you."

Kreer armed the console. "Sir, shall we set attack vector?"

"Yes, Lieutenant Kreer. Lock in on the nearest intruder. Full thrust," Cessil commanded.

The boxy hold tilted as the four main thrusters engaged vectoring. The three laser-tipped cockpits rotated on the front of the craft as the wings adjusted to the course. "Course set. Arming shieldshock missiles," Jacobin pronounced.

"Give me high incendiaries," Cessil demanded.

"Fly us in, President Chirac," Kreer crackled over the intercom. Chirac responded by spinning the rear of the craft three hundred-sixty degrees and angling the whole carrier toward the nearest walking titan of destruction.

"Hang on. That thing has a mouth. We shall open it. There is bound to be a weapon in there we can destroy," Cessil asserted.

"Yes, Sir. You have high incendiary controls. We have a full volley," Kreer added.

The *Anhaengen* turned on its side in a wide loop around the giant robotic construct. A swing of its mammoth fist nearly grounded the craft. Cessil pulled back on the yoke and swung the craft about. "Launch shieldshocks now," Cessil ordered. Two missiles screamed from the body of the *Anhaengen*. Both exploded slightly above the surface of the metal monster. The carrier was away from the blast, and the only effect the pilots witnessed was the glass shards and metal fragments from the behemoth's collapsed shielding raining across three cockpit viewports.

♟

Rowan watched the explosion from the tower. "Have you and your men found anything yet, Helmut?"

"They are being controlled by a satellite uplink. It is a very dense signal and we have no way to block it. Even our sleeper satellites are unresponsive, if they still exist at all," Verndestag said. "You know, Yarishnachov is not faring well. His people are being wiped out by both the invaders and the laserlike weapons that picked apart Moscow. Ming is here with me. His army is on perimeter duty, but we cannot fight them like this. I am deploying Arctic Fire along the invasion front. The prototypes are nearly exhausted. However, production is underway. If it fails, I put in my bid for a simultaneous nuclear strike against every major city in the Americas. Ming and Yarishnachov are both in support of a sea-based launch. That leaves you and Chirac for authorization."

"Not while we still have options. A strike that massive is tantamount to genocide," Rowan demanded. "I can tell you Chirac is on my side in this. Otherwise he would not be out there fighting these things. Besides, a nuclear strike would be an invitation to be incinerated."

"We are being destroyed anyway, my friend. We are out of viable options," Verndestag conceded heavily.

"That would be a choice of extinction. Just give me everything you have and keep me posted. Rowan out."

The *Anhaengen* was following a collision course with the construct's pseudo-face. The pendulum fists were set on a collision course with the carrier. At the last possible moment, the craft rolled away under Cessil's command, launching three high incendiary missiles right into the creation's mouth. The missiles, though, veered off in wind shear and missed their mark.

"Damn. We cannot pull that maneuver again. Give me one close pass, and we will move on to the next one," Cessil commanded.

"Affirmative, Sir," Jacobin responded.

The *Anhaengen* shot straight off of the invader. As the prehensile, whiplike appendage swung after it, the carrier spun and circled around. Cessil fired the shots again, and, this time, they struck their intended mark.

The explosion masked the face at first, but the glow faded to an internal flame. When the smoke cleared, the scarred construct was left with a gaping look of awe and only one eye. Sparks poured out of the hole once covered with a jaw. A mild cheer was heard inside the *Anhaengen*.

Then, the fist of the invader opened and tore the center cockpit cleanly off. It held the piece of the carrier remarkably gently. The rest of the carrier suffered mild smoking but veered quickly off, away from the construct. "Not so fast," the construct bellowed. "Thought you could just hit and run? That's a federal offense in some countries." The construct's other hand extracted Chirac, and the construct dropped the rest of the mangled cockpit. "I'm disappointed."

"Blade," Cessil roared, struggling uselessly in the unbreakable metal grip.

"Oh, you're too good at this. Hey, maybe this is *deja vu*, or is that just a French thing?"

The *Anhaengen* came back around, firing careful shots at the arm's support struts. Unfortunately, the shots just deflected to the ground. "Friends of yours?" The construct, suddenly under Blade's control, swung its prehensile appendage straight down through the left cockpit, where it held. Blade whipped the craft to the ground, and the titan crushed the remnants of the craft with its leg stand.

"I've been waiting a long time for this," the construct bellowed, straightening to its impressive full height. It flipped Cessil upside down, taking a foot in each metallic hand. "Hey, Chirac, make a wish."

CHAPTER 51

"WELL, I GUESS this is the place," Max said doubtfully.

"I thought you said you knew her." Leona pulled her elbow tighter through Max's.

"I did, but she disappeared a few years ago. I got to see her again just to watch her die," Max recalled. "Stone had this address scrawled on his laboratory system desktop."

"If you'll excuse me for asking, why are we here to see a dead woman?" Franklin James turned in his seat with his eyebrow cocked, his gloved hand still resting on the steering column. The cabin was small, but it was meant to be small. The independent chairs in the front were the only comfortable seats. Only the driver had any control, and a rotating machine gun in the cockpit covered the rest of the potentially occupied seats. Saint's suit made a sharp contrast to the dark interior, and it became apparent that Saint casually had a gun trained on the rotating base of the turret. The cabin tapered towards the back bench, which had a bar beneath it for handcuffing.

"Because if we're going to infiltrate the Neo-Colosseum, we'll need some weaponry," Max fired back. The transport slammed to a halt.

"Infiltrate the Neo-Colosseum? Who mentioned that?" Franklin James eyed Saint curiously.

"I just did. You don't think you're getting Stone's house for driving us here, do you?" Max ventured that his surprise would be taken well. At least it would be if he judged Franklin James correctly.

Franklin James actually looked shocked. Then his eyes flashed darkly. "This could be fun. What do you say, Saint? Oh, wait, think it over a while. We get to keep the arsenal, though," Franklin James said jovially with an enormous smile on his face.

Franklin James took the modified Continent Hopper, a wingless military jet, over the house and set it down in the cover of the surrounding structures. Two rows of shock struts descended and held the craft's belly off of the ground. Franklin James popped open his door and shut off the engine. He leapt out and pressed a button on his wrist. The hatch behind the driver's door opened, and two repeater rifles leveled themselves on the ground in front of the rear door.

"Forgive the guns. I'm not used to having such agreeable cargo," Franklin James apologized, still smiling.

"That's okay. The former occupant of this residence was an assassin. I bet you'll find some real nice security measures inside," Max responded.

"I love challenging work," Franklin James assured. Max and Leona cleared the vehicle, and four short range missile turrets came alive around the craft, scanning with motion and infrared sensors. Saint reached the door to the resident first, and, three shots later, they were inside.

"Duck," Franklin James said as he brought up two handguns. Four careful shots rang out from the guns in the mercenary's hand, and they could safely enter. "I've seen that one before. It scans for her particular body signature. If someone else's signature is present without hers, that nice harmless looking smoke detector pumps this room full of gas and ignites it. That stuff could flash fry steel."

"So, is everything safe now?" Leona was scanning the room nervously.

"Unless she has systems I've never seen," Franklin James conceded.

"So let me put it this way, Leona, if that is the case, I bet Kylie could have taught Stone a few things about over preparation," Max threw in.

"I wish I could have met her," Franklin James said admiringly, taking an exploratory step through the doorway with his guns still poised. Then, his face lit up like a child with a sugar high. "Look Saint, Christmas!"

Max looked around and quickly found the duffel bag near the holo/video screen. He examined the four halves of the disks. "I guess I can solder them with my joint splicer," Max muttered. He shot the toolbar out through the gap in his wrist plates and sparked it to life. Max ripped the wiring out from behind the holo/video screen and reattached only the power supply. The first disk launched successfully, skipping occasionally. Green lettering appeared on the screen reading "Unable to Connect."

"There's the offer," Max guessed. He placed the second disk in the slot. Suddenly, a wavering image of Stone displayed through the screen followed by an impressive sum and the words "Terminal Mark." "So, that's why you were so distraught. You agreed to kill my best friend. I thought he was your friend, too," Max cursed.

"Not to interrupt," Franklin James interrupted, "but your late friend had quite a penchant for illegal weaponry." He held up a small handgun with a bulging center. "This is a nuclear backwash emitter. It has been illegal since the last piece was put on the prototype. It emits the worst parts of a nuclear explosion in a single direction. Everyone involved in the project was just amazed the user didn't die with the victim. Mind if I keep it?"

"Why are you doing this, Franklin?" Max looked straight into the other's dark eyes.

"It's Franklin James," the mercenary corrected.

"Of course. Why are you doing this, Franklin James?"

"I just figure that a few minutes of congeniality is the least I can do," Franklin James began. He removed the glove from his free hand and undid the first two snaps of his shirt. "In return for this," he continued, pointing to the fist-sized scar on the left side of his chest.

Max backed up hastily, spinning the toolbar to find the sharpest object he could. In the process, he stumbled over the holo/video screen and sent both it and himself tumbling to the ground. Franklin James held up his hands apologetically. "No, no, no, no, no! You saved my life. You see, I did my tour of duty in Blade's army, and I paid the price. I thank you for the artificial heart. I'm convinced to this day that you're the only one who could have saved my life. I appreciate the upgrades, too, increased oxygenation and more efficient adrenaline circulation. Thanks," Franklin James said, smiling as ever.

"Sure," Max said dumbfounded, collecting himself again.

"How did she die, your friend?"

"She electrocuted herself with my own circuits," Max said, clicking his leg plates open and shut.

"There are worse ways, I suppose," Franklin James pondered. "It is my experience that when a lady must die, it should be in a manner that does not mar the beauty and wonder of her body. There is too little beauty out there, so what there is should always be preserved. Remember that."

"I'm glad you're engaged. Talk like that to Leona, and I'd have even less of a chance."

"Oh, worry not. Your position is quite secure, and don't forget, I'm a person who survives on observation," Franklin James said, walking back towards Saint. Max sighed in relief, admitting silently the respect and fear he had for the man in the long black coat. Leona walked toward Max from the private chamber. She carried a book and an uneasy expression.

"Max, I think you might want to see this," Leona said, handing Max an actual paper notebook.

"Well, look at this," Franklin James said from across the small chamber. "This is a genuine outlawed artifact: fifty-three stars and thirteen stripes. Long may she wave, eh? You know, I miss her sometimes, the United States. The old girl was a cesspool of corruption, greed, lawlessness, and, worst of all, politics. You have to admit, though, she was more fun than this place, and you got some freedom with her, too. It's too bad she slipped down the butt crack of society. May she rest in peace."

Max leafed through the pages once Franklin James had finished his commentary. "This is her diary, Leona. I have no right to-" Leona cut him off.

"Look at the last page," she insisted. Max reluctantly obeyed. "'I have nothing now,'" he read. "'My father is dead. My sister has disappeared. Now Blade has my mother, and if I don't kill his son, she'll die. So much for needing no one.'" Max looked at Leona. "She was forced into this. I should have known. Blade manipulated everyone so perfectly in this situation and he almost succeeded."

"Almost?" Leona looked at Max curiously.

"He didn't count on the fact that I will stop at nothing to avenge the deaths of my two best friends." Max steadily lifted a nearby weapon.

"And he didn't count on a dead lady giving us the tools to destroy him." Max hooked two handheld weapons to the stolen soldier's belt he still wore. He picked up a jagged assassin knife. "She could outfit an entire militia with this stuff," he said, cracking a pained smile.

"In a way, I guess she has," Leona laughed. She stepped closer to Max and put her hands on his shoulders. Slowly, she slid her arms around him and pulled him tighter. Max raised his human hand and stroked her soft hair down to the black tips. Franklin James smiled and nudged Saint. Saint did not respond, but his eyes seemed to soften for an instant. He then straightened his collar and glanced back over at Franklin James.

"Well, Hero, if you aren't in too big of a hurry to go, Saint found some popcorn," Franklin James announced, the darkness in his eyes flashing mischief.

CHAPTER 52

ROBERT STOOD UP from the rail, sweat drenching his face. He sighed in frustration and slung his sword over his back, remembering how much more comfort the blade offered him when he could actually die. Then again, rebirth was bad enough to warrant caution in keeping conditions livable for his body. He saw the tears in his uniform and the scars on his boots. By then, there were no wounds left beneath the tattered shirt. Robert saw the hole in his shirt over his heart. *That's the one that did it,* he thought, still breathing with effort. He had gotten used to injuries, but when his body was forced to reform as a whole, every pain receptor his natural body possessed fired at once and there was no mystic energy to keep him from that.

Then, he noticed that his shoulder pad hung loosely. He tore the strap from under his arm and pulled out the aging construct it had safeguarded for so long. He tossed the covering away, letting it fall the hundred feet from the railing to the pavement. He held the technological device in his hand, venturing a look up the railway system ascending to the height of the statue under construction. He concentrated ever so slightly. He had a climb ahead of him. *Wait until I get my hands on you, Marcus,* he thought angrily.

Robert gripped the hand railing, put the device in a pouch on his thigh, and began his ascension. At the first platform, he took out his frustrations on a hapless butterfly that dared to venture to that height. Robert effortlessly burst its exoskeleton from within. He swatted his hand after the mess and spat at Marcus. "I'm never having children again. I don't care how many centuries go by," Robert vowed. He reached for the next rung.

CHAPTER 53

ARDEN SHUREMAN WAS a soldier. He was one of a great many to serve under Blade Stone. Even though he was extremely efficient in his job, he wanted out. He had modeled himself after Blade's very own son, his first born son. Arden had been conscripted into service as opposed to being imprisoned. As a reward for his unfailing service, he got to personally lead the assault on the United Armies using the very weapon that killed his father, the Deathunter remote battle armor.

The suit itself was elegant enough, a sleek machine designed for effective, swift destruction. It was the result of the Genesis prototype, which was tested on the imprisoned populace of Atlanta, Arden's hometown. His father was among the long list of casualties.

Arden did not want to dawn the remote systems. He was disgusted enough at having been forced to coordinate the launch, but now he was controlling one of the mass executioners personally. He saw only through its scanners and cameras once he donned the helmet. His movements were its movements. He was actually immersed in a fluid basin with weapon controls at his thumb. His every ripple in the pool was replicated as a precise movement by the machine. However, he was experiencing technical difficulties.

"Confirm location," Arden ordered through his communications/ breathing apparatus. He heard a volley of coordinates in succession, all of which were well beyond the point of landing. Blade himself had commandeered one of the battle suits briefly, but apparently that stint was at an end. Arden wanted to scream in frustration. There had been others who had escaped the service. There was even a chance that Blade's son was alive somewhere after his bold challenge, but, despite attempts, Arden was nothing like Stone. He had made it to second in the line for the seat of power only by being consistently meticulous and constantly on edge.

Now, Arden saw his own death impending, and all of his dreams of freedom were little more than smoke in a gun barrel. He had gained sensor vision inside a laboratory. The construct he was controlling was sluggish in response, and his readouts told him he was down to the fifth level in places. It took him a good two hours to ram his way out through the building. He could not quite figure out why he allowed the scientists to live, but he did. His main concern was leaving the laboratory. He forced the construct to stand at full height once he got out in the open, but the construct was still crippled. He was two hours behind the invasion force's schedule, too. *So much for being second in line*, Arden thought. At least death at Blade's hands would end his suffering. Maybe Blade would give him a chance to die by combat, at least then he could die proud.

"Proceed to secondary attack coordinates," Arden ordered. He lurched his uneasy invader forward, and then came the worst part of the scenario: a high incendiary bomb erupted in the pit of the machine. Arden lost control of several more systems, and his ability to walk ceased. His frustrations came to full fruition. For some reason, Blade had given him specific orders to reach London ahead of the rest of the team. Now, he was stranded in the corporate sectors outlying the staging area. All he could do was coordinate the others until Blade killed him.

CHAPTER 54

ROWAN STOOD IN impotent rage inside the gutted corporate building. He witnessed the bloody end of France's greatest hero. He watched as his own British forces, the very ones that had crushed previous invasions of thousands, dwindled down to citizens with handguns protecting their families. Her Majesty's Royal Air Force was decimated before his eyes. He watched the reports coming from Verndestag on his screens. The German forces were holding their own at defense, but offense was out of the question. Yarishnachov's marred landscape flashed across the screen. Ming's bloodied forces fled for their lives before Rowan's eyes, and he had just received a petition from France's Parliament for a macronuclear strike to surgically eliminate every known American stronghold.

Rowan was officially the leader of a decimated force that once held grandeur as the United Armies. He was a broken man fighting an unstoppable enemy with a broken force that was itself divided against him. He was defeated, and he knew it. He thought bitterly that this must have been what the Americans felt on their side of the pond when Blade first rose to power. At least the evacuations had succeeded. He would not be the cause of death for the citizens who trusted him, the voters that cast their faith in him. He had not failed them completely, in that much at least.

"Lieutenant, patch me through to Vice President DePallo," Rowan ordered wearily.

"Ah, Prime Minister John Rowan," a voice echoed from the walls. Rowan would have sworn the temperature dropped noticeably in that instant. He turned to see the achromatic hologram of Blade Stone. "Alone in contemplation, are you?"

"What do you want now?" Rowan's face twisted involuntarily in pure hatred.

"Surrender. It is your only viable option. Your army is gone. You have nothing left. Give it up. You are getting too old for this anyway," Blade offered, sneering through the hologram.

"Never. If I surrender, then Cessil gave his life in vain. I promise you this: he will be avenged. If not by my hand, fine, but you will pay for the atrocities you have committed. By God, you will pay," Rowan roared.

"And you will die. As I bring in the last two carriers, consider this a front row preview of the fate of your United Armies," Blade said coldly. "Shhh! You can almost hear death approaching."

In that instant, Arden Shureman's Deathunter battle armor consumed itself in a nuclear explosion from its deepest core. Rowan did not even have time to draw another breath. Blade sat back in his throne and smiled. "And then there were three," he whispered grimly. "Bring in the last two carriers. Open the rear hatches. The artificial constructs are locked on their specific coordinates, correct Commander?" Blade rested his hand on the controls that brought up Arden's location.

"Yes, my lord, they are. Sir, I was unaware I had one of the nuclear devices inside the armor I was operating. I am sorry I did not make it to London, Sir," Arden apologized.

"No, you performed well under the circumstances. It turns out, fortunately for you, that Rowan was still within the blast radius. Get ready, Commander, the United Armies cannot possibly survive a nuclear strike of this magnitude. With these Deathunters as shells, there will be no way for the opposition to disarm them. Watch closely, Commander," Blade said confidently.

"I cannot, Sir," Arden said regretfully.

"What? How dare you?"

"I am blind, my lord. The nuclear explosion whited out my sensors and cameras. My eyes are ruined, my lord."

"You didn't get out of the tank?"

"You did not order me to, my lord. I had no idea what you were planning," Arden stammered.

"Lieutenant, escort Commander Shureman to the best

technogeneticist remaining in this complex," Blade ordered. "Get him seeing again no matter what or you will die with him."

"Sir," a female voice crackled over the speaker. "Our signature scanner just crashed around the entire perimeter, Sir."

"Keep me apprised of the situation. I'm going elsewhere," Blade snarled, disgusted.

CHAPTER 55

MARCUS STOOD ON the upper level of the Skyrail cargo hauler. It looked out over the city in a dizzying view. The shadow looming over him was cast by a statue, a statue Blade was having constructed of himself. "Arrogance to the point of madness," Marcus solemnly mused. He was still sore where the clasps had held him, and he had no idea how long he had slept. He looked up at the intertwining railway just in time to watch his attacker leap down upon him from the adjacent track.

The assailant kneed Marcus swiftly in the chest and forced the monk to the ground, binding his hands behind his head. "Now, maybe this time, you'll listen," Robert said above his breathless son. "I've been trying to tell you something, Marcus. That destiny you have been prepared for is at hand. You do remember your upbringing, don't you?"

Marcus wheezed an affirmative. "Your creation has a reason, Marcus. I took it upon myself to train you with the knowledge of centuries so that you could fulfill what is needed of you now." Robert released one of his hands and withdrew the technological device from the pouch in the front of his pants. "This is why you became what you are. I'll let you up to see if you don't throw me off the railway again."

Marcus agreed, and Robert released him. Marcus kept his word and got slowly to his feet. "Look familiar?" Robert held the device out.

"Yes, it is a holographic device from Stone's armor. Where did you get it?" Marcus eyed his mentor, his father, suspiciously.

"About sixty years in the past in a cave near the shore. The place is still underdeveloped. This was the only relic there. Of course, imagine what I thought when I first saw the thing, huh? Take a good look at the lock, too."

"His cross opens it," Marcus ascertained.

"The cross you gave him, the cross I gave you. The cross I carved with my own hands. You see, I could open the device, too. The image is Stone in full armor regalia, a fact I only recently discovered, but the message is clear enough. After I found it, I took it back to the monastery where I was studying, and they were convinced it warned of the Antichrist. Though understandably, they believed it to be the person in the image. That is something I believe I have only recently proven wrong. So you see, you do have a very important destiny, though it is not the one the rest of the monks and I believed it to be. Funny, isn't it? Technically, you were raised to kill your own pupil. Well, monks are wrong from time to time," Robert shrugged.

"What about an immortal?"

"I don't have all the answers. Even after all these years, I can't tell the future," Robert ceded. "Now, your final lesson is at hand."

"Is this from a mentor or a father?"

"Both," Robert said, raising an eyebrow at the fire in his son's spirit. He noticed, too, that his own anger had lessened in the climb, and his resolve had sharpened. "Let's just see how much of your father you have in you." He keyed the lift to rise to the tip of the statue.

CHAPTER 56

"WELL, HERE WE are. Let's keep this quiet," Franklin James whispered. All traces of his smile had vanished, and his repeater rifle was leveled perfectly still in his steely grip. The darkness in his eyes ran wild then.

Saint was absolutely statuesque. His spotless white suit, though conspicuous in its own right, almost adopted the shadows around it. He held an impulse weapon and a feedback tazer pistol. He was as cold as ice.

Max was the uneasy one. He kept control of his nerves as always, though. After all, combat was nothing new to him. However, this time it was two crazy gunmen and one crazy geneticist against the most lethal army in existence and the most dangerous man the world had ever produced. At least they had gotten this far smoothly. Franklin James had brought down the signature scanner with the aid of Max's pirated schematics. Saint got them through the back door, and there they were in the tunnels and recesses of Blade's command center, the Neo-Colosseum. Then there was Leona.

"Let her go, Max. We have a mission here, and it's one you're paying us well to complete," Franklin James whispered darkly. He was right; Max needed to focus on the task at hand. Leona could wait.

Saint fired three shots down the corridor, and three bodies hit the ground. "Well, I'd say we've been reported," Max whispered. Franklin James nodded and proceeded. Saint sped down the hallway with amazing agility. In a blinding instant, he put away the impulse pistol, drew his knife, and silently cut down four soldiers before any of them could get off a single shot.

"It brings the fight to us," Franklin James whispered.

"I guess so," Max agreed quietly. He opened the palm-sized

holographic device, and a partial schematic of the Neo-Colosseum sprang to life, one taken straight from Stone's archives. "Down the hall, left, and two doors up on the right," Franklin James gave his silent acknowledgement and caught up with Saint. Max put the device away and drew one of the guns at his side.

Max approached the two mercenaries cautiously, stepping over the fallen bodies of the soldiers and conscripted employees. He paused only to exchange his pistol for a serial issue Rioter. Franklin James fired through the door's lock, and the entire door fell inward off its hinges. "Thanks," Max smirked. Franklin James shrugged. "Give me a minute to finish the schematic from the terminal, and then get those bodies in here," Max requested quietly. Saint silently felled two more workers. "You know, we wouldn't have to kill everyone if we used some subterfuge," Max chided.

"Where's the fun in that? If you insist, though, he's about your size," Franklin James said, hoisting one of the fallen soldiers up by the chest plate. Max looked back down at the network terminal. He downloaded the map into a disk and plugged it into the small holographic matrix.

"This dark spot, it has to be something big. It might even be the Vault," Max said, pulling on the rest of the armor. "So that's where we go."

"Always good to have a plan. Oop!" Franklin James fired his rifle into the stomach of a uniformed worker. "That's going to stain," Franklin James said toward the bloody mess that was barely recognizable as human. "Well, to the dark spot." He shrugged with a smile tugging at his face.

The path was easier than expected. Max, disguised as a soldier, was the point man with the two mercenaries taking care of any trouble around them before it arose. The door of the unknown area was more obstinate than it should have been. It took four shots from Franklin James's rifle and a swift kick from Max's semiorganics to rend it free of its frame. The darkened room beyond obviously held a secret worthy of security.

Saint slid through the doorway. Max could discern a muffled scream and a gag from another location before Saint reemerged brandishing two bloody knives. Franklin James raised an eyebrow and tossed an ignited light globe into the dim room. Beyond was a twenty foot metallic behemoth. Franklin James reflexively fired at its sensor plate, but, to his great surprise, the shot of explosive ammunition was ineffectual.

Max's awe suddenly collapsed into horror. He recognized the construction from the message Stone had recorded in his private files. Max had run the schematic through the monitor after a long debate with himself. "Look for remote operation tanks and destroy them and whoever is inside," Max ordered soberly, staring at the construct. Max turned back, but Franklin James and Saint were already gone.

"Halt," Max heard from the hallway. It was followed by Rioter fire. Max brought his own weapon up and aimed it at the doorway. A loud rifle shot and two quiet bursts from a tazer pistol joined with and then ended the Rioter shots. A loud explosion rocked the walls nearby.

Shortly, Franklin James appeared in the doorway again, holding a pistol to an officer's forehead. Saint followed them into the room and quietly took up a position to cover the doorway. "He's blind and Saint wouldn't kill him. What do you think?"

"Franklin James, do you have any idea who that is?" Max was intrigued by the scenario that was evolving.

"The legendary Franklin James?" The blind man seemed awed but still unafraid.

"Yes, he is," Max answered, "and you are Commander Arden Shureman, are you not?"

"Yes, I am. And you are?"

"Max."

"Maximus Fitzgerald? What on Earth are two people at the top of Blade's most wanted list doing inside the capital? If I am in a position to ask, of course," Arden questioned, remembering himself.

"You aren't. Don't forget who's pressing a gun to your head," Franklin James snarled.

"Help me get out of here, and I will help you in any capacity I can," Arden offered.

"Quite the sudden turncoat, are you? Why exactly should we trust you?" Franklin James dug the barrel of the gun into Arden's neck. His coat flared in the motion, revealing the new bullet holes in its flaps.

"Because I have no choice but to trust you," Arden said, mustering his courage.

"Sounds reasonable enough to me. Where are the remote operations tanks and how many are there?" Max walked back to the battle armor, which occupied most of the room.

"They are in three adjacent rooms bordering this one, if this is the room housing the prototype. There are three hundred eighty-four tanks," Arden answered promptly.

"Try one hundred twenty-eight, give or take for blast radius," Franklin James said, dropping a handful of grenade pins to the floor.

"Nice," Max said, "but I must ask, Arden, why are you helping us?"

"Let's just say I've lost my faith in Blade Stone's organization," Arden said, biting back his anger.

Franklin James's wrist beeped just as two soldiers entered the room. Saint dropped them easily enough with two shots from his impulse pistol.

"Go ahead and answer your wrist, Franklin James. What's Arden going to do, run away?" Max looked carefully at Arden's face and detected the traces of a genuine smile. Franklin James spun away and hit a button on his wrist control panel, which usually stayed hidden under his coat sleeve.

"This isn't a real good time, Darling," Franklin James said to his hand.

"So what does this invasion consist of?" Max held Arden's shoulder.

"Four hundred remote battle suits, seventeen of which carry a nuclear payload at their core," Arden answered.

"That's sixteen operation tanks unaccounted for," Max said angrily.

"No, they are preprogrammed for surgical nuclear strikes."

"Can you stop them?"

"Yes, but I need to get to the third room to do it," Arden said.

"This had better not be a trap," Max growled.

"Trust me, I want out of here."

"That's the real issue here, isn't it? Trust," Max mused grimly.

"Well, Saint, time to go. That was Darm. The corporation has sent coordinates for a rendezvous; they're opening contract negotiation. Max, I trust we've earned our pay?" Franklin James looked questioningly at Max. Max nodded, "Much obliged, and I promise you this, Max: if you ever end up on the other side of my gun barrel, I shall give you time to make peace with God. That's all any man truly needs." With that, the mercenaries departed, Franklin James hoisting his Maker's Call rifle over his shoulder.

"How heavily defended are these rooms?" Max still held Arden's shoulder.

"There are only four guards and one officer in each room," Arden said. "Perhaps if you put on soldier's armor and led me there, they wouldn't suspect anything until we left."

"That still leaves one hundred twenty-eight of these monstrosities active," Max said disapprovingly. "Then again, who says that when we leave, we can't come back?" Max voiced, looking up at the construct before them labeled "Genesis." "Would you happen to know where the Vault is located?"

"Actually, I do," Arden said, his eyes staring blankly before him.

CHAPTER 57

MARCUS AND ROBERT rode silently up the railing. As it locked in place on the highest scaffold, Marcus saw the face of death. "Well, well, well. The one that got away and the one that sold out my son for his. What an unpleasant surprise," Blade roared. Marcus braced himself for the fight he knew was impending. Robert walked out onto the makeshift wooden platform.

"Just as I planned, Blade," Robert sneered. Blade merely turned to face him and grunted. Robert drew his sword and struck it into the wooden flooring. Blade smiled.

"It makes sense now, Robert," Blade growled. "You wanted to wait until you could displace both my son and me. It would make controlling my dominion that much easier. I am quite afraid, though, that you will have to pull yourself together first," Blade said darkly. In a swift motion, he jammed a spike between Robert's ribs and clipped a magnetic grenade to it. Blade lifted Robert by the collar and hurled him out over the statue below. Marcus heard the explosion, muffled by the distance, as the spilled blood on the platform chased after the pieces of its owner.

"You know, he can," Marcus laughed, feeling himself go cold. At that moment, he remembered every bit of the training to which he had been subjected since childhood. His will tempered his body into the perfect state for combat, even as he felt death's icy grip close in around him.

Blade withdrew and extended his considerable sword. Marcus leapt to the side to avoid Blade's initial strike. In doing so, Marcus found himself in an opportune position to grab his father's sword from the ground. As Marcus turned back, he swung the Crusader's sword up to cease the descent of its technologically enhanced counterpart.

Remembering the energy battery of altered electricity, Marcus pulled his father's sword back and leapt over the second strike.

Marcus knew the crushing weight of the weapon his opposition held, and the sword he himself wielded could not withstand the bombardment for long. As Blade parried and swung again, Marcus struck. He used his blade to catch a link in the chain gripping the hilt of Blade's sword. Marcus swung again in the direction of the momentum of Blade's swing. The increased pull along the arc ripped the sword from Blade's hand, and, as it neared the ground, Marcus used the Crusader's sword for leverage in flinging both weapons over the scaffolding.

Unperturbed, Blade pulled the two remaining spikes from his belt, each measuring eight inches in length. Marcus dodged the swipes with a combination of luck and skill. "Now I see where my son got his penchant for swordplay," Blade said, undistracted.

"You seem worse for wear since his departure," Marcus replied, equally focused. The two slight clicks did not register in Blade's ears. "That tends to be the case with abuse scenarios."

"Never. He was a reminder, nothing more," Blade spat. "I don't remember you being involved in this situation anyhow." Marcus took his only chance at retreat, and two explosions shook Blade and the scaffold. Marcus had been given the chance to steal, arm, and return Blade's magnetic grenades, and he had taken full advantage of it.

As Marcus got to his feet again, he saw Blade pulling his leg back through the hole it made in the flooring. A large piece of his chest plate was oddly contorted, and the armor beneath it appeared to have melted around the explosive device. Blade's cape was burning and spitting ashes on the wooden scaffold. Marcus discerned that Blade was favoring his left side and wheezing slightly. Blade's belt was fused to the rest of his armor, and the weapons were gone from his hands. "Clever," Blade growled.

Marcus spun and kicked Blade in the face. Still struggling with balance, Blade stepped backward, but, as Marcus poised to strike again, Blade hammered Marcus's shoulder with his fist. The impact broke Marcus's clavicle and dislodged his right arm from its socket. With his other hand, Blade batted Marcus across the platform.

Struggling with dizziness and the spastic pain of his right arm trying to fix itself, Marcus forced himself to stand. Through the hologram on

Blade's face, Marcus saw Blade's mouth bleeding. The armored ruler lumbered inexorably towards Marcus, and the fallen monk focused himself on a single spot.

Blade raised his fist high in the air. Marcus summoned the power he held within and tempered his strength accordingly. As the death blow began to fall, Marcus punched Blade's chest with such an impact that it dented the remaining armor and shattered his rib cage, impaling his heart with his own bones. The force of the attack threw the metal clad dictator back and sent him crashing through the scaffold onto the top of the unfinished statue below.

Marcus slowly stumbled to the opening to look down at the broken body below. "Destiny," he whispered, looking at his shattered left hand and ignoring his right arm completely. The armored body below was contorted in an unnatural position. The blood from Blade's body leaked from his mouth over the side and dripped upon the statue's cheek, where it continued its flow. To all who would observe the sight from afar, it would appear as though grim death were weeping for its own demise.

CHAPTER 58

"I HAVE A very bad feeling about this, Commander," the dark haired man with wires and plugs constituting the hair on the left side of his head trembled. The various plugs ran from his head to a pack at his waist. A red digital number gauge was spiraling well above ninety.

"Maybe we should listen to him, Commander," Aleece said, rising from her chair and stepping uncertainly back from the desk. The man with the bad premonition blinked the two glowing artificial eyes in his left eye socket and over his brow centre in acknowledgement.

"You two are insane. Aleece, you should know better. Our protection comes from Blade himself. And you, Edward, are mistaken. I don't care if you are a high level psychic, I don't buy it," Dakker croaked. "You're acting as if the world is about to fall apart."

"I say we listen to Edward on this one. My gut doesn't agree with staying here too much longer, either," Devron proclaimed.

"Youth. Defiance," Dakker spat.

At that moment, the roof came tumbling down on the Vault. Atop the resulting rubble, masked in the dust of the broken plaster and concrete, stood a battle suit built by the very people it now faced. "It's Genesis," Devron shouted. "This is impossible." The construct spun its sensor plate and a red gleam flashed behind one of its empty eye sockets.

"Anything's possible, for better or worse," Genesis proclaimed.

"Maximus Fitzgerald," Edward stated flatly, blinking the artificial eye over his brow centre.

"In the remote battle suit, as it were," Max said playfully. Genesis sealed the two visible exit doors with a series of welding laser bursts. "Survivor check," he said enthusiastically, backing Genesis away from the rubble pile that had covered the remains of the desk where the Vault once convened. Genesis clanged against the flooring, its hunched frame scraping the nearby walls with the movement. "What a shame, only four," Max said, using Genesis to roll a torn torso out from under a large piece of cutaway metal ceiling. "I charge you all with unspeakable crimes against humanity. The verdict is guilty. How do you plead?"

"We could accuse you of the same, Max, or are you so self-righteous now that you have forgotten your contributions to the advancement of this nation under President Blade Stone? Go ahead, deny it," Dakker charged.

"Yeah, well, we all have our burdens," Max shrugged, giving Genesis an unnatural gesture.

"Blade will never allow this," Devron proclaimed, backing closer to the wall.

"Yeah, Jonathan? Well, he pretty much has so far," Max said flatly. "Edward, scientific query: does this hurt?" Genesis swung its prehensile appendage over its shoulder and through Edward's chest, arcing electricity back through all of the direct brain interface wires. "Aleece, an acquaintance of mine told me that a woman's beauty should never be marred in death." Aleece sighed some relief. "Fortunately, you're not that pretty." Max fired a dual burst of the soldering laser through Aleece's midsection. Genesis grabbed Devron off of his feet. Dakker pressed a button against the wall, and an infrasonic weapon erupted against Genesis's outermost hull and sensors. "Ouch Dakker, that really hurt, especially considering the fact that I'm not inside." At that, Genesis hoisted Dakker from his feet and brought both men in its grip closer so their faces were turned to its camera plate. Genesis squeezed tighter. "This is for building every damn one of these things," Max spat. "Hey, Arden, would you prefer green eyes or brown?"

CHAPTER 59

"IT IS TIME. With Prime Minister Rowan's untimely demise, I am prepared to take the fight straight to Blade. Though I cannot fathom why the onslaught has ceased, I feel it is best to strike during the calm of this storm. This is our chance to prevent the attack's eventual continuation. My orders are as follows: deploy Arctic Fire against every one of those mechanical killers and set up launch vessels at every probable strike point. At this time, I do not care about production capital. Our forces are small, but they are yet effective. Do not forget that, Lieutenant. Gather every drone ship we have aboard the *Berlin Nacht Ein*. Program them all to swarm when we are twenty kilometers from the coast. I am departing for the bridge presently. Order the crew to arm three macronuclear warheads and equip eight turrets with a full complement of Arctic Fire. Set a course for New Charleston and prepare an emergency escape vector," President Verndestag ordered.

One hour later, the command vessel was approaching the shore of the Atlantic Ocean bordering the Americas. In perfect synchronization, thousands of tiny vessels roared from the hangars of the *Berlin Nacht Ein*. Each four-foot craft was heavily reinforced for various types of attacks. The only armament any of the drone ships had was a lock-back missile system that would target an enemy which had fired upon the computerized drone. A signal emitted by the mobile German capital kept the drones swirling in a frenzied swarm that became veritably impenetrable to attack as long as the drones' numbers held. Damaged drones could be recalled through an electromagnet to be recycled. Just as swiftly, the drones could be reprogrammed to expand their flight radius and form a cone of the same frenzied motion, allowing the *Berlin Nacht Ein* to escape through the Earth's atmosphere. No such secondary programming was required for this run, though. In a few nervous hours, they arrived at the Atlantic coast of North America.

"President Verndestag, why have they not attacked?"

"I do not know. Stay your course, Captain," Verndestag commanded nervously. His resolve was stronger than it had been in a long time, but there was something unsettling about the lack of an immediate military response to their arrival. Verndestag gripped the cold steel arm of his chair tighter. The two-hundred foot craft continued forward.

"President Verndestag, I have an interesting reading here, Sir. The biorhythm echo profiler reads a match to Blade Stone, only it says Blade is dead. I have another unknown in the area, unconscious," the ranking medical officer reported from across the bridge.

"Send down a pickup carrier. Bring the body aboard and confirm identification. Get the unknown in a holding cell. As much as we want the prospect of Blade's death to be correct, we must proceed cautiously. The unknown may yet be our enemy," Verndestag ordered with only a slight pause for consideration.

"Sir, we are detecting a broadband override signal in multiple formats. We can translate it. This one is going global, sir," the communications officer reported.

"Patch it through on the main intercom. I want to hear this," Verndestag demanded, his suspicion growing.

"Citizens, I ask your immediate attention. Under circumstances yet unknown to me, our esteemed ruler, His Excellency President Blade Stone has met his tragic demise. I have confirmed this fact with both the organic signature and his armor's signal. In light of this development, I order you to cease all further reprisals against the United Armies. With the recent death of Commander Alex Herring and the disappearance of President Stone's own son, you know well that I, Commander Arden Shureman, am placed in charge of the forces under President Stone's name. While my methods are not the same as his, I demand the same unquestioning service. My first official order, to your pleasure or contempt, is that the imprisoned populace of the cities be released to the homes they once knew. This is, above all, to be an orderly process. You will each receive your specific instructions on the matter shortly," Arden commanded. "Cut transmission," he said to Max. He sighed and fumbled lightly with the edges of the bandage across his eyes.

"'Tragic demise'?" Max quietly pulled out the handgun at his belt.

"Give the people what they want, and they are less likely to suspect your deeper motives. They just may listen, too," Arden said, facing toward the dead communications module.

"And just how much of that have you done with me?"

"Enough," Arden smiled, "but be assured that I am set on completing the objectives I have promised. Thank you, Max, for all that you have done for me. You are welcome here anytime you desire."

"Good, I'll be keeping my eye on you," Max said threateningly.

Arden smiled again, lifting himself on the sensor staff that would accompany him in his temporary blindness. "Time shall tell."

CHAPTER 60

ROBERT PICKED HIMSELF up from the pavement, finally recollected from seemingly endless points. He gnashed his teeth through the residual pain of being born again. He watched the wavering ship high above him and decided not to be seen. Naked, he walked to where his cloak was stowed away. Once he was covered again, he began his search for the sword which had been his only real companion through the ages. He knew his son was still alive, but Robert decided his quest for power could wait. He decided he was content to dwell in shadows a while longer. His chance would come again. After all, he had forever.

CHAPTER 61

"YOU KNOW THAT armor blew up our entire medical facility when my crew tried to remove it. As it stands now, I am the only medical officer aboard the ship. Now, I want to believe you. I have concluded by crude examination that it was you who did that man in. A recent broadcast by one Commander Shureman would tend to support your case. However, Blade is, quite truly, insanely clever," Lieutenant Wehrer said as he finished wrapping Marcus's hand in the plaster wrap. They were both sitting behind the tightly woven bars of the holding cell door.

With an all too familiar sensation, Marcus asked, "Where am I?"

Lieutenant Wehrer let his mouth open and shut before beginning. He smiled slightly. "Of course. I forgot to mention this. You are aboard the German capital and flagship to President Helmut Verndestag. I am Lieutenant Wehrer, ranking medical officer of this vessel. If you truly are the man who killed Blade Stone, then welcome aboard the *Berlin Nacht Ein*."

"The *Berlin Nacht Ein*? Then this is the most impressive command vessel in existence with its revolutionary swarming feature and a unique extraplanetary escape sequence that allows for reentry within miles of the intended destination at a tremendous cost of fuel," Marcus recited astutely.

"Impressive. How did you know these things? You might as well tell me, you are not going anywhere anyway," Wehrer said confidently, gesturing to the window panel in the floor that continued up the back wall. "Just a reminder of where you are."

"I am now quite aware of my location. You see, I have garnered everything I need to know from your own mind. It's a little trick my father taught me. Just like I know that every single bone in my hand is broken and my shoulder is going to take four weeks in a sling to recover at all. Since the clavicle is broken, though, it will have to be recast as soon as the shoulder resets."

"I am truly impressed. You merit further investigation," Wehrer said, rising to his feet from the steel slab.

"I think not, Lieutenant," President Verdestag interrupted. "Our computer experts retrieved some of the data flow from the pieces of the medical wing. DNA scans and age projections match every file we have on Blade Stone. Lieutenant, if you will, excuse me and allow me to salute the man who avenged the millions."

"Of course, President Verndestag," Wehrer said, clamoring out of the way.

"Thank you," Verndestag said, adopting the posture of a formal German salute.

"Bitte," Marcus smiled.

"You are free to leave. I will provide passage on my personal carrier to whatever location you wish, Mister ... Forgive me, I do not even know your name," Verndestag apologized.

"It's just Marcus," Marcus smiled, doing his best to return the salute. "If you would simply take me to the city of New Charleston, I shall find my way from there."

"Excellent. I have business there myself. I would speak to this Arden Shureman, so I will accompany you personally. If there will be nothing further, I must relay this news to the remaining forces in Eurasia. If you will forgive me, I must, for security reasons, keep you confined to one of the free housing units until we depart," Verndestag said without leaving room for discussion.

"As long as I get back to North America," Marcus said, struggling with his good shoulder.

CHAPTER 62

LEONA HEARD A knock at the door. She grabbed the nearest rifle and cocked it quickly. She slid the door open carefully and looked out to see Max. "Not this again," he said, looking down at the rifle barrel in his stomach. Leona smiled and kissed him soundly on the lips.

"Were you followed?"

"I don't think we have to worry about that anymore. I have a new friend in a very high place. Besides, I brought some insurance with me," Max said, gesturing back toward the unmoving Genesis, which was carrying its own remote control pod.

"Nice," Leona said, putting the gun down against the doorway. As soon as the barrel rested against the ground, Max grabbed Leona up in his arms.

"Lord." Max whispered softly in her ear as he pulled her closer to him, "Do you have any idea how good it is to hold you in my arms?"

"I'm just glad you came back," she cried.

"Have faith, Beautiful," he whispered.

"You? Faith?"

"I've realized something today: I have no choice in the matter if I ever want to see my two best friends again," Max ceded. He paused for a moment and drew himself out from her, sliding his hands to her elbows. "I think I love you, Leona," Max said, looking uncertainly for a response in her eyes.

"So this is what love feels like." Leona leaned forward and kissed Max so hard he nearly lost his balance. Neither of them had any concept of the passage of time. Leona asked, "What now?" She was still wrapped in Max's arms with her face warmly pressed to his cheek.

"Now, we have a future to build, for the ones who are left behind,"

Max said, smiling and holding Leona with no intention of ever letting go.

"First, I need to let Desyree out," Leona laughed lightly, snuggling further into Max's embrace.

CHAPTER 63

STONE PLACED HIS cross in the conforming lock of the hologram pod. He slid the helmet over his face. He calculated that the reporter should have received the letter by then. Planting his staff, he set the hologram pod on the ground. When the device activated, Stone began reciting the warning that would serve as his failsafe should he die in the forgotten era of his childhood before he could accomplish what he sought to do there. He recited the years of the war and the necessity of eliminating the threat of his father by any means necessary.

He finished and shut off the device resting at his feet. He locked the holographic recording into the main compartment of the time capsule and set the device to, in the event of Stone's demise, leech energy from any available source, most likely meaning Stone's dead body and broken armor, and catapult the hologram as far back in time as the available energy would allow. He placed the cross back around his neck and set his armor to meltdown on a dead man's switch. He picked up his staff again and began to pray. Then he had an appointment to keep.

CHAPTER 64

STONE SLAMMED THE chessboard onto the ground, flinging the remaining pieces about the room. He slammed his armored sole against the bent playing ground. "So chaos erupted from these sixty-four squares where order should have reigned. And so I am here, telling you this," Stone continued. "Now, you must do your part in that matter."

"Who are you?" The reporter adjusted in his chair with a newfound fear of the man before him.

"Finally," Stone reveled. "Well, I shall tell you. You see, in killing my own flesh and blood, I bear the weight of sin upon me. You named me well, Father, for I am Cain, and fratricide is my curse," Stone roared.

"Impossible," the young reporter Blade Stone demanded.

"Anything is possible in this world. I just wanted you to listen to me for once, to hear of the crimes you will commit and the lives you will destroy. Now, Father, you must pay for these genocidal horrors before you can inflict them upon this earth, and, by God, if I must sacrifice myself in the process, it shall be done. You will die this day," Stone said coldly, lowering the blade of his staff to his father's Adam's apple. The blade began to glow with vibrant energy. In a swift movement, Blade had a pistol trained on Stone's face. In desperate panic, Blade fired.

Stone's helmet closed over his face, and the bullet pinged harmlessly to the ground. Stone saw the pure terror in his father's face, and he weakened. Through all the punishment, all the abuse, and all the pain, Stone saw a man desperate to live and his vows against mercy wavered. Stone slid a tiny panel of his chest plate away directly beneath the cross. Blade adjusted his aim to that point, but the cross caught his eye before he could shoot again. Stone swung his staff back behind his head and began to propel it towards his father's neck as Blade gritted his teeth and struggled to steady the gun as he squeezed the trigger. So fell a king.

EPILOGUE

Dear President Verndestag:

I have done my best to revitalize this broken world, but the burdens of power do not sit well upon my shoulders. I have brought to life some semblance of economy within this fractured dominion, and I have reinstated the populace into its rightful place among the free. The known revolutionaries loyal to Blade alone have been dealt with appropriately, so let this serve as my official resignation from power and the commandment of my will that you receive the mantle of President in this country.

Allow me also to share with you the details of Cain Stone's disappearance. According to a trustworthy associate of mine, young Stone has made himself immortal to some extent. If he should succeed in whatever goal he has planned, our existence may yet be unceremoniously ripped from under us, for better or worse. I cannot fathom the depths of time travel, but if events are not altered, Stone has made his life a continuous loop in history. Yet, if he succeeds, there is hope that the evils wrought upon this world will be undone; I have been assured that his presence in the past can safely be classified as benevolent. In essence, he has made himself a symbol of hope, for no matter what transpires there remains the possibility that the slate can yet be wiped clean. Take it from a man seeing quite truly through new eyes, hope is a commodity of infinite value. Yet I am left to wonder about the undoing of Blade Stone. Was is simple chaos or Grand Design? God has a way of undoing the evils of this world, one way or another.

Arden Shureman,
President of the United Republic

AFTERWORD

Thank you, dear reader, for picking up the novel in your hand. I started writing this book when I was in high school back in 1997 and completed it the next year. I have picked it up to edit it several times since then but what you hold in your hand is very close to the original script. You may be wondering how the book actually ends, and I will get to that momentarily.

I was inspired as I sat in my high school English classes by a number of great suspense stories like *And Then There Were None* by Agatha Christie and powerful character stories like Fitzgerald's *The Great Gatsby* and Dickens's *Great Expectations*. I was, however, most influenced by a story called "The Lady, or the Tiger?" by Frank R. Stockton. I loved that it just ended at the crucial scene and left it to you as the reader to go forth with your imagination. I started writing a full length novel that would send readers off to do the same.

However, I could not be so cruel as to see you share your precious time with this book without some closure. A short story can be inspirational with such a sudden stop, but if you have invested in my cast of characters as I have, then you want to know conclusively whether Stone succeeded in his mission or not. Rest assured, there is an answer for those who want it and it is contained within the pages of the book itself. The evidence was clear though you had to know then what you know now to see what it meant. I leave the mental heavy lifting to you, dear reader, as it should properly be.

I maintain a small Website where I would love to hear your theories and reactions to this book:

www.trichardson.me

ACKNOWLEDGEMENTS

I offer my many thanks to you, dear reader, for choosing this book among the masses. It was the first book I ever wrote though it was not my first to be published. I would like to thank my parents, Debbie and Dan, for putting up with the late nights of writing when I had school the next day. I want to thank my grandparents, Leonard and Sylvia, for being my greatest fans and supporters through these many crazy years. I want to thank my darling Katherine for her editorial services and pushing me into print.

I also want to give credit to Cherry Pivik and Debbie Myers for stellar English and composition courses at John Marshall High School and to Dr. Larry Grimes for continuing their impressive work at Bethany College. I also want to thank Linda Brinkman for the years of speech and theater at John Marshall, which have made me a more effective communicator to this very day. Thank you also to Dr. Dirk Schlingmann and Dr. Song Wang for their mentorship and guidance to my full-time career in computing which has afforded me opportunities like this.

Thank you to all of my friends throughout these many, winding years. Wherever you are now, you have influenced me to be the person I am today.